Praise for *Ho*...

"A stirring, inspiring celebration of heroism in its many incarnations."
—*Family Circle*

"A heart-wrenching portrayal of one veteran's trials points out how much training goes into preparing for war—and how little is done to teach returning soldiers how to be parents again."
—*People* magazine

"May have readers emptying their Kleenex boxes . . . the losses in *Home Front* are real. But so are the gains, beautifully detailed in what is probably Hannah's best work yet."
—*The Seattle Times*

"Hannah's characters are believable and lively, and her skillful treatment of this difficult topic will leave readers feeling moved and affected by the human toll of war, not lectured to about politics. This new offering after a string of bestsellers is sure to garner a lot of attention, not only because of Hannah's track record with readers, but also because of its heartrending and timely subject matter."
—*Booklist*

"A wrenching depiction of war's aftermath."
—*Kirkus Reviews*

"By reversing traditional expectations, Hannah (*Night Road*) calls attention to the modern female soldier and offers a compassionate, poignant look at the impact of war on family."
—*Publishers Weekly*

"Kristin Hannah has written a passionate, inspired story of war's cost to a family—even more, the cost of silence. She seamlessly weaves the two sides of a soldier's heart—the damage and the horror inflicted upon it with the honor and pride that make it beat—in Jolene. She is a hero, and her life is a hero's journey, psychological and spiritual and physical. It's made with others, and it's a journey that we are privileged to share."
—*Shelf Awareness* (starred review)

"Fans of Kristin Hannah's books appreciate her ability to create entertaining stories that are also relatable. Her latest novel, *Home Front*, is no different. . . . Readers of *Home Front* may not know what it's like to have a loved one in the military, but they can likely relate to the idea of a relationship in trouble and the challenges of juggling career with family."
—Associated Press

"Hannah has written a remarkable tale of duty, love, strength, and hope that is at times poignant and always thoroughly captivating and relevant."
—*Library Journal* (starred review)

Praise for *Night Road*

"Hannah masterfully details the unraveling of a family."
—*People* magazine

"Hannah is superb at delving into the characters' psyches and delineating nuances of feeling."
—*The Washington Post*

"*Night Road* is a do-not-miss for fans of Jodi Picoult, and will stay with you long after you've turned the last page."
—*Justine Magazine*

"Kristin Hannah is back in top form with *Night Road*. . . . It will hook Hannah fans from start to suspenseful finish."
—*The Seattle Times*

"Hannah's gripping new novel centers around a tragedy that rocks a family to its core. . . . A breakout for popular novelist Hannah."
—*Booklist*

"A gripping, emotional read."
—*She* magazine

"Kristin Hannah lets loose here, daring her readers to keep the tears at bay."
—*The Star-Ledger* (Newark)

"*Night Road* is one special book that can transform the lives of readers by influencing how they think about certain important life issues. The reader becomes a firsthand witness to the pitfalls of parenthood, mortality, heartbreak, guilt, life choices, grief, forgiveness, and much more. In short, the entire range of human emotions is explored in this excruciatingly painful but hopeful book about the triumphant power of the human spirit in the process of forgiveness."

—*New York Journal of Books*

Praise for *Winter Garden*

"It's a tearjerker, but the journey is as lovely—and haunting—as a snow-filled winter's night."
—*People* magazine

"The author of *Firefly Lane* and *True Colors* has written another powerful story of misunderstanding, family love, and strong women. . . . A fascinating story that weaves fairy tales into reality—fairy tales that don't always have the expected endings."
—*The Herald-News*

"A gripping read."
—*Booklist*

"Readers will find it hard not to laugh a little and cry a little more as mother and daughters reach out to each other just in the nick of time."
—*Publishers Weekly*

"*Winter Garden* is Kristin Hannah's best-written and most deeply affecting novel yet."
—*The Huffington Post*

"A wonderful story about the mother–daughter bond—one you won't be able to put down."
—SheKnows.com

"This tearjerker weaves a convincing historical novel and contemporary family drama. . . ."
—*Library Journal*

Home Front

Kristin
Hannah

St. Martin's Griffin
New York

HOME FRONT. Copyright © 2012 by Kristin Hannah. All rights reserved. Printed in the United States of America. For information, address St. Martin's Press, 175 Fifth Avenue, New York, N.Y. 10010.

www.stmartins.com

The Library of Congress has cataloged the hardcover edition as follows:

Hannah, Kristin.
Home front / Kristin Hannah.
p. cm.
ISBN 978-0-312-57720-9 (hardcover)
ISBN 978-1-4299-4221-8 (e-book)
1. Domestic fiction. I. Title.
PS3558.A4763H66 2012
813'.54—dc23
2011033805

ISBN 978-1-250-02327-8 (trade paperback)
ISBN 978-1-250-03744-2 (Scholastic)

10 9 8 7 6 5

*This book is dedicated to the
brave men and women of the American armed services
and their families, who sacrifice so much to protect and preserve
our way of life.*

*And, as always, to my own heroes,
Benjamin and Tucker.*

Part One

From a Distance

There are some things you learn best in calm,
some in storm.
—WILLA CATHER

Prologue

1982

The way she saw it, some families were like well-tended parks, with pretty daffodil borders and big, sprawling trees that offered respite from the summer sun. Others—and this she knew firsthand—were battlefields, bloody and dark, littered with shrapnel and body parts.

She might only be seventeen, but Jolene Larsen already knew about war. She'd grown up in the midst of a marriage gone bad.

Valentine's Day was the worst. The mood at home was always precarious, but on this day when the television ran ads for flowers and chocolates and red foil hearts, love became a weapon in her parents' careless hands. It started with their drinking, of course. Always. Glasses full of bourbon, refilled again and again. That was the beginning. Then came the screaming and the crying, the throwing of things. For years, Jolene had asked her mother why they didn't just leave him—her father—and steal away in the night. Her mother's answer was always the same: *I can't. I love him.* Sometimes she would cry as she said the terrible words, sometimes her bitterness would be palpable, but in the end it didn't matter how she sounded; what mattered was the tragic truth of her one-sided love.

Downstairs, someone screamed.

That would be Mom.

Then came a crash—something big had been thrown against the wall. A door slammed shut. That would be Dad.

He had left the house in a fury (was there any other way?), slamming the door shut behind him. He'd be back tomorrow or the next day, whenever he ran out of money. He'd come slinking into the kitchen, sober and remorseful, stinking of booze and cigarettes. Mom would rush to him, sobbing, and take him in her arms. *Oh, Ralph . . . you scared me . . . I'm sorry, give me one more chance, please, you know I love you so much . . .*

Jolene made her way through her steeply pitched bedroom, ducking so she wouldn't konk her head on one of the rough timbered support beams. There was only one light in here, a bulb that hung from the rafters like the last tooth in an old man's mouth, loose and unreliable.

She opened the door, listening.

Was it over?

She crept down the narrow staircase, hearing the risers creak beneath her weight. She found her mother in the living room, sitting slumped on the sofa, a lit Camel cigarette dangling from her mouth. Ash rained downward, peppering her lap. Scattered across the floor were remnants of the fight: bottles and ashtrays and broken bits of glass.

Even a few years ago, Jolene would have tried to make her mother feel better. But too many nights like this had hardened her. Now she was impatient with all of it, wearied by the drama of her parents' marriage. Nothing ever changed, and Jolene was the one who had to clean up every mess. She picked her way through the broken pieces of glass and knelt at her mother's side.

"Let me have that," she said tiredly, taking the burning cigarette, putting it out in the ashtray on the floor beside her.

Mom looked up, sad-eyed, her cheeks streaked with tears. "How will I live without him?"

As if in answer, the back door cracked open. Cold night air swept into the room, bringing with it the smell of rain and pine trees.

"He's back!" Mom pushed Jolene aside and ran for the kitchen.

I love you, baby, I'm sorry, Jolene heard her mother say.

Jolene righted herself slowly and turned. Her parents were locked in one of those movie embraces, the kind reserved for lovers reuniting after a war. Her mother clung to him desperately, grabbing the plaid wool of his shirt.

Her father swayed drunkenly, as if held up by her alone, but that was impossible. He was a huge man, tall and broad, with hands like turkey platters; Mom was as frail and white as an eggshell. It was from him that Jolene got her height.

"You can't leave me," her mother sobbed, slurring the words.

Her father looked away. For a split second, Jolene saw the pain in his eyes—pain, and worse, shame and loss and regret.

"I need a drink," he said in a voice roughened by years of smoking unfiltered cigarettes.

He took her mother's hand, dragged her through the kitchen. Looking dazed but grinning foolishly, her mother stumbled along behind him, heedless of the fact that she was barefooted.

It wasn't until he opened the back door that Jolene got it. "No!" she yelled, scrambling to her feet, running after them.

Outside, the February night was cold and dark. Rain hammered the roof and ran in rivulets over the edges of the eaves. Her father's leased logging truck, the only thing he really cared about, sat like some huge black insect in the driveway. She ran out onto the wooden porch, tripping over a chain saw, righting herself.

Her mother paused at the car's open passenger door, looked at her. Rain plastered the hair across her hollow cheeks, made her mascara run. She lifted a hand, pale and shaking, and waved.

"Get out of the rain, Karen," her father yelled, and her mother complied instantly. In a second, both doors slammed shut. The car backed up, turned onto the road, drove away.

And Jolene was alone again.

Four months, she thought dully. Only four more months and she would graduate from high school and be able to leave home.

Home. *Whatever that meant.*

But what would she do? Where would she go? There was no money for college, and what money Jolene saved from work her parents invariably found and "borrowed." She didn't even have enough for first month's rent.

She didn't know how long she stood there, thinking, worrying, watching rain turn the driveway to mud; all she really knew was that at some point she became aware of an impossible, unearthly flash of color in the night.

Red. The color of blood and fire and loss.

When the police car pulled up into her yard, she wasn't surprised. What surprised her was how it felt, hearing that her parents were dead.

What surprised her was how hard she cried.

$\mathcal{O}ne$

April 2005

On her forty-first birthday, as on every other day, Jolene Zarkades woke before the dawn. Careful not to disturb her sleeping husband, she climbed out of bed, dressed in her running clothes, pulled her long blond hair into a ponytail, and went outside.

It was a beautiful, blue-skied spring day. The plum trees that lined her driveway were in full bloom. Tiny pink blossoms floated across the green, green field. Across the street, the Sound was a deep and vibrant blue. The soaring, snow-covered Olympic mountains rose majestically into the sky.

Perfect visibility.

She ran along the beach road for exactly three and a half miles and then turned for home. By the time she returned to her driveway, she was red-faced and breathing hard. On her porch, she picked her way past the mismatched wood and wicker furniture and went into the house, where the rich, tantalizing scent of French roast coffee mingled with the acrid tinge of wood smoke.

The first thing she did was to turn on the TV in the kitchen; it was already set on CNN. As she poured her coffee, she waited impatiently for news on the Iraq war.

No heavy fighting was being reported this morning. No soldiers—or friends—had been killed in the night.

"Thank God," she said. Taking her coffee, she went upstairs, walking past her daughters' bedrooms and toward her own. It was still early. Maybe she would wake Michael with a long, slow kiss. An invitation.

How long had it been since they made love in the morning? How long since they'd made love at all? She couldn't remember. Her birthday seemed a perfect day to change all that. She opened the door. "Michael?"

Their king-sized bed was empty. Unmade. Michael's black tee shirt—the one he slept in—lay in a rumpled heap on the floor. She picked it up and folded it in precise thirds and put it away. "Michael?" she said again, opening the bathroom door. Steam billowed out, clouded her view.

Everything was white—tile, toilet, countertops. The glass shower door was open, revealing the empty tile interior. A damp towel had been thrown carelessly across the tub to dry. Moisture beaded the mirror above the sink.

He must be downstairs already, probably in his office. Or maybe he was planning a little birthday surprise. That was the kind of thing he used to do . . .

After a quick shower, she brushed out her long wet hair, then twisted it into a knot at the base of her neck as she stared into the mirror. Her face—like everything about her—was strong and angular: she had high cheekbones and heavy brown brows that accentuated wide-set green eyes and a mouth that was just the slightest bit too big. Most women her age wore makeup and colored their hair, but Jolene didn't have time for any of that. She was fine with the ash-gold blond hair that darkened a shade or two every year and the small collection of lines that had begun to pleat the corners of her eyes.

She put on her flight suit and went to wake up the girls, but their rooms were empty, too.

They were already in the kitchen. Her twelve-year-old daughter, Betsy, was helping her four-year-old sister, Lulu, up to the table. Jolene kissed Lulu's plump pink cheek.

"Happy birthday, Mom," they said together.

Jolene felt a sudden, burning love for these girls and her life. She knew how rare such moments were. How could she not, raised the way she'd been? She turned to her daughters, smiling—beaming, really. "Thanks, girls. It's a beautiful day to turn forty-one."

"That's so *old*," Lulu said. "Are you sure you're that old?"

Laughing, Jolene opened the fridge. "Where's your dad?"

"He left already," Betsy said.

Jolene turned. "Really?"

"Really," Betsy said, watching her closely.

Jolene forced a smile. "He's probably planning a surprise for me after work. Well. I say we have a party after school. Just the three of us. With cake. What do you say?"

"With cake!" Lulu yelled, clapping her plump hands together.

Jolene could let herself be upset about Michael's forgetfulness, but what would be the point? Happiness was a choice she knew how to make. She chose not to think about the things that bothered her; that way, they disappeared. Besides, Michael's dedication to work was one of the things she admired most about him.

"Mommy, Mommy, play patty-cake!" Lulu cried, bouncing in her seat.

Jolene looked down at her youngest. "Someone loves the word cake."

Lulu raised her hand. "I do. Me!"

Jolene sat down next to Lulu and held out her hands. Her daughter immediately smacked her palms against Jolene's. "Patty-cake, patty-cake, baker's man, make me a . . ." Jolene paused, watching Lulu's face light up with expectation.

"Pool!" Lulu said.

"Make me a pool as fast you can. Dig it and scrape it and fill it with blue, and I'll go swimming with my Lu-lu." Jolene gave her daughter one last pat of the hands and then got up to make breakfast. "Go get dressed, Betsy. We leave in thirty minutes."

Precisely on time, Jolene ushered the girls into the car. She drove Lulu to preschool, dropped her off with a fierce kiss, and then drove to the middle school, which sat on the knoll of a huge, grassy hillside. Pulling into the carpool lane, she slowed and came to a stop.

"Do *not* get out of the car," Betsy said sharply from the shadows of the backseat. "You're wearing your *uniform*."

"I guess I don't get a pass on my birthday." Jolene glanced at her daughter in the rearview mirror. In the past few months, her lovable, sweet-tempered tomboy had morphed into this hormonal preteen for whom everything was a potential embarrassment—especially a mom who was not sufficiently like the other moms. "Wednesday is career day," she reminded her.

Betsy groaned. "Do you *have* to come?"

"Your teacher invited me. I promise not to drool or spit."

"That is so not funny. No one cool has a mom in the military. You won't wear your flight suit, will you?"

"It's what I do, Betsy. I think you'd—"

"Whatever." Betsy grabbed up her heavy backpack—not the right one, apparently; yesterday she'd demanded a new one—and climbed out of the car and rushed headlong toward the two girls standing beneath the flagpole. They were what mattered to Betsy these days, those girls, Sierra and Zoe. Betsy cared desperately about fitting in with them. Apparently, a mother who flew helicopters for the Army National Guard was très embarrassing.

As Betsy approached her old friends, they pointedly ignored her, turning their backs on her in unison, like a school of fish darting away from danger.

Jolene tightened her grip on the steering wheel, cursing under her breath.

Betsy looked crestfallen, embarrassed. Her shoulders fell, her chin dropped. She backed away quickly, as if to pretend she'd never really run up to her once-best friends in the first place. Alone, she walked into the school building.

Jolene sat there so long someone honked at her. She felt her daughter's pain keenly. If there was one thing Jolene understood, it was rejection. Hadn't she waited forever for her own parents to love her? She had to teach Betsy to be strong, to choose happiness. No one could hurt you if you didn't let them. A good offense was the best defense.

Finally, she drove away. Bypassing the town's morning traffic, she took the back roads down to Liberty Bay. At the driveway next to her own, she turned in, drove up to the neighboring house—a small white manufactured home tucked next to a car-repair shop—and honked the horn.

Her best friend, Tami Flynn, came out of house, already dressed in her flight suit, with her long black hair coiled into a severe twist. Jolene would swear that not a single wrinkle creased the coffee-colored planes of Tami's broad face. Tami swore it was because of her Native American heritage.

Tami was the sister Jolene had never had. They'd been teenagers when they met—a pair of eighteen-year-old girls who had joined the army because they didn't know what else to do with their lives. Both had qualified for the high school to flight school helicopter-pilot training program.

A passion for flying had brought them together; a shared outlook on life had created a friendship so strong it never wavered. They'd spent ten years in the army together and then moved over to the Guard when marriage—and motherhood—made active duty difficult. Four years after Jolene and Michael moved into the house on Liberty Bay, Tami and Carl had bought the land next door.

Tami and Jolene had even gotten pregnant at the same time, sharing that magical nine months, holding each other's fears in tender hands. Their husbands had nothing in common, so they hadn't become one of those best friends who traveled together with their families, but that was okay with Jolene. What mattered most was that she and Tami were always there for each other. And they were.

I've got your six literally meant that a helicopter was behind you, flying in the six o'clock position. What it really meant was *I'm here for you. I've got your back.* That was what Jolene had found in the army, and in the Guard, and in Tami. *I've got your six.*

The Guard had given them the best of both worlds—they got to be full-time moms who still served their country and stayed in the military and flew helicopters. They flew together at least two mornings a week, as well as during their drill weekends. It was the best part-time job on the planet.

Tami climbed into the passenger seat and slammed the door shut. "Happy birthday, flygirl."

"Thanks." Jolene grinned. "My day, my music." She cranked up the volume on the CD player and Prince's "Purple Rain" blared through the speakers.

They talked all the way to Tacoma, about everything and nothing; when they weren't talking, they were singing the songs of their youth— Prince, Madonna, Michael Jackson. They passed Camp Murray, home to the Guard, and drove onto Fort Lewis, where the Guard's aircraft were housed.

In the locker room, Jolene retrieved the heavy flight bag full of survival equipment. Slinging it over her shoulder, she followed Tami to the desk, confirmed her additional flight-training period, or AFTP; signed up to be paid; and then headed out to the tarmac, putting on her helmet as she walked.

The crew was already there, readying the Black Hawk for flight. The helicopter looked like a huge bird of prey against the clear blue sky. She nodded to the crew chief, did a quick preflight check of her aircraft, conducted a crew briefing, and then climbed into the left side of the cockpit and took her seat. Tami climbed into the right seat and put on her helmet.

"Overhead switches and circuit breakers, check," Jolene said, powering up the helicopter. The engines roared to life; the huge rotor blades began to move, slowly at first and then rotating fast, with a high-pitched whine.

"Guard ops. Raptor eight-nine, log us off," Jolene said into her mic. Then she switched frequencies. "Tower. Raptor eight-nine, ready for departure."

She began the exquisite balancing act it took to get a helicopter airborne. The aircraft climbed slowly into the air. She worked the controls expertly—her hands and feet in constant motion. They rose into the blue and cloudless sky, where heaven was all around her. Far below, the flowering trees were a spectacular palette of color. A rush of pure adrenaline coursed through her. God, she loved it up here.

"I hear it's your birthday, Chief," said the crew chief, through the comm.

"Damn right it is," Tami said, grinning. "Why do you think she has the controls?"

Jolene grinned at her best friend, loving this feeling, needing it like she needed air to breathe. She didn't care about getting older or getting wrinkles or slowing down. "Forty-one. I can't think of a better way to spend it."

The small town of Poulsbo, Washington, sat like a pretty little girl along the shores of Liberty Bay. The original settlers had chosen this area because it reminded them of their Nordic homeland, with its cool blue waters, soaring mountains, and lush green hillsides. Years later, those same founding fathers had begun to build their shops along Front Street, embellishing them with Scandinavian touches. There were cut-work rooflines and scrolled decorations everywhere.

According to Zarkades family legend, the decorations had spoken to Michael's mother instantly, who swore that once she walked down Front Street, she knew where she wanted to live. Dozens of quaint stores—including the one his mother owned—sold beautiful, handcrafted knick-knacks to tourists.

It was less than ten miles from downtown Seattle, as a crow flew, although those few miles created a pain-in-the-ass commute. Sometime in the past few years, Michael had stopped seeing the Norwegian cuteness of the town and began to notice instead the long and winding drive from his house to the ferry terminal on Bainbridge Island and the stop-and-go midweek traffic.

There were two routes from Poulsbo to Seattle—over land and over water. The drive took two hours. The ferry ride was a thirty-five-minute crossing from the shores of Bainbridge Island to the terminal on Seattle's wharf.

The problem with the ferry was the wait time. To drive your car onboard, you had to be in line early. In the summer, he often rode his bike to work; on rainy days like today—which were so plentiful in the Northwest—he drove. And this had been an especially long winter and a wet spring. Day after gray day, he sat in his Lexus in the parking lot, watching daylight crawl along the wavy surface of the Sound. Then he drove aboard, parked in the bowels of the boat, and went upstairs.

Today, Michael sat on the port side of the boat at a small formica table, with his work spread out in front of him; the Woerner deposition. Post-it notes ran like yellow piano keys along the edges, each one highlighting a statement of questionable veracity made by his client.

Lies. Michael sighed at the thought of undoing the damage. His idealism, once so shiny and bright, had been dulled by years of defending the guilty.

In the past, he would have talked to his dad about it, and his father would have put it all in perspective, reminding Michael that their job made a difference.

We are the last bastion, Michael, you know that—the champions of freedom. Don't let the bad guys break you. We protect the innocent by protecting the guilty. That's how it works.

I could use a few more innocents, Dad.

Couldn't we all? We're all waiting for it . . . that *case, the one that matters. We know, more than most, how it feels to save someone's life. To make a difference. That's what we do, Michael. Don't lose the faith.*

He looked at the empty seat across from him.

It had been eleven months now that he'd ridden to work alone. One day his father had been beside him, hale and hearty and talking about the law he loved, and then he'd been sick. Dying.

He and his father had been partners for almost twenty years, working side by side, and losing him had shaken Michael deeply. He grieved for the time they'd lost; most of all, he felt alone in a way that was new. The loss made him look at his own life, too, and he didn't like what he saw.

Until his father's death, Michael had always felt lucky, happy; now, he didn't.

He wanted to talk to someone about all this, share his loss. But with whom? He couldn't talk to his wife about it. Not Jolene, who believed that happiness was a choice to be made and a smile was a frown turned upside down. Her turbulent, ugly childhood had left her impatient with people who couldn't choose to be happy. Lately, it got on his nerves, all her buoyant it-will-get-better platitudes. Because she'd lost her parents, she thought she understood grief, but she had no idea how it felt to be drowning. How could she? She was Teflon strong.

He tapped his pen on the table and glanced out the window. The Sound was gunmetal gray today, desolate looking, mysterious. A seagull floated past on a current of invisible air, seemingly in suspended animation.

He shouldn't have given in to Jolene, all those years ago, when she'd begged for the house on Liberty Bay. He'd told her he didn't want to live so far from the city—or that close to his parents, but in the end he'd given in, swayed by her pretty pleas and the solid argument that they'd need his mother's help in babysitting. But if he hadn't given in, if he hadn't lost the where-we-live argument, he wouldn't be sitting here on the ferry every day, missing the man who used to meet him here . . .

As the ferry slowed, Michael got up and collected his papers, putting the deposition back in the black lambskin briefcase. He hadn't even looked at it. Merging into the crowd, he made his way down the stairs to the car deck. In minutes, he was driving off the ferry and pulling up to the Smith Tower, once the tallest building west of New York and now an aging, gothic footnote to a city on the rise.

At Zarkades, Antham, and Zarkades, on the ninth floor, everything was old—floors, windows in need of repair, too many layers of paint—but, like the building itself, there was history here, and beauty. A wall of windows overlooked Elliott Bay and the great orange cranes that loaded containers onto tankers. Some of the biggest and most important criminal trials in the past twenty years had been defended by Theo Zarkades, from these very offices. At gatherings of the bar association, other lawyers still spoke of his father's ability to persuade a jury with something close to awe.

"Hey, Michael," the receptionist said, smiling up at him.

He waved and kept walking, past the earnest paralegals, tired legal secretaries, and ambitious young associates. Everyone smiled at him, and he smiled back. At the corner office—previously his father's and now his—he stopped to talk to his secretary. "Good morning, Ann."

"Good morning, Michael. Bill Antham wanted to see you."

"Okay. Tell him I'm in."

"You want some coffee?"

"Yes, thanks."

He went into his office, the largest one in the firm. A huge window looked out over Elliott Bay; that was really the star of the room, the view. Other than that, the office was ordinary—bookcases filled with law books, a wooden floor scarred by decades of wear, a pair of over-stuffed chairs, a black suede sofa. A single family photo sat next to his computer, the only personal touch in the space.

He tossed his briefcase onto the desk and went to the window, staring out at the city his father had loved. In the glass, he saw a ghostly image of himself—wavy black hair, strong, squared jaw, dark eyes. The image of his father as a younger man. But had his father ever felt so tired and drained?

Behind him, there was a knock, and then the door opened. In walked Bill Antham, the only other partner in the firm, once his father's best friend. In the months since Dad's death, Bill had aged, too. Maybe they all had.

"Hey, Michael," he said, limping forward, reminding Michael with each step that he was well past retirement age. In the last year, he'd gotten two new knees.

"Have a seat, Bill," Michael said, indicating the chair closest to the desk.

"Thanks." He sat down. "I need a favor."

Michael returned to his desk. "Sure, Bill. What can I do for you?"

"I was in court yesterday, and I got tapped by Judge Runyon."

Michael sighed and sat down. It was common for criminal defense attorneys to be assigned cases by the court—it was the old *if you require an attorney and cannot afford one* bit. Judges often assigned a case to whatever lawyer happened to be there when it came up. "What's the case?"

"A man killed his wife. Allegedly. He barricaded himself in his house and shot her in the head. SWAT team dragged him out before he could kill himself. TV filmed a bunch of it."

A guilty client who had been caught on TV. Perfect. "And you want me to handle the case for you."

"I wouldn't ask . . . but Nancy and I are leaving for Mexico in two weeks."

"Of course," Michael said. "No problem."

Bill's gaze moved around the room. "I still expect to find him in here," he said softly.

"Yeah," Michael said.

They looked at each other for a moment, both remembering the man who had made such an impact on their lives. Then Bill stood, thanked Michael again, and left.

After that, Michael dove into his work, letting it consume him. He spent hours buried in depositions and police reports and briefs. He had always had a strong work ethic and an even stronger sense of duty. In the rising tide of grief, work had become his life ring.

At three o'clock, Ann buzzed him on the intercom. "Michael? Jolene is on line one."

"Thanks, Ann."

"You did remember that it's her birthday today, right?"

Shit.

He pushed back from his desk and grabbed the phone. "Hey, Jo. Happy birthday."

"Thanks."

She didn't scold him for forgetting, although she knew he had. Jolene had the tightest grip on her emotions of anyone he'd ever seen, and she never *ever* let herself get mad. He sometimes wondered if a good fight would help their marriage, but it took two to fight. "I'll make it up to you. How about dinner at that place above the marina? The new place?"

Before she could offer some resistance (which she always did if something wasn't her idea), he said, "Betsy is old enough to watch Lulu for two hours. We'll only be a mile away from home."

It was an argument that had been going on for almost a year now.

Michael thought a twelve-year-old could babysit; Jolene disagreed. As with everything in their life, Jolene's vote was the one that counted. He was used to it . . . and sick of it.

"I know how busy you are with the Woerner case," she said. "How about if I feed the girls early and settle them upstairs with a movie and then make us a nice dinner? Or I could pick up takeout from the bistro; we love their food."

"Are you sure?"

"What matters is that we're together," she said easily.

"Okay," Michael said. "I'll be home by eight."

Before he hung up the phone, he was thinking of something else.

That evening, Jolene chose her clothes carefully. She and Michael hadn't had dinner alone, just the two of them, in forever, and she wanted this evening to be perfect. Romantic. After feeding the girls, she bathed in scented water, shaved, slathered her skin with a citrus-scented lotion, and then slipped into a pair of comfortable jeans and a black boatnecked sweater.

Downstairs, she found Betsy seated at the coffee table, doing homework, while Lulu was on the sofa, wrapped up in her favorite yellow "blankee," watching *The Little Mermaid*. The remnants of their impromptu birthday party were still on the dining room table—the cake, with its candle holes; the pink journal Betsy had given Jolene; the sparkly barrette that had been Lulu's gift; and a pile of wrinkled paper and discarded bows.

"She's not the boss of me," Lulu said when Jolene walked into the room.

"Tell her to shut up, Mom. I'm trying to do homework," Betsy responded. "She's singing too loud."

And it started. Their voices climbed up and over each other, rising in volume.

"She is *not* the boss of me," Lulu said again, more adamantly. "Tell her."

Betsy rolled her eyes and left the room, stomping up the stairs.

Jolene felt a wave of exhaustion. She hadn't known how *tiring* it could be to parent a preteen. How much eye rolling could one girl do? If Jolene had tried that, her father would have smacked her across the room.

Lulu ran over to the toy box in the corner of the room and rummaged around inside it. Finding the kitten-ears headband that had been a part of last year's Halloween costume, she put it on and turned around.

Jolene couldn't help smiling. There stood her four-year-old daughter, wearing gray cat ears that were beginning to look worn in places, with her hands on her hips. The sharp little gray triangles framed Lulu's flushed face and made her look even more elfin than usual. For no reason that anyone could explain, Lulu thought she was invisible when she wore the headband. She made a mewing sound.

Jolene frowned dramatically and looked around. "Oh, no . . . what happened to my Lucy Lou? Where did she go?" She made a great show of looking around the room, behind the television, under the overstuffed yellow chair, behind the door.

"Here I am, Mommy!" Lulu said with a flourish, giggling.

"There you are," Jolene said with a sigh. "I was worried." She picked up Lulu and carried her upstairs. It took Lulu forever to brush her teeth and get into her pajamas, and Jolene waited patiently, knowing her youngest had a strong independent streak. When Lulu was finally ready, Jolene climbed into bed beside her, pulled her close, and reached for *Where the Wild Things Are*. By the time she said, "the end," Lulu was almost asleep.

She kissed Lulu's cheek. " 'Night, Kitten."

" 'Night, Mommy," Lulu murmured sleepily.

Then Jolene walked down the hall to Betsy's room, knocked, and went inside.

Betsy was sitting up in bed, with her social studies book open in her lap. Her corn silk blond hair fell in fusilli curls along her bare, skinny arms. Someday Betsy would prize her porcelain skin and blond hair and brown eyes, but not now, when straight hair was all the rage and pimples had ruined her complexion.

Jolene went to her daughter's bed and sat down on the edge. "You could be nicer to your sister."

"She's a pain."

"So are you." Jolene saw how Betsy's eyes widened, and she smiled gently. "And so am I. Families are like that. And besides, I know what this is really about."

"You do?"

"I saw how Sierra and Zoe treated you this morning at school."

"You're always spying on me," she said, but her voice broke.

"I watched you walk into school. That's hardly spying. You three were best friends last year. What happened?"

"Nothing," she said mulishly, pressing her lips together, hiding her braces.

"I can help, you know. I was twelve once, too."

Betsy gave her the you-must-be-crazy look that had become familiar in the last year. "Doubtful."

"Maybe you should hang out with Seth after school tomorrow. Remember how much fun you used to have?"

"Seth's weird. Everyone thinks so."

"Elizabeth Andrea, don't you dare act like a mean girl. Seth Flynn is not weird. He's my best friend's son. So what if he likes to wear his hair long and if he's . . . quiet. He's your friend. You should remember that. You might need him one day."

"Whatever."

Jolene sighed. She'd seen this movie before; no matter how often she asked, Betsy wouldn't say anything more. *Whatever* meant *the end.* "Okay." She leaned forward and kissed Betsy's forehead. "I love you to the moon and back."

The words were the slogan of this family, their love distilled into a single sentence. *Say it back to me, Bets.*

Jolene waited a moment longer than she intended and was immediately mad at herself for hoping. Again. Motherhood in the preteen years was a series of paper-cut disappointments. "Okay," she said at last, standing up.

"How come Dad's not home yet? It's your birthday."

"He'll be here any minute. You know how busy he is these days."

"Will he come up to say good night to me?"

"Of course."

Betsy nodded and went back to reading. When Jolene was to the door, she said, "Happy birthday, Mom."

Jolene smiled. "Thanks, Bets. And I love the journal you gave me. It's perfect."

Betsy actually smiled.

Downstairs, Jolene went into the kitchen and put the last of the dishes away. Her dinner—a rich, savory pot of beef short ribs braised in red wine and garlic and thyme—bubbled softly on the stove, scenting the whole house. The girls hadn't loved it, but it was Michael's favorite.

Wrapping a soft pink blanket around her shoulders, she poured herself a glass of soda water and went outside. She sat down in one of the worn bent-twig chairs on the porch and put her bare feet on the weathered coffee table, staring out at the familiar view.

Home.

It had begun with meeting Michael.

She remembered it all so clearly.

For days after her parents' deaths, she had waited for *someone* to help her. Police, counselors, teachers. It hadn't taken long for her to realize that in her parents' deaths, as in their lives, she was on her own. On a snowy Wednesday morning, she'd wakened early, ignoring the cold that seeped through the thin walls of her bedroom, and dressed in her best clothes—a plaid woolen skirt, Shetland sweater, kneesocks, and penny loafers. A wide blue headband kept the hair out of her eyes.

She took the last of her babysitting money and set off for downtown Seattle. At the legal-aid office, she'd met Michael.

His dark good looks and easy smile had literally taken her breath away. She'd followed him to a shabby little office and told him her problem. "I'm seventeen—eighteen in two months. My parents died this

week. Car accident. A social worker came by and said I would have to
live with foster parents until I turned eighteen. But I don't need anyone.
Certainly not some fake family. I can live in my own house until June—
that's when the bank is repossessing it—and then I'll be done with high
school and I can do . . . whatever. Can you make it so I don't need to go
to a foster family?"

Michael had studied her closely, his eyes narrowed. "You'd be alone
then."

"I *am* alone. It's a fact, not a choice."

When he'd finally said, "I'll help you, Jolene," she'd wanted to cry.

In the next hour, she'd told him a tidied-up version of her life. He'd
said something about attorney-client privilege and how she could tell
him anything, but she knew better. She'd learned a long time ago to keep
the truth secret. When people knew she'd grown up with alcoholic parents, they invariably felt sorry for her. She hated that, hated to be pitied.

When they were done and the paperwork was filled out, Michael had
said, "Come back and see me in a few years, Jolene. I'll take you out to
dinner."

It had taken her six years to find her way back to him. By then, she'd
been a pilot in the army and he'd been a lawyer in partnership with his
father, and they'd had almost nothing in common. But she'd seen something in him that first day, an idealism that spoke deeply to her and a
sense of morality that matched her own. Like her, Michael was a hard
worker and had a keen sense of duty. True to his word, Michael had
taken her out to dinner . . . and that had been the beginning.

She smiled at the memory.

In the distance, lights came on along the shore, golden dots that indicated houses in the darkness. Gauzy clouds wafted across the moon;
in their absence, it shone more brightly. It was full night now, and dark.
She glanced at her watch. Eight thirty.

She felt a pinch of disappointment and pushed it away. Something
important must have come up. Life was like that sometimes. Things
were rarely perfect. He would show up.

But . . .

Lately, it seemed that their differences were more pronounced than the things they shared. Michael had always hated her commitment to the military. She'd left active duty for him and gone into the Guard instead, but that hadn't been good enough for Michael. He didn't want to hear about her flying or her drill weekends or her friends who served. He'd always been antimilitary, but since the war in Iraq had started, his opinions had grown stronger, more negative. Their once-companionable silences had become awkward. It was pretty lonely when you couldn't talk to your husband about the things that mattered to you. Normally, she looked away from these truths, but tonight they were all that occupied the chair beside her.

She got up and went back inside.

8:50.

She opened the heavy yellow pot lid and stared into the meal she'd made. The rich sauce had reduced too far; it looked a little black around the edges. Behind her, the phone rang. She lunged for it. "Hello?"

"Hey, Jo. I'm sorry I'm late."

"Late was an hour ago, Michael. What happened?"

"I'm sorry. What can I say? I got into work and forgot."

"You forgot," she said, wishing it didn't hurt.

"I'll make it up to you."

She almost said *how?* but what was the point? Why make it worse? He hadn't meant to hurt her feelings. "Okay."

"I'll try to get home quickly, but . . ."

Jolene was glad they were on the phone; at least she didn't have to smile. The thought came to her that he hadn't been trying hard enough lately, that his family—and his wife—seemed not to matter to him. And yet she still loved him as deeply as the day he'd first kissed her, all those years ago.

Time, she thought. *It will be okay next week or next month.* He was still grieving over the loss of his father. She just needed to be understanding.

"Happy birthday," he said.

"Thanks." She hung up the phone and sat down at the kitchen table. In the shadowy room, decorated with her family photos and mementos and the furniture she had salvaged and restored herself, she felt alone suddenly. All dressed up, sitting in this darkened room. Lonely.

Then there was a knock at the door. Before Jolene even stood up, the kitchen door opened. Tami walked into the house, holding a bottle of champagne. "You're alone," she said quietly.

"He got caught up at work," Jolene said.

"I was afraid of that." Sadness passed through Tami's eyes, and Jolene hated how it made her feel. Then Tami smiled. "Well. It's no good to turn forty-one without an audience," she said, kicking the door shut behind her. "Besides, I'm dying to know if you'll start wrinkling up right in front of me, like Gary Oldman in *Dracula*."

"I am not going to start wrinkling up."

"You never know."

"Champagne?" Jolene said, arching one eyebrow.

"That's for me. *I* don't have alcoholic parents. You can guzzle soda water, as usual."

Tami popped the champagne bottle effortlessly, poured herself a glass and headed into the family room, where she plopped down on the overstuffed sofa and raised a glass. "To you, my rapidly aging best friend."

Jolene followed Tami into the family room. "You're only a few months younger than I am."

"We Native Americans don't age. It's a scientific fact. Look at my mom. She still gets carded."

Jolene sat down in an overstuffed chair and curled her bare feet up underneath her.

They looked at each other. What swirled between them then, floating like champagne bubbles, were memories of other nights like this, meals Michael had missed, events he'd been too busy to attend. Jolene often told people, especially Tami, how proud she was of her brilliant, successful husband, and it was all true, but lately he seemed unhappy. His father's death had capsized him. She knew how unhappy he was, she just didn't know how to help.

"It must hurt your feelings," Tami said.

"It hurts," Jolene said quietly.

"You should talk to him about it, tell him how you feel."

"What's the point? Why make him feel worse than he already does? Shit happens, Tami. You know Michael's work ethic. It's one of the things I love about him. He never walks away from responsibility."

"Unless it's a family obligation," Tami said softly.

"He's just really busy right now. Since his father's death . . ."

"I know," Tami said, "and you two don't talk about that, either. In fact, you don't talk."

"We talk."

Tami gave her an assessing look. "Marriages go through hard times. Sometimes you have to get in there and fight for your love. That's the only way for it to get better."

Jolene couldn't help thinking of her parents, and the way her mother had fought for a man's love . . . and never gotten it. "Look, Tami. Michael and I are fine. We love each other. Now, can we please, *please* talk about something else?"

Tami lifted her half-full glass. "To you, my friend. You look fabulous for being so freakishly old."

"I look fabulous, period."

Tami laughed at that and launched into a funny story about her family.

It was ten forty before they knew it, and Tami put her empty glass down on the table. "I have to get home. I told Carl I'd be home for *Letterman.*"

Jolene got to her feet. "Thanks for coming, Tam. I needed it."

Tami hugged her fiercely. Together, they walked to the back door.

Jolene watched her friend cut across the driveway and head toward the adjoining property. At last, she closed the door.

In the quiet, she was alone with her thoughts, and she didn't like their company.

It was midnight when Michael pulled into the garage and parked next to Jolene's SUV. On the seat beside him lay a dozen pink roses bound in cellophane. He'd been on the ferry, already on his way home, when he remembered that Jolene preferred red roses. Of course. Soft and girly wasn't her style, never had been, not even on that first, sad day when she walked into his life.

She'd been seventeen. A kid, dressed in thrift-store clothes, with her long blond hair a mess and her beautiful green eyes puffy from crying, and yet, with all of that, she'd walked into the legal-aid office with her back straight, clutching a ratty vinyl purse. He'd been an intern then, in his first year of law school.

She had seemed impossibly brave to him, a girl refusing help even in the worst days of her life. He'd fallen a little in love with her right then, enough to ask her to come back and see him when she was older. It had been her boldness that spoke to him from the beginning, the courage she'd worn as easily as that cheap acrylic sweater.

Six years later she'd walked back into his life, an army helicopter pilot, of all things. He'd been young enough to still believe in love at first sight and old enough to know it didn't happen every day. He'd told himself it didn't matter that he was blue state and she was military, that they had nothing in common. He'd felt so loved by her, so adored, that he couldn't breathe. And their lovemaking had been amazing. In sex, as in everything, Jo had been all in.

He picked up the roses and the small Tiffany's box beside it, wondering if the expensive gift would redeem him. She would see that he'd bought it before—that he'd remembered her birthday in time to have her gift engraved—but would that be enough? He'd missed her birthday dinner—forgotten.

It exhausted him, just thinking of the scene that was coming. He would use his charm to make her smile, beg for her forgiveness, and she would grant it with a grace and ease that would make short work of the whole thing, but he would see the hurt in her green eyes, in the way her smile wouldn't quite bloom, and he would know that he'd disappointed her again. He was the bad guy here; there was no doubt about that, and she would remind him of it in a million tiny ways until he could hardly look at her, until he rolled away from her in bed and stared at the wall and imagined a different life.

He got out of the car and went into the house. In the shadowy kitchen, he found a vase and put the roses in it, then carried them up the stairs.

The master bedroom lights were off except for a small, decorative lamp on the desk by the window. He set the flowers on the antique dresser and went into the bathroom, where he undressed and got ready for bed. Climbing in, he pulled the heavy down comforter up to his chest and lay there in the dark.

It used to soothe him, listening to his wife's breathing, but now every sound she made kept him awake.

He closed his eyes and hoped for the best, knowing before he even tried that it would be hours before he fell asleep and that, once found, his slumber would be haphazard at best, plagued by dreams of a life unlived, a path unchosen.

When he woke, hours later, he felt as if he hadn't slept at all. Watery light came through the windowpanes, making the sage-colored walls look gray as driftwood. The dark wood floors swallowed whatever sunlight came their way.

He pushed up to his elbows, felt the coverlet fall away from his chest.

Jolene lay awake beside him, her blond hair tangled to one side, her pale face turned slightly toward him.

The hurt was already in her eyes.

"I'm sorry, Jo." He leaned down and kissed her quickly, then drew back. "I'll make it up to you."

"I know. It's just a birthday. Maybe I made too much of it."

He got out of bed and got the Tiffany's box off the dresser and brought it back to her.

It occurred to him that she'd asked for something for her birthday, something special. Not a gift, either; that wasn't Jolene's way. She wanted . . . something. He couldn't remember what it was, but he saw the slight frown dart across her face as she saw the box; then it was gone, and she smiled up at him.

"Tiffany, huh?" She sat up in bed, positioned her pillows behind her, and then opened the box. Inside, a sparkling platinum and gold watch was curled around a white leather bed. A single small diamond took the place of the number twelve.

"It's beautiful." She turned it over, to the back, on which *Jolene, happy 41st* was engraved. "Forty-one," she said. "Wow. Time is going fast. Betsy will be in high school in no time."

He wished she hadn't said that. Time wasn't his friend lately. He was forty-five—middle-aged by any standard. Soon he'd be fifty, and whatever chance he'd had to become another version of himself would be gone. And he still had no idea what that other version would look like; he just knew that the color had gone out of who he was.

He sat down on the bed beside Jolene. He looked at her, needing her suddenly, wanting to feel about her the way he used to. "How did you get through . . . their deaths? I mean, really get through it? You had to change your life in an instant."

He saw her flinch, turn slightly away. The question was like a blow that glanced off her shoulder, bruised her. When she looked at him again, she was smiling. "What doesn't kill you makes you stronger. I chose happiness, I guess."

He sighed. More platitudes. Suddenly he was tired again. "I'll make you breakfast in bed, and then maybe we can all go for a bike ride."

She set the watch, still in its box, on the nightstand. "Tonight's my birthday party at Captain Lomand's house. You said you might come."

And there it was: the thing she'd asked for. No wonder he'd forgotten. "I have nothing in common with those people. You know that." He stood up and walked over to the dresser, opening his top drawer.

"I am those people," she said, and just like that they stumbled onto the familiar and rocky terrain. "It's a party for me. You could come just this once."

He turned to face her. "We'll go out to dinner tomorrow night. How's that? All four of us. We'll go to that Italian place you like."

Jolene sighed. He knew she was considering another volley across the net of this old argument. She wanted him to be a part of her military life—she'd always wanted it, but he couldn't do it, couldn't stand that rigid world of one for all and all for one. "Okay," she finally said. "Thanks for the watch. It's beautiful."

"You're welcome."

They stared at each other. Silence gathered in the air, as bitter and rich as the scent of coffee. There were things to be said, he knew, words that had been withheld too long, hoarded in the dark and spoiled. Once he gave them voice, said what he really felt, there would be no going back.

Later that afternoon, carrying a foil-covered casserole dish, Tami walked into Jolene's kitchen. "Well?" she asked, kicking the door shut behind her.

Jolene glanced back into the family room, making sure her kids weren't around. "He's really sorry," she said. "He brought me roses and a beautiful watch."

"He's the one that needs the watch," Tami said. At Jolene's look, she shrugged. "Just sayin'."

"Yeah," Jolene said. "I asked him to come to the party. He doesn't want to."

"I'm sorry," Tami said.

Jolene managed a smile. She couldn't help thinking how different life was for Tami. Although Carl wasn't in the military, he supported Tami fully, came to every event, and often told her how proud he was of her service. Tami's military pictures decorated the walls of their house, were hung alongside Seth's school pictures and shots from their family gatherings. All the pictures of Jolene in uniform were hidden away in drawers somewhere.

She turned away from the disappointed look in Tami's eyes and walked to the bottom of the stairs. "Girls!" she yelled up. "Come on down. It's time for the party."

Lulu came down the stairs, grinning, dragging her blanket. She was dressed for the party in a pink princess dress, complete with a tiara. Betsy appeared at the top of the stairs with her arms crossed.

"Pleeease don't make me go," Betsy pleaded.

"Ticktock, ticktock."

"Dad doesn't have to go."

"He's working," Jolene said. "You're not."

Betsy stomped her foot and spun around. "Fine," she said, marching back to her room.

"I remember how much I wanted a daughter," Tami said, coming up beside Jolene. "Lately I'm not so sure."

"Nothing I do or say is right. Honestly, she breaks a little piece of my heart every day. She swears she'll skip school if I go to career day. Apparently a mother in the military is only slightly less humiliating than one in prison."

Tami leaned against her. "You were raised by wolves, so you don't know this: it's normal. My mom swore she tried to sell me to gypsies at twelve. No takers."

"Is Seth coming today?"

"Of course. He's a boy. They're like puppies; girls are like cats. He just wants to make me happy and play video games. Drama has not yet made an appearance at our house. Although, he does miss Betsy."

Jolene glanced up the stairs. "I hope she's nicer to him."

Tami nodded. "My son is a fashion disaster. He's a geek boy who gets excited to answer a question in biology. Betsy wants to hang with the popular girls. I get it. I do. He's social suicide, and the fact that they used to be best friends does not help her any. Still, *he* doesn't get it. He wonders why she quit skateboarding and doesn't like to look for sand crabs anymore. He still has the birthday poster she made him tacked up on his wall."

Jolene didn't know what to say to that. Before she'd thought of anything, Lulu came to the last step and hurled herself forward. Jolene scooped up her youngest daughter and settled her on her hip, carrying her out to the SUV. After Jolene strapped Lulu into her car seat, she went back into the house. "Come on, Betsy!"

Betsy stomped down the stairs, looking mutinous, with her iPod's earbuds firmly in place. The message was clear: *I'm coming, but I won't like it.* Jolene let the little defiance pass, and followed her daughter to the SUV.

"Where's Seth?" Betsy yelled, opening the passenger door.

Jolene climbed into the driver's seat. "He and Carl are meeting us there. They went fishing this morning. Be nice to him."

Betsy already wasn't listening. She put on her seat belt and started fiddling with her iPod.

"Music?" Jolene asked Tami.

"The queen today, I think. In your honor."

"Madonna it is." Jolene popped a CD into the player and drove off to the familiar beat of "Material Girl."

She and Tami alternately talked and sang; Lulu talked nonstop; Betsy didn't say a word.

In no time, they were pulling into the Gig Harbor subdivision called Ravenwood, which was about forty minutes from the post. The Guard crew came from all over this part of the state—some of the people would have driven hours to get here.

The captain lived in a pretty Wedgwood-blue tract house with white trim and a wraparound porch. Kids ran around the yard, their voices raised into a single, echoing squeal. The house and yard were a reflection of the family—of the man—who lived here. Everything was trimmed and well cared for. Fifty-year-old Captain Benjamin Lomand was one of the best men Jolene had ever met.

Most of the flight crew and their families were already here; Jolene could tell by the multicolored snake of cars parked in the cul-de-sac. Though she couldn't see the backyard from here, she knew that the men—and the female soldiers—would be gathered around the barbecue, holding bottles of domestic beer or cans of Coke, while the wives stood in groups, talking to one another and herding children. Everyone would be smiling.

Jolene pulled up to the side of the driveway and parked. Tami's husband, Carl, and her son, Seth, were standing outside the garage. Waving, they strode down the driveway toward the car. Dressed in baggy jeans and a Seahawks jersey, with a baseball cap down low to conceal his thinning hair, Carl looked like one of those slightly heavy, solidly built men who'd been a high school football star and gone on to work on the line at Boeing. That image was surprisingly accurate, except that he was a mechanic who owned his own garage.

Seth looked nothing like his dad. At twelve, he was a strange and gawky kid, with a pronounced case of acne, eyes that seemed just a little too big for his narrow face, and jet-black hair that fell almost to the middle of his back. Today he was wearing tight Levi's (everyone knew that baggy pants were "in") and a huge Nine Inch Nails tee shirt that accentuated the thinness of his arms.

Tami got out of the car at her husband's approach, taking a foil-covered casserole dish with her.

"And here's the love of my life," Carl said, opening his arms. Tami grinned and handed him the dish. No doubt it was her famous seven-layer dip.

"Happy belated birthday," Carl said to Jolene when she got out of the car.

"Thanks, Carl." She opened the back door and unhooked Lulu's car seat. It was like loosing the Kraken. Lulu skipped off, squealing in delight, looking for someone to play with.

Betsy stepped out of the car slowly, her earbuds still in place. When she saw Seth, her eyes widened in shock at what he was wearing; her mouth compressed. Jolene knew her daughter was terrified to be seen talking to her childhood best friend. So she gave her a little push.

Betsy stumbled forward, almost fell into Seth. He reached out, steadied her, saying, "Whoa . . ." The single word cracked, came in two volumes.

"I hope no one saw that," Betsy said, pulling away from him, walking off. Seth stared after her for a long moment, then shrugged and headed over to a place in the grass. There, he sat down cross-legged and played some electronic game.

Jolene made a mental note to talk to Betsy again about being nice to Seth. Honestly, she didn't understand how her daughter could be so mean.

Carrying the foil-covered glass bowl full of coleslaw she'd made, Jolene followed Carl and Tami into the backyard. They stepped around the corner of the house, and there they were: the flight crew—her friends.

They gathered together often, this group that had trained together for so many years. In the "outside" world, they were from all different walks of life—dentists and loggers and teachers and mechanics. But for one weekend a month and two weeks a summer, they were soldiers, training side by side, serving their country with pride. Although Michael would roll his eyes at it, the truth was that Jolene loved these people. They were like her; they'd joined the military because they believed in serving their country, in being patriots, in keeping America safe. They *believed*. There wasn't a member of this crew who wouldn't give his life for Jolene's, and vice versa.

At her arrival, everyone started singing "Happy Birthday."

Jolene laughed, feeling a rush of pure, sweet joy. There was only the smallest of nicks in her happiness; she wished Michael were here with her. She would have loved to turn to him right now and tell him how much these friendships meant to her. How much this moment meant to her. God knew, her birthdays had never mattered to her parents.

When the song ended, she made the rounds, thanking everyone, talking. As she put her coleslaw down on a table already groaning under the weight of salads, casseroles, desserts, and condiments, Owen "Smitty" Smith offered her a glass of lemonade. He was the newest member of their crew—a freckle-faced twenty-year-old kid who had joined the Guard to pay for college.

"Thanks, Smitty," she said.

He grinned, showing off a full set of braces. "Happy birthday, Chief," he said. "You're the same age as my mom."

"Thanks," she said, laughing, and then he was gone, hurrying off to catch up with his latest girlfriend.

"Warrant Officer Zarkades," Jamie Hix said, sidling up to her at the table, tilting a Corona at her. He was the other gunner on her crew. Twenty-nine and newly divorced, Jamie was trying to get joint custody of his eight-year-old son from his ex-wife, Gina. Their recent divorce was becoming increasingly contentious. "Forty-one, huh?"

She plucked a raw carrot from the vegetable tray in front of her, swiping it in ranch dressing. "Hard to believe."

"Too bad Michael couldn't make it today."

She wasn't surprised by the sentiment; she knew that most of her friends here wondered why Michael rarely made an appearance at their functions. They were protective of her. They'd all drilled together so long there weren't many secrets between them. "He works hard, and his job is important."

"Yeah. Gina didn't come around much either."

She didn't like the comparison between their spouses, however subtle. She was going to say so, but the compassion in Jamie's eyes made her feel suddenly lonely. Saying something—she wasn't quite sure what—she moved away, made her way past the barbecue, where everyone seemed to be laughing, and came to the captain's rose garden. She looked down at the bright, tightly coiled pink buds. Pink. Her favorite was red. Michael used to know that.

"Are you okay?" Tami said, sidling up to her, bumping her hip to hip.

"Of course," she answered too quickly.

"I'm here for you," Tami said softly, as if she knew everything that was turning through Jolene's mind. "We all are."

"I know," Jolene said, looking around at the people who mattered so much to her. Everyone she looked at smiled and waved. They loved her, cared about her; these people were as much her family as Michael and the girls. She had so many blessings in her life.

It was okay that Michael wasn't here; they were married people, not conjoined twins. They didn't have to share every aspect of their lives.

$\mathcal{T}hree$

On Wednesday morning, Jolene returned from her run to find Betsy standing on the porch, wearing a robe she'd outgrown over flannel pajamas and a pair of pink Ugg boots. Her face was scrunched in irritation—a familiar expression these days.

Jolene ran up the driveway, breathing hard, her breath clouding in front of her. "What's wrong?"

"Today's Wednesday," Betsy said in the same tone of voice you'd use to whisper the words *you have cancer.*

Oh. That. "Shoo." Jolene herded Betsy back into the house, where it was warm.

"You can't go, Mom. I'll say you are sick."

"I'm going to career day, Betsy," Jolene said, turning on the coffeepot.

Betsy practically shrieked with displeasure. "Fine. Ruin my life." She stomped out of the kitchen and up the stairs. She slammed her bedroom door shut.

"Oh, no, you don't," Jolene muttered, following her daughter's route up the stairs. At the closed bedroom door on the second floor, she knocked hard.

"Go away."

Jolene knocked again.

"Fine. Come in. You will anyway. There's no privacy in this stupid house."

Jolene accepted the lovely invitation and opened the door.

Betsy's bedroom was a reflection both of the twelve-year-old who currently inhabited it and the tomboy who'd lived here only a few months ago. The walls were still the pale wheat-yellow color that Jolene had chosen nearly a decade ago. Long gone were the white crib and dressing table and framed Winnie the Pooh prints. In their place were a four-postered bed covered in denim bedding, an antique yellow dresser with blue knobs, and posters of mop-headed boys from teenybopper bands. The war between childhood and adolescence showed everywhere: on the nightstand lay a tangle of makeup (which she wasn't allowed to wear outside the house), a mason jar full of beach glass and agates, and a once-favorite bug catcher that Seth had given her for her eighth birthday. Piles of clothes—tried on and discarded before school yesterday—lay in heaps on the floor.

Betsy sat on her bed, looking pissed off, with her knees drawn up to her chest.

Jolene sat down on the edge of the bed. Her heart went out to her daughter, who had been so undone by middle school. This once-buoyant, confident tomboy had become lost in a sea of mean girls and impossible social choices; lately she was so unsure of herself that nothing came easily and no decision could stand without peer approval. Nothing mattered more than fitting in, and clearly that was not going well.

"Why don't you want me to go to career day?"

"It's embarrassing. I told you: no one cool has a mom who's a soldier."

Jolene didn't want to let it hurt her, and she was mostly successful. It was just a tiny sting, like the prick from a needle. "You don't know embarrassing," she said softly, remembering her own mother, stumbling drunkenly into a parent-teacher conference, saying *whad she do* in a slurry voice.

"Sierra will make fun of me."

"Then she's not much of a friend, is she? Why don't you tell me what's happening, Bets. You and Sierra and Zoe used to do everything together."

"You don't let me do anything. They get to wear makeup and go to the mall on the weekends."

This old argument. "You're too young to wear makeup. Thirteen is our deal for makeup and pierced ears. You know that."

"Like I agreed," Betsy said bitterly.

"If they don't like you because you don't wear mascara—"

"You don't understand *anything*."

"Bets," Jolene said in her gentlest voice. "What happened?"

That did it, the gentleness. Betsy burst into tears. Jolene scooted over on the bed and took Betsy in her arms, holding her while she cried. This had been a long time coming. Betsy cried as if her heart were breaking, as if someone she loved were dying. Jolene held her tightly, stroking her curly hair.

"Si-Si-erra brought cigarettes to school last week," Betsy said between sobs. "Wh-when I told her it was against the rules, she ca-ca-lled me a loser and dared me to smoke one."

Jolene took a calming breath. "And did you?"

"No, but now they won't talk to me. They call me Goody Two-shoes."

She wanted to hold her daughter until these dangers passed, until Betsy was old enough to handle them with grace and ease. Jolene needed to say the right thing now, the perfect motherly thing, but she was out of her element. Until the army—with its rigid rules of behavior—she had never fit in anywhere. The kids in her school had known she was different—probably it had been the out-of-date clothes or the events she could never go to, or maybe it had been because she couldn't invite anyone home. Who knew? Kids were like Jedi in that way; they could sense the slightest disturbance in the Force. Jolene had found a way even then, as a girl, to compartmentalize her feelings and bury them.

So she didn't know about wanting to fit in so desperately you felt sick at the smallest slight. Ordinarily, she would talk to Betsy about inner strength now, about believing in herself, maybe even about cutting her friends some slack.

But smoking on the school grounds changed all that. If Betsy's friends, ex-friends, were smoking, Jolene needed to be more firm.

"I'll call Sierra's mother—"

"Oh, my GOD, you will not. Promise me you won't. If you do, I'll never tell you anything again."

The fear in Betsy's eyes was alarming.

"Promise, me, Mom. Please—"

"Okay," Jolene said. "I won't say anything for now. But, honey, if Sierra and Zoe are smoking cigarettes at school, you don't want to follow their lead. Maybe you need to make new friends. Like the girls on your track team. They seem nice."

"You think everyone seems nice."

"How about Seth?"

Betsy rolled her eyes. "Puh-lease. Yesterday he brought his guitar to school and played it at lunchtime. It was superlame."

"You used to love listening to him play his guitar."

"So what? I don't now. People were laughing at him."

Jolene stared at Betsy; her daughter looked utterly miserable. "Ah, Betsy. How can you be mean to Seth? You know how much it hurts when Sierra and Zoe are mean to you."

"If I'm his friend no one will like me."

"You have to learn not to be a lemming, Bets."

"What's that, a rodent? Are you saying I'm a rodent?"

Jolene sighed. "I wish I could make all this easier on you. But only you can do that. You need to be your best self, Betsy. Be a good friend and you'll have good friends."

"You want to make it easier on me? Skip career day."

And just like that, they were back to the beginning. "I can't. You know that. I made a commitment. When you make a promise to someone, you follow through. That's what honor is, and honor—and love—matter more than anything."

"Yeah, yeah. Be all that you can be."

"I won't volunteer next year. How's that?"

Betsy looked at her. "Promise?"

"I promise." Jolene tried not to care that she'd finally drawn a reluctant smile out of her daughter by promising *not* to be a part of her life.

Career day was as bad as expected. Betsy had been mortified by Jolene's appearance at the middle school. Jolene had tried to be as quiet as possible, modulating her voice carefully as she told the kids about the high school to flight school program she'd entered at eighteen. The kids had loved hearing about the missions she flew in state, like last year's rescue of climbers on Mount Rainier during a blizzard. They questioned her about night-vision goggles and guns and combat training. Jolene tried to underplay everything, including the coolness of flying a Black Hawk, but all the while, she saw Betsy slinking downward in her seat, trying her best to disappear. At the end of the event, Betsy had been the first one out the door. On the other side of the gymnasium, Sierra and Zoe had pointed at Betsy and laughed.

Since then, Betsy had been even more hormonal and moody. She yelled; she cried; she rolled her eyes. She had stopped walking and begun stomping. Everywhere. In and out of rooms, up the stairs. Doors weren't shut anymore; they were slammed. When the phone rang, she lunged for it. Invariably, she was disappointed when the call turned out to be for someone else. No one was calling her, which for a twelve-year-old was the equivalent of being stranded on an ice floe. Jolene might be overreacting, but she was worried about her daughter. Anything could set her off these days, send her spiraling into depression.

"And today is the first track meet. You know what that means. Potential humiliation. I'm worried," she said to Michael that morning. He was beside her in bed, reading.

She waited for him to respond, but it quickly became apparent that he had nothing to say, or he wasn't listening. "Michael?"

"What? Oh. That again. She's fine, Jolene. Quit trying to control everything." He put down his newspaper and got out of bed, heading into the bathroom, closing the door behind him.

Jolene sighed. As usual, she was on her own for family matters. She got out of bed and went for her run.

When she was finished, she took a shower and dressed quickly, tying her wet hair back in a ponytail as she awakened the girls. Downstairs, in the kitchen, she poured herself a cup of coffee and started breakfast. Blueberry pancakes.

"Morning," Michael said from behind her.

She turned and looked at him.

He smiled, but it was tired and washed out, that smile; it didn't reach his dark eyes. In fact, it wasn't his smile at all, really, not the one that had coaxed her so completely into love once upon a time.

For a moment, she was struck by how good-looking he was. His black hair, still without a trace of gray at forty-five, was damp and wavy. He was the kind of man who drew attention; when Michael Zarkades walked into a room, everyone noticed—he knew it and loved it.

"You'll make the track meet, right? I know how busy you are at work, and normally I get that you can't come home, but just this once I think it's important, okay? You know what a daddy's girl she is," she said.

Michael paused, the coffee cup inches from his mouth. "How many times are you going to remind me?"

She smiled. "I'm a little obsessive? What a surprise. It's just that it's important that you be there. On time. Betsy is fragile these days and I—"

Betsy shrieked "Mom!" and skidded into the kitchen. "Where's my orange hoodie? I *need* it!"

Lulu ran up beside her, looking sleep-tousled, holding her yellow blanket. "Hoodie, hoodie."

"Shut *up*," Betsy screamed.

Lulu's face crumpled. She shuffled over to the kitchen table and climbed up into her chair.

"I washed your good-luck hoodie, Betsy," Jolene said. "I knew you'd need it."

"Oh," Betsy said, sagging a little in relief.

"Apologize to your sister," Michael said from his place at the counter.

Betsy mumbled an apology while Jolene went to the laundry room and retrieved the hoodie—a gift from Michael that had become Betsy's talisman. Jolene knew it wasn't unrelated—the source of the gift and the magic that went with it. Betsy needed attention from her father, and sometimes the hoodie was all she got.

Betsy snatched the orange-sherbet-colored hoodie from Jolene and put it on.

Jolene saw how pale her daughter was, how shaky. She glanced over at Michael, to see if he'd noticed, but he had gone back to reading the newspaper. He was in the room with them but completely apart. How long had it been that way? she suddenly wondered.

Betsy went to the table and sat down.

Jolene patted Betsy's shoulder. "I bet you're excited about the meet. I talked to your coach and he said—"

"You *talked* to my coach?"

Jolene paused, drew her hand back. Obviously she'd gone wrong again. "He said you'd been doing great at practice."

"Unbelievable." Betsy shook her head and stared down at the two pancakes on her plate, with their blueberry eyes and syrup mouth.

"I want pancake men," Lulu yelled, irritated not to be the center of attention.

"It's natural to be nervous, Bets," Jolene said. "But I've seen you run. You're the best sprinter on the JV team."

Betsy glared up at her. "I am *not* the best. You just say that because you're my mom. It's, like, a rule or something."

"The only rule that I have is to love you," Jolene said, "and I do. And I'm proud of you, Betsy. It's scary to put yourself out there in life, to take a chance. I'm proud of you for trying. We all are," she said pointedly, her words aimed at Michael, who stood by the counter, reading his paper. Beside him, tacked to the wall, was Jolene's calendar that listed everything she needed to do this week, and everywhere she needed to be. TRACK MEET was written in bold red on today's date.

Betsy followed Jolene's look. "Will you be at the meet, Dad? It starts at three thirty."

A silence followed, a waiting. How long did it last? A second? A minute? Jolene prayed that he would look up, flash that charming smile, and make a promise.

"Michael," she said sharply. She knew how important his job was, and she respected his dedication. She rarely asked him to show up to any family event, but this first track meet mattered.

He looked up, irritated by her tone. "What?"

"Betsy reminded you about her track meet. It's at three thirty today."

"Oh, right." He put down his newspaper and there it was, the smile that had swept so many women, including Jolene, off their feet. He gave it to Betsy, full power, his handsome face crinkling in good humor. "How could I forget my princess's big day?"

Betsy's smile overtook her small, pale face, showing off her braces and big, crooked teeth.

He walked over to the table, leaned down, and kissed the top of Betsy's head and ruffled Lulu's black hair and kept moving toward the door, grabbing his coat off the back of the chair and his briefcase off the tile counter.

Betsy beamed under his attention. "Did you know—"

He left the house, the door snapping shut behind him, snipping Betsy's sentence in half.

She slumped forward, a rag doll emptied of stuffing.

"He didn't hear you," Jolene said. "You know what it's like when he has to catch the ferry."

"He should have his hearing checked," Betsy said, shoving her plate aside.

Four

Michael stood at his office window, staring out. On this cold, gray day, Seattle simmered beneath a heavy lid of clouds. Rain obscured the view, softened the hard steel edges of the high-rise buildings. Far below, messengers on bicycles darted in and out through traffic like hummingbirds.

Behind him, his intercom buzzed.

He went back to answer it. "Hey, Ann. What's up?"

"An Edward Keller is on the phone."

"Do I know him?"

"Not to my knowledge. But he says it's urgent."

"Put him through." Michael sat down behind his desk. Urgent calls from strangers were a fixture of criminal defense.

The phone rang; he picked it up.

"Michael Zarkades," he said simply.

"Thank you for taking my call, Mr. Zarkades. I understand you're my son's court-appointed attorney."

"Who is your son?"

"Keith Keller. He was arrested for killing his wife."

The case Judge Runyon had assigned to Bill. "Right, Mr. Keller. I was just getting up to speed on the facts of the case." He rifled through the piles of papers and folders on his desk, looking for the Keller file. When he found it, he said, "Oh, right. In fact, I have an appointment with your son today at two."

Two o'clock.

Shit.

The track meet.

"I'm worried about him, sir. He won't talk to me. I'd like to come in and talk to you, if you don't mind. You need to know what a good kid he is."

Murder notwithstanding. "I'm sure I'll need to talk to you soon, Mr. Keller," Michael said. "But I need to speak with my client first. Did you give my secretary your number?"

"I did."

"Good."

"Mr. Zarkades? He is a good kid. I don't know why he did it."

Michael wished he hadn't said that last sentence. "I'll get back to you, Mr. Keller. Thanks."

Michael hung up the phone and glanced at his watch. It was 12:27. He'd forgotten about this appointment with Keller—he should have cancelled it because of the track meet.

He still could. Or he could go early. It wasn't like Keller had a full social calendar.

He looked at his watch again. If he left now, he could be at the jail by 12:45, interview his new client, and still make the 2:05 ferry.

The room in the King County jail was dank and dreary. There was no *CSI* two-way mirror on the wall; instead, there was a pair of green, banged-up light fixtures hanging above a desk that had been marked up through years of use and a small metal trash can in the corner. Nothing that could be used as a weapon. The table legs were bolted to the concrete floor.

Michael sat in the chair across the table from his new client, Keith Keller, who was young, with short blond hair and the kind of build that hinted at either steroids or obsessive weight lifting. His cheekbones were sharp and his lips looked like he'd been biting at them.

The wall clock kept a steady record of the minutes that passed in silence.

Well, not silence.

Keith sat as still as a stone, his gray eyes strangely—disturbingly— blank.

They'd been sitting here alone, the two of them, for over thirty-five minutes. Keith hadn't said a word, but the kid breathed loudly, a rattling, phlegmy kind of breathing.

Michael glanced at the clock, again—1:21—and then down at the paperwork on the wooden table in front of him. All he had so far was the arrest report, and it wasn't nearly enough upon which to base a defense. According to the police, Keith had gone on a rampage, shooting up everything until his neighbors called for help. When the police arrived, Keith barricaded himself in his house for hours. At some point in all of this, he'd—allegedly—shot his wife in the head. The report indicated that he'd threatened to kill himself before the SWAT team captured him.

It didn't make sense. Keller was twenty-four and a half years old, with an unblemished record. Unlike most of Michael's clients, Keller had never been arrested for anything before this, not even shoplifting as a teen. He'd graduated from high school, joined the Marines, and been honorably discharged. Then he'd gotten a job. He had no known gang affiliations, no history of drug abuse.

"I need to understand what happened, Keith."

Keith stared at the same spot on the wall that had held his attention for three-quarters of the last hour.

And that awful, shuddering breathing.

Michael sighed and looked at his watch. If the kid didn't want to help himself, that was his business. Michael had to leave right now or he'd miss the ferry—and the start of the track meet. "Fine, Keith. I'm going to ask the court for a psych eval on you. You won't be competent to stand trial if you can't participate in your own defense. Would you rather be in a psychiatric hospital than the jail? It's your choice."

Still, nothing.

He waited another moment, hoping for a response. Getting nothing from his client, he stood up and gathered his files. "I'm on your side, Keith. Remember that."

Putting his papers in his briefcase, he closed it up, grabbed the handle, and went toward the door. He was just about to push the button for the guard when Keith spoke.

"Why bother? I'm guilty."

Michael stopped. Of all the things the kid could have said, that was probably the least productive. A criminal defense attorney didn't actually want to know that—it limited the defenses he could offer. He turned around slowly, expected to see Keith looking at him, but the kid was staring at his own fingers, as if the secret to immortality lay in the dirty nail beds. "When you say guilty . . ."

"I shot her in the head." His voice broke on that. He looked up. Michael had grown used to grief, and he saw it in the young man's eyes. "Why would you be on my side?"

Shit.

Now he had to explain the attorney-client relationship and the idea of American jurisprudence, the whole innocent-until-proven-guilty thing. He looked down at his watch. 1:37. There was no way he was going to make the start of the track meet, but he could be late, couldn't he?

He went back to the desk and sat down, pulling a pad and paper out of his briefcase. "Let me explain how this works . . ."

At 2:20, Jolene pulled up in front of her mother-in-law's gardening shop, the Green Thumb, and led Lulu inside.

A bell tinkled gaily overhead. The small, narrow shop—once an old-fashioned drugstore, complete with a soda fountain—was a treasure trove for gardeners. Michael's mother, Mila, had opened the shop ten years ago—just for fun—but in the months since Theo's death, it had become her sanctuary. Like her son, Mila had a strong work ethic, and lately she spent long hours here.

"*Yia Yia!*" Lulu yelled, yanking free. She charged forward with her usual enthusiasm. "Where are you?"

Mila pushed through the shimmering glass-bead curtain of the back room. "Do I hear my granddaughter?"

"I'm here, *Yia Yia!*" Lulu squealed.

Mila wore her usual work outfit: a thigh-length tee shirt, a green canvas apron (designed to camouflage her weight), and jeans tucked into orange rubber boots. Heavy makeup accentuated the dramatic beauty of her face—arching jet-black eyebrows, sparkling brown eyes, and full lips that smiled easily. She looked as Greek as she sounded, and she spoiled her grandkids as much as she'd spoiled her son. She had also become the mother Jolene always wanted.

As a young mother, Jolene had spent hours hunkered down in the rich black dirt with her mother-in-law beside her. At first she'd thought she was learning about weeds and the importance of a solid root system and levels of sunlight needed for growth; in time, she'd realized that her mother-in-law was teaching her about life and love and family. When it had come time for Jolene and Michael to purchase a home in which to raise their own family, she had never questioned the location. This town had become "home" for Jolene the moment Mila first hugged her and whispered, "*You're the one for him, but you know that, don't you?*"

"Hello, Lucy Louida," Mila said, swinging her granddaughter up into her strong arms and setting her on the counter by the cash register.

"Hi, *Yia Yia*," Lulu said, grinning. "You want to play patty-cake?"

"Not now, *kardia mou.*"

Jolene came up behind her mother-in-law and hugged her tightly. For as long as she lived, the scent of Shalimar perfume would remind her of this woman.

Mila leaned back into the embrace. Her dyed black hair—piled up à la an aging Jersey girl—tickled Jolene's cheek. Then she clapped her plump hands together. "Now it is time to watch my granddaughter run like the wind. I'm ready to go." Mila gave some instructions to the older man who was her assistant manager, and in no time they were headed to the middle school, where, finally, the sun had brushed the clouds away.

The track was a hive of activity; all around them, students and teachers and parents were readying the track and football field for the events. The opposing team was huddled at the opposite end of the field. Betsy was with her team beneath the goalposts, dressed in her blue and gold sweats. At their arrival, she looked up, waved, and ran up to them.

Betsy grinned. "Hi, *Yia Yia*."

Jolene smiled down at her daughter, who for just a second looked proud that they were here to watch her run. She felt a little catch in her throat. This was such a big moment for her daughter; the first school athletic event. Jolene leaned forward and kissed Betsy.

"Oh. My. God." Betsy gasped and stumbled back, her eyes huge.

"Sorry," Jolene said, trying not to smile. "No one saw."

Mila laughed. "The horror. The horror. Your father used to hate it when I kissed him in public also. I did not care about his horror, either. I told him he was lucky to have a mother who loved him."

"Right," Betsy said. She glanced over at the team, and bit her lower lip nervously.

Jolene moved forward. "You're ready for this, Bets."

Betsy looked up, and in that instant Jolene saw her little girl again, the one who'd loved digging in the sand and capturing caterpillars. "I'm going to lose. Just so you know. I might even fall."

"You are not going to fall, Betsy. Life is like an apple. You have to take a big bite to get all the flavor."

"Yeah," Betsy said, looking miserable. "Whatever *that* means."

"It means good luck," Mila said.

"We'll go up into the stands to watch," Jolene said.

"Where's Dad?" Betsy asked.

"He'll be here," Jolene said. "The ferry is just landing now. Good luck, baby."

Jolene slung Lulu onto her hip and carried her over to the stands. There were probably forty people in the bleachers, mostly moms and kids. They climbed up to a seat in the middle and sat down. About five minutes later, Tami showed up, a little out of breath and red-faced.

"Did I miss anything?" she said, sliding to sit next to Jolene.

"Nope."

At exactly three thirty, a gun went off and the first event started—the boys' mile run.

Lulu screamed at the sound. She lurched to her feet and ran back and forth in the bleachers, yelling, "Look at me, Mommy!"

"Where is Michael?" Mila asked worriedly. "I reminded him yesterday."

"I'm sure he's on his way," Jolene answered. "He better be."

Tami shot her an are-you-worried look.

Jolene nodded.

The mile race finished. Then they called the girls' mile.

Jolene fished her phone out of her purse and dialed Michael's cell phone. It went straight to voice mail. She tapped her foot nervously.

Come on, Michael . . . get here on time . . .

At 4:10, they called Betsy's event—the hundred-meter dash. *Runners, take your spots . . .*

Jolene's phone rang. It was Michael. She picked up fast. "If you're in the parking lot, you need to run. They just called her race."

"I'm at the jail," he said. "My client—"

"So you'll miss it," she said sharply.

Below, on the track, Betsy approached the starting line. She bent over, placed her palms on the track, fit her feet into the blocks.

"Damn it, Jo—"

The starting gun went off. Jolene said, "I gotta go," and hung up on him. Getting to her feet, she cheered for Betsy, who was running hard, pumping her arms and legs, giving it her all. Pride washed through Jolene, brought tears to her eyes. "Go, Betsy, go!"

Betsy was the second one across the finish line. Afterward, she bent over, breathing hard, and then she looked up into the stands. She was beaming, her smile triumphant as she looked up at her family.

Slowly, her smile faded. She saw that Michael wasn't there.

Then she ran off to be with her team.

Jolene sank slowly back onto the bleacher seat. She knew what it was like to need a parent's attention and be denied, how much that hurt. She had never wanted her children to know that pain. She knew she was overreacting—it was just a track meet, after all—but it was the start. How long would Betsy remember this, be wounded by it? And how easily could Michael have made a different choice?

There was another race—the 220—and Betsy gave it her all, but her sense of triumph was gone; so was her smile. She came in fourth. After that, the races went on and on, and Lulu kept running back and forth in the bleachers, but the three adults just sat there.

"I don't understand it," Mila said at last. "I reminded him twice."

"I saw your twice and doubled it," Tami said. "The only way he could legitimately have forgotten was if he had a brain tumor. Sorry, Miz Z, I'm just saying . . ."

"He is like his father in this," Mila said. "I begged Theo to come to Michael's school functions, but he was always working. Their jobs are important."

"So is the family," Jolene said quietly.

Mila sighed. "Yes. This I told his father, too."

Lulu twirled in front of Jolene, banging into the seat. Her eyes sparkled in that I'm-either-going-to-scream-or-fall-asleep-any-second kind of way.

When the meet ended at five fifteen, Jolene took Lulu's small hand in hers and stood. "Well. Let's go."

They made their way down the bleacher steps and onto the field, where athletes from both schools milled around.

"There she is," Lulu said, pointing to Betsy, who stood alone, beneath the football goalpost.

Jolene pulled Betsy into a fierce hug. "I am so proud of you."

"Second place. Big deal," Betsy said, pulling back.

Jolene could see the hurt turning into a brittle shell of anger. That seemed to be Betsy's modus operandi these days—any sharp emotion turned into anger.

"I have never seen such running, *kardia mou*. You were like the wind."

Betsy didn't even try to smile. "Thanks, *Yia Yia*."

"How about if we go out for pizza and ice cream?" Mila suggested, clapping her hands together.

"Sure," Betsy said glumly.

They walked out together. It was obvious to Jolene—and certainly to Betsy—that everyone was trying to talk at once, hoping to mask Michael's absence. For the next hour, they pretended, laughing a little too loudly, making jokes that weren't funny. Jolene lost track of the times someone told Betsy how amazing she had been. The words hit her daughter's brittle wall, failing to evoke even a small smile. There was an empty seat at the table and all of them felt it keenly.

By the time they left the restaurant and drove home, Jolene was as mad at Michael as she'd ever been.

He could disappoint her—hell, she was an adult, she could take it. But she wouldn't let him break their daughter's heart.

Mila was the only one who addressed the white elephant in the car with them. At her house, before she got out of the car, she turned to Betsy and said, "Your father wanted to be here today. I know he did."

"Big deal," Betsy said.

Mila seemed to consider a response to that, but, instead of saying anything, she smiled sadly, unhooked her seat belt, and got out of the car.

At home, Jolene parked in the garage and unhooked Lulu's car seat.

"Where's Daddy?" Lulu said sleepily.

"He was too busy to come," Betsy said sharply. "Not that I care." On that, she slammed the car door shut and ran into the house.

Jolene pulled Lulu into her arms and carried her up the stairs. She readied her youngest for bed, read her a story, and tucked her in. Lulu was asleep before her head hit the pillow.

Then she went to Betsy's room, knocked on the door, and went inside.

Betsy was already in bed, her pimply face pink from scrubbing. Her blue and gold tracksuit was a tangled heap on the floor. The red ribbon she'd won lay on the nightstand.

Jolene got into bed beside her. Betsy eased sideways to make room and then leaned against her.

"What's his excuse this time?"

What could Jolene say? That Michael's work ethic and sense of duty sometimes trumped his family? She could hardly fault him for that: it was one of the things they shared. And he'd learned it from his father. The Zarkades men could disappoint their wives and children, but they never let down a client. "Ah, baby . . . sometimes we have to forgive the people we love. That's all there is to it. And you know how important his work is. People's lives depend on him."

"I don't care anyway," Betsy said, but her eyes filled with tears.

Jolene held Betsy close. "Of course you care. You're mad at him, and you have a right to be. But he loves you, Betsy."

"Whatever."

"You pretty much rocked today, you know that, right?"

She felt Betsy relax a little. "I sort of did."

They lay there for a long time, saying nothing of importance. Finally, Jolene kissed her daughter's temple, said good night, and went downstairs.

She sat on the cold brick hearth, with the black, empty fireplace behind her, and stared down at her hands. In her mind, she yelled at Michael, railed at him for disappointing their daughter.

This time, she'd say it all. She'd get his attention and make him understand that there were moments in life that could simply be lost. Too many and a relationship could founder.

It was just past nine o'clock when she heard his car come up the driveway. Moments later, he walked into the kitchen, looking harried. "Hey, Jo. Sorry I'm late, but once I missed the track meet, I figured, why hurry home?"

Jolene got to her feet. "Really. Is that what you thought?"

"I had to—"

"*You* had to do something. How utterly surprising. And in a balancing of needs, yours won out. I'm shocked."

"Damn it, Jo, it wasn't intentional. If you'd just listen—"

"You hurt her feelings," she said, moving toward him. He was a tall man—six feet, but in her shoes, Jolene was only an inch shorter. "Why aren't we important to you anymore, Michael?"

A change came over him. He took a step backward, eyeing her hard. "Don't start a conversation you don't want to have, Jo."

"What does that mean?"

"You don't care *why* I did it, and you don't trust me to have a good reason. An important reason. I'm tired of you defining every second of our life. We live here because it's what *you* wanted. You make all the rules—where we live, where we vacation, how we spend our weekends. When was the last time you asked what *I* wanted?"

"Don't you *dare* try to turn this into my fault. We picked this house together, Michael. You and me, back in the days when we did things together. And if I manage our family, it's because *someone* has to. All you ever seem to care about lately is your work."

"You're not even listening to me. I'm trying to say something here."

"What could you possibly say, Michael? Your daughter needed you today, just this one time. You should have quit whatever you were doing and gotten here. But no, you put us on the back burner again."

She hadn't meant to say us; she'd meant to say *her*. Our daughter. This wasn't about them.

"Damn it, Jo, it's a track meet, not her wedding. My dad didn't make it to every game, but I knew he loved me."

"Is that the kind of father you want to be? Like yours? He was too busy to get to your high school graduation." She knew instantly she'd gone too far; she saw it in the way he stiffened. "I'm sorry. I didn't mean that. I know how much you loved him, but . . ."

"I can't do this anymore," he said softly, shaking his head.

Jolene frowned. "Do what?"

"I don't want this anymore."

"What the hell is going on here, Michael? You screwed up tonight. Why can't you—"

He looked at her. "I don't love you, Jo."

"What?"

"I don't love you anymore."

"But . . ." It felt as if something inside of her were tearing apart, ripping muscle from bone. She grabbed the counter edge for support. In the roar of noise in her head, she heard a small, indrawn breath. She turned slowly, slowly, slowly, thinking, *please, God, no* . . .

Betsy stood in the family room, holding her second-place ribbon. She gasped quietly, her eyes widening slowly in understanding. Then she turned and ran up the stairs.

$\mathcal{F}ive$

Michael couldn't believe he'd said the words out loud.

I don't love you anymore.

He hadn't meant to say it; the words had formed in anger and spilled out without warning. But they'd been there, waiting for him, building inside him. And he'd thought them before, more often than he'd like to admit.

He could say he was sorry and she'd forgive him, maybe not instantly, but soon. Their family, this family, was everything to her, and she loved him. He knew that, had always known it; even tonight, as he'd wounded her, she still loved him.

He *wanted* to love her. But that wasn't the same thing, and it wasn't enough for him anymore. If he backpedaled now, retrieved those sharp words and softened them, shaped them into something different, nothing would change. He would keep living this life where too often he felt constricted by her rules and regulations, emasculated by her strength.

He couldn't seem to measure up to Jolene. It wasn't enough for her that he loved his children and had a successful career and did his best. She demanded more, in that silent, competent way of hers; he had to compensate somehow for all the love she hadn't had as a child, and it was too much for him.

He was done pretending to be the man she wanted. It was time—finally—to find out who *he* wanted to be.

The decision freed him. He wanted to tell her all this, make her understand so he could feel better, but now was not the time. He needed to get out of here. He was reaching for his car keys when she said, "Go talk to Betsy."

In all of this, he'd forgotten. He looked at her for the first time since he'd said *I don't love you anymore.* "Me?"

She looked like one of those marble statues in the Louvre. Already she was retreating emotionally, pulling her feelings back inside where they'd be safe.

"She's your daughter, Michael, and you hurt her. If there's any chance of making her feel better, it lies in you. Maybe *she'll* forgive you."

He heard the emphasis she placed on the pronoun. "I haven't asked for your forgiveness, Jo," he said.

He saw how deeply that hurt her. "No, Michael, you haven't. Do you want a divorce?"

"I don't know. Maybe."

"Maybe."

He saw the way she looked at him then. When it came to love, Jolene was like a recovering alcoholic, a zealot. Love was either there, hot as fire, or it was dead, as cold as ash. She saw no middle ground, and she had no patience for uncertainty. It made him feel small, the way she looked at him, and he almost hated her for that. She was always so damned strong, even now, when he had broken her heart. Had he wanted her to fall apart and say she loved him?

He walked away from her, went up the stairs.

Outside Betsy's closed door, he paused, then knocked.

"Go away, Mom."

He opened the door, saying, "It's me."

She saw him and started to cry. "I don't wa-want you in h-here. G-Go away."

"Don't cry, Lil Bit," he said. At the childhood nickname, so long unused, she cried harder.

He went to the bed, sat down facing her. He felt unable to sit straight in her presence; his shoulders slumped forward, as if his spine had begun to go soft. "Betsy," he said tiredly.

She sniffed, looked at him from beneath heavy lashes.

In her teary eyes, he saw the full import of what he'd done, what he'd said. His love for Jolene was only a part of their life together, the skeleton of their family; but there was more. Their children were the sinew and muscles. The heart. How could one love be extracted from the other without it all collapsing?

"I'm sorry I missed your race."

"It was stupid anyway. I didn't win" was what she said, but in her eyes, he saw heartbreak.

"You ran the race, that's what matters. There will be lots of winning and losing in your life. All of it makes you who you are. I'm proud of you."

She wiped her eyes and studied him.

He could see what she was thinking. He sighed, pushed a hand through his hair. Turning slightly, out of his depth, he glanced out the window.

"Grown-ups fight," he said, too ashamed to look at her. Was he lying? He didn't even know. Ten minutes ago it had been so clear to him—he had fallen out of *in love* with his wife. Now he saw that it had been a drop of water, that moment, falling into the ocean of their connected lives. "You and Lulu fight all the time and you still love her, right?"

"But you said—"

"Just forget it, Betsy. I didn't mean it."

"It was a mistake?"

He looked at her at last. "A mistake," he repeated, hearing the word as something unfamiliar. "I'm sorry you heard our fight, and I'm sorry I missed your track meet. Forgive me?"

Betsy stared at him so long he thought maybe she was going to say no. Finally, though, she nodded solemnly.

He leaned forward and drew her into his arms. He felt her start to cry again, so he held on, let her be. When she finally quieted, he let go of her and eased off the bed, standing beside her.

She looked up at him. "You love Mom, too, right?"

He said yes—the right answer—but he could tell by the sadness in her eyes that he had waited too long, that the silence convinced her of more than his words had.

Leaving her, he went back downstairs, steeling himself to face Jolene, but she wasn't down there, waiting. She'd picked up the room and turned off the lights.

That was Jolene, cleaning up even while life was falling apart.

Jolene made it up the stairs and into her bedroom without coming apart, although how she did it, she wasn't quite sure. Somehow, her heart was still beating and her brain was still sending signals of the most rudimentary kind—breathe, lift your foot, step forward.

She closed the door quietly behind her, wondering for a split second why she didn't slam it shut. Maybe a sound like that, a *crack,* would make her feel better.

Through her window, she saw a block of night and the Big Dipper, slanted on its side.

She meant to sit on her bed, but she missed, was off by inches, and so she slid down to the floor.

She sat there, her knees drawn into her chest, staring into the darkness.

I don't love you anymore.

It hurt so much she thought her heart might stop.

She leaned back against the bed she shared with her husband.

She didn't want to think about that, or him, but how could she help herself now?

He had changed her, completed her. Or so she'd thought.

In the army, she'd found herself; in the air, she'd found her passion. But it wasn't until she met Michael that the missing part of her began slowly, cautiously to fill back in.

Tami had encouraged her to go in search of the young lawyer who'd helped her, and flight school had given her confidence to do it. He'd been easy to find at Zarkades, Antham, and Zarkades.

You came back, he said when he saw her standing in the lobby. Those were the very first words he spoke. He said it, smiling, as if the six years in between had passed in a breath. She knew then that he'd been waiting, too, in his way. *I came back,* she answered, not even surprised when he reached for her hand. It had been more than a start; love was a deep blue sea and they dove in. She hadn't known how to believe in love, but he'd swept her away; it was as simple as that. With their first kiss, she'd forgotten the love that had been her birthright and begun to believe in him and forever.

Somewhere along the way, she'd forgotten that love had a dark underside. Too many years in its sunlight had blinded her. She'd handed Michael her heart, wrapped it up and placed it in his hands, and she'd never bothered to worry that he might be careless with it. Even as he'd pulled away from her in the last few years and spent more hours at the office, she'd believed in the durability of their vows and made excuses for him. *Like Pollyanna, always believing . . .*

Downstairs, she heard a door slam shut, then a car engine start. She stumbled over to her window and stood there, watching him drive away, wondering if he would come back.

He didn't.

Jolene spent the restless, unbearable hours of the night cleaning and doing laundry. She vacuumed, dusted, polished silver, and scrubbed toilets—anything to keep her mind off his *I don't love you anymore.*

Not that it worked. The words had changed her perception of her life, if not herself.

Five words to change a world, to dissolve the ground beneath a woman's feet. It was a tidal wave, that sentence, whooshing in without warning, undermining foundations, leaving homes crumbled in the aftermath.

By morning, she was so exhausted she could barely stand and so wired she didn't bother making coffee. More than anything, she wanted to escape this too-quiet house and get in her helicopter and fly away. Instead, in the pink and lavender light of a rising dawn, she went for an eight-mile run, but it didn't help.

When she got back, she took a long shower, dressed in worn jeans and a gray army sweatshirt, and then went to wake up Betsy. She knocked on the door and went inside. "Hey, Betsy," she said, forcing a smile. She should have spoken to her daughter last night—that was what a good mother would have done, a stronger mother, but Jolene had been afraid of breaking down in front of her child, of crying, of scaring Betsy even more.

"Don't say anything," Betsy said dully.

"I know Daddy talked to you. I thought—"

"I do NOT want to talk about it."

Jolene stopped, unsure of what to say anyway. How did you talk to a child about such adult things? She'd never been good at knowing when to push with Betsy and when to back off. Invariably, she pushed when she should have let go. It was one of Jolene's flaws: she was good at holding on. Letting go, not so much.

But one thing she saw clearly: Betsy was afraid and confused, and so she was angry. There was nothing Jolene could offer that would help. How could she talk about what she herself didn't understand?

Instead, Jolene went to her daughter and pulled her to her feet and took her into her arms. It took a supreme act of will not to layer words onto the hug, but she managed it, just let it be.

She felt Betsy's haggard sigh, and knew how her daughter felt. It was terrifying to see your parents fight. She knew Betsy would remember last night, and she would notice Michael's absence this morning.

Lulu walked into the bedroom, dragging her favorite yellow blanket behind her. "Hey, I want a hug, too."

Jolene opened one arm and Lulu rushed forward, folding her little body alongside her sister's. They stood there a second longer; then Lulu pulled back. She scratched her tangled black hair, pushed it out of her eyes. "Can I have Cap'n Crunch?"

"No Captain Crunch. That's for special mornings," Jolene answered automatically.

"Today could be special," Lulu chirped.

"It's the opposite of special," Betsy said bitterly.

"Why?" Lulu wanted to know.

Jolene sighed. "Come on, girls. Let's get breakfast going."

As they made their way downstairs, Jolene felt Betsy's gaze on her. In the kitchen, Betsy seemed to notice everything—the way Jolene's hands shook just a little when she got out the flour and eggs for pancakes, the way she kept sighing, the way she opened the fridge and just stared inside. Finally, she couldn't take it anymore, being under this scrutiny. She poured the girls Cheerios.

"Where's Daddy?" Lulu asked, concentrating on getting the right number of Cheerios in her spoon.

"At work," Jolene said, wondering what she'd say if he stayed away tonight, too.

Betsy looked up sharply. "He left already?"

Jolene turned to pour herself more coffee. "You know what it's like when he has to catch an early ferry," she lied, not looking at her daughter.

The moment seemed to draw out; she could feel Betsy's suspicious gaze on her back. "Hurry up," she said. "We need to leave in twenty minutes."

As soon as breakfast was over, Jolene herded the girls upstairs to finish getting ready. They left right on time, and by nine fifteen, she was home again.

She parked in her garage and then walked next door. Waving to Carl, who was working on a Ford truck, she went to the front door, opened it, and said, "Hey, Tam," at the same time she went inside.

Tami was in the living room, in a fraying blue robe and sheepskin slippers, sipping coffee from a huge insulated mug. Behind her, the wood-paneled walls were studded with dozens of family photographs, all framed in white. Dead center was Tami's military portrait.

"Hey, flygirl," Tami said, grinning. She sat on the blue plaid sofa, her slippered feet propped on the glass coffee table.

She looked at Tami, and for a second she couldn't say it, couldn't force the words out.

Tami frowned and put down her coffee cup. "What is it, Jo?"

"Michael said he doesn't love me anymore," she said quietly.

"You don't mean—"

"Don't make me say it again."

Tami walked forward slowly, put her arms around Jolene, and held her. It took Jolene a minute to lift her own arms, to hold on to Tami, but once she did, she couldn't let go. She wanted to cry, was desperate for a way to release this pain, but no tears came.

"What did you say to him?"

"Say?" Jolene stepped out of the embrace. "After *I don't love you,* what is there to say?"

Tami sighed. "Couples fight, Jo. They yell, they say things they don't mean, they storm off and come back. Granted, Michael said a stupid thing, but he didn't mean it. You can forgive him. This isn't the end."

Jolene heard the undertone of pain in Tami's voice, knew her friend was remembering the affair Carl had had ten years ago. "I know about forgiving people and loving them anyway, even after they hurt you."

She did know. Jolene had spent a childhood forgiving her parents, hoping that tomorrow or next week or next month they would change. But they hadn't changed and they hadn't loved her. She'd started to get better when she accepted that simple truth. She'd stayed whole, become whole, by not needing their love anymore. She knew what Tami was saying; hell, it was what Jolene would have said if the situations were reversed. One sentence couldn't end a marriage. But she couldn't hang on alone, either. Hadn't she learned that from her mom?

"He didn't mean it. Michael loves you."

"I want to believe that," Jolene said quietly, and it was true; she wanted to believe in Michael and his love for her, but her faith had been shaken. She was afraid to trust him so completely again. If he could just fall out of love with her, what did it all mean?

"I'm sure—"

Before Tami could finish, her phone rang. She went to the kitchen and answered. "Oh. Hi. Yes, sir." She turned to Jolene, mouthed *Ben Lomand,*

and then said into the phone, "Really? I see. When, sir? So soon? Oh. Okay, Jolene and I will handle the phone tree. Thank you, sir." Tami hung up the phone slowly and turned to face Jolene.

"We're being deployed."

$\mathcal{S}_{ix}$

When Jolene and Michael had first seen the house on Liberty Bay, it had been a beautiful sunlit July day. They'd been out driving, enjoying their time together after an afternoon barbecue at his parents' house. They hadn't been looking for a house.

But there it was, just sitting at a bend in the road, waiting for them, a for-sale sign stuck haphazardly by the mailbox. A quaint little farmhouse in need of love, a sagging wraparound porch, and three green acres that cascaded down to the black ribbon of a quiet country road. Across the road, there was a small patch of land, an afterthought really, that lay tucked between the road and the sweeping gray crescent of beach.

It was the little bit of beachfront that drew them in. The first thing they did to the property was build a deck above the sand. They built it with their own hands, she and Michael, laughing and talking and dreaming the whole time.

We'll barbecue out here on the Fourth of July . . . and show Betsy how to find sand dollars . . . and eat dinner from paper plates while the sun sets into the water . . .

It was only a thin strip of grassy land stitched alongside a winding ribbon of asphalt, but it was Jolene's dream, her slice of paradise. The smell of the sea and the sound of the waves comforted her. She had always come out here to think, to recharge. Especially in those long, barren years between Betsy and Lulu, when Jolene had been so desperate to conceive another child. Here, alone, month after month, she'd cried when her period started. And here was where she'd come to thank God when her prayer had finally been answered.

Now, she sat in one of the Adirondack chairs that flanked a rusted metal fire pit. It was raining, but she hardly noticed. She stared out at the flat gray waters, pockmarked by falling rain, and thought: *How will my children handle this? How will I? How will Michael?*

How much a world could change in three hours . . .

They'd always known she could be deployed; at least since September Eleventh they'd known it, and yet she and Michael had never discussed it. How could they? Michael didn't want to hear about her career in the military. Every time she even brought up the idea of other soldiers deploying, he'd gone off on a rant about the wrongheadedness of sending troops to Iraq.

She knew what he thought, what he saw—the military's dark side, the mistakes, the way the brass let down soldiers and veterans. That was politics, though. Separate, somehow. For her, it was different. The Guard was her family, too.

Honor. Duty. Loyalty. These were more than words to Jolene; they were part of her. She'd always been two women—a mother and soldier—and this deployment ripped her in half, left a bloody, gaping tear between the two sides of her.

Who would help Betsy through the rocky terrain of adolescence, give her advice about bad boys and mean girls and all the kids in between? Who would walk Lulu into kindergarten and hold her when she woke, sobbing, from a nightmare?

And there was the risk. Jolene was a helicopter pilot. She would tell Michael and the girls that she wasn't allowed in combat, that she would be far from harm's way, but she knew it wasn't true. Helicopters were shot down all the time.

We'll come home, Tami had said.

Jolene had nodded, smiling, although she knew—they both did—that no such promise could be made. It didn't matter now anyway. Tomorrow and the future wasn't something they could control. For now, they had a job to do, a job they'd been trained for. Civilians didn't understand, maybe they couldn't, but a soldier stepped up when he or she was needed. Even if she was afraid, even if her children needed her. It was Jolene's time to give back to the army, her time to serve her country.

She placed a hand over her chest, feeling the slow, even beating of her heart. She closed her eyes, hearing her heartbeat mingle with the whooshing of the waves on the pebbled beach and the exhalations of her breath. Tears stung her eyes, fell down her cheeks, mixing with the rain. She imagined all of it—the good-bye, the missing, the loss. She pictured her daughters crying for her, reaching out for her, unable to really understand her absence.

But she had no choice to make. At that, she felt a kind of peace move through her, an acceptance of the situation and a realization of who she was. She had given her word that if called to serve, she would go.

She hated leaving her children—hated it with a passion that could have crippled her if she gave in to it, but she had no choice. She would go to Iraq for a year, do her job, and come home to her family.

That was what she would tell them . . . what she would believe.

She was prepared, had always been prepared, for this moment. For more than twenty years, she'd trained for it. A small part of her even wanted to go, to test herself. She wanted to go . . . she just didn't want to leave.

She pulled her hand slowly away from her chest, let it fall in her lap. At her feet, a small collection of dried white sand dollars lay in a cloverleaf pattern, a reminder of last summer. She bent down, plucked one up, rubbing the pad of her thumb over the porous surface. Then she stood up.

She was going to war.

At one o'clock Jolene called the preschool and arranged for Lulu to stay later, and then she called Michael at work. He kept her waiting long enough that she began to think he wasn't going to answer, and when he did finally take the call, he sounded preoccupied.

"Hi, Jo. What is it?"

"I need you to come home tonight," she said.

He paused; she heard him breathing. "I have a lot of work to do. I think I'll sleep at the office tonight."

"Don't, please," she said, hating how it sounded as if she were begging. "Something has come up. I need to talk to you."

"I think we need some time apart."

"Please, Michael. I need to talk to you tonight."

"Fine. I'll be on the six o'clock boat."

For the next few hours, she tried not to think about the future, but it was impossible. As the time for carpool approached, she found her spirits lagging. The thought of seeing her children—looking at them, seeing their bright smiles, and knowing the pain that was coming their way— was terrible. She kept losing her balance, stumbling. Once, in the kitchen, she'd looked at the yellow-school-bus framed photo of Betsy's school years, and she actually had to sit down.

Help me through this, she prayed more than once.

At the preschool, she parked out front and went inside slowly, hearing the high-pitched buzz of children's laughter before she even reached the gate that led to the backyard.

"Mommy!" Lulu said, shrieked really, throwing her hands in the air and scrambling to her feet. She ran at Jolene, threw herself into Jolene's arms.

"Do you have something in your eye, Mommy?" Lulu asked. "Cuz I gotted sand in my face at lunch and it made me cry."

"I'm fine, Lucy Louida," Jolene said, grateful that Lulu didn't hear the thickening of her voice. She carried Lulu out to the car, strapped her into the seat in the back, and drove across town to the middle school. As usual, Betsy was one of the last ones out of the school. She hung back from the other kids, as if she didn't want to be seen. Then she ran to the SUV and climbed into the backseat, slamming the door shut.

Jolene stared at her daughter in the rearview mirror and felt a flutter of panic. *She's so fragile now . . .*

"Are you going to just sit here all day?" Betsy said, crossing her arms.

How would Betsy get through seventh grade without her mom? What would happen when she started her period? Who would help her?

"Mom," Betsy said sharply. "Are you brain-dead?"

Jolene drove into the stream of carpool traffic. She meant to start a conversation, say something, but her throat felt tight. When she pulled up to Mila's house, her eyes stung with tears that didn't fall.

Her in-laws' house was a small L-shaped rambler built in the late seventies. It was small in comparison with the newer houses on either side of it, but the land was stunningly beautiful. Set on a deep, treed waterfront lot, it overlooked the placid waters of Lemolo Bay. Giant evergreens studded the landscaping; here and there, mounds of multicolored flowers grew around their rough brown trunks. Mila had turned this yard into a showpiece; every year it was on the local home and garden tour as a magnificent example of Northwest landscaping. The water out front was shallow and clear; in the summer, it warmed enough for swimming.

"Why are we here?" Betsy asked.

Jolene didn't answer. Instead, she parked in front of the garage and let the girls out of the car. Before they even reached the front door, Mila came around the side of the house. She waved, smiling brightly, wearing a big flannel shirt over jeans tucked into bright orange rubber boots. A multicolored scarf covered her poofy black hair, à la Liz Taylor, and fist-sized silver hoops dangled from her ears. In her left hand was an enameled watering can. "Hey, girls," she said.

"I'm sorry to call at the last minute like this," Jolene said, bumping the car door shut with her hip.

Mila shook the dirt from her gardening gloves; it rained onto her boots. "Ah, honey, what's family for?"

Lulu got out of the car and put on her kitten-ears headband, mewing loudly for attention.

"Not *this* again," Betsy said, pushing past her sister.

Mila put down her watering can and glanced around. "Hmmm. Where is my granddaughter, Jolene? Did you leave her at home? In the car?"

Lulu giggled.

"What was that noise?" Jolene said.

Lulu whipped off the headband. "I'm here! *Yia Yia.*"

Mila picked Lulu up and held her.

For a moment, Jolene couldn't say anything. The weight of her future pressed down on her chest so hard she couldn't breathe.

Mila frowned. "Are you okay, Jo?"

"I'm fine. Michael and I need to talk, that's all. I'll pick the girls up tomorrow if that's okay?"

Mila stepped closer. "You tell my son he needs to do better. Work is important, but so is family. I tried to teach his father this lesson, too, but . . ." She shrugged. "You will do a better job of it than I did."

Jolene could only nod. It seemed a lifetime had passed since the missed track meet. She almost blurted out—*I'm being deployed.* She needed to tell Mila, needed to feel a mother's embrace, but she couldn't do it, couldn't be comforted yet.

She mumbled good-bye and went back to her car. By the time she got home, she was sick to her stomach.

This deployment changed everything. He would see that. Whatever their problems were—had been—they would have to be set aside. She and Michael would have to come together now, for the children, for their family. And she would need him now, really need him. His love would save her over there, keep her warm at night, just as her children's love would bring her home.

She thought about what Tami had said. *Couples fight. They say things they don't mean; they stomp off.*

They come back.

She wanted to believe that, believe *in* that, even though she'd never seen it. She wanted to forgive Michael and find a way to scrub his declaration from her brain so they could go back to who they'd been.

All she had to do was give him a chance.

She could do it; she could be strong enough to let him know she still loved him. These were the things she told herself as she waited for him.

And waited.

Finally, at seven o'clock, he came into the kitchen and immediately poured himself a scotch.

"Hey," Jolene said, rising from her seat on the hearth.

He turned. In the ambient light from above the stove, he looked more than tired. His hair was a mess. The skin beneath his eyes had a violet cast, as if he'd slept as badly as she had last night.

"Jo," he said quietly; there was a gentleness in his voice that surprised and saddened her. It swept her back, in a breath, to who they used to be.

She ached for that—needed it, needed him. "I'm being deployed."

Michael went so still it was as if he'd stopped breathing.

"You're kidding, right?" he finally said.

"Of course I'm not kidding. Who kids about going to war?" Jolene's voice cracked. For a split second, her strength wavered. She realized how desperate she was to have him take her in his arms and tell her they'd be okay through this. "I'm going to Fort Hood first for combat training, then it's off to Iraq."

"You're in the Guard, for Chrissake. You're not a real soldier."

Jolene flinched. "I'm going to do you a favor and forget you said that."

"You are not going to war, Jo. Come on. You're forty-one years old—"

"*Now* you remember."

"People are *dying* over there."

"I'm aware of that, Michael."

"Tell them you're a mother. They can't expect you to leave your children."

"Men leave their children to go off to war every day."

"I know that," he snapped. "But you're a mother."

"I was a soldier first."

"This is not a damn game, Jo. You are not going to war. Tell them thanks but no thanks."

She looked at him in disbelief. "I would be court-martialed for that. I'd go to *jail*. You don't say no."

"Quit then."

He didn't know her at all if he could say that to her. Honor was just a word to him, and lawyers made a game of playing with words. He had no real idea what a dishonorable discharge meant. "I gave my word, Michael."

"And what was 'I do'?" he snapped back.

"You son of a bitch," she yelled at him. "For all these years, I've loved you. Adored you. And last night you tell me you don't love me anymore, that maybe you want a divorce. And then, because you're a selfish prick who doesn't know me at all, you tell me to quit the Guard."

"What kind of mother could leave her children?"

She drew in a sharp breath. It would have hurt less to be smacked across the face. "How *dare* you say that to me? *You*, who are the least reliable person in this family. It breaks my heart to leave them, but I have to." Her voice broke. "I have to."

"So you're going to war," he said.

"You make it sound like a choice, Michael. There's no choice here. Either I go to war or I go to jail. How can you not understand this? I'm being deployed."

"And you're surprised I'm pissed off. I never wanted you in the stupid military in the first place."

"Thanks so much for minimizing what I do."

"War—and this war in particular—is a waste, and I might not be Colin Powell, but I know that helicopters are big targets in the sky that get shot at. What am I supposed to say? 'Good for you, Jolene. You go off to Iraq and be careful. We'll be waiting for you.'"

"Yeah," she said quietly. The fight drained out of her. "That would have been really nice."

"Well, you married the wrong man then."

"Obviously. Look on the bright side, Michael. You wanted time apart."

"Fuck you, Jo."

"No. Fuck *you*, Michael." On that, she turned on her heel and walked out of the room. She didn't run, although she wanted to. She kept her chin up and her shoulders squared as she walked up the stairs and into her bedroom.

Downstairs, a door slammed. She was reminded of her childhood and all the fights she'd heard from a distance. She'd never imagined she would grow up to be a wife listening to her own husband leave. But even with the pain of that sad and pathetic echo, she thought *Go, Michael, run.*

She should have known better anyway. She knew better than to count on anyone to stand beside her, to *stay*. And yet even knowing that, knowing that she was alone again and that she was strong enough to take it, she felt herself breaking inside. She sat down on her bed, unable to stand any longer.

Sometime later, the floor outside her bedroom door creaked, and the door opened. Michael stood there, looking both angry and defeated. His hair was a mess, as if he'd run his hands through it repeatedly, which he probably had. It was a nervous habit. A half-full drink—scotch, no doubt—hung from one hand. She found herself looking at that hand for a moment; his fingers were long, almost elegant. She'd often said he had pianist's hands, painter's hands. She'd loved what those hands could do to her body.

But they were uncalloused, those hands, unused to manual labor. A thinking man's hands, unlike her own. Maybe it all came down to that. Maybe she should have seen this scene unfolding the second she first held his hand.

"You're going," he said, and his voice was thin, tinged with the kind of banked anger she'd never heard from him before.

"I have to," she said.

"Does it matter that we need you here?"

"Of course it matters."

He finished his drink and came into the room. Putting the empty glass on the nightstand, he sat down on the bed beside her, but not close enough to touch. With a sigh, he slumped forward. The wavy mass of his hair spilled forward. Seeing him now, his sharp profile, his defeated shoulders, she was reminded of the week in which his father had lain dying. Michael had been unable to stand seeing Theo that way, gray and hollow and in pain, connected to life by machines. He'd tried to sit by the bed, but he could never do it for long. More often than not, Jolene had found him pacing in the hallways, beating himself up for his weakness. She had gone to him then, taken him in her arms and held him until he could breathe again. To her, it had been second nature, caring for him when he was hurting. But now she saw what she had never dared to see before: this love of hers was one-sided. She was the one who took care; he was the one who took.

"Okay, then," he finally said.

Jolene felt a profound sense of relief. She didn't realize until right now, when her breath rushed out, how nervous she'd been, sitting beside him, waiting. "So you'll wait for me," she said.

"How long until you leave?"

"Two weeks. That's quicker than usual. Special circumstances."

"And you'll be gone for a year."

She nodded. "I'll get Leave in six months. I'll be able to come home for two weeks."

He sighed again. "We'll tell the girls tomorrow. And my mom."

"Yeah," Jolene said, but it was barely above a whisper, that word; there was so much more to say, plans to be made, problems to be solved, but neither one of them said anything.

They sat on the bed in which they'd made love so many times, silent, each staring out at nothing, until it was time to turn out the lights.

Seven

The next morning, Michael and Jolene drove to Mila's house.

He pulled into the driveway and turned off the car's engine. For the first time all morning, he looked at her. "Are you ready to do this?"

Jolene saw the banked anger in his eyes and it made her feel empty and painfully alone. She didn't bother to answer. Instead, she reached for the handle and opened the door and got out. As they walked to the front door, she couldn't help noticing how far apart from her he stood.

Michael knocked on the door. In moments, the sound of footsteps came from inside. Then the door swung open and Mila stood there in a fuzzy pink bathrobe, with her black hair a tangled mess. Behind her, the room was a wash of pale green walls, windows to the water view, and rattan furniture from the fifties positioned on wide-planked pine floors. The overstuffed cushions were in muted tones of celery and rose and white. "Oh, you're early!" she said, stepping aside to let them in to a living room strewn with toys and books and DVDs.

Lulu jumped up from her place on the cream-colored shag rug. She was wearing the kitten headband.

"Someone has embraced her invisibility," Mila said quietly, smiling.

Jolene frowned thoughtfully and made a great show of looking around. "Hmmm . . . Mila, have you seen Lulu? I wonder what happened to my kitten? Has anyone seen my Lucy Louida?"

Lulu giggled.

Michael frowned. "What are you talking about? She's right—"

Lulu whipped off the headband and grinned. "I'm here, Mommy!"

Jolene rushed forward and took Lulu in her arms. "You sure are." Jolene buried her nose in Lulu's velvety neck, smelling her little girl sweetness, trying to memorize it.

"Mommy," Lulu whined, kicking to be free. "You're smovering me."

Jolene loosened her hold on Lulu, let her wiggle to the floor.

"Are you hungry?" Mila asked, picking up an empty DVD case, frowning, looking around for the disc.

"Actually, we have something to tell you and the girls," Michael said tightly.

"Oh?" Mila looked up. "Is something wrong?"

Michael actually stepped aside. "This is Jolene's show, Ma. She's the one with the news."

Mila frowned. "Jo?"

"Where's Betsy?" Jolene said, unable to get much volume out of her voice. She could fly helicopters and shoot machine guns and run ten miles with a full pack on her back, but the thought of saying these few words to her children made her feel weak.

"I'll go get her," Lulu said and ran off, screaming, "Bet—sy! Get out here!"

Mila looked from Jolene to Michael, and back to Jolene.

Then Betsy came into the living room, trailing behind Lulu, looking sleepy, rubbing her eyes. She was wearing a huge tee shirt and white ankle socks. "Why did you wake me up?"

Jolene picked Lulu up, carried her to the sofa, and sat down. "Have a seat, Betsy. We need to talk to you guys. It's important."

Michael sat down on the sofa beside Jolene.

Betsy stopped suddenly. "Are you getting divorced?"

"Elizabeth Andrea," Mila said. "Why would you say such a—"

Michael sighed. "Just sit down, Betsy."

Betsy knelt on the ivory-colored shag rug in front of them, crossing her arms, jutting her chin out. "What?"

They were all looking at Jolene. She almost lost her nerve; she looked at Michael, who shrugged.

She was alone in this. What a surprise. With a sigh, Jolene looked at Betsy and then down at Lulu. "You remember the story I told you about when I joined the army?" she said. "I was eighteen and had no direction. My parents had just died. I was so alone. You can't imagine how alone. Anyway, you all were a dream I had, but of course, you were in my future then."

Betsy sighed impatiently. "Duh. Can I go back to sleep now?"

"I'm not doing this well," Jolene said.

"Just tell them," Michael said.

Lulu started bouncing on Jolene's lap. "Tell us what?"

Jolene took a deep breath. "I'm going to Iraq to help—"

"*What*?" Betsy said, clambering to her feet.

"Huh?" Lulu said.

"Oh, Jolene," Mila whispered, bringing a hand to her mouth. She sank into the celery-colored, overstuffed chair by the window.

"No *way*," Betsy said. "Oh my *God*, no one has a mom in the war. Will people know?"

"*That's* your concern?" Michael asked.

Jolene was losing control of this.

"But you're a *mom*," Betsy cried out. "I *need* you here. What if you get killed?"

Lulu's eyes filled up with tears. "What?"

"That won't happen," Jolene said, trying to keep her voice even. "I'm a woman. They don't let women in combat situations. I'll be flying VIPs around, moving supplies. I'll be safe."

"You don't know that. You *can't* know that," Betsy said. "Tell them you won't go. Please, Mommy . . ."

At that, the small *Mommy*, Jolene felt a tearing in her heart. She wanted to hold Betsy close, reassure her, but what comfort could she offer? This was a time for strength. "I have to go. It's my job," Jolene said at last.

"If you go I won't forgive you," Betsy said. "I swear I won't."

"You don't mean that," Jolene said.

"You love the army more than us," Betsy said.

Beside her, Michael made a sound. Jolene ignored him.

"No, Bets," she said quietly. "You and Lulu are the air in my lungs. The blood in my veins. Without you, my heart stops. But I have to do this. Lots of working women have to leave their kids sometimes—"

"Ha!" Betsy screamed. "I'm not stupid. Do those moms get shot at on their business trips?"

"You'll come home, right, Mommy?" Lulu asked, biting her lower lip.

"Of course I will," Jolene said. "Don't I always? And in November I'll be home for two weeks. Maybe we could even go to Disneyland. Would you like that?"

"I hate you," Betsy said and ran out of the room, slamming the door shut behind her.

Mila got slowly to her feet. She started to walk toward Jolene, then stopped dead, as if she couldn't make her legs work quite right. "How long will you be gone?" she asked. Her voice wobbled with the effort to appear strong.

"One year," Michael answered.

Lulu frowned. "How long is a year? Is that like next week?"

Jolene turned to her husband. "Maybe you should talk to Betsy."

"Me? What the hell am I supposed to say to her?"

That single question brought it all crashing down on Jolene and scared her as much as everything else combined. How would he be a single father? Would his children be able to count on him in a way that Jolene no longer could?

Jolene stood up. She tried to put Lulu down, but the child clung like a barnacle. So she said nothing to Michael or Mila, just walked out of the living room and down the hallway to the guest bedroom, carrying Lulu. It wasn't ideal, trying to talk to the girls together, but nothing was ideal about this situation.

She knocked on the door.

"Go away," Betsy yelled.

"I am," Jolene answered. "That's why we need to talk now." She waited a moment, collected herself, and then went into the room, which was papered in a wild 1970s foil paper and decorated with a collection of whitewashed furniture.

Betsy sat on one of the wicker twin beds with her knees drawn up. She looked royally pissed off.

"Can I sit down?" Jolene asked.

Betsy nodded mulishly and scooted sideways. Jolene and Lulu sat down beside her. Jolene wanted to jump into the ice-cold water of the conversation, but she knew Betsy needed to find a way through this, so she waited quietly, stroking Lulu's hair.

Finally Betsy said, "Moms aren't supposed to leave their children."

"No," Jolene said, feeling the sharp point of those words sink deep into her. "They aren't. And I'm sorry, baby. I really am."

"What if you said you wouldn't go?"

"They'd court-martial me and put me in jail."

"At least you'd be *alive*."

Jolene looked at her daughter. There it was, the fear that lay beneath the adolescent fury. "It's my job as a mom to keep you safe and be with you and help you grow up."

"That's what I'm saying."

"But it's also my job to show you what kind of person to be, to teach you by example. What lesson would I teach you if I ran from a commitment I made? If I was cowardly or dishonorable? When you make a promise in this life, you keep it, even if it scares you or hurts you or makes you sad. I made a promise a long time ago, and now it's time to keep that promise, even if it breaks my heart to leave you and Lulu, and it does . . . break my heart."

Jolene willed her tears away. Nothing in her life had ever hurt like this, not even hearing Michael say he didn't love her anymore. But she had to keep going, had to make her daughter understand. "You've grown up safe and loved, so you can't know how it feels to be truly alone in the world. When I joined the army, I had nothing. Nothing. No one. I was all alone in the world. And now my friends need me—Tami, Smitty, Jamie. The rest of the Raptors. I have to be there for them. And the country needs me. I know you're young for all this, but I believe in keeping America safe. I really do. I have to keep my promise. Can you understand that?"

Tears sprang into Betsy's eyes. Her lower lip trembled mutinously. "I need you," she said in a quiet voice.

"I know," Jolene said, "and I need you, baby. So much . . ." Her voice caught again; she had to clear her throat to keep going. "But we'll talk on the phone and e-mail, and maybe we'll even write good old-fashioned letters. I'll be home before you know it."

Lulu tugged on her sleeve. "You'll be home before I start kindergarten, right?"

Jolene closed her eyes. How was she going to do this, really?

"Mommy?" Lulu said, her voice shaking.

"No," Jolene said finally. "Not for kindergarten, Lulu, but your daddy will be home for that . . ."

Lulu started to cry.

Michael sat on the couch, alone now, and looked up at his mother. He could see the concern in her eyes, the unasked question. She wondered why he was out here while Jolene was handling this alone.

She stared at him for a long, assessing moment. Then she walked out of the living room and came back a few minutes later, carrying a cup of coffee in one hand and a plate full of baklava in the other. Of course. Food. Her answer to everything.

She put the cup and plate on the table beside him and then sat down on the sofa next to him. She placed her hand on his knee. "When I was young . . . during the war . . . it was a terrible time in Greece. My father and uncles and cousins were all gone. Many of them did not come back. The family stayed strong, though, and faith kept us together."

He nodded. He'd heard her stories all his life. World War II had seemed distant to him, barely understandable; now he thought of the relatives he'd lost to enemy fire. They'd been just names in a book before. Without thinking, he reached over for a baklava and began eating it. God, he wished his father were here now.

"I will move into the house and take care of the girls."

"No, Ma. There's no bedroom for you, and you've got the Thumb. I'll hire someone."

"You most certainly will not. No stranger will take care of my grandbabies. I will hire another part-time employee for the store."

"The store can't afford that."

"No, but I can. I will be at your house after school each weekday. I'll pick Lulu up from preschool and meet Betsy's bus. We will be just fine. You can count on me, and the girls will count on you."

"Every day, Ma? That's a big job."

She smiled at him. "I am a big woman, as you may have noticed. I need to help you, Michael. Let me."

He didn't know how to respond: he still couldn't wrap his mind around how completely his world had changed.

"These are details, though, and not the thing that matters most." She looked at him. "You should be with her now, telling your children they will be fine."

"Will they . . . be fine?"

"It's not your children you should be worrying about right now, Michael. Their time will come."

"And Jo?" he said. "Will she be fine?"

"She is a lioness, our Jolene."

Michael could only nod.

"Already you are letting her down. Your father was like this, God rest his soul. He was selfish. This is a time for you to see beyond yourself." She touched his cheek, resting her knuckles against his skin as she'd done so often in his youth. "You be proud of her, Michael."

He knew he was supposed to nod and agree and say that of course he was proud of his wife, but he couldn't do it.

"I'll do what needs to be done," he said instead, and knew that he'd disappointed his mother.

How many more people would he let down before this was over?

. . .

Michael spent the weekend watching his life as if from a distance. Betsy alternated between being blazingly pissed off and desperately clingy. Lulu was so confused she became overwrought and cried at everything. Michael couldn't bear any of it, could hardly look at the pain in his daughters' eyes, but Jolene was a warrior, as strong as tested steel. He saw how carefully she treated the girls, how tenderly. It was only when they weren't looking that her pain was revealed; tears welled in her green eyes, and when they did she turned away quickly, dashing the moisture away with the back of her hand.

An hour ago, she'd put them to bed. God forgive him, but Michael had let her do it alone.

Now he was in the family room, standing in front of the fireplace. Bright orange and blue flames danced across a tepee of logs, sending off waves of heat, and yet still he was cold. Frozen, really.

He glanced through the kitchen. In the window above the sink, he could see moonlight skating across the bay.

"They're asleep," Jolene said, coming into the room. "We can talk now."

Michael wanted to say *no, I don't want to talk, not about this, not yet, not anymore.* He knew it was selfish of him, and small, but it pissed him off to be left here as Mr. Mom. Not that he could tell anyone this. He'd look like an asshole if he admitted that he didn't want this job that had fallen in his lap, didn't know if he could even do it. How was he supposed to manage a sixteen-person legal firm, defend his clients, and handle the day-to-day minutiae that came with raising two kids? Carpool. Field trips. Meals. Laundry. Homework.

Just the thought of it overwhelmed him.

"How the hell am I supposed to do it?" he said, turning to her. "I've got a job to do."

"Your mom will be a huge help. She said she'll hire someone for the store, and that's perfect. I don't want a nanny taking care of the girls—they'll be so scared and confused," Jolene said. "Especially Betsy, she's fragile these days, and kids can be cruel. She'll need you, Michael. They both will. You'll have to be really present. I want—"

"You want." Already he was losing patience with that sentence. "Classic, Jo. You're the one leaving—but not before you tell me how you want me to handle things while you're gone."

"Not things, Michael. My children."

He heard the way her voice broke on that and knew how deeply his words had cut her. Not that long ago, he would have turned to her and taken her in his arms and apologized. Now, he just stood there, dropping his chin forward, staring dully at the scuffed hardwood floor beneath his stockinged feet. The echo of that word—*divorce*—hung like smoke in the air between them.

She waited a long time. Her breath sounded like waves breaking along a shore, ragged and uneven. He could feel her judging him. Then, quietly, she left the room.

On Monday morning, Tami showed up after carpool, and honked her horn.

Jolene walked down the driveway and climbed into her friend's big white truck.

They looked at each other, and in that look—unaccompanied by words—they revealed their fears, their hopes, their worries.

Tami sighed. "How was it?"

"Brutal," Jolene said. "For you?"

"I barely survived." She put the truck in reverse and backed down the driveway. In no time, they were speeding down the interstate toward Tacoma.

"Seth tried to act cool when I told him," Tami said after an unfamiliar silence that had gone on for miles. "He asked what would happen if I didn't come back. He's not even thirteen. He's not supposed to have to ask his mom a question like that."

"Betsy was pissed off. She said she wouldn't forgive me if I left her. That I love the army more than I love her."

"Carl cried," Tami said softly after another long silence. "I've never seen him cry before. It was like . . ." Her voice broke. "Man, this is hard."

Jolene swallowed the lump in her throat. "What's worse," she said quietly, "a man who cries when you go to war or one who doesn't?"

At that, they both fell silent. The miles passed quickly, and in no time, they were at the post, driving up to the checkpoint.

They handed over their IDs, nodded to the soldier, and drove onto the post.

In the hallway outside the Black Hawk classroom, they found several members of the unit seated in chairs along the wall. No one was saying much of anything, except for the younger men, who seemed amped up and eager. Smitty—young, young Smitty, with his braces and pimples and puppy-dog buoyancy—was grinning, going from man to man, asking what combat was like, saying they were going to kick some ass over there. Jolene wondered how his mother felt right now . . .

Jolene and Tami leaned back against the concrete-block wall, waiting their turns.

The classroom door opened. Jamie Hix strode out. His army-issue hair—short and dirty blond—stood up from his tanned, broad forehead. Lines fanned out from the corners of his gray eyes—they were new, those lines, etched in the days since their deployment had been announced. No doubt he was thinking about his young son. Would his ex-wife use this deployment to take his son away from him? "Your turn, Jo," he said.

With a nod, Jolene walked into the classroom, where she found a man in dress uniform seated at a long desk with papers spread out in front of him.

"Chief Zarkades?" he said, looking up at her. "At ease. Have a seat. I'm Captain Reynolds. Jeff."

She sat down in a chair facing him, her back ramrod straight, her hands in her lap.

He pushed a stack of papers toward her. "Your family plan is in place. Your daughters, Elizabeth Andrea Zarkades and Lucy Louida Zarkades, will be cared for by your husband, Michael Andreas Zarkades. Is that correct?"

"Yes, sir."

"Your mother-in-law is also available, I see."

"Yes, sir."

The lawyer looked down at the paper, tapped his pen. "Deployment can be difficult on a marriage, Chief. Is there any cause to worry about this plan?"

"No, sir," Jolene said.

The captain looked up. "Do you have a will?"

"Yes, sir. I'm married to an attorney, sir."

"Good." He pushed a stack of papers toward her. "Sign and date your family plan. And the funeral arrangement addendum. I assume you want Michael notified in the case of your death. Anyone else?"

"No, sir."

"Okay, then, Chief. That's all. Dismissed."

She stood. "Thank you, sir."

"Oh, Chief? We recommend you write letters . . . to your loved ones."

Jolene nodded. Letters. Good-byes. They *recommended* she write letters in which she said good-bye to the people she loved most in this world. She tried to imagine that . . . Betsy opening a letter one day in the blurry future, seeing her mother's handwriting, reading her last words— and what would they be, those last words, written now, before she knew all that she had to say, before they'd had this lifetime together? Lulu would be crying, wailing, yelling, *What? She's gone where?* her small heart-shaped face scrunching up, tears forming in her dark eyes as she tried to understand what that even meant.

"Be safe, Chief. God bless."

The next two weeks passed so quickly Jolene half expected to hear a sonic *boom* echoing along behind. She wrote and edited and rewrote at least a dozen to-do lists, filled a three-ring binder with every bit of information she could think of. She canceled the magazines she wouldn't receive, hired a neighbor's son to mow the grass in the summer and check the generator next winter, and she paid as many bills in advance as possible. All of this she did at night; during the day she was at the post, preparing to go off to war. She and her unit flew so many hours they had begun to breathe as one. By the first of May, she—and the rest of the unit—were actually getting itchy to leave. If they were going to do this thing, they wanted to *go*. It was the only way they'd start marking off the time until their return.

At home, life was an endless series of poignant moments and elongated good-byes. Every look, every hug, every kiss took on the weight of sorrow. Jolene didn't know how much longer she could stand it. Every time she looked at her babies, her throat tightened.

And then there was Michael.

In this short time they had left together, he had pulled away even further, spent even more time at the office. She rarely caught him looking at her, and when she did she saw resentment in his eyes and he looked away quickly. She had tried to talk to him about all of it, the deployment, her feelings, his feelings, her fear, but every volley had been met with retreat until finally, exhausted, she'd given up.

It seemed he'd told her the truth: he didn't love her anymore.

Sometimes, late at night, when she lay in bed beside him, unable to sleep, afraid to touch him and aching for him to touch her, she wondered if she even cared anymore. She wanted to give him the benefit of the doubt, interpret his coldness as fear and concern, but in the end her innate optimism failed her. She needed him now, maybe for the first time, and he had let her down. Just like her parents.

Tonight, after a long day at the post, hours spent getting ready to leave, she pulled her SUV up into the garage and parked, sitting in the darkness for the minutes it took to find strength. When she felt sure she could be herself, she got out of the car and went inside.

The house was filled with golden light and the scent of lamb stewing in tomato and spices. A hint of cinnamon sweetened the air. She could hear the girls talking somewhere, but their voices were muted. No one seemed to have much to say these days. They were all holding their breath for the last good-bye. Betsy had taken it particularly hard; she'd begun acting out, throwing tantrums, slamming doors. Supposedly someone in class had made fun of her for having a mom who was going off to fight "in that stupid war," and Betsy had had a near breakdown. She'd come home begging Jolene to quit the military.

Jolene hung her coat on a hook in the mudroom and went into the kitchen, where she found Mila at the sink, washing up the dinner dishes. Michael was still at work—lately, he rarely got home before ten o'clock.

At 8:10, the sun was beginning to set; the view through the window looked like a Monet painting, all bronze and gold and lavender pieces juxtaposed together.

Jolene came up behind Mila, getting a waft of the woman's rose-scented shampoo as she touched her shoulder. "Hey, Mila. Moussaka?"

"Of course. It is your favorite."

That was all it took these days for Jolene to feel melancholy. She squeezed her mother-in-law's upper arm. "Thanks for coming over tonight."

"Yours is in the fridge. It needs about three minutes in the microwave," Mila said, drying the last plate, setting it on the counter. "How was training today?"

Jolene drew back. "Great. I couldn't be more ready to handle myself over there."

Mila turned, looked up at her. "Pretend with Betsy and Lulu and even my son, if you must, but not with me, Jo. I don't need your strength. You need mine."

"So I can tell you I'm a little afraid?"

"You forget, Jo, I have lived through a war before. In Greece. The soldiers saved our lives. I am proud of what you are doing, and I will make sure your daughters are proud, too."

It meant so much to hear those few simple words. "And your son?" Jolene asked at last.

"He is a man, and he is afraid. This is not a good combination. He loves you, though. This I know. And you love him."

"Is that enough?"

"Love? It is always enough, *kardia mou*."

Love. Jolene turned the word around in her mind, wondering if Mila was right, if love was enough at a time like this.

"We will be waiting for you to come home, safe and sound. Do not worry about us."

Jolene knew that she had no choice in this matter. She had to let go of the people she loved back here. She could miss her family, but the emotion—the longing—would have to be buried deep. "I can do it," she said quietly. She'd been compartmentalizing her emotions all her life. She knew how to put fear and longing in a box and hide it away. "I have to."

"My son will rise to the occasion," Mila said. "He is like his father in that way. Michael would never shirk his duty. He will not let you down."

"How do you know?"

Mila smiled. "I know."

Eight

During the first week of May, Michael handled the Keller arraignment, put in a not guilty plea to the charge of murder in the first degree, and set about discovery on the case. He needed to find all the facts he could—and his client still wasn't talking. Keith had said "I'm guilty" that day in the jailhouse interview and then pretty much gone silent again, responding to each of Michael's questions with a glazed look. Now and then he mumbled, "I killed her," but that was it. And hardly helpful.

Meanwhile, at home, Jolene kept handing him to-do lists. Every time she caught his eye, she rapid-fired some chore at him: don't forget to wrap the pipes in November . . . to fertilize the plants . . . to clean the barbecue grates. This was how she filled their evenings together. During the day she was at the post, preparing to go off to war. He could tell that she was starting to get itchy to leave. Last night she'd told him she wanted to *go, do this thing so it could be over, and I can come back.*

Soon she'd have her wish.

In two days he would say good-bye to his wife, watch her walk onto a military bus and disappear.

He wanted to be stoic and sturdy and true. But he'd learned something about himself in the last month: he was selfish. He was also worried and scared and pissed off. Truth be told, he was pissed off most of all. He was angry that she had chosen the military over their family, angry that she hadn't quit years ago, angry that he had no choice in any of this.

He'd gone to the ridiculous family-readiness group meeting that Jolene had recommended. What a debacle *that* had been. He'd been running late all day, and getting to the meeting was no exception. He'd been breathless when he finally arrived, a little harried, going through the papers in his briefcase, looking for the contact name when he walked into the room.

Women. That was what he saw. There had to be at least fifty women in the room; most were busy wrangling screaming, crying children. On an easel, a big poster board read: *Support Your Soldier*. Below it was a bullet-pointed list. *Care Packages. Phone Calls. Loneliness. Sex. Financial Help.* As if he were going to talk to these strangers about the problems he encountered with his wife's deployment.

At his entrance, every woman in the room looked up. The place fell silent.

"Sorry," he mumbled, "wrong place," and left.

He'd had no intention of sitting in that room, hearing those women talk about how to be good wives while their soldiers were gone.

Everywhere he went, it seemed the news preceded him. He hated the way people looked at him when they heard Jolene was going to Iraq. *Your wife is going off to war?* He could see them frowning, picturing him in an apron, mixing cake batter in a silver bowl. His liberal, intellectual friends didn't know what to make of it. They quickly turned the conversation to George W. and the politics behind the war, concluding that she was risking her life for nothing. And just what in the hell was Michael supposed to say about any of it?

He knew he could support the warriors and not the war. That was the position he was supposed to take, the honorable position, but he couldn't do it with regard to his wife. He couldn't make himself support her decision.

She knew it, too, recognized his anger and his resentment. They knew each other too well to hide such contaminated emotions. Without love to protect them, they were both as raw as burn victims; every touch hurt.

So he didn't look at her, never touched her, and buried himself in work. That was how he'd survived the last two weeks. Absence. He left for work early and stayed as late as possible. At night, he and Jolene lay on separate sides of the bed, breathing into the darkness, saying nothing, not reaching out. Neither of them was sleeping much, but both pretended to find solace there. Jolene had reached out for him just once, wanting to make love, saying quietly, *I'm leaving, Michael.* He'd turned away, too angry with her to attempt intimacy. The next morning, he'd seen the pain and humiliation in her eyes, and it shamed him, but he couldn't change the way he felt.

On his desk, the intercom buzzed. It was his secretary telling him that the King County prosecuting attorney was here, on time, for their appointment.

"Send him in," Michael said, straightening in his chair.

Brad Hilderbrand, the prosecuting attorney, strode into the office. Michael knew Brad well: beneath the politician's slick veneer beat the heart of a zealot. Brad had been elected to be hard on crime and harder on criminals, and he did his job well because he believed in the party line. "Michael," he said, smiling, his hand outstretched.

They shook hands. Michael could tell from Brad's smile that there was trouble coming.

"I want to let you know that a witness has come forward in the Keller case," Brad said. "In the interest of full disclosure—"

"And a possible plea bargain."

"We wanted you to have the information as soon as possible. Keller confessed. That's why I brought it down myself."

"Really?"

He tossed a manila file folder on the desk. "That's Terry Weiner's statement. He is Keller's cell mate."

The courthouse snitch. Ever popular with prosecutors and police. "So let me get this straight. You're suggesting that Keith Keller, who in the past few weeks of his incarceration has not spoken to his father, his lawyer, or the court-appointed psychiatrist, suddenly opened up to his cell mate."

"He said—and I quote: 'The bitch wouldn't shut up, so I smoked her.'"

"Short, to the point, and easy to remember. I see. And let me guess, the so-called witness has been let go."

"He was only in for possession."

"A drug addict. Perfect." Michael picked up the manila folder and opened it, skimming the statement. "I'll need a copy of the wit's arrest record."

"I'll have it sent over."

"Is this little bit of fiction all you have?"

"It's plenty, Michael, and we both know it." Brad paused meaningfully, looked at him. "I heard about your wife. Going off to war, huh? I didn't know you were a military family."

"A military family? I wouldn't call us that."

"Really? That seems odd. Anyway, I guess you're going to have your hands full with the kids."

Was there a smirk in Brad's voice? "Don't worry about me, Brad. I can drive carpool, make dinner, and still kick your ass across the courtroom."

After dinner, Jolene stood at the kitchen sink with her hands deep in the hot, soapy water, staring out at the view from her own backyard. It was impossibly beautiful tonight—a star-spangled sky, waves dipped in moonlight, fence rails that seemed to glow from within. She knew that if she closed her eyes, she would recall a thousand memories played out across this very view, hear her daughters' laughter, feel a small hand pulling at hers.

Good-bye. She'd said it in her mind so many times in the past two weeks. To views, memories, moments, pictures, people. She had spent hours trying to memorize all of it so that she could take it with her, a scrapbook in her mind of the life she'd left behind . . . the life that was waiting for her.

She pulled her hands out of the water, dried them off, and let the water out of the sink. Then, slowly, she left the empty kitchen.

The family room was brightly lit—every light was on and a fire danced in the grate—and the television played a sitcom that no one was watching. She turned off the TV and hated the sudden silence, so she turned it back on again. Walking up the stairs, she noticed the creaking sound of the risers and kept going. Betsy was in her room, doing homework, and Lulu was asleep already. She paused at Betsy's door, let her fingertips brush the oak door. She had the idea to go in, to sit with her older daughter and try again to make her understand this deployment. But there was something else to do tonight—something she'd already put off as long as she could.

She went into her bedroom, turned on the light, and closed the door. As she stood there, looking at the room she shared with her husband, memories came to her. *That's the bed, Michael, let's get it . . . look how sturdy it is, we can make babies in that bed . . .* And the dresser they'd found at a garage sale in the old days, and the oriental rug that had been their first major purchase.

With a sigh, she went to the dresser and fished the video camera out of her sock drawer. Setting it up on the tripod she'd bought, she aimed the lens at the big king-sized bed, then hit the Record button. Climbing into bed, puffing the pillows up around her, she forced a smile, as if this were an ordinary bedtime story. "Hey, Lulu." Her voice snagged. She drew in a deep breath, and tried again. "I'm making this tape for you." She held up Lulu's favorite book, *Professor Wormbog in Search for the Zipperump-a-Zoo.* Opening the big colorful book, she began to read the story out loud, using all the voices and drama at her command. When she was done, she closed the book and looked into the camera, tears stinging her eyes. "Lucy Louida, I love you to the moon and back. Sleep tight, baby girl. I'll be home before you know it."

She climbed out of the bed and snapped the camera off. She removed that tape and put in another one. This time, she sat at the end of the bed and looked directly into the camera. "Betsy," she said softly, "I don't even know how to say good-bye to you. I know how much you need me right now. You're dealing with so much stuff at school, and I want to give you all the advice you'll ever need to get through life, but we don't have time for that, do we? How can we not have time?" She sighed. "I know you're mad at me, Lil Bit, and I'm so so sorry for that. I only hope that someday you'll understand. Maybe you'll even be proud of me, as I am proud of you. So proud of you. You're strong and beautiful and smart and loyal. You will have a lot of hills to climb while I'm gone, and it will be hard. I know it will be hard. But you'll be okay." Jolene closed her eyes for just a moment, thinking that there was so much more she wanted to say. For the next ten minutes, she gave her daughter the best advice she could, about boys and girls and classes and starting your period and wearing makeup. When she came to the end of it all, she was drained. There was so much more . . . and no time. "I love you, Betsy, to the moon and back. And I know you love me. I know," she said simply, and she smiled.

Rising tiredly, she went to the camera and changed the tape again. This time, it was for Michael, but as she sat at the end of the bed, looking up into that small black lens, she felt a rush of loss. After all their years together, she had no idea what to say to him now and no idea if he would even listen or care. She got up and turned off the camera. She placed the two tapes on her dresser, writing LULU on one and BETSY on the other.

And now.

She went to the desk in the corner of the room, remembering the day she'd found it, how Michael had laughed and said, *It's the ugliest thing ever, how many times has it been painted?* And she'd taken his hand and pulled him toward it and said, *Look deeper, baby.*

She sat down at the desk and opened the bottom drawer. In it was the green metal lockbox that she'd bought specifically for her deployment. She lifted it out, set it on the burnished mahogany desktop. Then she took out the stationery she'd bought this week and set about the task of writing her last letters. Hopefully, they would never be read.

To my beloved Elizabeth Andrea, writing this letter is the hardest thing I've ever had to do. Not because I don't know what to say

*(although I don't, not really), but because I cannot stand the idea that
you will read it, that I will be gone, that you will know how it feels to
be a motherless girl . . .*

She wrote and wrote and wrote, through her tears, until she couldn't
find a single additional word to say. And still it wasn't enough. When
she finished, her hands were trembling. Lulu's letter was no easier; with
every word written, Jolene thought about a child who would forget her
mother almost completely . . .

Michael, she wrote at last in this third letter, pausing, her pen held
above the paper, her tears dripping now, hitting the paper in small gray
bursts. *I loved you, beginning to end. Take care of our babies . . . teach them
to remember me.*

She folded the letters, slipped each one into its own envelope, and
put them in the metal box along with her wallet and her driver's license.

After she put the lockbox away and closed the drawer, she sat there,
staring out at the night, feeling empty. She got to her feet—she was unsteady now, weak in the knees—and went to her closet, where she found
her big green army-issued duffle bag. Throwing it onto the bed, she began to pack.

She was so intent on finding the things she had put on her list and
folding her uniforms in precise thirds that she didn't hear a knock at the
door, but suddenly Betsy was beside her, staring down at the gaping
duffle bag, unzipped and full of desert camo ACUs and sand-colored
boots and army-green tee shirts.

"Hey, Bets," Jolene said.

Betsy walked woodenly toward the bed, her gaze fastened on the
small silver tangle of dog tags that lay beside the duffle bag. She picked
them up, looked down at the rectangular bit of steel that recorded the
facts of Jolene's service.

"Sierra said you were going to kill people," she said softly, her voice
catching. "And then Todd laughed and said, 'No she won't, women can't
shoot—everyone knows that.'"

"Betsy—"

"I saw a movie once, where a soldier was identified by dog tags. Is that what they're for? To identify you?" Her eyes filled with tears.

"Nothing's going to happen to me, Betsy."

"You shouldn't be going."

Jolene swallowed hard. She wanted to pull Betsy into her arms and hold her tightly and vow to stay home. "I wish I weren't."

"Swear you'll come home okay."

"Oh, Betsy . . ." Jolene tried to find the right words, the way to make an unkeepable promise to a girl who would never forget what was said right now. "I love you so much . . ."

Betsy looked stricken. She made a strangled sound and burst into tears and said, "That's not a promise!" Then she threw the dog tags to the floor and ran out of the room and slammed the door shut behind her.

Jolene bent slowly to retrieve her dog tags. Putting them around her neck, she sighed tiredly. She would finish packing and then go to Betsy, and try—again—to make her daughter understand.

Tonight was their last night together. Jolene had spent the day with her daughters. She'd let Betsy skip school. The three of them had seen a movie, gone ice-skating, and had lunch at Red Robin.

Now the sun was beginning to set.

Jolene had a plan for this last evening together. She wanted to go to the Crab Pot for dinner. They needed—she needed—one last perfect memory to carry forward like an amulet into the separation that was coming.

For years, the Crab Pot had been "their" restaurant. In the hot, lazy days of a Northwest summer, they'd walked there, strolled along the beach at low tide, often having contests along the way. There were prizes awarded, usually a two-scoop ice cream cone, for the first one to find an agate, a sand dollar, a perfect white rock.

In years past, Michael had come with them. He'd carried brightly colored buckets, plastic shovels, armloads of towels, and bags of sunscreen. But in the months since his father's death, he'd changed. Maybe if he could go back in time for just a second, just long enough to remember, he could give Jolene the one thing she needed most tonight: her family together before she left. She needed to know that Michael would do a good job with the girls, and that he would be waiting for her return, that she still had a husband to come home to.

"Come on, you guys," Jolene said again. "Let's go to the Crab Pot for dinner."

Only Lulu cheered.

"It's too cold," Betsy said, thumbing through the songs on her iPod, adjusting her earbuds. "No one goes to the Pot until summer. Only old people will be there."

Michael pointed the remote at the TV, flipping through channels. In the silence, he shrugged.

That was enough agreement for Jolene. "Perfect. We're going, then. Get your coats, guys. It might be cold out." She spent the next ten minutes herding her family through the checklist—coats, boots, and blankets. She threw four beach chairs in the back of her car, just in case, and ten minutes later they were driving down the winding road that followed the shoreline.

The Crab Pot diner was a local institution. Built fifty years ago by a Norwegian fisherman, it was a small, shingled building positioned on a perfect lip of land between the road and the sand. A weathered gray deck fanned out all around it, decorated with picnic tables and surrounded by fencing draped in fishing nets and strung with Christmas lights. In the summer, red and white plastic tablecloths covered the tables, but in the off-season, when only the locals stopped by, the tables were bare.

Inside, the uneven floor was a thick layer of sand, reportedly brought in from the wild coast near Kalaloch. The wooden walls were barely visible beneath multicolored bits of memorabilia—pictures, expired fishing licenses, dollar bills. Whatever someone wanted to tack up was fine. There were even a few bras and panties stuck in amidst the papers.

Lulu knew just where to go. She marched into the place as if she owned it, went right to the window by the cash register, and pointed up. "That's us," she said to anyone who might be listening. There were only a few patrons in the restaurant, and none of them looked up.

The waitress, a white-haired woman who'd been there as long as anyone could remember, said, "Of course it is, Lulu. It's my favorite picture of you, too."

Lulu beamed.

The waitress—Inga—led them to a table by the door. "You want the usual?" she asked, pulling a pen out of her hair. It was just for show, that pen; no one had ever seen Inga actually write down an order.

"You bet," Jolene said, trying to sound happy. "Two Dungeness crabs, four drawn butters, and two orders of garlic bread."

They took their places on the twin benches—Michael and Betsy on one side, Lulu and Jolene on the other. All through the meal, Jolene tried to keep up a lively conversation, but, honestly, by the time they were taking off their plastic bibs, she was disheartened. Really, only she and Lulu had talked. Michael and Betsy had pretty much communicated by shrugs and grunts. They were both unhappy on this last night, and they wanted Jolene to know it. At least that was what she figured. Michael was paying the bill when the Flynns walked into the restaurant.

"Perfect," Betsy said, slumping forward in her seat, letting her hair fall across her face.

"Tami!" Jolene got to her feet and stepped around the table, hugging her friend tightly. She should have known they'd all show up here together. Pulling back, she smiled, said, "Photo op!"

Tami and Seth and Carl immediately came together, looped their arms around each other and smiled brightly for the camera. Jolene captured their image in the clunky old Polaroid camera the Crab Pot kept for its guests' use. It was another part of their tradition; every visit included a family photo to be tacked on the wall. "Got it," she said. The Flynns gathered around her, watching their picture develop. When it was done—and it was a good one—Carl pinned it to the wall by the door.

"Your turn," Tami said, taking the camera from Jolene.

Jolene gathered with her family, put her arm around Betsy (how thin her elder daughter was, how gangly) and Lulu (her baby). Michael stepped in behind her. At Tami's *say cheese,* they smiled.

Flash.

Then Betsy and Michael drifted away, went outside. Jolene stood there, watching them leave.

Tami took her hand, squeezed it. "Hey there," she said softly.

Jolene shook her head a little, forced a smile. They walked out to the deck, still holding hands. By now, it was dark. A full moon illuminated the sharp, jagged, snow-covered peaks and sent streamers across the waves.

At the end of the deck, Carl stood beside Michael. Even from here, it was easy to see how uncomfortable they were with each other, these two men with nothing in common except their wives' friendship. Michael's hands were shoved deep in his pockets; he bounced slightly on the balls of his feet. The cool night air ruffled his black hair.

Seth walked down to the beach with Lulu. At the waterline, they crouched down, looking at something. Jolene could tell that Betsy wanted to follow, but she held back.

"Go on, Betsy," Jolene urged quietly. It took a moment, but Betsy finally started moving, walked down the deck steps and across the sandy beach. At her approach, Seth looked up, smiled shyly.

"What are they going to do without us?" Jolene said quietly.

"What are we going to do without them?" was Tami's reply.

They stood there until the air turned cold in their nostrils and the breeze graduated to a wind, until Carl and Michael had stopped pretending they had something to say to each other. Then the Flynns went into the restaurant and Jolene's family went home.

By the time they'd parked the car and gone back into the warm, golden house, the mood had grown solemn. Even Lulu seemed affected.

"Mommy," Lulu said as they came into the family room. "You'll be back for my birthday, won't you?"

Betsy rolled her eyes.

"Not before your birthday, Lulu. But Daddy's going to make sure you have a nice party."

"Oh." Lulu scrunched her face in thought. "What if I lose a tooth? You'll come home for that, won't you?"

Michael sat down and turned on the TV.

Betsy made a sound of pure frustration and left the room. The sound of her footsteps on the stairs reverberated through the house.

"What about bedtime stories? Who will read to me?" Lulu said, frowning.

"Lulu, honey, put your toys away. I'll be right back."

Feeling shaky, Jolene followed Betsy up the stairs and knocked on her door.

"Go away," Betsy screamed.

"You don't mean that," Jolene said. "Not tonight."

There was a long pause, then: "Fine. Come in."

Jolene walked into the bedroom and went to the bed.

Betsy didn't move sideways, but Jolene sat down beside her anyway. She put an arm around her daughter and pulled her close.

"I'm trying, Mom," Betsy said at last.

"I know."

"On the news—"

"Don't watch the news, Betsy. It won't help."

"What will?"

Jolene sighed. "I'll tell you what. Let's synchronize our watches' alarms. That way when the alarms go off, we'll think of each other at that second."

"Okay."

In silence, they set their alarms.

"I shouldn't have said that about the dog tags . . ." Betsy said, her voice uneven.

"It's okay, Betsy."

"I'll miss you," Betsy said after a minute. "I don't know why I'm being so mean to you . . ."

"I know, baby. I was twelve once. And you've got a lot to worry about right now." Jolene kissed Betsy's cheek.

They sat there, holding each other for a long time. In the quiet, Jolene felt as if she were coming undone. How could she leave tomorrow, walk away from her family, say good-bye to her children?

She wanted to tell Betsy everything she would need to know for her whole life—just in case, to warn her about sex and boys and drugs and makeup, about social politics and college admissions and bad choices. But it was too early—and too late.

Finally, she kissed her daughter's cheek, said, "Are you ready to come back downstairs?" and got up.

"I don't feel like watching TV. I think I'll read," Betsy said.

Jolene could hardly challenge that. She didn't really want to go back downstairs, either. "Okay."

She went downstairs, where she found Michael watching TV while Lulu sat beside him on the sofa, doggedly asking him questions about how long Mommy would be gone.

"Come here, Lucy Lou," Jolene said, scooping her daughter into her arms. "It's time for your bath."

Jolene carried Lulu upstairs, gave her a long, play-filled bath, then got her ready for bed.

As she looked around for last night's book, she saw Lulu scamper out of bed, put on her ratty gray cat-ear headband, and climb back into bed.

So Lulu wanted to play. Jolene turned to the bed and stopped suddenly. "Oh, no. Lulu, where did you go? Did the fairies steal you?"

Lulu made a sound and clamped a hand over her mouth.

"Was that the wind?" Jolene went to the window, opened it. "Lulu, are you out there?"

Lulu took off her headband and burst into tears. "I want to stay inbisible 'til you come home."

"Aw, Lulu," she said, climbing into Lulu's narrow bed, taking her baby into her arms.

"Who will find me if you're gone?"

Jolene tightened her hold, thinking of all the things she'd miss.

Lulu would start kindergarten and ride the bus and make new friends, all without Jolene beside her. "I love you, Lucy Louida. You remember that, okay?"

"Okay." Lulu snuggled under the covers and closed her eyes. In minutes, she was asleep.

Jolene kissed her cheek and left the bedroom. On her way out, she snagged one of Lulu's yellow plastic barrettes from the dresser and slipped it into her pocket.

As she went downstairs, she was struck by the quiet in her house.

"Michael?"

She got no answer. Moving from room to room, she didn't find him anywhere, but his car was in the garage. Finally, she caught a glimpse of something out front.

She stopped at the kitchen window and looked out. Moonlight glanced off a figure seated on their dock.

She slipped into the pair of boots that were always at the mudroom door. Zipping up her hoodie, she left the house and walked along the fence line down to the main road.

On the other side, she followed the wooden steps down to their dock. The full moon lit her way. She stepped on something that made a loud, cracking sound.

"I guess you found me," Michael said, lifting a bottle to his lips.

Jolene sat down in the chair beside him. He'd built a fire in the metal pit off to the side, and some heat wafted her way.

"I'm sure you'll tell me getting drunk is a bad idea."

Jolene sighed. How had they come to this place, and how would they ever find their way back?

They wouldn't.

She reached out, said, "May I?" and took the bottle from him, taking a sip of the bitter scotch. It burned all the way down.

"You must be upset," he said.

She nodded. Normally she stayed away from alcohol, both because of her family history and because of her career. A DUI would ground her, and she would never do anything to risk her ability to fly. "I'm human, Michael. In fact, getting drunk sounds good right now."

"I'm scared, Jo," he said quietly. "I don't know if I can handle it."

She waited for him to say something more, maybe reach for her. When he didn't, she turned to look at him.

In profile, his features sharpened by moonlight, he looked remote and cold. She saw the way he held his lips pursed in disapproval, as if the slightest relaxing would undo him, and she hated that she was leaving him now when their marriage was in trouble. She needed to believe he still loved her, or that he could love her again.

"Look at me," Jolene said.

He took another long drink from the scotch bottle and then turned to her.

They were close enough to kiss; all it would have taken was the slightest movement by either one of them, but neither leaned toward the other.

"Don't get hurt over there, Jo," he said, his gaze steady.

She heard a caring in the words she'd thought was gone, and it filled her with a sweet and tender hope. Maybe they *could* fix it, maybe one perfect moment could put them back on track. She needed him so much right now she couldn't stand it; she needed to be able to take his love with her.

Slowly, she put a hand around his neck and pulled him closer, kissing him, but even as her heartbeat sped up and passion flared inside her, she felt him holding back. It was like kissing a stranger.

She drew back, humiliated. "Take care of my babies," she whispered.

But he was drinking again, staring out at the rolling waves.

"It's too bad you think you have to say that," he said.

She got up and returned to the house, alone.

Nine

※

Michael woke up alone. At some point, long before dawn, he'd heard Jolene awaken and climb out of bed. Without turning on the lights, she had dressed in her camo fatigues—ACUs—grabbed her duffle bag, and left the bedroom, quietly shutting the door behind her. He had pretended to be asleep. Later, he'd heard a horn honk outside; Tami had come to pick Jolene up.

Afterward, Michael lay alone. He thought he'd never fall asleep again, but somehow he had, and he'd been wakened hours later by the alarm bleating beside his bed.

Now, it was The Day. He woke the girls up and then took a long, scaldingly hot shower.

He had no idea what to wear for a deployment ceremony, so he went for the ever-popular charcoal slacks and matching V-neck cashmere sweater, but when he looked in the mirror, he saw a stranger. His dark eyes had a haunted look, and the shadows beneath attested to the fact that he hadn't slept well in weeks.

"Dad?" Betsy walked into the room, wearing white knee-length leggings, a long pink sweater cinched tight at the waist by a wide silver belt, and Ugg boots. Her long blond hair hung in frizzy ringlets to the middle of her back.

She looked like she was trying out for some Disney kid show where people burst into song at the drop of a hat.

"Is that what you think you're wearing?" he asked.

"You can't tell me what to wear."

"Why not? I'm your father."

Betsy rolled her eyes. "I came to tell you that Lulu isn't coming with us."

"What do you mean? She's four years old."

"I *know* her age, Dad. I just said she won't come. And she's wearing the headband."

Michael had no idea what difference a headband could make. "Fine." He sighed—he was exhausted already and it was barely past eleven. "Come on," he said to Betsy and headed down the hallway.

Lulu's room appeared to have been ransacked. There were toys and clothes everywhere; all of the bedding had been pulled off the bed and lay heaped on the floor.

She sat in the corner, wearing her ragged gray kitten Halloween costume, with her skinny legs drawn up to her chest. Her eyes were red and watery from crying and her cheeks were blotchy.

He looked at his watch. They were late. "Get up, Lulu. We don't have time for this. We have to say good-bye to your mom."

When he reached down for her, she screamed, "You can't see me!"

Michael frowned.

Betsy grabbed his wrist. "Lulu's invisible when she has the headband on."

"Oh, for God's—"

"Lulu," Betsy said in a singsong voice. "Where are you? We need to go."

Lulu didn't answer.

Michael felt acutely out of his depth already and Jolene hadn't even left yet.

"I know how afraid Lulu must be to say good-bye, but Mommy needs our kisses to keep her safe," Betsy said.

Lulu burst into tears. Taking off the headband, she stood up. "I don't want her to go. Will she be back for dinner?"

Betsy took her sister's hand. "No."

"My birthday?" Lulu said hopefully, clutching the ratty cat-eared headband. It was at least the fiftieth time she'd asked this question.

"Come on," Michael said tiredly. "We need to change your clothes, Lulu."

"No!" she screamed, scrambling away from him. "I want my kitty costume!"

"You should give in, Dad. Trust me," Betsy said.

"Fine," Michael said, sighing. He picked Lulu up, and the three of them went out to the car.

They drove away in a heavy, awkward silence.

When they picked up his mother, she tried to fill the silence with chatter, but her buoyant pretense at optimism soon faded. Michael turned on the radio, let Clint Black be their voice.

At the guard tower, he eased to a stop and handed his and his mother's IDs over to a very serious-looking young man in uniform.

"Go ahead, sir," the guard said finally, handing him back the two licenses.

The post was a hive of activity. Cars and trucks and uniformed soldiers were everywhere. Betsy read the instructions and guided them to a parking area, where they found a sign about the deployment ceremony to be held in the hangar.

The four of them were silent as they walked out to the hangar, which was a huge, open-sided building full of helicopters and cargo jets and smaller airplanes. One section had been cleared of aircraft, and rows of metal chairs had been placed in their space. Along the back wall, they'd set up a wooden dais. There was a giant TV screen to its left. A large banner hung from the rafters. It read: BE SAFE RAPTORS.

A pair of Black Hawk helicopters were in the center of the hangar; they were crawling with kids and parents. In front of them, a long, low table offered pamphlets on everything from PTSD to suicide prevention to summer camps for kids.

They took seats in the front row. Lulu sat curled on Michael's lap, sucking her thumb—she no longer even pretended she'd given it up. In the next thirty minutes, the place filled up with people—mostly women and children and older men—who held posters and flowers. Over by the helicopters, a news crew gathered; a pretty woman in a blue suit talked into a microphone.

Then the side door opened and the crowd went still. Music started; five soldiers marched out single file, wearing camouflage fatigues tucked into lace-up sand-colored boots and jauntily slanted berets, playing instruments. At the end of the song, the band formed a line along the wall. They stood straight and tall, their shoulders broad, their chins high, at attention in front of a row of flags.

On the dais, a man in uniform approached the mic and welcomed everyone to this important day. Then he turned and gave an order, and the giant hangar doors began slowly, slowly to open. The rollers made a grinding, pinging sound that filled the room. The doors parted to reveal the uniformed soldiers, all seventy-six of them, who made up the Raptors flight unit.

They stood outside, stone-faced, looking ready to go. There was his wife, in the front row, so tall, so strong-looking amid her other family. Chief Warrant Officer 3 Zarkades. He hardly knew her. She was the officer in charge of a forty-million-dollar aircraft and countless lives.

A soldier stood in front of the troops, said something that ended in "present arms!" and the Raptors saluted and marched into the hangar.

"Ladies and gentlemen, will you please rise for the national anthem?"

Michael watched it all as if from some great distance. At the close of the national anthem, the unit members who were being deployed assembled and stood with their legs apart and their hands behind their backs as the base commander introduced the speaker. A couple of uniformed men conducted a ceremony with a flag—they rolled it into a case and put it away. It would not be brought out again until the troops returned from war.

The governor of Washington State stepped up to the podium. The hangar was quiet, except for the crying of babies in their mothers' arms.

"The brave men and women standing in front of me are known to all of you," he began. "They are our brothers, our sisters, our neighbors, our parents, our children, and our friends. They are our heroes. To the soldiers, and to the families, and to all of those who are supporting our troops, no words can adequately express the depth and breadth of our gratitude. We left at home, the protected, are acutely aware of and thankful for your courage and your sacrifice." The governor looked up from his notes and leaned closer to the microphone. "Standing before me are the members of Charlie Company that are being deployed today. We can all be proud of their willingness to serve this great country of ours and take comfort from the certainty that each soldier is ready, is trained, is prepared to succeed in this endeavor. But we in this room know that there is more than courage being asked of these soldiers and of you, their families. I have been privileged to speak privately with many of our state's brave soldiers, and the question I always ask them is, 'What is your greatest concern with this deployment?' You will not be surprised to hear that none has expressed concern for their personal safety. They worry about *you*. Saying good-bye to loved ones is the most difficult act for any soldier." The governor paused. "There are no words that we, a grateful nation, can offer to Charlie Company except thank you." He looked at the troops. "Your willingness to put yourselves in harm's way to protect us here at home is humbling. We say thank you, and pray that you will be safe. God bless this unit and God bless America."

A soldier called out: "First Sergeant. Release the warriors to their families."

Whatever was said next was lost in the rush of applause. The audience was on their feet, clapping and crying, rushing in a herd toward the troops.

Michael couldn't make himself move. He looked at the soldiers walking past him, going in search of their families; none looked afraid. They looked proud. Strong. Certain.

Up ahead, he saw Jolene and Tami come together. A news crew was talking to them. As he approached, he heard the reporter say, "Two best friends who are female and just happen to fly Black Hawks. That's quite a story . . ."

Jolene said, "It's not as unusual as you would think. Excuse me, ma'am." She ducked out of camera range and headed toward Mila, who was pushing through the crowd.

Everywhere he looked, he saw heartbreak and courage. He saw a man in uniform, holding an infant who couldn't be more than a month old. The soldier stared at his baby intently, his eyes moist, as if trying to imagine all the changes that would be made in that small face while he was gone. Beside him, a pregnant woman hugged her husband, sobbing, promising that she would be okay without him.

And there was Jolene, hugging his mother so tightly it looked like they'd fused together.

Lulu tightened her hold around Michael's neck. "Hurry, Daddy. She might go."

Michael walked toward his wife. He hadn't expected any of this. How was that? He prided himself on his intelligence, but he'd been wrong, blinded by selfishness or politics or intellectualism. For years, he'd watched news reports about the global war on terrorism and followed images of soldiers in the desert and he'd thought about the politics of it all, about weapons of mass destruction and George W.'s declaration of war and the wisdom of arming and sending out troops. He'd argued with colleagues about it—while he sat safe and warm and protected in his country. He'd argued about the true cost of war.

He hadn't known shit. The cost of war was here, in this room. It was families being torn apart and babies born without their parent at home and children forgetting their mother's face. It was soldiers—some of them his age and others young enough to be his sons—who would come home wounded . . . or not come home at all.

His *wife* was going off to war. *War.* How was it he had missed the most important part of that? She could die.

"Breathe," Jolene said gently.

Michael stared at her, his eyes bright with tears he was trying to hold back. "How can you do this? Any of you . . ."

Lulu leaned out of his arms, toward Jolene, her arms outstretched. "Don't leave me, Mommy. I'll be good. I won't be inbisible anymore."

Jolene pulled her youngest into her arms and held her fiercely. "You are the best girl in the world, Lucy Lou . . ." She pinned a small golden set of wings on Lulu's costume. "When you look at these wings, you'll know I'm thinking of you, Lulu. Okay?"

Michael reached out, took Jolene's hand. He should have done that before, told her he'd be here for her. She grasped his hand so tightly it hurt. He wanted to wrap his arms around both of them, but he didn't dare. If he got close enough to kiss her, he might fall apart and be the only man in the room who cried. His kids didn't need to see that.

Betsy stood back, her arms crossed, one hip flung out, her mouth pulled into a tight frown.

"I'll send videos and e-mails. I'll call as much as I can," Jolene promised them all.

"We'll be fine," Mila said to Jolene, hugging her, taking Lulu into her arms. "Don't you worry about us."

Jolene moved toward Betsy, caressed her cheek, forced her to look up. "I have my watch set. Do you?"

"Seven o'clock," Betsy said firmly, looking away.

Jolene bent down, looked Betsy in the eyes. "I love you to the moon and back." She paused. Michael knew she was waiting. He thought: *say it back to her, Bets,* but the silence just hung there, until Jolene straightened, looking unbearably sad.

Behind them, a voice came through the speakers, telling the soldiers to gather at the buses. The crowd started to move like a wave, swelling toward the doors.

And then they were outside, this crowd of straight-backed soldiers with duffle bags, amid their weeping families and reaching children. A row of buses waited on the tarmac.

"I'll be good," Lulu said, crying hard.

Jolene kissed her daughters and held them tightly and then . . . let them go.

Michael watched her move toward him. For a split second it was just the two of them in his mind—no kids, no soldiers, no crying babies. Everything around them was a blur of sound and fury.

He didn't know what to do or say. He couldn't repair a broken marriage with a kiss or a touch, but he was ashamed of what he'd done to get them here, and it was too late to fix it.

"Michael," she said and he felt the sting of tears. "Take care of yourself."

It was so little, that good-bye; more evidence of the shoals they'd wrecked on.

"You take care of *yourself*. Come home to . . ."

"Them?"

"Just make sure you come home." He took her in his arms at last, holding her tightly. It wasn't until she walked away that he realized she hadn't hugged him back.

With one last agonizing look, Jolene disappeared into the crowd of soldiers and boarded the bus.

Betsy cried out, "MOM!" and ran the length of the bus, following her mother's progress. Her voice was lost in the din.

Michael picked up a sobbing Lulu and tried to soothe her, but she was hysterical.

In the back row of the bus, Jolene put down her window. She gazed down at her family; the smile she gave them faltered as the bus drove away.

And then she was gone.

"I didn't say 'I love you,'" Betsy said, bursting into tears.

In the months before his wife left, Michael had slept on "his side" of the bed. He'd seen the river of rumpled white cotton between them as a no-man's-land where passion had gone to die. Now, on this morning when he woke up truly alone, he saw how false that had been. In all those nights, he'd had a wife beside him, a partner with whom he'd shared his life. Alone was different from separate, infinitely different. Often last night he'd reached out for her and found only emptiness.

His first thought when he woke: she's gone.

He sat up in bed. Beside him on the nightstand was her "bible," the huge three-ring binder that housed the endless list of his new responsibilities. In it, she'd put everything she thought he might need— appliance warranties, recipes, lists of mechanics and housecleaners and babysitters. He reached for it and opened it to the "Daily Planner" section.

Make breakfast. (Each morning came with its own carefully constructed meal plan.)

Get girls dressed. Make sure they brush their teeth.

Get Betsy on school bus. Arrival: 8:17.

Drop Lulu off at preschool. 8:30. She had provided him with an address, which pissed him off, both because she assumed he would need it and because, in fact, he did.

He threw back the covers and got out of bed, stumbling toward the bathroom. After a long, hot shower, he felt ready to start his day. Dressing in navy wool slacks and a crisp white Armani dress shirt, he left the room.

As he walked down the darkened hallway, he knocked on the girls' doors, yelling for them to get up.

Downstairs, he made a pot of coffee, realizing too late that he'd made enough for two. Then he stood there, waiting impatiently. As soon as it was done, he pulled out the glass carafe and poured himself a cup.

Only it wasn't done; coffee dripped down, splattering and burning on the warming pad below. He shoved the carafe back into place, ignoring the steaming sizzle, and looked at his list.

Today was "clown" pancake breakfast day.

Ha.

Instead, he rifled through the cupboards, found some cereal, and thumped it down on the table. Tossing some bowls and spoons alongside it, he grabbed the newspaper from the porch and sat down to read it.

The next time he looked up, it was 8:07.

"Shit." He threw down the paper and ran up the stairs, opening Betsy's door.

His daughter was still asleep.

"Damn it, Betsy, get up."

She sat up in bed slowly, blinking, and glanced sleepily at the clock by her bed and then screamed.

"You didn't wake me up in time!" The horror on her face would have been funny any other time. He knew how precise Betsy was, just like her mom; she hated to be rushed.

"I knocked on your door and yelled at you," he said, clapping his hands. "Get going."

"I don't have time. I don't have time." She jumped out of bed and looked in the mirror. "My hair," she groaned.

"You have five minutes to be at the table for breakfast."

"No shower?" Again, the horror. "You can't mean it."

"Oh. I mean it. You're twelve. How dirty can you be? *Go.*"

She glared at him.

"Move it." He strode down the hall to Lulu's room. As usual, his youngest daughter slept spread-eagle on top of the blankets with a zoo of stuffed animals gathered around her. He threw the toys aside and kissed her cheek, pushing her tangled hair aside. "Lulu, honey, it's time to wake up."

"I don't wanna," she said, rolling away from him.

"Time to go to preschool."

"I don't wanna."

He turned on the light and went to her dresser. Opening the top drawer, he pulled out some tiny pink-flowered underwear and a pair of small elastic-waisted yellow corduroy pants and a green sweater. "Come on, Lulu, we need to get you dressed."

"Those are summer clothes, Daddy. And they don't go together. Get the yellow sweater."

"This is what you're wearing."

"Am not."

"Are, too."

"Mommy lets me pick—"

"Come here, Lucy," he said sternly.

Scrunching her face up, she climbed out of bed and padded toward him. All the time he was dressing her, she was complaining.

"There," he said when she was dressed. "Pretty as a picture."

"I look ugly."

"Hardly."

She reached up for the pair of wings on the dresser top. "Pin it on me, Daddy. It means she's thinking of me. Ow! You poked me."

"Sorry," he mumbled. Picking her up, he carried her downstairs and into the kitchen. There, he put her in her chair and poured her a bowl of cereal.

"It's clown pancake day," she informed him crisply, looking down at her wings. "Look at the calendar."

"It's Captain Crunch day."

"That's for special. Is Mommy coming home?"

"Not today." He poured the milk into her bowl.

Betsy came running into the kitchen and stopped dead. "I can't go to school like this," she cried, flinging out her arms dramatically. "Look at my hair."

She *did* sort of look as if she'd just undergone electric shock therapy. "Put a twisty thing in it."

Betsy's eyes widened at the thought, her face paled. "You're ruining my life already."

"Mommy's not coming home yet," Lulu said and burst into tears.

"Eat," Michael snapped to Lulu; to Betsy, he said, "Sit down. Now."

Outside, he heard the grinding of gears, the rattling of an old engine. He looked through the kitchen window and saw the yellow blur of a school bus pull up at the end of his driveway.

"I'm *late*," Betsy howled. "See?"

Michael ran to the back door and flung it open, yelling, "Wait—"

But it was too late. The bus was pulling away.

He slammed the door shut. "When does school start? *That* wasn't on her damn list."

Betsy stared at him. "You don't even know?"

"Eat. Then go brush your teeth. We're leaving in two minutes."

"I'm not going to first period," Betsy said. "Ooooh no I'm not. Zoe's in that class. And Sienna. When they see my hair—"

"You're going to school. I have a ferry to catch." Michael looked at the wall clock and grimaced. He was going to miss his ferry, which meant he was going to miss his first meeting of the day.

Betsy crossed her arms. "I'm on a hunger strike."

"Fine," he snapped. "Be hungry." He grabbed the dishes and put them in the sink, cereal and milk and all. In the mudroom, he found Lulu's pink rubber boots and picked them up.

In the kitchen, Betsy hadn't moved. She sat in the chair, looking mutinous, with her chin jutted out and her eyes narrowed.

"I'm not going in late. Everyone will stare at me," she said.

"Who do you think you are, Madonna? A bad hair day doesn't stop school. Get your backpack."

"No."

He looked at her. "Get your backpack and get ready, Betsy, or I'll walk you in to first period, holding your hand."

She opened her mouth in horror, then clamped it shut. "Whatever. I'm going."

He looked through the kitchen to the family room, where Lulu lay curled on the couch, with her blanket and a stuffed orca, watching the video of Jolene reading her a story. "Lulu, come let me put your boots on you. Lulu. Come here."

"She's wearing the headband," Betsy said primly.

Michael marched into the family room and picked Lulu up. At the movement, the headband slid off her head.

"I'm inbisible!" she screamed.

He carried her screaming and squealing out to the car and strapped her into her car seat. Betsy, silent and glowering, climbed in beside her.

Lulu burst into tears. "I want my mommy!"

"Yeah," Michael said, starting the car. "Don't we all?"

The first week without Jolene almost drove Michael into the ground. He'd had no idea how much there was to do around the house and with the kids. If his mother hadn't had such boundless energy, he would have had to hire full-time help. She'd been a lifesaver, no doubt about it. Jolene had enrolled Lulu in after-preschool day care, which lasted until four o'clock. That meant his mother could work until almost four, and then pick Lulu up from day care, and get to Michael's house in time to meet Betsy so that she never came home to an empty house—one of Jolene's strictest rules. By the time Michael got home at six, his mom had usually started dinner and done some laundry. She was shouldering a big part of his burden.

Even so, he wasn't doing well. Betsy was a whirling dervish; he never seemed to be able to anticipate her reaction to the simplest of things. She could burst into tears over nothing and then be mad as a hornet five seconds later. And Lulu wasn't much easier to handle. She had taken to wearing her ratty gray cat ears almost all the time. She swore she was going to stay "inbisible" until Jolene came home, and when Michael ignored the game and picked her up anyway, she screamed like a banshee and sobbed that she missed her mommy.

And then there was the Keller case, which was showing all the signs of becoming a disaster. Keith still hadn't spoken to anyone, not even his court-appointed psychiatrist. Michael had waived his client's right to a speedy trial, but at the moment competency to stand trial was a legitimate concern.

His intercom buzzed. "Michael? Mr. Keller is here to see you."

"Send him in." Michael closed up the file and opened a pad of paper.

Edward Keller walked into the office slowly, looking nervous. He was a big man with close-shaved black hair and a bushy black Tom Selleck mustache. He was pale and sweaty-looking in his plaid shirt and Wrangler jeans.

Michael stood up, extended his hand. "Hello, Ed. I'm Michael. It's nice to finally meet you."

Ed shook his hand. "My wife wouldn't come. She tried . . . she just can't talk about it yet. Emily was like a daughter to us. It's hard . . ."

"I understand," Michael said, and he did. He lived in a world of crime and victims; he'd seen time and again how terrible a grief came with the realization that a loved one had committed a heinous crime. Ed and his wife were the forgotten victims in a case like this.

"He won't talk to me," Ed said. "He just sits there, staring at the wall."

"To be blunt, Ed, that's our real problem now. The only one doing the talking is the prosecuting attorney, and I don't like what he's saying. They've charged Keith with murder in the first degree, and they claim to have a witness who will testify that Keith confessed to the murder."

Ed looked miserable. The man slumped in his chair. "He was such a good kid. Popular. Friendly. The kind of kid who asks you if you need help carryin' in the groceries and how your day was. He dated lots of girls, cheerleader types, and had fun in high school, but when he met Emily, he knew right away she was the one."

"When did it start going wrong?"

"What?"

"The marriage."

"Oh. It never did."

"Ed," Michael said evenly. "Something went wrong."

Ed looked down at his own hands. "We've asked ourselves that question a million times. *Did he seem depressed? Did you ever hear them arguin'? Did he ever say he was unhappy?* Our family has looked at it six ways to Sunday. They had a happy marriage; that's what we think. She couldn't wait for him to get home from Iraq. She wrote him every day."

Michael looked up sharply. "Iraq? There's no mention of him serving in Iraq in what I've got here. It just says he's an honorably discharged marine."

"He did two tours. When he came home the second time, he wasn't the same."

"What do you mean?"

"We all saw that he was changed. If you startled him—and that was easy to do—he could turn on you fast enough to take your breath away. I know he didn't sleep much. Emily told me that he'd started keepin' a loaded gun by the bed. God help me, I told her a man needed to protect his family."

Michael wrote down *PTSD* and underlined it. "Did he ever hit Emily, to your knowledge?"

"In the last few days, before the . . . you know, I wondered about that. Keith was so edgy and upset. At a family dinner, he blew up at his brother over nothing. And the look in his eyes scared us all. It wasn't our Keith. When I asked him about it, he told me he'd had too much coffee, but I didn't believe him. I think whatever happened to him in Iraq is why he killed Emily."

Michael added: *What happened in Iraq?* to his notes. *Diminished capacity?* "Did he get help?"

"He tried. The VA sent him away with a prescription for Prozac."

Michael tapped his pen on the desk, thinking. So his client had tried to get help from the military and been denied. That was good. And hardly surprising. "Okay, Ed. I'll do some research based on what you've just told me, but I need to talk to Keith, and I need Keith to talk to a psychiatrist. And I need it to happen quickly."

"He won't—"

"If he doesn't, Ed, he'll go to prison. Probably for life."

Ed looked stricken by that, as Michael had intended. In the silence that followed, Michael sighed. "I don't want to scare you, but I can't help your son if he won't talk to me. There are two sides to every story. I need his."

"I'll get him to talk," Ed said.

Michael stared at him. "Do that, Ed, and fast."

Ten

The first week at Fort Hood passed in a blur of classes, assignments, paper pushing, and lectures. It had been so many years since her active army days that Jolene had forgotten how much bureaucracy there was in ordinary military life, how much of a day was spent "hurrying up to wait." She'd spent the last seven days standing in one line or another—or so it seemed. They stood in line for supplies, for lectures, for paperwork to be signed. There was the SRP—soldier readiness process—and more medical tests and examinations and shots, finance reviews, and updating of personnel records.

The day started early here at Fort Hood; breakfast was at 0430. Immediately afterward were classes on anything and everything they would need to know in Iraq: spiders and scorpions and IEDs—improvised explosive devices—sexual harassment, chemical warfare. The list went on and on. The worst of the lines were at the phones. Jolene had been advised to leave her cell phone at home, since it wouldn't work in Iraq anyway. Following that advice had been a mistake. As it was, she spent much of her off-duty time standing in line to call home. More often than not, by the time it was her turn to use the phone, it was too late to talk to the girls. The few conversations she'd had with Michael had been short and stilted. Neither had said *I love you* before hanging up. Afterward, she felt more lonely than she had before the calls.

Now, Charlie Company was out beneath the blazing hot Texas sun, in full gear, walking along a dirt road the color of old blood. Jamie was in the lead. A lone hawk circled overhead curiously, no doubt wondering why these uniformed, helmeted adults, armed with M-16s and 9 mils, were running around in this heat. They kept pulling to the side of the road and looking for fictitious IEDs.

She knew it was important, lifesaving, even, but they were an aviation unit going in to provide support—backfill—for a combat aviation brigade. If she found herself on a road in Sadr City or Baghdad, in a Humvee, something had gone wrong enough that an IED would be only one of the worries.

And man it was hot.

By the time they finished that drill and made it out to the rifle range, Jolene was sweating so badly under her helmet that moisture ran into her eyes.

"Zarkades, get the hell down here!"

"Roger that, sir."

She hustled to her place on the gun range and lifted her rifle. Aiming, she pulled the trigger.

"Good shot, Chief. Ten more just like that and you can start the live-fire course."

For the next four hours, Jolene did as she was ordered: stand, sit, crawl, shoot, run. Afterward, she and Tami headed across the post, hoping the phone lines would be a little shorter at this hour.

They were wrong. At least forty soldiers were already in line, standing under the waning heat of the sun, reading, talking, listening to music.

Jolene slowed. "Damn." She was about to turn around when she saw Smitty wave at her. He was fourth in line. Even with dirt and sweat running down his face, he looked young enough to be her son.

"Hey, Smitty," Jolene said, heading toward him.

He smiled, showing off his braces. "Hey, Chiefs."

Tami came up beside Jolene. "Are you calling your mom or is there some girlfriend pining away for you?"

"I'm holding this spot for you two," he said. At their surprised look, he added: "I just remembered, my girlfriend's still at work. I can't call her for another hour. And besides"—he gave them both a sheepish grin—"I know I'd want to hear from my mom."

Smitty backed away, leaving an opening in line.

"You sure you don't have anyone you want to call?" Jolene asked. "What about your folks?"

"Nope. They're driving to see my grandma today."

Jolene looked at Tami, who gave her a big smile. "You're the man, Smitty," Tami said.

The women stepped into line; Smitty walked away, whistling.

When the phone was free, Tami stepped forward and made her call. As Jolene listened to the singsong sound of her friend's voice, she tapped her foot impatiently, flicked her fingers against the rough fabric of her pants, and then, finally, it was her turn. Tami hung up, and Jolene lurched forward, picked up the old-fashioned receiver, hot from so many hands, and called home.

Betsy answered, said "Hello?" and then yelled, "It's Mom."

Jolene leaned against the sun-warmed side of the building, trying to ignore the line of soldiers behind her, but it was impossible. She could hear them moving around, talking, laughing. "Hey, Bets. How's your week been? I'm sorry I couldn't call yesterday. They had us busy all day and night."

Betsy launched into a breathless story about a trauma at school. Apparently Betsy had been chosen last for volleyball teams in PE. Sierra and Zoe had been behind the humiliation, had pointed and laughed until Betsy screamed at them to shut up and then received detention for her outburst. "Me! I got detention and it was all their fault. Can you call my PE teacher and get me out of it?"

Jolene had ten minutes on the phone, and Betsy had already used up six of those minutes telling her story. "Oh, honey, I can't do that, but if you—"

"I get it. You're too busy. Don't worry about it, Mom. Lulu! Your turn!"

"Don't be that way, Betsy," Jolene said, her guilt surfacing again. "We get so little time to talk."

"Obviously."

"I'll write you an e-mail as soon as I can, okay?"

"Like I said, Mom, don't worry about it. I don't need you. Here's Lulu."

"Betsy. I love you."

There was only breathing on the other end; then Lulu was on the phone, sounding like a mouse on helium. At the end of a story about something she made for Jolene out of macaroni and string, Lulu said, "I want you to read me a story tonight."

"I can't, baby."

Lulu burst into tears. "Daddy, she's not coming home yet . . ."

"Hey, Jo," Michael said a second later, sounding as tired as she suddenly felt.

"Lulu didn't say good-bye or 'I love you.' "

"She's upset, Jo. She'll be fine. How are you?"

Jolene had been on the phone eleven minutes. The soldiers behind her were starting to get restless. "Is she having nightmares again? Because if she is, she needs her yellow blanket and her pink ribbon."

"Come on, Jo. Did you think the girls would say good-bye to their mother, watch her march off to war, and be fine?"

Behind her someone yelled out, "Come on, ma'am. We all have families."

There was so much she wanted to say and no time to say it. Michael's silence gnawed at her nerves. "I'll write Betsy an e-mail tonight. Can you make sure she reads it before school?"

"Sure. So, your time's up now?"

"It is."

"Great talk, Jo," he said in a voice she could barely hear.

She whispered "Good-bye," and hung up the phone. Another soldier moved in next to her, picked up the receiver.

Jolene backed away; she felt Tami coming up beside her. They began the walk back to their barracks.

"Betsy spent ten minutes telling me about her day and asking if I'd call her teacher to get her out of detention," Jolene said.

Tami laughed quietly. "So we go off to war and motherhood pretty much stays the same. And Michael?"

"He asked me why I thought the girls would be fine after I went off to war."

"We're not even at war."

Jolene sighed. "How's Seth?"

"He loves me and misses me and he's proud of me. At least that's what he says. According to Carl, he isn't sleeping and he unplugged his Xbox and won't play video games anymore—he doesn't want to see cartoon people getting blown up. And when I think of how many times I told him to get off that idiot box . . ."

"How are we going to get through this?" Jolene asked quietly.

Tami had no answer for that. At their barracks, they grabbed their dopp kits and headed for the showers. Afterward, they walked over to the dining facilities—DFAC—and sat down with several of the members of Charlie Company, including Jamie and Smitty. They were surrounded by the smell of gravy that had been on a burner too long and sweet corn cooked down to mush. The drone of soldiers' voices was like a jet engine.

Smitty was shoveling creamed corn into his mouth at an alarming rate, talking at the same time about the rifle range. Jamie stared down at his food, poking the meatloaf with his fork. He seemed far away from all of them, and Jolene understood his distance.

"We need to get our heads in the game, Jo," Tami said. "We're soldiers first now. That's the way it has to be or . . ."

"We'll die," Jolene said softly. She knew Tami was right; she'd thought the same thing several times. No doubt it was what occupied Jamie's thoughts now, too. The point of war games was, ultimately, war. Jolene needed to put her feelings for her family in a compartment and hide it away. "I don't know how to stop missing them. I feel guilty all the time.

I keep thinking that if I can say just the right thing on the phone, we'll all be okay."

"Carl and I talked about this before I left. He told me I had to stop being a part of him and start being a part of this. He said he knew I loved him and that my job was to think about me and the men and women around me." Tami looked at her. "Two weeks from now we'll be in-country, Jo. You've got to cut yourself loose from Poulsbo. Trust Michael to keep everything together."

"Trust Michael," she said dully.

"You have no choice."

Jolene knew Tami was right, but letting go was easier said than done. She knew how it felt to be abandoned in childhood, and although this was different, profoundly different, she wasn't certain her children would really understand why she had left them. "How have men done it all these years, gone off to war and left their kids behind?"

"They had wives," Tami said simply.

Late that night, after Tami had fallen asleep, Jolene opened her laptop. She was so tired, she had trouble keeping her eyes open, but she had to write to her daughter.

Dear Betsy:

I'm so sorry I can't help you with your detention. You won't want to hear what I have to say about it, either. The bottom line is that you broke the rules. There's always a consequence for our actions. You might as well learn that early. Of course Sierra and Zoe are wrong to have goaded you and mean to have made fun of you. But how you respond is what will make you who you are.

I have so many things to say about that, and it kills me that we aren't together. Mothers and daughters are supposed to curl up on the couch and talk about anything and everything. And we will soon. You'll see. Until then, I wish I knew how to tell you how to get through the tough times in middle school. I know so much about mean girls.

*When I was your age, no one liked me. I was always the girl with
the ratty clothes and no lunch money. I was too ashamed to invite
anyone home, so I didn't make friends. It was terrible. Lonely. I don't
want that for you.*

*I know how it feels to be ignored and teased. So I ignored those
girls right back, and it just made me feel bad about myself.*

*You know what helped? Joining the Army, and not because they
taught me to fly (or not only because of that), but because that's
where I met Tami.*

*I was afraid to talk to her in the beginning. She was so confident.
She didn't seem to care that we were the only women in flight school.
For the whole first week, I ignored her because I figured she wouldn't
like me. And you know what?*

She was WAITING for me to talk to her.

*That's when I learned how much one smile can matter. Let people
know you're ready to be their friend, and if they give you a chance,
take it—don't be afraid. With Tami, all I had to do was find the
courage to say hi, to sit by her in the mess hall. You never know when
a sentence, a hello, can change your life.*

*I wish I were there to tell you how beautiful and smart and
talented you are, but for now, these words on a blue screen will have
to do it. Be strong, Betsy. Believe in yourself and you'll be okay.*

I love you to the moon and back.

It wasn't enough. Not nearly. But it was all there was, all she could
say from here.

Tomorrow, she'd write to Lulu.

She yawned and hit Send.

On the last Thursday in May, Michael woke early and got breakfast ready.
He thought that if he could just get ahead of the curve, get a smooth
schedule going with the girls, he would be okay. Ever since Jolene's departure, he'd been running behind—late to meetings, late for the ferry,

late for dinner. Something was always going wrong. Today, he was determined to have a nice, peaceful morning.

He knew he'd wasted his time when Betsy came into the kitchen wearing more makeup than a Vegas showgirl.

"You have got to be kidding me," he said, putting down his paper.

Betsy turned her back on him. "What?" she said, opening the fridge.

"You are not wearing that makeup to school."

She faced him. "What makeup?"

"I wear reading glasses, Bets. I'm not blind. Go wash your face."

"Or what?"

"Or . . ." He narrowed his gaze. "I'll offer to volunteer in your class today. Social studies. Aren't you guys reading the Constitution?"

"You wouldn't."

"Try me."

She stared at him a long minute, then stomped her foot and marched out of the room. When she returned, she was a real pain in the ass, slamming cabinet doors, muttering under her breath, being mean to Lulu, who cried through most of breakfast and kept asking when Mommy was coming back.

At work, he spent the day catching up on all the work he'd missed in the past few weeks, but there was too much. Between managing the firm and defending his clients, he was overworked, plain and simple. Now, he was dictating a discovery request for Keith Keller's military record. Something he should have done weeks ago.

He buzzed his secretary. "Ann? Have we heard anything from Keith Keller?"

"No, Michael."

"Thanks." He glanced back down at the papers spread out across his desk. As he reached for a pen, his cell phone rang.

"Hi, Michael," his mother said. "I'm sorry to call you at work, but I just got a flat tire. I'm out by the Tacoma Mall for that gardening gift show. There's no way I can make it home in time to pick up Lulu and be at your house in time to meet Betsy."

"Are you okay?"

"Fine. Fine. Just waiting for AAA. Sarah Wheller is doing carpool today—she'll drop Betsy home after track practice. About five o'clock. And Lulu needs to be picked up by four thirty."

He looked at his watch. It was 3:33. The next ferry left in twelve minutes. If he missed it, Betsy would come home to an empty house—a no-no according to Jolene's über list. Although, honestly, why a twelve-year-old needed someone to welcome her home was beyond him. "Okay, Ma. Thanks."

"Sorry to do this to you. Oh, darn, my phone is beeping. Does that mean my battery is going out? Michael? Did you hear me?"

"I'm here, Ma. No problem. Thanks." He flipped his phone shut, gathered up what work he would need, and left his office. "I left some dictation on my desk for you. And try Keller's father again, remind him I really need to speak to his son," he said to Ann as he passed her desk. "I'll be on my cell if you need me."

"Your four fifteen appointment—"

"Cancel it. I have to leave right now," he said over his shoulder and kept walking.

Outside, a steady rain drizzled from a low-slung sky. Car headlights glowed in the falling rain, looking like an endless stream of fuzzy yellow balls inching down wet streets. As he drove away from his office, blurry neon signs attested to the city's rough-and-tumble past—gun shops and X-rated bookstores and dark, seedy bars. He followed the stop-and-go traffic to the ferry terminal, cursing at every red light, checking his watch.

He knew he was in trouble when he saw the ticket line. All at once he remembered that today was the Thursday before Memorial Day weekend. The tourists were out in droves, already heading to Bainbridge Island and the beautiful Olympic Peninsula. Tapping his fingers on the leather-covered steering wheel, he inched forward, following the car in front of him until it was his turn to buy a ticket. "Which ferry?" he said tightly.

"Six twenty."

"Shit." Michael calculated quickly: if he waited for the ferry, he wouldn't get home until at least 7:20.

But he could drive around; although the Kitsap Peninsula was only a thirty-five minute ferry ride from downtown Seattle, one could also drive through Tacoma and come into Poulsbo from the mainland. He could drive home in a little under two hours. And it was only three forty-five. He'd be through Tacoma before the rush-hour traffic hit.

"Thanks." He pulled out of line and drove back through the city. In less than ten minutes, he was rocketing onto I-5 South. He flipped open his phone and called his mom, who didn't pick up. Her battery had probably gone dead. Then he called the day care and told the teacher that he'd be late picking up Lulu.

Four o'clock.

And yes, he wouldn't be home when Betsy got there.

He knew what Jolene would say, the disappointed look she'd give him, but he would only be a few minutes late—fifteen or twenty. Betsy was twelve years old, for God's sake, she could be home alone for fifteen minutes. Thirty at the most.

He cranked up the music—a U2 concert album—and concentrated on driving through the now pouring rain. He was making good time until he came to the Narrows Bridge. The soaring green stanchions looked like huge ladders in the falling rain.

And the traffic was stopped. Up in the distance, he could see the flash of red ambulance lights.

"Damn it," he cursed, opening his phone. He dialed home, left Betsy a message: "I'm stuck in traffic, Betsy. Just sit tight. I'll be home as soon as I can. Six o'clock at the very latest. Call me if you want. I'm on my cell."

He sat . . . and sat . . . and sat in the middle of a clog of cars, with rain blurring his windshield. All the while, he felt his blood pressure rising, but there was nothing he could do about it. At 5:40, he called home again. "Damn it, Betsy, pick up." When she didn't, he snapped the phone shut and dialed his mom at home. She didn't answer either, so he left another message.

It was almost 6:20 when the barricades were cleared and traffic started up again. Michael hit the gas—too hard—and gunned for home. He had a pounding headache by the time he pulled into the day care parking lot. Inside the small well-tended house, he found the teacher waiting for him. "I'm sorry," he said, raking the hair back from his face. "There was an accident on the Narrows. Ugly. I got here as quickly as I could."

She nodded. "Things happen. I know. But Lulu's upset." She stepped aside.

Through an open door, Michael saw Lulu sitting all alone in a brightly colored playroom surrounded by dolls and stuffed animals.

"You're late," she said, looking up at him. "All the other mommies were already here."

"I know. I'm sorry." He helped her into her coat, said good-bye to the teacher, and carried her out to the car.

Lulu didn't talk to him all the way home, but to be honest the last thing he had to worry about these days was pissing off a four-year-old.

In the house, he patted her butt and told her to be good. "Betsy! I'm home," he yelled, closing the door behind him. "I know you're pissed, but come down and talk to me."

He tossed his briefcase on the kitchen table and loosened his tie. "Betsy?" he yelled again.

"She's not here," Lulu said, coming into the room.

"What?" Michael looked down. "What do you mean?"

Lulu stood there, holding her ratty yellow blanket. "Betsy's not home."

"What?" He yelled it so loud Lulu looked startled. He ran past her and up the stairs; at Betsy's room, he shoved the door open, yelling for her.

No answer.

He ran through the house, yelling until he knew: she wasn't here.

Downstairs, Lulu was crying. "She's gone. Oh, no . . . someone stoled her."

"No one stole her," he muttered angrily as he went to the phone and called his mom at home. When she picked up, he said, "Why don't you listen to your messages? Is Betsy with you?"

"What? I just got home. What's going on?"

"I got home late," he said, cursing under his breath. "She's not here." He hung up before his mom could answer. Fear latched into him, deep and profound. "I'll call her friends," he said, picking up the phone again, then pausing. "Lulu, quit crying, damn it. Who are Betsy's friends?"

Lulu wailed. "I don't know. She's *gone*."

He called the school and listened to the after-hours message. With a curse, he hung up.

"Maybe she ranned away," Lulu said.

Michael went out to the porch. The rain was falling hard; it studded the grass, collected in muddy puddles in the driveway. He thought about the bay, the deep cold of the water and its allure for his children. "Betsy! Where are you?"

The more he yelled her name, the more Lulu cried and the more Michael panicked. What in the hell had he been thinking? He should have left his car downtown and walked on the damn ferry and taken a cab. Or he could have called Carl. Why hadn't he thought of that then? *Damn.* What if some guy had watched Betsy get out of the car, followed her up to an empty house . . . ?

Yelling her name again, he grabbed Lulu as if she were a football, perpendicular to his body, and ran through the rain toward the neighbor's house. Resettling her as he ran, he made it to Carl and Tami's house in less than a minute. He pounded on the door.

Carl opened the door. "Michael, what's up?"

Michael wiped the rain from his eyes. "Betsy's not home and she should be. I thought maybe she came over here."

Carl slowly shook his head, and Michael felt his stomach plunge. He thought for a second he might be sick.

Seth walked into the living room, chewing on a Tootsie Pop. Holding a tattered copy of *Stranger in a Strange Land,* he was wearing tight jeans and high-tops and a ratty Gears of War tee shirt. His black hair was drawn back from his narrow face in one of those samurai knots. "What's up?"

"Betsy's not at home," Carl said. "Michael's worried."

"I bet I know where she is," Seth said.

"Really?" Michael said. "Where?"

Seth tossed his book on the sofa. "Wait here." He ran past Michael and went outside.

Michael and Lulu followed him down the driveway. Carl grabbed an umbrella and joined them at the mailbox. Seth paused at the street, looked both ways and then crossed, climbing down to the beach.

She's not supposed to go near the water alone. Rain thumped the umbrella overhead, drowning out the sound of their breathing.

Minutes later—minutes that felt like hours—Seth appeared again, with Betsy beside him. They were climbing up the beach path toward the road. Both of them were soaked.

Michael's relief was so great he almost fell to his knees. "Betsy, thank God."

As they neared, he could see how angry his daughter was, and how hurt. "How *could* you?"

"I'm sorry, Betsy."

She shoved the wet hair out of her face. "You're supposed to *be* here when I get home."

"I know. I know."

"I'm *never* supposed to come home to an empty house."

"I'm sorry. But I think you're old enough to come home by yourself."

"Aaagh!" She pushed past him and stalked into the house, slamming the door shut behind her.

He looked gratefully at Seth. "Thanks, Seth."

"It's the big tree by the Harrisons' dock. She always goes there when she's upset."

"Oh. Well. Thanks." It shamed him that the neighbor kid would know Betsy better than he did. He turned and went into the house. There, he wrapped Lulu in a big towel and put her in front of the TV before he went up to Betsy's room.

Her back was to him. Rainwater dripped down from her wet hair, darkening her shirt. She was staring out the window. "I'm sorry, Bets. If you had just listened to—"

She spun to face him. "Don't you get it? I thought you were dead."

"Oh." How had he not expected this? Jolene would have known Betsy's fear and protected against it. Of course Betsy would worry about losing the only parent here. "I'm sorry, Betsy. I screwed up. I won't do it again. Okay?"

Betsy's eyes filled with tears. She wiped them away impatiently.

"I'll always be here for you."

"Ha."

Downstairs, the phone rang.

A moment later, Lulu shrieked: "It's Mommy!"

Betsy pushed past Michael and ran downstairs.

Reluctantly, he followed. This was not good timing for a call.

"Mom," Betsy said, holding the phone to her ear, looking furious. "Dad wasn't here when I got home today. He forgot me. If *you* were here this wouldn't happen."

Lulu threw herself at Betsy. "Give it back! I was talking to her—"

Betsy pushed her away. Lulu plopped onto her butt and screamed. "I wanna talk!"

"Betsy," he said, "let Lulu talk, too."

Betsy made a face, but let Lulu into the conversation. The two girls sat down together at the table, talking over each other.

Sighing, Michael went into the kitchen and poured himself a drink. Within ten minutes, Betsy was handing him the phone. "She wants to talk to you, Dad. She doesn't have much time for us. Like always."

He took the phone and went into the family room, sitting down. "Hey, Jo."

"Really, Michael? You forgot her?"

"If you want to bitch me out, don't bother, Jolene. I feel bad enough."

There was a pause, then, "You scared her, Michael."

"Tell me something I don't know."

Another pause. "We're leaving tomorrow," she said. "For Iraq."

"Has it been a month already?"

"Yes, Michael."

In the insanity of the last four weeks, he'd forgotten this date, almost forgotten that she was going to war. He hadn't *really* forgotten, of course; the knowledge had been a shadow, rarely glimpsed in the hectic mess of his days. Up until now she'd been safe, so it had been easier to think about himself.

"I don't know what communication will be like at Balad, or how long we'll be there. I'll keep in touch as best I can." She paused. "Michael, it would be really nice if the girls could send me letters or e-mails if we have Internet."

He thought about her days over there, how empty a part of her would be without her girls. It was kind of shameful that she'd had to ask this. Especially since he knew how hard it was for her to ask for favors from him or anyone. "I'll make sure," he said.

"Thanks. Well. I gotta go now, the natives are getting restless."

"Jo?"

"Yeah?"

"Be safe," he said. "Take care of yourself."

She sighed. "Good-bye, Michael."

"Good-bye."

All he wanted to do was go to the counter, retrieve his drink, and finish it. He even thought fondly of getting drunk.

Instead, he dialed the local pizza shop, ordered dinner, and went upstairs.

Betsy's bedroom door was open. He peeked in, saw that she wasn't there, and walked down the hall to the bathroom.

She was peering into the mirror, messing with her face.

"I don't think you're supposed to squeeze those things," he said.

She pivoted, screamed, "GET OUT," and slammed the door shut in his face.

He stood there a long time, waiting for her to change her mind and apologize.

Nothing.

Finally, he went back downstairs and found Lulu watching Jolene's good-bye video again.

He groaned.

The pizza arrived, and he paid the kid and slapped the pie on the table, yelling, "Dinner."

"Pizza is for birthdays, Daddy. Not dinner," Lulu said with a sigh. She walked past him and climbed up to the table just as his mother walked into the house, looking irritated.

"Don't you ever hang up on me again, young man. Is Betsy okay?"

"She's here," he said. "I don't know how okay she is."

"Thank God. From now on—"

"Please, Ma. Yell at me tomorrow. It's been a hell of a day."

His mother stared up at him. "You need to do better, Michael," she said evenly.

"Yeah. I'm aware."

Before she could say anything to make him feel worse, he left the kitchen and walked into his office, where, thankfully, it was quiet. He closed the door behind him and sank into the chair by his desk.

He didn't think he could do this. And *this* was taking care of his children.

What in the hell was wrong with him? How could he be such a success in the courtroom and in his office and with his clients but fail so completely with his own family?

He sighed. His wife had been gone less than a month, and already he was tired of feeling like a failure in his own home.

Eleven

The next morning, Betsy still wasn't talking to him. Michael awoke early, started breakfast, and got the girls to school on time. When he finally got to his desk—late—he was already tired. But at least he felt competent here.

At eleven o'clock, the call he'd been waiting for came in.

Keith had requested an interview. Finally.

Michael grabbed his notes and left the office. Fifteen minutes later, he arrived at the King County jail and took a seat in a dingy interview room.

Keith came into the room, wearing the orange jail jumpsuit, his wrists shackled in front of him, leg chains scraping and jangling across the stone-tiled floor.

"Leave us," Michael said to the guard. "And uncuff him."

"Sir—"

"Uncuff him," Michael repeated. "I understand the risks."

The guard frowned but did as he was asked, then left the room to stand guard just outside the door.

Keith sat down at the table across from Michael, rigidly upright. In the pale overhead lighting, he looked surprisingly young and fresh-faced. His crew cut had grown out, stood up now like a jagged blond crown above his face. "My father says I have to talk to you."

"I'm trying to keep you out of prison. You're not making my job easy, by the way."

"Did you ever think I don't deserve to be saved?"

"No," Michael said evenly. "I didn't. And neither has your father. Or your mother, who I hear cries herself to sleep at night."

"Low blow."

Michael opened his pad and uncapped a pen. "You know why I'm here, Keith. You promised your dad you'd tell me what happened that day. And I hear you military types are big on keeping promises."

"I killed the love of my life," Keith said, and finally there was emotion in his eyes. "I must have."

"What? What do you mean, 'you must have'?"

"I'm crazy," Keith said quietly. "I must be. I can't remember shooting my own wife. Does that sound sane to you?"

Michael studied his client. Honestly, this was the first good news he'd gotten on this case. He hated that he was analytical enough to hear pain and think *good,* but that was his job, sorting through heartache for reason. Although the law was a codified set of rules, justice was far from set in stone. In court, there was always room for ambiguity, for emotion, for sympathy. "Tell me what happened, Keith. Minute by minute."

Keith stared dully at the wall. Michael saw that blank look come back into the young man's eyes.

"She wanted to go to Pike Place. I knew it was a bad idea, but I didn't know why, I couldn't say why. And you know, I love . . . loved Emily and we did what she wanted, especially after I got back from Iraq."

"Why then specifically?"

"I was hard to live with. I was constantly having to make shit up to her. Anyway, we went to the market." He paused so long Michael was about to prompt an answer when Keith started talking again. "It was sunny that day. The market was crowded. Piano players, jugglers, magicians, fish throwers, bums. You couldn't walk a foot without someone bumping into you or running out in front of you or trying to sell you something."

He looked down at his shaking hands. "I started to get edgy, tight. So I had a straight shot of tequila at the Athenian, but it wasn't enough to calm me down. I got so jumpy. I get jumpy a lot lately. That day, every movement startled me, got my heart pumping—and there were a lot of movements. I kept thinking people were after me. So, while Emily was picking out flowers, I zipped back into the Athenian, and had a few more shots."

"How many?"

"A lot." Keith sighed. "I *know* drinking doesn't help. It's something Emily and I had been fighting about. She thought I drank too much and got mean. And I could feel it that day, me getting mean."

"Did you drink much before Iraq?"

He shrugged. "I guess not."

"Afterward?"

"Lots. Sometimes it made the . . . yelling in my head quiet down. But it didn't help that day."

"It made it worse."

Keith nodded. "We were leaving the market—I was pissed and pretty drunk by this time—and this homeless guy jumped out at me. Emily said he just walked up, but it didn't seem like that to me. Or, he came up *fast*, and he was a skuzzy-looking guy with all this long black hair and a Jesus beard and I hit him so hard he went down. I saw blood spray up from his nose. Emily started screaming that she didn't know me anymore and there was this . . . shaking that made it impossible for me to stand still. The next thing I remember is seeing Emily lying on the floor in our living room." In his lap, his hands clenched and unclenched. "It was like I woke up in someone else's nightmare. There was blood everywhere, on me, on the wall, on Em. Half of her head was just . . . gone. I bent down and tried to give her mouth to mouth and I did compressions. The whole time I was screaming and crying. It wasn't until I saw the gun—my gun—that I knew what I'd done."

"And that's all you remember."

"That's it."

"Okay. I'm going to need you to talk to a psychiatrist. Will you do that for me, Keith?"

"Sure. It won't make a difference, though. I don't need a doc to tell me I'm crazy."

Michael looked at his client, thinking, *This kid needs my help.* He knew how heavily the deck was stacked against them, and for the first time in a long time, he felt hopeful. This could be the kind of case that mattered. He wished his dad were here to hear about it. "I'll set up the appointment."

Dear Mom:

You are NOT going to believe this. Dad bought me a cell phone. My very own one. Yesterday I was in the lunch room and I put it down on the cafeteria table and you should have seen Sierra's face. She couldn't STAND it. Only the high schoolers have cell phones. I told Sierra she could make a call if she wanted and she did and then she walked to class with me. You said one smile could make a difference—maybe you're right. Maybe she'll want to be my friend again. I really miss her. Well, I have to go now, Dad's yelling for me. Like always. He is totally stressed. Yesterday he forgot to put the garbage out for the truck. Everyone misses you. Xo Betsy

Dear Betsy:

I'm glad to hear about your cell phone. It will be good for emergencies. Take good care of it and use it wisely. I wouldn't be me if I didn't say that if you have to bribe someone into liking you, she's not much of a friend, but we can talk more about this later. I'm FINALLY leaving for Iraq today. I'll write again when I land. Love you to the moon and back.
Mom

P.S. I hope you're helping your dad around the house . . .

. . .

When Jolene stepped off the cargo jet and onto the flat sand at Balad, it was like stepping into a furnace. Tiny sand granules moved invisibly on the hot wind, insinuating themselves into everything—eyes, ears, nostrils, hair, throat. Jolene wanted to cover her mouth and nose in protection, but she stood tall, eyes watering, waiting.

There was a lot of waiting: for orders, for supplies, for transport. Their trip seemed to have taken forever. From Texas to Germany to Kuwait to Tallil to Al Kut to, finally, Balad Air Base.

Wind blew through the base, hot as fire. In seconds, Jolene was sweating. After what felt like hours of waiting, she and Tami were assigned to a small trailer with wood-paneled walls that were pockmarked with tack and nail holes from previous tenants. A pair of sagging beds and a pair of scarred-up metal lockers were the only furniture.

Jolene dropped her heavy duffle bag on the floor: dust puffed up around it. Dust, she knew already, was one of the many new facts of her life. She sat down on the narrow bed, holding her rough, newly issued bed linens and the pillow she'd brought from home. The bed squeaked beneath her.

"We need some pictures and posters," Tami said, coughing as she sat down on her own bed. "Like Keanu or Johnny."

Jolene sighed and looked at her friend. The trailer smelled of dust and heat and of the men who'd inhabited it before them. Wind rattled the room, plied at the windows and doors, trying to come in.

Suddenly an alarm sounded.

Jolene was first to the door. She opened it for Tami, grabbed her friend's wrist and pulled her through. The alarm and speakers were on a pole just outside their trailer and the repeated announcement—GET TO THE BUNKERS!—was so loud she couldn't hear anything else.

There were dozens of cement bunkers positioned around the base. Jolene and Tami ran for the nearest bunker and went inside.

There was no one else in here. They sat on the floor inside, in the dark, while mortar fire exploded all around them. Shards of cement rained down. Somewhere close, a rocket hit hard and exploded. The acrid smell of smoke slipped through the cracks in the door.

And then it was over.

Jolene stood up, not surprised to find that her legs were a little shaky.

"You notice we're the only ones in here?" Tami said. "Where is everyone?"

Jolene opened the door. Sunlight, bright as a starburst, blinded them. Black smoke hung in the air, burned their eyes. Everywhere she looked, she saw troops acting as if nothing had happened. They were riding bikes from one trailer to another, standing in line at Porta-Potties, playing football. She turned to Tami. "They told us Balad was called Mortaritaville. I guess now we know why."

The alarm sounded again. Mortar fire erupted to their left, a cement wall exploded. Smoke wafted their way.

"That'll take some getting used to," Tami said when it was quiet again.

Jolene looked at her best friend and knew they were both thinking the same thing. For the next year, they could be killed any second of any day— while they were sitting in their trailer or playing cards or taking a shower.

How did you handle knowing that any moment you could be killed, maimed, blown to bits? Worse than her fear was worry for her children. For the first time, she really thought, *What if I don't make it home? How will my children survive without me?*

That night, after a long day spent filling out paperwork, meeting the men and women she'd be serving with, and listening to endless lectures about everything from the scorpions on base to the use of CSEL survival radios, Jolene finally made it to the showers at eleven o'clock. Because there were so few women on base, the shower lines weren't long, but a woman didn't walk there in the dark alone. The army had come a long way—but not far enough. "Battle buddies" were encouraged.

After their showers, she and Tami walked back to their trailer in silence.

Once inside, Tami collapsed on her bed and was sound asleep in no time.

Jolene was well past the point of exhaustion, but she was too wired to sleep, so she got out her laptop and started a letter home. She wasn't connected to the Internet yet, might not be for some time, but she could type the letter tonight and figure out how to send it from the comm center tomorrow. She needed to connect with her family right now, and this was the only means available to her.

She imagined them in detail, completely; the family, *her* family, gathered on the sofa, with the letter bringing them together. Betsy would read it aloud.

The base was bombed four times today and we just got here.

Jolene imagined their reaction to that . . . and knew what her letters home had to be.

My loves, she wrote, missing them so sharply it was difficult to go on. She drew in a deep breath.

> *It was a long flight over here, and I have to admit that I'm tired. Betsy, you wouldn't believe how flat it is, and how everything is the same color, like dying wheat. And man is it hot. I think I was sweating before I even got off the plane.*
>
> *Tami and I are roommates in a little trailer. It's kind of how I imagine college would be. So we need photos and posters to make it homey. Can you help us out? I'll send pics when I can . . .*

Jolene wrote everything she could think of to say. When she ran out of steam, she closed the laptop and put it in her locker. That was when she noticed the pink journal Betsy had given her for her birthday. Reaching out, she brought it to her lap and opened it. She'd intended to give this journal back to Betsy when she got home, but after less than twenty-four hours, she knew that wouldn't happen. She needed a place where she could be honest because from now on, she was Chief Zarkades, and she couldn't show fear or hesitation any more than she could tell her family the truth.

She opened the diary and wrote.

MAY 2005

> This journal was supposed to be for you, Betsy. I intended to write down all my feelings over here, so that when I come home,

I could give it to you, say here, this is everything I thought while we were apart. I thought I'd give you all the advice you would need, that I'd be wise and helpful. The perfect mother, even from a world away.

But the truth is that being your mother is breaking my heart. I have to figure out how to be strong, how to put my love for you and Lulu aside. If I can't, I won't be any good to anyone.

Here, between these pages you gave me, I'll have to talk to myself. Hopefully writing about my fear will lessen it. Maybe someday I'll give it to you, when you're old enough not to judge me too harshly.

The base was attacked four times today. By the fourth time, when the alarm sounded, Tami and I just looked at each other and shrugged and stayed in our trailer. I kept putting away my clothes, but I could hear the whistling of missiles and mortar fire exploding, and I thought will I have a chance to say good-bye to my girls? and then it was over.

Over.

It's a word that seems to crop up more and more in my life lately. Like my marriage.

Over.

I feel so alone over here, without Michael. Sometimes I pretend that he's still waiting for me back home. That he still loves me.

Then I wake up to the sound of bombs. I've been in-country a day and here's what I think: I'm going to die over here.

Why didn't I think that before?

Michael left the office at about noon and drove north of the city. He pulled up to the street and checked the address he'd been given. He peered through his car's side window, frowning. Yes, this was the place.

The psychiatrist's office did not inspire confidence. It was housed in a run-down midcentury house on a bad stretch of Aurora Avenue. Traffic streamed past it, honking.

Michael parked between a rusted pickup truck and a shiny green electric car. Following a cracked, weed-patterned sidewalk to a slightly sagging front porch, he stopped at the front door and knocked.

The door was opened almost immediately by a lanky older man with shoulder-length gray hair and an elongated, wrinkled face. In a blue plaid suit, at least two decades out of date, and lime green shirt, he looked like a cross between Ichabod Crane and a low-rent British rocker. He was probably seventy years old, but there was something strangely youthful about him.

Michael hoped this wasn't the doctor. Juries liked their experts to look like experts.

"You must be Michael Zarkades," the man said, extending his hand. "Christian Cornflower. Most of my patients call me Doctor C. Come in."

The doctor stepped back. In the front room, a young woman with purple hair and a silver nose ring sat at a whitewashed antique desk, her fingers clacking on a keyboard while she talked on the phone. Nodding at her as he passed, the doctor led Michael through an office that was full of comfortable, overstuffed chairs and old-fashioned oak tables. Rose-patterned paper covered the walls, which were further decorated with needlepoint samplers sporting pithy sayings like *today is the first day of the rest of your life.*

Finally, they came to what probably used to be the home's master bedroom. A big window framed the limbs of a beautiful old apple tree, decked out in bright green leaves and dotted with tiny new fruit. The walls here were 1970s wood paneling, decorated with more samplers and framed diplomas from Harvard, Johns Hopkins, and Berkeley.

The doctor took his seat behind an antique mahogany desk.

Michael sat in a comfortable, overstuffed red-velvet tufted chair, facing the desk. "I have to say, Doctor Cornflower, you come highly recommended. I'm defending a young man—"

"Keith Keller."

Michael frowned. "I didn't name my client over the phone."

Christian shrugged eloquently. "I may look like I was at Woodstock—which, sadly, I missed—but don't mistake my demeanor. I'm a smart man, Michael. You took on the seemingly impossible defense of Keith Keller, who shot his wife in the head and then barricaded himself in his home for hours, threatening to kill himself. It was on television, for God's sake. A SWAT team brought him out, splattered in blood, with cameras rolling. Everyone knows he did it. I knew that if you were smart—and I hoped you were—that sooner or later you'd end up at my door."

"And why is that?"

"I specialize in post-traumatic stress disorder. The minute I heard Keith Keller was a former marine, I looked into his case. He did two tours of duty in Iraq." He shook his head. "The Department of Veterans Affairs is absolutely criminal in its negligence in helping the troops coming back from Iraq. By the time this damn war's over, we'll have hundreds of thousands of severely traumatized soldiers trying to put the pieces of their lives back together. This thing with Keith will become, sadly, too common, if we don't start helping these young men and women."

Michael took out a notebook. "Go on."

"I was in 'Nam. 1967. I saw firsthand how good men could be swallowed by war. And in Vietnam, at least you could go somewhere to blow off steam. In Iraq, nothing and nowhere is safe. The woman who smiles and waves can blow up the soldier who tries to help her cross the street. This was occasionally true in Vietnam; it's commonplace in Iraq. The roads are rigged with IEDs—improvised explosive devices—that kill anyone who passes by. Bombs are in garbage heaps, in animals, in people, in ditches. You're not safe anywhere over there. Our soldiers are returning with extreme post-traumatic stress disorder."

"Could extreme PTSD diminish one's capacity for reasonable thought?"

"Absolutely. That's the question that begs to be asked in this case. It's not some random bad guy shooting his wife and claiming he's crazy. Keith Keller served his country and, while he came back physically undamaged, it may not be the end of the discussion. I'd have to speak with him to make an accurate diagnosis, however."

"Can you tell me a little more about PTSD, how it works?"

"It's entirely possible Keith didn't even know he *was* killing his wife. He could have been disoriented enough not to know where he was or what he was doing. I can't say, of course, specifically until I speak with him. But I can say with authority that too many of our troops are coming home with devastating PTSD and that this condition can cause a soldier to snap. By all accounts, Keith Keller sounded like a good man before the war."

Michael tapped his pen on the pad of paper, thinking through the possibilities. Cornflower had just handed him a defense to murder one, but it was tricky. Jurors were notoriously reluctant to accept a diminished-capacity defense. And they hated insanity.

Christian pressed his fingertips together. "PTSD is a legitimate psychiatric disorder and has been for decades. A person can literally be incapacitated by the disorder. What's happening over there . . . well . . . you should know as well as anyone."

Michael frowned. "What do you mean?"

"I understand you're a military family. Your wife is a helicopter pilot serving in Iraq right now, isn't she?"

"You really do your homework."

"I like to know who I'm talking to. Your wife, is she telling you much?"

Michael didn't like the way the doctor was studying him. He shifted uncomfortably in his seat. "She just got there, but they don't let women in combat situations. Mostly she'll be ferrying VIPs around."

"Ah," he said, eyeing Michael. Then he smiled. "She's a mother. Her instinct is to protect. Of course." He paused.

"Of course, what?"

"Here's what you need to know: some clichés are true, and war is definitely hell. It's being afraid all the time, and when you're not afraid it's because you're so pumped full of adrenaline you could literally burst. It's watching people who you love—really profoundly love—get blown to pieces right next to you. It's seeing a leg lying in the ditch and picking it up to put it in a bag because no man—or part of a man, your friend—can be left behind. It's the dark night of the soul, Michael. There's no front line over there. The war is all around them, every day, everywhere they go. Some handle it better than others. We don't know why, but we do know this: the human mind can't safely or healthily process that kind of carnage and uncertainty and horror. It just can't. No one comes back from war the same."

"Will you meet with Keith, assess him? I'll need a diagnosis if I'm going to go for a PTSD defense."

"Of course," Christian said. "I would be honored to help this young man."

Honored. That was a word Michael hadn't heard in connection with one of his clients in a long time. So many of them were guilty as hell. He was proud to be a part of the criminal justice system—an important part—but he was rarely proud to defend an individual client.

It made him think of Jolene, for whom honor was so important. She would have liked that he took this case. He rose to his feet, shaking Dr. Cornflower's hand, saying, "Thank you."

All the way home, he thought about Keith, and this new defense . . . and what had happened to this formerly good and decent young man in Iraq.

What happened to him over there?

And then, he thought: *Jolene, what's happening to you?*

He was late getting home, as usual, and he knew by the look on Betsy's face that she'd been counting the minutes, adding them up to hold against him. The thought of another angsty teenaged tirade, which he deserved, was more than he could stand.

His mother came into the kitchen. "I had no problem staying an extra hour. Don't worry about it."

"Thanks, Ma."

As he said it, the phone rang.

Somewhere, Betsy screamed—actually screamed—"I'll get it!"

He heard footsteps thundering down the stairs.

Michael smiled ruefully, walking his mother to the back door. "Thanks again, Ma."

She kissed his cheek. "By the way, an e-mail came in from Jolene. Lulu is dying to read it, but I reminded her of the rules—no reading it until you got home—and she's a bit . . . excited."

Michael kissed his mom and watched her walk out to her car. He thought, not for the first time, that he couldn't have handled this without her. When she'd left, he went into the kitchen and poured himself a drink.

Lulu marched into the kitchen. "We got an e-mail from Mommy. Can we read it now?"

"Can I have a drink and change my clothes first?"

"No, Daddy, I've been waiting FOREVER."

Michael glanced at Jolene's calendar, seeing that tonight dinner was supposed to be baked chicken and rice. He thought a can of mushroom soup was involved. "Okay. Go get your sister. I'll meet you at my computer."

Lulu ran upstairs. Mere seconds later, she was back, her little face scrunched up tightly, her cheeks red. "She's on the phone."

"Tell her to hang up."

"She won't."

"Well, we can wait—"

"NONONONO!" Lulu wailed. Tears filled her eyes.

Michael knew he was the boss here, but frankly, the thought of a Lulu tantrum was more than he could handle right now. With a sigh, he went upstairs, found Betsy in her room, talking on the phone. "Can you call her back, sweetie? We're going to read Mom's letter before your sister levitates."

Betsy turned her back on him and kept talking.

"Betsy," he said in a warning tone.

"Get out, Dad, I'm on the PHONE."

He took the phone from her, said, "She'll call you back in ten minutes," and hung up.

You would have thought he pushed the red button on a nuclear warhead. Betsy screamed, *That was Sierra!* so loud he went momentarily deaf.

"We're reading the letter now. Come downstairs." He left her standing there, so mad she was practically emitting smoke, and went down to his office.

There, he planted Lulu on the chair at his desk and went to the sofa to wait for Betsy. It didn't take long. She stomped down the stairs and swept into the room like the Red Queen, muttering, *Fine, where's the stupid letter?*

Betsy scooted Lulu sideways and sat down, then Lulu scrambled onto her sister's lap, saying, "Read, Betsy."

Betsy pulled up the e-mail, opened it.

A photo filled the computer screen. In it, Jolene and Tami were standing in front of some open-air market stall with their arms around each other. Everything was washed out, a little colorless, as if maybe it was raining or really windy. But you couldn't miss how bright their smiles were.

"Mommy." Lulu pointed at Jolene.

Betsy scrolled down and started to read the letter out loud. "It was a long flight over here . . ."

> . . . *and I have to admit that I'm tired.*
>
> *Betsy, you wouldn't believe how flat it is, and how everything is the same color, like dying wheat. And man is it hot. I think I was sweating before I even got off the plane.*
>
> *Tami and I are roommates in a little trailer. It's kind of how I imagine college would be. So we need photos and posters to make it homey. Can you help us out? I'll send pics when I can.*
>
> *We had dinner at the DFAC tonight—the dining facilities. Lulu, they had your favorite—peach pie. It wasn't as good as* Yia Yia Mila's, *but it made me think of home.*
>
> *We are what's called backfill (an army word for substitutes, kind of) for the 131st. Everyone we've met is great. I'm sure we'll make lots of friends.*
>
> *Well, guys, I better get some sleep.*
>
> *I'm thinking of you all the time and loving you to the moon and back.*
>
> *XXXOOO*
> *Mom*
>
> *P.S.: Good luck on your math test, Bets. I know you'll rock it. I'm proud of you!* ☺

"Read it again," Lulu said. "My part. Daddy, make her read it again," she whined.

"There, I read it. Big deal. It's hot," Betsy said. She turned to look at Michael. "Can I go back upstairs and call Sierra now?"

"Fine," Michael said, barely listening. As she ran past him, he got up from the chair and went to stand in front of the computer.

He stared at the picture of two women in uniforms smiling for the camera.

"She looks happy," Lulu said.

Michael thought about what he'd learned today and he couldn't reconcile it with this photograph. He thought about the descriptions of the war he'd heard, about finding your friends' body parts and roadside bombs and raining shrapnel.

Two women, best friends, smiling for the camera.

He understood suddenly what Cornflower had meant. *She's a mother. Her instinct is to protect.*

This photograph was a lie, as was everything she'd told him about her deployment. *There's no front line over there,* Cornflower had said. So there was no safe place.

Jolene—always the hero, always the mother—was sugarcoating her life to prove there was nothing for them to worry about. She'd planted the seeds early. *They don't let women in combat. I'll be flying VIPs around, nothing dangerous.*

He'd bought it because he wanted to. He'd looked away. He shouldn't have, for God's sake. He'd known it was a *war.* Maybe it was the political backlash about imaginary weapons of mass destruction, or the bait and switch with Saddam Hussein. He didn't know why he'd imagined this to be a lesser war, maybe, one that would be over soon and with few American casualties.

He'd seen the photos on the news of soldiers walking with Iraqi children, handing out water, posing for pictures, and he'd read about suicide bombers, but somehow he'd imagined those two things as separate. He'd let himself believe Jolene when she told him that she would be far from combat.

What an idiot she must think him.

He'd been so busy thinking about himself, being pissed off about how her choice impacted *his* life, that he'd barely considered the truth of where she was and what she was doing.

How did she feel, lying in bed at night, alone and far from home, knowing any second a bomb could hit her trailer and she could be killed?

June slipped away from Michael; days fell like rain, disappearing in the ground at his feet. At home, he thought about work; at work, he thought about home. He was always rushing and almost invariably arriving late. *I'm sorry* was his new default sentence. He'd said it more in the last few weeks than in the last few years.

At the end of the school year, he'd had to recalibrate his schedule. His mom was still a huge help with the girls, but summer was her busy season at the Green Thumb, and she couldn't be at his house as much as before. So he'd shortened his workweek to four days. Friday through Sunday he worked from home, struggling to juggle the demands of fatherhood with those of his job. When he wasn't grocery shopping or cooking dinner or washing dishes, he was writing briefs and researching cases. He sent the girls to as many day camps as possible, and still he didn't have time to get everything done. Driving them from one place to another—or finding someone else to drive them—took an inordinate amount of time. Last week, he'd finally admitted that he wasn't getting as much work done as he needed to. He'd handed off most of his smaller cases to associates.

That gave him more time to work on the Keller defense.

Today, his plan was to work on the deposition questions for the policemen who'd arrested Keith, as well as the jailhouse snitch.

He woke early and went downstairs to make breakfast. At ten o'clock, he was going to drop the girls off at the Thumb, where they would "help" his mother until he picked them up at two o'clock. It wasn't much time to work, but these days, he took what he could get.

Lulu's questions started first thing: *It's sunny today, Daddy. Can we*

go to the beach? Mommy almost always takes us to the beach when it's
sunny. I could make a sand castle. Do you know how to make a sand castle,
Daddy?

The questions came at him so fast he mumbled something and walked
away, choosing to drink his coffee standing in front of the TV.

Another mistake. CNN reported that a suicide bomber had killed six
people in a market in Baghdad.

The phone rang.

Lulu screamed, "I'll get it!" in a voice so loud the neighborhood dogs
probably came running.

He saw Lulu run for the phone, pick it up, say "Mommy?" Then her
smile fell and her shoulders slumped. She hung up the phone and shuffled back into the kitchen and climbed up into her chair. "It's Sierra," she
said glumly. "Betsy is talking to her."

Fifteen minutes later, Betsy came thundering down the stairs. "I'm
going to the mall with Sierra to see a movie."

Michael leaned forward, switched off the television. "Can you please
rephrase that in the form of a question?"

"Sure. Can I have some money?"

Michael turned around, ready to say, *Don't you mean please, Dad,*
may I go to the mall? but when he saw her, the teasing question fell
out of reach.

She had on enough makeup to be an extra in the *Rocky Horror Pic-*
ture Show, and her outfit was equally unacceptable: pink Ugg boots, a
jean skirt so short it could have been a valance, and a white sweatshirt
that had been cut off to reveal an inch of her stomach.

"What the hell are you wearing?"

She glared at him. "Uh. Clothes."

"Your mother wouldn't let you out of the house in that getup."

"She's not here."

"And what's all over your face?"

"Nothing."

"You're wearing makeup."

"No, I'm not."

He couldn't believe she could stand there and lie to him. "No, you're not? You look like Tootsie waiting for a close-up."

"Whatever *that* means."

"It means, young lady, that you are not leaving the house like that."

"Oh, yes, I am. Sierra's brother is picking me up in a half an hour."

"Sierra's *brother*? And how old is he?"

"He's a senior."

"Well, I hope you mean senior citizen, because no eighteen-year-old boy is taking you to the mall."

"You are ruining my *life*."

"I know. You've said so before. Give me Sierra's number and I'll call her mom. If you dress like a human, I'll drive you girls there."

"I'd rather die."

"Really? Well, I feel the same way about a trip to the mall. It's up to you, kiddo." He shrugged and turned the TV back on, changing the channel. An ad for the new Spielberg movie, *War of the Worlds*, filled the screen.

War. It was everywhere.

Betsy stomped her foot.

Michael ignored her. In the past weeks, he might not have learned everything he needed to know about parenting a preteen, but he'd learned a few valuable lessons: don't back down. And use peer pressure. Oh, and try to be calm. Two crazies did not make for a good day.

"Fine. I'll go take off the makeup I'm not wearing."

"And change your clothes."

"Aaagh!" she yelled, running up the stairs. He could hear her stomping around up there.

Michael shook his head. So much drama.

He walked into the kitchen, where Lulu sat at the kitchen table, kneeling on a pillow she'd placed on one of the chairs. Her *My Mommy Fights for Freedom* coloring book was open in front of her, along with a pick-up-sticks tangle of crayons. She was furiously adding red streaks to an American flag.

"How come we don't have a flag up, Daddy?" Lulu said. "Mommy's gone."

Michael stopped. How was it possible that he'd never considered this before? All the things he'd learned from Cornflower and Keller slipped into his mind again.

They were a military family.

He heard that all the time; people said it to him and he shrugged it off, thinking, no, not really; my wife is just in the Guard. Because HE wasn't in the military, it hadn't felt real to him, and God knew he'd never liked her commitment or supported it.

Still, they were a military family, and his wife was at war. And a four-year-old had seen the truth of that before he had.

He tousled Lulu's hair, watching her color a scene of a girl waving good-bye to a woman in uniform. "We'll put one up," he said quietly.

Betsy stomped back into the room, coming up behind him. "I look sufficiently gross now. Can I go?"

He turned.

Betsy was dressed in cutoffs that were too short in his opinion, but not enough to fight about, a tee shirt that read *Oops! I Did It Again*, and flip-flops. She'd taken off most of the makeup, but was still wearing blue mascara and blush.

Did she think he couldn't *see* it?

"Well?" she demanded, and at that her voice broke. He saw how much this meant to her, and he was lost. The games these preteen girls played with each other seemed ridiculous to him. Betsy could go from smiling to ballistic in a second, all based on some under-the-breath comment from a former friend. God forbid someone laughed at her hair. "Come on, Dad, it's Sierra. I've waited so looong for her to call. I need to go. Pleaaaase."

Call him a coward, but he couldn't deny her. She looked so damned desperate and lonely, and he knew now how much this turnaround with Sierra meant to Betsy. "You look fine, Betsy. And you can go to the mall. Just let me call Sierra's mom."

"I already called. It was *so* embarrassing to say that my dad wouldn't let me ride with Tod."

"Horrifying," he agreed.

"Anyway, Mrs. Phillips is picking us up in ten minutes. So can I have money?"

"How much do you want?"

"Fifty."

"*Dollars?*"

"Okay." She sighed dramatically. "Twenty-five."

Michael dug into his pocket and pulled out his wallet. While he was counting his bills, Betsy shrieked.

"They're here! Give me the money, Dad. Now! Hurry! They might leave."

"I'm walking you out to the car."

"No!"

He smiled.

She grimaced. "Fine."

He walked her out of the house and down the driveway, where a blue minivan waited.

Sure enough, a woman was driving.

"Here, Betsy," he said, handing her thirty dollars. She swiped it like a raptor taking prey and mumbled something that might have been good-bye.

The driver rolled down her window. "Hi," she said to him. "I'm Stephanie. I understand Betsy thought Tod would be driving." She smiled. "Hardly."

Michael smiled back. "That's good to hear. I remember being eighteen. Focus behind the wheel was not my strength."

"My husband says the same thing." Stephanie glanced in the backseat, then leaned closer. "It's good to see the girls together again. How's Jolene?"

People asked him that all the time. He never really knew what to say. "Fine."

"Tell her I said hi."

"Will do." He backed away, watching the car back down the driveway and then drive away.

He walked back up to his house. On the porch, he stopped, looked around. Sunlight spilled across the white slats, brightening the faded chair cushions. The grass out front was still a deep, rich green—summer's heat hadn't found its way here yet. Down below, across the road, he could see a family gathering, building a fire and setting up chairs for a day at the beach. In a normal year, Jolene would be down there already, setting up coolers and chairs.

He went back inside. "Hey, Lulu," he said, closing the door behind him. "Want to help me find our flag?"

Twelve

Dear Mom:

I had the best weekend EVER! You won't believe what happened. I'll start at the beginning. First, I got my phone—you remember that—and Sierra thought it was so cool and we sat together. Then she talked to me in PE, and THEN she got in a fight with Zoe because Zoe like, totally, lied to her about what Jimmy said about her. So Sierra is my friend again! Last week we went to the mall together and saw War of the Worlds, *which was so cool.*

And guess what? Zoe was there and we didn't even talk to her.

Dad says Sierra and me can go to kayaking camp together in July. Cool, huh?

Anyway, that's everything. Things are okay here.

Lulu doesn't think she's invisible all the time anymore, so that's good. We made Daddy put up a flag.

Well, I gotta go. Dad is ordering pizza for dinner again and I want pineapple on it. Be careful, Mom.

Love, B.

P.S.: Sierra wants to know if you've shot anybody yet. Have you?

Dear Betsy:

Wow. That's a lot of news! I am so glad to hear about you and Sierra working on your friendship. You two have been friends for a long time, and those relationships are important. BUT I want you to be careful, too. I haven't forgotten about Sierra's thing with the cigarettes, and honestly, I think she can be kind of a mean girl sometimes. Be careful.

Also, you should think about how it felt when Sierra and Zoe froze you out. Do you really want to be the kind of person who treats someone like that, who hurts a girl's feelings for sport? Be nice to Zoe. Be the kind of girl I know you can be.

Glad you're having a fun summer already, though. I wish I were there. I sure do miss you guys.

And don't worry about me. I know you saw that report on CNN, but I'm fine. It's dangerous over here, that's true. But mostly, Tami and I are flying way away from the bad areas. We fly a bunch of VIPs around, and supplies. You don't need to worry about me. Honest.

Love you to the moon and back. Mom

P.S. Tell your dad enough pizza! And no, I haven't shot anyone. Did Sierra really ask you that?

JULY 2005

I once read a Stephen King book that used the term SSDD. Same shit, different day. That's pretty much what the last month in Iraq has been. Day after day of rising at 0 dark thirty, getting mission orders, checking my aircraft, and flying out.

Today I was on duty for more than fourteen hours all together. Honestly, Tami and I are so tired most of the time that we hardly talk before we fall asleep. The heat and dust are unbearable. It's over 125 degrees most days, and when you consider that I'm wearing a helmet, gloves, and Kevlar. Well, the way I smell after a mission cannot be good.

We've been flying at night a lot, and that's better, at least with regard to the heat. Sometimes we're supporting the medevac guys, and I have to say, that's no easy job. I can't get the images out of my mind—soldiers blown apart, bleeding, screaming for help.

Only yesterday, I ended up sitting with a kid outside one of the hospital tents. He was young—no more than twenty-five—and I knew he wasn't going to make it. I'm no doctor, and even now I can't describe his wounds, they were too horrific. I knew, that's all. Anyway, I held his hand and listened to him talk, and mostly what he kept saying was "tell my wife I love her." I told him I would, and I'll write her a letter—what else can I do? But when I left him, when he died, and I was standing there, listening to the war going on and the doctors yelling and a helicopter landing somewhere close by, I thought: What would I say at the end like that? Of course I'd be thinking about my children, whom I love more than the world, but what about Michael? I know he doesn't love me anymore—if words hadn't been enough to prove it, the lack of letters since I went away certainly make his position clear—but do I still love him?

The truth is, at the end, I'd be reaching for him. I know I would. Reaching out for a man who no longer wants to be there.

Just like my mother.

By late July, Michael and the girls had settled into a manageable routine. This week, Betsy was away at a weeklong summer camp on Orcas Island, where she was learning to kayak; Lulu was spending the weekend with her grandmother. Last he'd heard, they were making stuff out of dry macaroni.

Without them, the house was quiet. Maybe too quiet.

It was growing late; night was beginning to fall. After a long day at the office, Michael had come home, eaten a bowl of Raisin Bran, and then gone back to work. He'd finally received a copy of Keith Keller's military records, and he had the documents laid out on his kitchen table, alongside interview transcripts. In the past week he'd spoken with Ed and his wife, as well as Dr. Cornflower. There was also a list of prospective witnesses, military and civilian.

By all accounts, Keith had been an ordinary small-town boy before he went off to war. He'd won local scholarships and hit home runs and graduated from high school. He'd fallen in love, almost literally, with the girl next door. They'd had a country club wedding, complete with DJ and no-host bar, and gone to Honolulu for their honeymoon.

And then: September Eleventh.

That day had changed the course of Keith's life. He'd had a friend on Flight 93, a classmate who had gone east to check out colleges. When Keith heard about the crash, and the sudden, unexpected danger of terrorism on American soil, he'd enlisted in the Marines.

He was that kind of guy, Ed had said, shaking his head. *Keith wanted to be part of the solution.*

So off Keith went to boot camp and then to war. He'd done two tours in Iraq, and with each return, Ed said he saw less of the boy he'd raised.

Michael flipped through the research his team had put together. Keith had been in the Sunni triangle, one of the deadliest regions of the war. *Roadside bombs hit my brigade at least twice a day, every day, for a year,* Keith had said. *That's a lot of shit blowing up around you. A lot of your friends dying . . . when I got home, sounds were the worst. When someone slammed a door or a car backfired, I hit the ground. Sudden light could totally freak me out.*

Michael sat back. Why was it he hadn't known all this, about the deaths and the devastation, about the wounds our soldiers were suffering? This was 2005, for God's sake. The war had been going on for a while. The truth should have been more apparent. The nightly news should have been showing images of flag-draped coffins being carried onto cargo jets, of heroes coming home in boxes.

He got up, walked away from the table. The Keller case was beginning to trouble him deeply, and not for the usual reasons. The more he read about his client, the more he worried about Jolene.

He grabbed a Corona from the fridge, popped its cap, and went out to stand on the porch. There, he touched the fraying white wicker back of the chair beside him. *Why get new furniture?* Jolene had said when they'd found this chair abandoned by the side of the road. Back then, they'd had more love than money, and he'd been unable to deny her anything, even a crappy used chair. *I want a chair that tells a story.*

The night was quiet around him. Somewhere, a coyote howled; it was a mournful, elegiac sound.

On the road below, a bicycle turned onto the Flynns' driveway—Seth. Michael had a sudden memory of years ago, when Betsy and Seth had ridden their bikes together constantly, and Jolene had worried so much . . .

Michael waved at Seth.

Seth saw him and pedaled from one driveway to the other.

"Hey, Seth," Michael said as the kid rode into the light thrown by the fixtures at the garage. As always, Seth looked thin and odd, with his flat cheeks and straight black hair. Tonight he was dressed all in black. Not a great idea when biking at night.

He got off his bike, held it beside him. "Hey, Mr. Z."

"How are you, Seth?"

The kid shrugged. "Fine, I guess. My grandma's staying with me. She rented a movie for tonight. It's probably G-rated and stars a talking dog. Dad had to go to Ellensburg this week for some car part. Is Betsy still at kayak camp?"

Michael nodded. "'Til Sunday."

"Oh."

Michael frowned. "You want a Coke?"

Seth grinned, showing off his braces. "Rad."

Michael took that as a yes and went inside for a soda. When he returned to the porch, Seth was leaning back against the railing; his bike lay on its side in the gravel driveway.

Michael sat down. He should have known this kid really well—he had been around forever; once, he and Betsy had been inseparable—but honestly, Michael had barely shared ten words with Seth in all the years he'd been coming around. It was like with Carl. Michael just didn't have much in common with them. Until now.

"So, Seth, what's the deal with you and Betsy? One day you guys were thick as thieves, and the next thing I knew you were gone."

"She started hanging with some girls—I call 'em the bitchwolves. Sierra and Zoe. They think I'm a loser. I guess Betsy agrees now."

Michael frowned. "I don't think she'd say that."

"Think again," Seth mumbled. "I'm not the most popular kid in school."

"Neither was I," Michael said. "And the quarterback—Jerry Lundberg, by the way—is doing time. High school was probably the highlight of his life."

Seth took a drink of Coke. Then he said, "There was a bombing yesterday. I saw it on CNN. A helicopter went down. Did you know that when one of our soldiers is killed, they shut down communications on base until the relatives can be notified? I was, like, waiting for a call. They're fine though."

Michael had been in court all day. He hadn't watched the news when he got home. "I didn't know," he said, his voice tight.

"Mom keeps sending me these pictures of her and Jo. They're like vacation photos; girls just want to have fun. She thinks I'm stupid."

"No," Michael said quietly. "That's not the reason."

Seth looked at him. "My dad says we need to believe she'll be fine and she will be."

"Yeah," he said, glancing down at his half-empty beer.

"I'm afraid I'll forget her."

Michael looked away. He understood how that could happen, how you could forget someone. Hadn't he done it himself, hadn't he forgotten Jolene while she was standing right beside him?

Michael didn't realize how long he'd been silent, but then Seth cleared his throat and said, "Thanks for the Coke, Mr. Z. I better get home. My grandma calls the National Guard when I'm late—and in our family, that's no joke. She calls Ben Lomand, and he chews me out."

Michael smiled. "Good to talk to you, Seth. Tell your dad I say hi."

When the kid walked away, Michael added, "You should come around sometime, see Betsy."

Seth turned to him. The sadness in his dark glance surprised Michael. "I wish."

. . .

If Dante had lived in modern times, Michael had no doubt that going to the mall with your daughters would have qualified as one of the circles of hell. Especially when you were there to find a birthday present for your twelve-year-old daughter's on-again best friend. So far, they'd been here an hour and found nothing. He was so tired of looking at glittery headbands and ripped-neckline tee shirts and posters of boy bands he could scream.

They were in Wal-Mart now, drifting through the makeup aisle. Lulu was like a pitbull straining on a leash; she kept grabbing Michael's hand and surging forward, yanking him toward some cheap, sparkly thing.

"There," Betsy said, pointing to a small, neon-pink case that held an array of makeup items. "She'd like that."

"Is Sierra allowed to wear makeup?"

Betsy gave him the Look. "I'm the only one who can't."

He looked at her, seeing the mascara smudges beneath her eyes and the blush that looked like war paint. "Right. And you don't. Fine. Get it. Let's go."

"It's expensive."

"Get it." He would have paid anything, really, just to get out of there.

Lulu said, "I want something, Daddy," and tugged at his hand.

"I need wrapping paper and a card," Betsy said.

Michael was pretty sure he groaned aloud. Still, he followed her out of the makeup aisle and toward whatever came next, all the while listening to Lulu shout: *Stop, Dad! I want that and that and that!*

In the gift-wrap aisle, Betsy stopped so suddenly Michael ran into her. Lulu yelled, "Geez, Betsy—"

"I have to go to the bathroom," Betsy said.

"Come on, Betsy, can you wait 'til—"

She turned on him. "*Now.*"

She said it so forcefully, he frowned. With another sigh, he followed her to the restrooms, although it set Betsy off, caused her to hiss at him to stop following her, but what could he do? Lately he'd developed an irrational fear that he'd lose one of the kids. He had nightmares where he said to Jo, *I don't know, I just looked away for a second.*

He sat down in one of the uncomfortable chairs to wait.

"Daddy, play patty-cake," Lulu said, raising her hands like a mime. "Huh?"

Before Lulu could start whining, Betsy came out of the bathroom, looking pale and terrified. She moved awkwardly, as if her knees didn't bend right anymore.

He rose, instantly worried. "Betsy?"

She glanced around. When he said her name again, louder, she flinched. "Shhhhh."

He moved closer. "Honey? What is it?"

Betsy looked up at him. Her mouth was unsteady, her eyes huge. "I started my period."

Michael's stomach literally dropped. "Oh."

"What's a period?" Lulu said loudly and Betsy clamped a hand over her sister's mouth.

Lulu immediately shrieked.

"Stop it, Lulu," Michael hissed. To Betsy he said, "What do we do?"

"I need . . . something."

"Something. Right." What she needed was a woman, but that wasn't going to happen. He took hold of her hand and led her back through the store. She walked woodenly, kept putting her hands behind her, hiding the back of her pants.

Feminine Products.

There was no doubt about that. He stared at the rows of multicolored packaging, trying to figure out what she needed. *Wings! Adhesive strips! Absorbent!*

Betsy looked like she was ready to vomit. "Hurry, Dad. Pick one."

Come on, Michael. Step up to the plate. She needs you now. "Okay," he said firmly, moving closer to the products, reading the packages.

"Dad," Betsy said under her breath, bouncing on the balls of her feet. "Come on."

He had no idea what made one product better than the other, so he chose the most expensive and handed it to her.

Betsy gasped. "I can't buy it. What if someone I know is there? Oh, my *God*."

"Right." He nodded. "I'll meet you at the restrooms."

Betsy flushed with gratitude and ran off. Michael hefted a wiggling, complaining Lulu into his arms. All the way to the checkout, she sang "periodperiodperiod" at the top of her lungs. He smiled awkwardly at the lady who rang up the sale, and then hurried back to the bathrooms, carrying a small plastic bag.

Betsy waited for him by the back wall, tapping her foot.

"Do you . . . uh . . . know how to use these?" he asked.

"It's not rocket science, Dad." He could tell that she wanted to be sarcastic, but her voice wasn't sharp enough. She took the package and ran into the restroom.

At least fifteen minutes later, Betsy came out of the bathroom slowly, staring at Michael. She looked scared and young; ironic, since this was supposed to be the start of womanhood. Slowly, she turned around. "Can you see anything?"

"No," Michael said softly. "Your pants are fine."

"Phew," Betsy said.

"Can we *go* now?" Lulu whined.

Michael picked up his youngest, and off they went, headed once again for the gift-wrap aisle. By the time they'd picked out the paper and the card and bought Scotch tape and ribbon, Lulu was out of control, but her wailing and pointing was easier to take than Betsy's silence.

Michael's heart went out to her. He knew this was one of those moments that would be filed away and remembered as a day her mother had been disappointingly gone and her father had let her down.

He wanted to give her something that would take the sting out of this memory when she looked back on it. He was thinking that as they passed the jewelry counter. "Hey, Betsy," he said, "do you want to get your ears pierced? They're having a special today."

Betsy gasped and then grinned, showing off the red, white, and blue rubber bands on her braces. "Mom says I have to be thirteen."

"You're close enough. And you're . . . a woman now, I guess," he mumbled, uncomfortable saying it. "And we don't have to tell your mom."

Betsy threw her arms around Michael and hugged him tightly. "Thanks, Dad."

"What? Me TOO!" Lulu said, her voice rising.

Michael winced. Really, his youngest daughter had a screech worthy of some prehistoric bird caught in a trap. He looked around, sure people were staring. *Please, Daddy, pleasepleaseplease . . .*

Dear Mom:

Dad says I have to write you a letter so I am. I started my period. In Walmart. With Dad.

He bought me pads that were like twin mattresses. Sierra's mom says that's what happens when you send a man to do a woman's job Ugh.

Thanks for not being there when I needed you.

AUGUST

Man, it's hot. I am getting so used to my own sweat and stink that I don't even smell it anymore. I'm starting to dream about ice. When I sleep, that is.

The commander called a meeting last night. He told us what we already knew—the missions are getting more dangerous. We're getting shot at all the time and we land under fire. We're going to be doing a lot more air assaults, apparently. Yay.

And Betsy started her period without me. Honestly, I can't even write about that, it makes me feel so bad. I'm missing her life. Missing it.

In the middle of August, Dr. Cornflower delivered his psychiatric evaluation on Keith. His diagnosis: extreme post-traumatic stress disorder. Further, the doctor gave the opinion that Keller was competent to stand trial, that he fully understood the nature of the proceedings.

That meant the trial was a go. A court date had been set.

Michael looked out at the collection of eager, ambitious young faces seated around him. They were at a conference table. Each of the three associates chosen for the defense team had graduated at the top of his or her class and worked at least sixty hours a week. To be a great criminal defense attorney, you had to be hungry, and they were.

"So we have our start. PTSD, as you know, is a diminished-capacity defense, which means we will use it to negate intent. We'll prove that Keith couldn't form the specific intention to kill his wife; without intent, it's not murder one. I don't have to tell you all that anything less would be a victory in this case. However, juries don't like diminished capacity much more than they like insanity, so we'll need experts, eyewitnesses, and statistics." He assigned tasks—some would research sentencing, some jury instructions, some precedents in Washington State and elsewhere. Others would draft the crucial pretrial motions. "I want to find *any* case *anywhere* where PTSD—especially with regard to Iraq—was successful and any case in which it was argued. I will want a draft of our notice to raise the defense by Monday. Hilary, you get started on that. You have all the reports and expert information you need. Make sure you meet all the evidentiary rules. Are there any questions?"

Silence.

"Good."

Michael stood, and the team did the same. As they walked out of the conference room, he repacked his briefcase and headed back to his office. For the next few hours, he worked at his computer, pulling up every case with a PTSD defense that he could find.

On the ferry ride home, he was still at it. He read Cornflower's report again, specifically focusing on Keith's telling of his own story.

In Ramadi, we used to bet on whose tent would be hit by mortar next . . . I was walking back from taking a piss when a mortar landed in our Howitzer . . . we couldn't do shit . . . they burned up alive in there, screaming . . . And there was bagging—picking up body parts . . . legs, arms . . . we put 'em in bags and carried 'em back. It's weird to grab your buddy's arm . . .

Michael put down the report. *What was happening to Jolene over there? What was she seeing?* Once the question arose, he couldn't ignore it. He thought about his wife, and for the first time he imagined the worst . . .

It was still light outside—lavender and beautiful—when he parked in front of the Green Thumb.

His mother met him at the door, looking worried.

"Sorry I'm late," he said.

She brushed his apology aside with an impatient wave. "Betsy is upset. That girlfriend of hers—Sierra—called her an hour ago and told her that a female helicopter pilot was shot down today. I tried to calm her, but . . ."

Michael glanced past his mother; he saw Lulu in the corner, seated at a garden display table, pretending to serve her doll tea in a paper cup. "Where is she?"

"Outside, by the big rock."

Michael nodded. "We're going to the Pot for dinner. You want to join us?"

"I'd love to, but I can't. Helen and I are changing the window display tonight. Labor Day's coming up—the big sale starts."

He leaned down and gave her a kiss on the cheek. "Thanks, Ma." With a sigh, he headed through the store, past the shelves full of knick-knacks and planters and gardening tools. At the back door, he paused for just a moment, gathering his strength, and then he went out to the parking lot that ran between the Front Street stores and the marina. A huge gray boulder sat on a patch of grass overlooking the docks. For as long as he'd lived here, kids had scrambled up, down, and around the rock. Now, he saw his daughter sitting on top of it, her blond hair tousled by the warm summer breeze, her gaze turned out to sea. Hundreds of boats bobbed on the flat calm waters below.

He came up beside the rock. "Hey, you," he said, looking up.

She looked down at him, her pale, pimply face ravaged by tears. There was an alarming flatness in her eyes. "Hi, Dad. You're late."

"Sorry."

As he stood there, trying to dredge up some words of wisdom, her watch alarm bleeped. Betsy yanked the watch off and threw it to the ground.

He bent over and picked it up, heard the *beep-beep-beep* that his wife was listening to at this very moment, a world away. For a moment, he imagined it, imagined *her*, looking down at her watch, probably feeling so far from home.

"Your mom's fine," he said at last. Honestly, all of this had been easier before the Keller case, when he could believe in Jolene's optimistic letters and assurances of safety. Now, he knew better. How was he supposed to comfort a child when her fears were reasonable and he shared them? "It wasn't her, Betsy."

Betsy slid down from the rock. "It could have been."

"But it wasn't," he said quietly.

Her eyes watered at that, her mouth wavered. He could see her composure crumbling. "This time," she said.

"This time."

"I'm forgetting her," Betsy said, reaching into her pocket for the latest picture Jolene had sent, lifting it. "This . . . this isn't her. She isn't only a soldier."

What could he say that wasn't a lie? "Let's go to the Crab Pot and look at the picture of her. That will make you remember."

She nodded.

It wasn't enough.

He reached for her hand. Sometimes holding on was all you could do.

After dinner, Michael led the girls into the house and watched them run upstairs. He felt drained. He should have known how affecting dinner at the Crab Pot would be. Jolene's spirit had been so strong there. Lulu and Betsy had spent a good ten minutes staring up at the Polaroid picture of their mom tacked to the wall. Lulu wouldn't even eat—she just held on to that little wings pin and cried.

He poured himself a drink and stared out the window at the night just beginning to fall across the bay. He heard Lulu come up behind him. She climbed monkeylike up his body, attaching to his hip. "Betsy is crying, Daddy," she said in that squeaky voice of hers.

He kissed her forehead, sighing.

"It's about Mommy," she said, then burst into tears. "She got losted or hurted, right?"

He tightened his hold on Lulu. "No, baby. Mommy's fine."

"I miss my mommy."

He rocked her back and forth, soothing her until her tears dried. When she was calm again, he put her down on the sofa and started *The Little Mermaid* DVD. That would keep Lulu busy for a while. She should be in bed, of course. It was late. But all he could think about was Jo, and what could have happened.

He didn't really make a decision; rather, he found himself moving toward his office. He went inside and shut the door. His hands were shaking; ice rattled in his glass.

It could have been.

He slumped onto the sofa and bowed his head. Betsy was worried that she was forgetting her mother. But Michael had forgotten Jolene long before, hadn't he? He'd lived with her, slept with her, and still somehow had forgotten the woman he'd married. He glanced to his left and saw a framed picture of him and Jolene; it had been taken years ago, at the arboretum in Seattle. They had been young then, and so in love. *Look at the family of ducks, Michael, that will be us one day, waddling along with our babies in tow . . .* In that one image, in Jolene's bright smile, he remembered her.

He was a little unsteady as he got to his feet. At the bookcase, he withdrew a leather-bound photo album and an old VHS tape. Tucking them under his arm, he went into the family room, asked Lulu to follow him, and went upstairs.

He knocked on Betsy's door. "Can we come in?"

"Okay."

He picked up Lulu, carried her into the room, and sat down on the bed beside Betsy. Settling a girl on each side of him, he opened the album.

Centered in the first page, covered by a shiny piece of see-through plastic, was one of the few pictures he'd ever seen of his wife as a young girl. She stood on a rocky outcropping, wearing faded jeans and a cheap V-neck sweater. She was turned slightly away from the camera, looking into some invisible distance, with messy strands of long blond hair pulled across her face by the wind. Off to the left was a man walking away; all you could see was a ragged jeans hemline and a scuffed black boot.

Jolene had often said she'd chosen this photo to begin her life's trail because it was so representative: her mother was missing and her dad was leaving. He'd seen this picture lots of times, but now he really looked at it, saw how sharp she looked, how thin. Her hair looked as if it hadn't seen a comb in weeks, and the loss in her eyes was wrenching. She was watching the man walk away. Why hadn't he noticed that before?

"She's about fifteen here. Not much older than you, Bets."

"She looks sad," Betsy said.

"That's cuz we aren't borned yet," Lulu said, repeating what Jolene always said about this photograph.

Michael turned the pages slowly, taking his girls on a journey down the road of Jolene's life. There were pictures of Jolene in her army uniform, seated in a chopper, out playing Frisbee. In each successive photograph, she looked taller, stronger, but it wasn't until their wedding picture that he saw *her*, the woman with whom he'd fallen in love. She'd smiled and cried through the ceremony, and told him it was the happiest day of her life.

Our lives, he'd said, kissing her. *We will always be in love like this, Jo.*

Of course we will, she'd said, laughing, and they'd believed it for years and years, until . . . they hadn't. No, until *he* hadn't.

"She looks pretty," Lulu said.

He knew all that Jolene had lost in her life, and the things she'd never had and the things she'd overcome, and yet in all of these pictures, she looked incredibly happy. He'd made her happy; that was something he'd always known. What he'd forgotten was how happy she'd made him.

"When is she coming home?" Lulu asked. "Tomorrow?"

"November," Betsy said with a sigh. "For just two weeks."

"Oh." Lulu made a small, squeaking sound. "Will I be five by then?"

"Yep," Betsy said. "But she won't be here for your birthday."

Before Lulu could start crying, Michael got up and put a tape in the TV. Since Jolene's deployment, the girls had obsessively watched the "good-bye reels," as he liked to call them—the tapes she'd made for each of the girls. But they hadn't seen this one in years.

He hit Play and the movie started. The first scene was Jolene, bleary-eyed, holding a baby girl who was no bigger than a half gallon of milk. "Say hi to your fans, little Elizabeth. Or will you be Betsy? Michael? Does she look like a Betsy to you . . ."

Now Betsy was walking for the first time, wobbling forward, laughing as she plopped over . . . Jolene was clapping and crying, saying, "Look, Michael, don't miss this . . ."

Twelve years of his life, passing in forty-two minutes of tape.

He hit Stop.

There she was, his Jo. Her beautiful face was distorted, pixellated by the stop-motion, but even through the grainy, muted colors, he saw the power of her smile.

He saw the whole of his life in her eyes, all his dreams and hopes and fears.

I don't love you anymore.

How could he have said that to her? How could he have been so cavalier with their life, with the commitment they'd made?

He wanted to tell her he was sorry, but time and distance separated them now. Whatever he had to say, it would have to wait until November. Would she even want to listen?

"Let's go shopping tomorrow and send her a care package," Betsy said.

"Yay!" Lulu said, clapping her hands.

Michael nodded, saying nothing, hoping they didn't see the tears in his eyes.

. . .

Strapped in place and weighed down by the thirty pounds of Kevlar plating in her vest, Jolene piloted the Black Hawk toward Baghdad. Sweat collected under her helmet, dampened her hair, ran down the back of her neck. Her skin was flushed; she had a little trouble breathing. Inside the gloves, her hands were slick and damp. Even with the helicopter's doors open, it was a damn oven in here. The water in her bottle was at least 122 degrees—hardly refreshing. Tami was in the right seat.

They flew a combat spread formation, three helicopters strong, hurtling through the darkening sky. Below, the confusing sprawl of Baghdad fanned out on all sides.

"Blue rain . . . blue rain . . ." came the other pilot's voice through the radio.

It meant that the zone into which they were flying was hot, inhospitable. It could be anything—mortar fire, a missile, an RPG (rocket-propelled grenade), a gunfight of some kind.

Jolene said on comm, "Raptor eight-nine veering east. ETA to Green Zone, four minutes."

She moved the cyclic; the helicopter responded instantly to her touch, dropping its nose, picking up speed, hurtling forward.

Ra-ta-ta-tat. Bullets hit the helicopter in a spray. The sound was so loud that even wearing a helmet and earbuds, Jolene flinched.

"We're taking fire," Tami said sharply.

"Hang on," Jolene said, banking a hard left turn.

She heard the *tink-tink-tink* of machine gun fire hitting her aircraft. One first, then a splatter of hits, close together, sounding like a hard rain on tin. Smoke filled the helicopter.

"There," Tami said. "Three o'clock."

A group of insurgents was on a rooftop below, firing. A machine gun set on a tripod spit yellow fire.

Jolene banked left again. As she made the turn, the helicopter to her right exploded. Bits of burning metal hit the side of Jolene's aircraft. Heat billowed inside, and the aftermath rocked them from side to side.

"Knife oh-four, do you copy?" Tami said into the radio. "This is Raptor eight-nine."

The helicopter next to them spiraled to the ground. On impact, a cloud of black smoke billowed up. For a split second, Jolene couldn't look away.

Tami radioed the crash coordinates into the base. "Knife oh-four, do you copy?"

Jolene made a series of fast turns, evading, varying her airspeed, changing her altitude. Up, down, side to side.

When they were out of range, she turned to look in the back bay. "Is everyone okay?" she said to her crew, hearing back from all of them.

Jolene followed the other Black Hawk into Washington Heliport, landing behind it. She was shaking as she unhooked her MCU vest and seat belt.

She climbed out of the seat and stepped down onto the tarmac. The sky was gunmetal gray, but even in the gloom she could see the thick black smoke still rising up from the crash site. She closed her eyes and said a prayer for the fallen airmen, even though in her heart she knew that no one had survived that explosion. Seconds later, the roar of jet engines filled the night sky; bombs exploded in bursts of red fire. As soon as possible, she knew that a medevac helicopter would go to the site and try to locate survivors and victims.

She couldn't help thinking that if you *were* alive and hurt in enemy territory with your bird on fire, it would be the longest wait of your life.

Could she have done something differently? Would a different choice on her part have changed the outcome? They flew in formation to protect one another, but Jolene hadn't protected her partner aircraft; soon, somewhere across the world, a casualty assistance team would gather to give a family the worst possible news.

Tami and Jamie came up to stand beside her. They stood in front of their helicopter, which was scarred with bullet holes.

No one spoke. Each of them knew that one bullet in the right place, one RPG hit, and they could have been the aircraft on fire in the desert.

"Who's hungry?" Jamie said, taking off his helmet.

"I'm always hungry," Smitty said, coming up beside them, coughing. He gave everyone his trademark grin, but it didn't reach his eyes.

Tonight, for the first time, Smitty looked old. "I sure could use me a Mountain Dew."

Jamie, as always, kept up a steady stream of conversation as they walked through the Green Zone. Everything he said was funny, and each of them wanted something to smile about. They ate made-to-order stir-fry and homemade milkshakes while the maintenance crew patched up their helicopter. All the while, they talked about anything except what was on their minds.

By midnight, they were back in the air, flying over Baghdad again. They skirted the most dangerous parts of the city. Now and then gunfire rang out—coming from opportunistic insurgents who could hear the helicopter and shot skyward, hoping to hit what they couldn't see. They landed back at Balad without incident.

Jolene shut down the engine. The rotors slowed by degrees, the *thwop-thwop-thwop* more drawn out in every rotation.

Jolene finally relaxed in her seat. Through her night-vision goggles, the world looked distorted. Here on the black tarmac, she saw ghostly green images moving in front of her.

Absurdly, she thought of souls, walking away from their bodies; that reminded her of the crew they'd lost.

"My son has chicken pox," Jamie said from behind her. "Did I tell you that?"

It was what she needed: a reminder of home. "Kids get over that fast. He won't even remember it in a year. Betsy wanted strawberry Popsicles for every meal."

"Will he remember that I wasn't there?"

Jolene had no easy answer for that.

She unhooked the goggles from her helmet and unstrapped from the seat. When she stepped onto the tarmac, a wave of exhaustion overtook her, and it was not an ordinary tiredness; this was bone deep, a kind of standing death.

She wanted to know she'd done everything possible tonight, that she was not in any way at fault, but there was no one to tell her that, no one she could believe, anyway. The thought isolated her, reminded her of how alone she was over here. She wished she could call Michael, tell him about her day and let his voice soothe her ragged nerves. So many soldiers over here had that, a marital lifeline. Like Tami and Carl.

There was little privacy over here, and since Tami and Jolene routinely stood in the phone lines together, they heard each other's conversations. She heard Tami whispering, *I love you so much, baby, just hearing your voice makes me strong again.*

She remembered when she and Michael had been like that, each a half of the whole. Tami came up beside her, bumped her hip to hip. "You okay?"

"No. You?"

"No. Let's call home. I need to hear my husband's voice," Tami said.

They walked across the base to the phones. Amazingly, the line was short. There were only two soldiers in front of them.

Jolene let Tami go first, heard her friend say, "Carl? Baby? I miss you so much . . ."

Jolene tried not to listen. The truth was she needed Michael right now, needed him to say he loved her and that he was waiting for her, that she wasn't as alone over here as she felt, that she still had a life at home.

When it was finally Jolene's turn, she dialed home, hoping someone was there. Back there, it was two fifteen on a Saturday afternoon.

"Hello?"

"Hey, Michael."

She closed her eyes, imagining his smile. She wanted to tell him more, share her feelings, but how could she? He would never understand. He wasn't like Carl; he wasn't proud of what she did over here. He didn't understand how deeply she cared about the other soldiers with whom she served. At that, she felt even more separate, more distant.

A world away, she heard the creaking of his chair as he sat down, and that simple, ordinary sound reminded her acutely of the people she'd left behind and how they'd gone on with their lives, making memories that didn't include her.

"How are you, Jo?"

She felt her mouth tremble. His tone of voice was so tender; she had to remind herself that he didn't really want to know. When had he ever wanted to hear about her service? She couldn't tell him that her friends had been killed tonight, that maybe it was even her fault, a little. He'd just tell her it was a ridiculous war and the soldiers had died for nothing. She straightened, cleared her throat. "How are my girls? Is Lulu excited about her birthday?"

"They miss you. Betsy heard about a helicopter pilot who'd been shot down. She was pretty upset."

"Tell her I'm a long way from the front line."

"But are you?"

She thought about tonight and winced. "Of course. I'm safe." That was what he wanted to hear. "Can I talk to the girls?"

"Mom took them to a movie."

"Oh."

"They'll be so disappointed. They miss you so much, Jo. Lulu keeps asking if you're going to be home for her party."

They miss you. "I better go."

"Don't. I want to say—"

It was always about what he wanted. The thought exhausted her. She'd been a fool to need him. "I have to go, Michael. There's a line behind me."

"Take care of yourself," he said after a pause.

"I'm trying." Her voice cracked. She hung up the phone and turned back around.

Tami had heard every word. "How about a hot shower?" her friend said, putting an arm around her.

Jolene nodded. They walked to their trailer, grabbed their dopp kits, and headed for the showers. Jolene kept meaning to say something to Tami, make some idle chitchat to gloss over the emotions that lay beneath, but she couldn't.

Even at this late hour, the base was a busy place. Thirty thousand men and women lived here. That didn't even include the contract people who came and went.

Jolene wore her flip-flops into the shower and turned on the water.

Cold.

Trying not to think about the shower—and the hot water—she had at home, she washed quickly, scrubbing the sweat and sand from her skin. After she dried off, she redressed in her dusty, dirty ACUs.

"Cold wasn't exactly what I had in mind," Tami said, smiling tiredly.

"Yeah."

They walked out of the shower trailer and headed back to D-Pod.

Jamie and Smitty were waiting for them, sitting on a pair of over-turned crates outside the door of their trailer, which was across from Tami and Jolene's. Beside Smitty was a small blue and white cooler full of pops. "Wanna drink?" he said. Jolene could see how hard he was try-ing to smile. He might be a great gunner and a courageous soldier, but he was still just a twenty-year-old kid, and tonight had shaken him. He probably wouldn't sleep well; none of them would.

Tami and Jolene sat down beside them—Tami on the steps in front of the door, Jolene on the crate beside Smitty. Behind them, the metal still radiated some of the day's heat, even though it was cold out here now. On either side of the door, sandbags were piled high—rows and rows of them provided some protection from the near-constant mortar fire. Across from her, not more than eight feet away, was the door to their trailer.

"Bill Diehler was on Knife oh-four," Tami said solemnly.

Jolene pictured Bill: a big florid-faced "old school" Guard pilot out of Fort Worth. Just last week he'd shown her a picture of the daughter who was waiting for him to walk her down the aisle.

She closed her eyes and immediately wished she hadn't; she saw the last few seconds again—the roof sniper, the shooting. She'd banked left, turned sharply away from Knife 04.

"Wally Toddan was the crew chief," Jamie said. "His wife just found out she's pregnant. Yesterday, he went to the Haji Mart and bought the kid a football. He hasn't even mailed it yet."

Jolene didn't want to think about that, a child who would never know his father.

"They were heroes," Jamie said solemnly.

"Heroes," Jolene said, thinking about the word and all that it meant.

They clanked their pop cans together in a silent tribute to their fallen friends. After that, they fell silent. Finally, Tami stood up. "I'm going to bed. 0430 is going to come mighty fast. Jo?"

Jolene turned to Smitty and Jamie. "You guys okay?"

Jamie grinned. "Right as rain, Chief. I'll keep the kid out of trouble."

Smitty grinned at that. "He's too old for trouble any way."

Jolene and Tami got up together, crossed the small walkway, and went into their dark, smelly trailer. Once there, Tami flicked the light on and then looked at Jolene. "You did everything you could have, you know. Nothing tonight was your fault."

Jolene had never loved her friend more. Afraid her voice would shake if she tried to speak, she nodded.

"I'm worried about you," Tami said, sitting down on her bed, looking up. "Hell, I'm worried about both of us. I want to make it home."

Jolene sat down on her own bed. She saw the fear in Tami's dark eyes, and it did something to her, uncoiled something that had been tied down. "Me, too," she said quietly.

"If we don't . . ."

Until tonight, Jolene would have stopped Tami right then, but now she remained silent, waiting.

"If I don't make it," Tami said softly, "I am counting on you with Seth. You make sure he knows who I was."

Jolene nodded solemnly. "And my girls will need you."

Tami nodded.

"But we'll make it back," Jolene said.

"Of course we will."

They smiled at each other. Jolene didn't know how she looked, but she saw the fear in Tami's eyes. Neither one of them was as certain of that as they'd been before.

AUGUST

How do I write about a colleague's death? How do I use words to expel the fear and confusion that's uncoiling slowly inside of me? I can't. I don't want to write about it. I don't want to remember the smell of smoke or the terrible sound of ripping metal or the rattle of gunfire. I don't want to think about Wally Toddan and his young widow or the baby who will never know his daddy's smile. Or the bride who will walk down a church aisle without her father.

RIP Knife 04, that's what I can say. All I can say. You were heroes and you will be missed.

Thirteen

After a long, excruciatingly hot day of flying—mostly moving people and Iraqi troops in and around Baghdad, Jolene was exhausted. While they'd been gone, Balad had been attacked again, and this time there had been some serious damage. It was amazing what shrapnel did to wood and metal—Humvees and buildings had been destroyed.

She walked away from the helicopter, with Tami on one side of her and Jamie on the other. No one said anything.

"I need to go to the comm center," Tami said. "See if they've gotten the Internet connection back up yet. If I don't hear from my family, I'm going to lose it."

The three turned slightly, walked down the dark, dusty way between trailers.

It was past midnight, and even this late, the base was busy. At the communication's trailer, Tami said, "Wait here," and went inside. She was out a moment later, looking disgusted. "Internet is still down. Damn it."

Jolene sighed. They headed across the base; Jamie peeled off from them and went to the DFAC, while Tami and Jolene went into their trailer.

Too tired for conversation, each flopped onto her bed and opened her laptop. They were going to write letters tonight, which—hopefully—they'd be able to send tomorrow.

My loves, Jolene typed.

> *Thank you for the care package. I can't tell you what it means to me to get mail. I can tell that Betsy picked out the shampoo—love that strawberry scent—and Lulu chose the sparkly barrette. It looks so pretty in my hair.*
>
> *We've been flying a lot lately. Usually I leave my trailer at 4:30 in the morning, ride my bike to the DFAC (meal trailer), and then go to the helicopter. We're lucky if we get back to base before nine p.m. We are pooped by then. But I'm thinking of you all the time. Especially when my watch alarm goes off, Betsy. I hope you're thinking of me then, too. ☺*
>
> *Yesterday I tried to call home, but the phones weren't working, so I guess it's e-mail to the rescue! I bought you presents at the Haji Mart—it's a kind of street fair set up inside the base. It's crazy, I can tell you. I bet you're not surprised that Tami and I have found a little time to shop. Girls will be girls, I guess. ☺*
>
> *Tomorrow we're having a party out by the burn barrel. I hear there's going to be hot dogs and baked beans, just like a beach party at home!*
>
> *I know I'm super far away, but I'll pretend that I'm with you for Lulu's birthday party. I hope the present gets there in time! Think of Mommy when you blow out your candles, baby girl. ☺ I love you.*
>
> *Well, I'm sort of starting to fall asleep on my feet, so I guess I better go to bed. 4:30 will come mighty early.*
>
> *Betsy, don't forget to remind Daddy about your orthodontist appointment. You need to go in next week. Lulu, can you send me a picture from your party? I have the last one up on my wall.*

Her fingers lifted from the computer keys. She wanted to say something to Michael, but what? He hadn't written her once while she'd been here. Reaching out to him made her feel like her mother, grasping to bring closer a man who didn't love her.

I think of you every day and I love you. To the moon and back.

Remember: Only ninety-one days till I get to see you again. Disney-land???? xxxooo
     Mom

Jolene had never even imagined heat like summer in Iraq. Dust was everywhere—in her hair, her eyes, her nose. Her sweat was gritty, and as soon as she showered, she started to sweat again.

From her first day in-country, she'd known that every breath could be her last, and her nights were no better. She dreamed of fires and mortar and babies who forgot their mothers' faces. She'd made an uneasy peace with death.

Injuries terrified her even more: the RPGs and IEDs ripped bodies apart, flung arms and legs into the sky and the dirt.

Never was her fear closer than on a day like today.

She was on a "hero mission," which meant that she had flown across the desert to pick up the remains of soldiers who had died.

She had been doing far too many of these lately; each time she watched the ceremony, she imagined herself or her crew lying in one of these makeshift surgical hospitals, irreparably broken, waxy faced, crying.

Now she stood back from the hospital tent's opening, among the crews that had been sent on the mission. All of them stood tall and straight, even in the pounding, pulverizing heat. Jolene and Tami, as pilots, could have stayed with their aircraft, but it never seemed right to them. So they were here, standing with their crew, to show respect.

The outlying-combat surgical hospital baked under the noonday heat. The hospital was a row of dirty white canvas tents, connected by a network of wooden sidewalks. Inside, the floors were cement, stained with dark smears of blood. Jolene didn't go inside; she was here to wait. The hero-mission procedure was very precise.

Besides, she knew what it looked like in there: cot after cot filled with the damaged and the dying. Gruesome, devastating injuries were survivable in this modern age. The field docs were nothing short of miracle workers.

It wasn't just soldiers, either. Inside lay rows of Iraqi civilians, children and women, who'd been too close to an exploding IED or been hit by mortar fire. The smell was terrible, made worse by the unrelenting heat.

A doctor ducked through the tent's canvas opening and held it open behind him. Six soldiers followed him out, pushing four gurneys. On each lay the black-bagged remains of a soldier.

Jolene and Tami immediately stood at attention and saluted. The look that passed between them was as solemn as the mood: each was thinking of how it would feel if the other were in that bag. Somewhere close by a mortar round hit, exploded through concrete. No one even flinched.

The doctor looked as weary as Jolene felt. He placed a hand on each one of the bagged bodies in turn and said simply, "Thank you."

Jolene's throat tightened. She looked down at the gurneys, knowing that the lost soldiers deserved this last measure of respect from all of them. One of the bags was small, too small, a bad thing. It meant that pieces were missing. The result of an IED or RPG probably. Beside each body was a small clear bag containing personal effects. Even though the bag was marked with bloody fingerprints, she could see the watch and dog tags and wedding ring inside.

It made her think of Betsy, holding up Jolene's dog tags, asking if they would identify her . . .

The silence stretched a second more, and then someone said "Captain Craig" inside the tent, and the doctor went back inside.

Led by the gurneys and their silent watchmen, the two Black Hawk crews walked across the base to the waiting helicopters. Here again, the exact manner of transport was prescribed.

At Jolene and Tami's helicopter, Jamie and Smitty saluted the bodies again; then they loaded the fallen soldiers onto the helicopter, using exquisite care, placing them just so.

As the loading went on, soldiers came from all over, some in uniform, some in civilian clothes, and formed two straight lines out from the helicopter's open side door, saluting their fallen friends one final time.

She wondered who these fallen soldiers were. Husbands? Fathers? Mothers? Did their families know yet that their worlds had changed?

Jolene and Tami nodded to each other and climbed into the aircraft. Tami was left seat today. She leaned forward, placed the white hero-mission card in the windshield.

Jolene strapped herself into the right seat and began the preflight checklist. The helicopter doors were closed. Within moments, they were taking off amid a swirl of beige sand.

Below, the soldiers began to disperse.

On the flight to the Baghdad airport the crew was quiet, as they always were on hero missions. The deaths weighed heavily on their minds. The war had begun to heat up in the past few months. It had begun to be normal to be shot at, to be hit. Jolene heard the *ping!* of machine gun fire hitting a helicopter in her sleep and often woke up screaming. Last week, a bullet had gone through the window beside her head, shattering it, and bounced off her helmet. She'd felt the slightest *thwack* to her head and kept flying. Only later did she begin to have nightmares about it, to imagine her head exploding, her body coming back to her children in a black bag that was twelve inches too short.

By the time they made it back to Balad, Jolene was beyond exhausted. She hadn't slept well in weeks, and it was beginning to take a toll on her. She couldn't remember the last time there hadn't been a middle-of-the-night mortar attack. She slept through the shelling but woke to the sound of the blaring alarm.

After the end of the mission, the maintenance crew swarmed to check out the helicopter. Jolene and her team walked away. On this dark night, there was no camaraderie, no "let's go to the DFAC for pie." Each of them, like Jolene, was thinking how thin a piece of luck separated them from the bodies they'd transported today.

"You okay, Tami?" Jolene said as they reached their trailer.

Tami stopped. "No. Not really."

They walked into the trailer. Tami flipped a light switch; on came the fluorescent bulb on the ceiling. Instantly, the dark little space was illuminated. There were family photographs everywhere—and a movie poster of Johnny Depp from *Pirates of the Caribbean* on the wall.

Tami sat down on her bed. It sagged in the middle; dust puffed up from the army-green bedding. The alarm sounded.

Jolene heard footsteps running past her trailer. She sat down opposite Tami.

Somewhere, something exploded; the lights in the trailer flickered and remained on.

When the alarm stopped and the world stilled, Tami went on as if nothing had happened: "Carl says Seth is having a hard time. Kids are making fun of him because of us. It makes me want to kick some preteen ass."

"Michael just says the girls are fine."

Tami looked up. "It's not like you're telling him the truth, either."

"We're hardly talking. He hasn't sent me a single e-mail." Jolene bent over, began unlacing her boots.

"You are getting a care package once a week. Who's buying all that stuff and mailing it?"

"My guess? Mila. And the girls."

"Have you written him?"

Jolene sighed. "You know I haven't. What would I say?"

"Maybe he's thinking the same thing."

"I'm not the one who said I wanted a separation."

"Are you really going to play chicken with your marriage from here?"

"I didn't start it."

"Who cares? Look at what we did today." She snapped her fingers. "That's how fast it happens, Jo. Dead. Alive." She snapped again. "Dead. This is the time to say what needs to be said, not to play games. Your parents were losers who scarred you. I get it, I really do. But you have to find the cojones to talk to your husband or you guys are going to lose everything."

"That's easy for you to say, Tam. Your husband loves you."

"It's not easy, Jolene. None of this is easy, you know that. Michael loves you," Tami said. "I know it."

"No. I don't think he does."

"Do you love him?"

There it was, the question she'd spent months avoiding. Leave it to Tami to throw it out like the first pitch in a baseball game. "I don't know how to stop loving him," she answered quietly, surprising herself. "It's in my blood. But . . ."

"But what? Isn't that your answer?"

"No." Jolene sighed. Really, she didn't want to think about this, or talk about it. "Love is only part of it. Like forgiving is only part. Even if I could forgive him, how would I forget? He stopped loving me, Tam. Just stopped. He looked me in the eyes and said he didn't love me anymore. How can I trust him again? How can I believe in our marriage, in forever together, if our love has some expiration date?"

"Just don't give up. That's all I'm saying. Write him a letter. *Start.*"

Jolene knew it was good advice. She believed in fighting for love; at least she once had. Lately, she had trouble remembering what she believed and who she used to be. "I'm afraid," she said after a long silence.

Tami nodded. "He broke your heart."

Jolene looked at her friend, sitting across from her in their dingy, smelly trailer, and she thought how lucky they were to have each other over here. "I'm glad you're here with me, Tam. I don't know what I'd do without you."

Tami smiled. "I love you, too, Jo."

$\mathcal{F}ourteen$

W e've got an emergency situation that's going bad fast," the captain said. "We need to run search and rescue in a very tight spot. Reports give us a narrow weather window. We need two helicopters in the air in fifteen minutes or less." He turned to point at a map. "Here. We've got two army rangers trapped by enemy fire."

"We can be up in ten," Jolene assured him. She looked at Tami, who nodded sharply, and led the way to the tarmac. There was no conversation along the way.

As they walked across the base, a sharp wind blew up dust that bit into skin and eyes; it raked the flag overhead, whipped it into a frenzy. After a quick check of her craft, Jolene climbed into the left side of the cockpit and took her seat.

She was the first one inside, but within seconds, the crew was all in place. Jolene ran the preflight check, cleared departure with the tower, and started the engine.

The aircraft climbed slowly into the air as she worked the controls—

her hands and feet in constant motion. With each mile flown, the dust storm intensified. Wind smacked their windshield.

"Deteriorating viz," Jolene said. She reached over, flipped a toggle switch, and glanced at her instrument readings. Wind gusted against them, pushed the Black Hawk sideways. A pothole of air sucked at the rotors; the helicopter dropped two hundred feet in a plunging, heart-stopping second. "Hold on, guys," Jolene said into her mouthpiece. She clung to the bucking, jerking controls and steadied the Hawk.

At the search vector, it took all of Jolene's upper-body strength to descend evenly in the maelstrom. Below them, the land was craggy, broken.

"There's nowhere to land," Jamie called out.

"Roger that," Jolene said. She worked the two foot pedals, finding the delicate balance between the tail and main rotors.

"There!" Smitty said. "At one o'clock."

Jo held the helicopter in a hover, but every second was a fight. Wind clawed at them, kept battering the aircraft. On the rugged desert floor below, she could just make out the two soldiers. They were obviously taking heavy fire. Bullets pinged off the aircraft.

Jamie shoved the door open and laid down a heavy cover of fire.

"All clear," he said after a few seconds. "Good to land."

A blast of dust and wind gusted through, swinging the Hawk side to side.

"Low and slow," Jolene said into her mic. She lowered the aircraft slowly to the ground. The other helicopter remained in the air, covering them.

Jolene watched her gauges closely as they rescued the two army rangers.

When the soldiers were safely loaded in the back bay, Jolene finally breathed a little easier. In seconds, they were back in the air, flying toward the base.

There, they heard about another helicopter that had gone down near Baghdad, killing the whole crew.

That night, she couldn't sleep. Everytime she closed her eyes, she saw helicopters hurtling to the ground, heard people screaming. She saw children, dressed in black, huddled around a flag-draped casket; a soldier in dress uniform walking to her front door . . . Finally, she gave up trying. Turning on her small light, she reached for her journal.

AUGUST

I love flying. I've always loved it, and I'm proud to be here, doing my job, helping my country. But there's this fear in me lately, a terrible, frightening thing, like a bird flapping to get out of my chest. I have a bad feeling.

The things I've seen stay with me. Even in sleep, I can't get rid of them—arms and legs blown off, soldiers dying, pictures of children pinned to trailer walls, curling in the heat. Every time I take off, I wonder: will this be it? I imagine my family getting the worst news.

Tami keeps telling me I need to reach out to Michael. She tells me how much Carl is helping her cope with what we're facing. She says I am being stubborn and playing chicken with my marriage.

But how can I take her advice? How can I talk to Michael—Michael, whom I loved from the moment he first kissed me—Michael, who is my family. Or was, until he said he didn't love me anymore. I watched my mom do that, year after year, reach out for a man who'd stopped loving her. It ruined her. I never thought I'd be like her. Am I?

Am I losing myself out here or just falling out of love with him? Or is this just a part of war? I know that no one at home can matter too much. My friends over here are the people who have my six, the people who will save me and cover me.

It's not enough sometimes, though. Sometimes, I need . . . Michael.

I need him. But I don't want to. I don't trust him to be there for me. Not anymore.

No wonder I feel so alone. And now my damn watch alarm is going off, reminding me . . .

August passed in a blur of hot, lazy blue-skied days. Betsy and Lulu were busy almost all the time, going to day camps and spending time at the Green Thumb with Mila. Lulu's fifth birthday party had gone off without a hitch, although it had been a quieter version of earlier parties.

On this Thursday morning, the sun rose hot and bright into a cloudless blue sky. It would be a glorious summer day. At nine thirty, Michael pushed away from his home computer and went upstairs. He knocked on the girls' bedroom doors, saying, "Wake up, sleepyheads, *Yia Yia* will be here in a half an hour to pick you up."

Then he went downstairs and put breakfast on the table. French toast with fresh blackberries. "Come on, girls," he yelled again.

Sipping his coffee, he turned on the TV in the family room.

". . . in heavy fighting last night near Baghdad. The helicopter, a Black Hawk flown by female warrant officer Sandra Patterson, of Oklahoma City, was hit by an RPG and crashed within seconds, killing everyone on board . . ."

Pictures of bright-eyed soldiers in uniform filled the screen, one after another . . .

"I thought women weren't allowed in combat," Betsy said quietly behind him.

Michael thought, *God help me.* It was bad enough that he'd just heard the report, and now he had to comfort his daughter. How could he reassure her when the truth was obvious to both of them?

What would Jolene do? What would she want him to do?

He turned slowly, saw the tears in Betsy's eyes. She looked as fragile and shaky as he felt right now.

"She's lying to us," Betsy said. "All those letters and pictures . . . they're lies."

He reached out for Betsy, took her hand, and led her over to the sofa, where they sat down together. "She doesn't want us to worry."

"Are you worried?"

He looked at her, into her scared eyes, and knew that she would re-member what he said next. Would he tell her a lie? He knew how to bend the truth, but for once he wanted more of himself. "I'm worried," he said at last, pulling her onto his lap.

"Me, too." Betsy coiled her arms around his neck as if she were a little girl again, buried her face in his neck. He felt her crying—the shudder-ing of her slim shoulders, the dampness on his skin, and he said noth-ing more.

When she finally drew back, shaking, her pale face streaked with tears, he felt a surge of love as powerful as any he'd ever known. "I love you, Betsy, and we're all going to be okay. That's what we have to believe. She'll come home to us."

Betsy nodded slowly, biting her lower lip.

"Hey," Lulu said, coming into the room. "I want a hug."

Michael opened his other arm and Lulu scampered up beside her sister. "I think I should take my girls to the beach today," he said after a moment.

Lulu drew back, her eyes big. "You?"

"But it's a workday," Betsy said.

"I've worked enough," Michael said. The unfamiliar words loosened something in him, made him feel buoyant. He reached for the phone on the end table and called his mom. "Hey, Ma, I'm going to stay home with the girls today. We're going to hang out at the beach. You want to come?"

His mother laughed. "I've got a bunch of stuff to do at the store. I'll meet you there?"

"Perfect," Michael said, hanging up. Then, to his stunned daughters, he said, "Why are you sitting there? I thought we were going to the beach."

"Yay!" Lulu yelped, bouncing off his lap and running upstairs.

In the garage, Michael found that Jolene had everything organized neatly—folding beach chairs, marshmallow-roasting sticks, lighter fluid, coolers. He had an entire cooler packed by the time Betsy and

Lulu came back downstairs, wearing their bathing suits and carrying beach towels. "I got Lulu ready," Betsy said proudly.

After breakfast, Michael grabbed the cooler, directed the girls to get the buckets and shovels, and down they walked, toward the beach. At the street—quiet this morning—they crossed holding hands and went to their small dock.

They spent the whole day on the beach, making sand castles, looking for shells, wading in the cold blue waves. Sometime around noon, he built a fire in the round, metal, portable pit on their small deck, and in no time at all they were roasting hot dogs over an open flame.

At about one o'clock, his mom showed up and joined in the fun. For the first time in months, Betsy dropped her preteen attitude and became a kid again, and come evening, when the sky turned lavender and a ghostly moon came out to see who played on the beach below, they sat in chairs pulled close together, with blankets wrapped around them.

"Daddy," Lulu said, tucked in the lee of his arms. "I'm scared about starting school. When is next week? Can Mommy come home?"

An emotion moved through him, tightened his chest. "I know your mommy would love to walk you into school, but she can't. I'll be there, though. Will that be good enough?"

"Will you hold my hand?"

"Of course."

"How come I have to go all day? Mommy said I would be done by lunchtime."

"It's different now, baby. You need to be in the all-day program."

"Cuz she's gone?" Lulu asked sleepily, fingering the small metal wings pinned to her bathing suit.

"Right."

"What if I get scareded?"

"It's always scary on the first day," Betsy said quietly. "But everyone will like you, Lulu. And you have a great teacher—Ms. MacDonald. I loved her."

"Oh," Lulu said, sounding unconvinced.

Michael smiled. "Let me tell you what it's like . . ."

As he talked to his youngest daughter about kindergarten and teachers and cubbies and recess, it was as if he were another man from another life. For years, he'd strived to make a difference in the world, and he'd worked like a dog to make that happen, and yet here he was, a man sitting on a dock with his children, and never had he felt more certain that his words mattered.

That was what Jolene had been trying to tell him every time he missed an event. *It matters,* she'd said.

"Okay, Daddy," Lulu said at last. "I guess I can do that 'cause I'm a big girl now. If you hold my hand. And I'm taking my pink ribbon."

"Ah, Lulu," he said. "I wouldn't miss it for the world."

Much later, when the girls had fallen asleep in their chairs, while the waves lapped along the pebbled shore and the stars shone down on them, his mother looked at him. "Jolene would be proud of you today," she said quietly.

Michael looked at her, over Lulu's dark head. "I let her down," he said.

His mother nodded, smiling sadly, as if she'd known this all along.

September was a bloody month in the war. It seemed that every day a helicopter came back to base shot up. Hero missions and suicide bombers were commonplace now. Jolene had begun to avoid the Haji Mart altogether; she couldn't stand thinking that the cute boy selling videos might someday have a bomb strapped to his chest. It had begun to rain in the past few days; the base had become a huge mud hole. The trailer's cement floor looked like dirt. There was no way to get the viscous red mud off your boots.

Tonight, the sky was clear and black, spangled with stars. It occurred to her that only a few months ago a sky like this had made her think of her family at home, sleeping peacefully beneath the same stars. These days, she didn't dwell on what was happening at home. She was too busy and exhausted to think about that. She was in the air constantly now, flying units into location, transporting workers to job sites, and flying

Iraqi troops and civilian and military VIPs. More and more often, she flew air-assault missions, carrying troops to their mission-landing zones.

She walked beside Tami toward the trailer that housed the Charlie Company flight-planning room. They didn't bother to talk; they were both too tired to make the effort. It was 2200, and they'd already flown two missions today. Yesterday had been even busier.

Jolene stepped up the muddy wooden steps and entered the trailer. The walls were covered with pieces of paper—schedules, reports, flyers, calendars. Every aircraft's route was tracked from here. Computer screens sat on every desk. Here was where they stored all their machine guns and ammo and flight gear.

As she stepped into the trailer, the electricity snapped off and everything went dark. She heard someone say, "Shit. Again?"

Jolene knew the generator would kick in soon, but she was supposed to be at the helicopter in five minutes. "Zarkades, sir," she said into the darkness. "You have a mission plan for Raptor eight-nine?"

There was a rustle of paper, then the creaking of footsteps on the plywood floor. "Air assault, Chief. You and Raptor four-two are going to Al Anbar. We have a marine unit trapped in a ditch. They're taking heavy fire."

The generator started up; the lights came on.

Captain Will "Cowboy" Rossen was standing in front of her, holding out her orders.

"Yes, sir."

The captain nodded. "Be safe."

Jolene and Tami went to the small room attached to the op center and retrieved their things. Jolene put on her heavy vest with the Kevlar plating and grabbed her flight bag. As they walked down the muddy streets, it started to rain. She looked up, saw a layer of pale gray clouds cover the stars.

"Shit. Viz is deteriorating," Jolene said.

They increased their pace, boots sloshing through the mud. Jolene felt Jamie come up beside her, but neither of them said anything as they headed to their aircraft. Then Smitty showed up, strapping his helmet on as he walked.

"Your turn in the left seat?" Tami said when the bird was checked out and ready to go.

Jolene nodded and climbed into the left seat and strapped herself in. She clicked the night-vision goggles onto her helmet and pulled them into place.

In less than five minutes they were taking off, rising to just below the cloud cover.

It was a two-helicopter mission. They flew together, always in contact, across the black expanse of desert, over Baghdad to Al Anbar province, just past Fallujah.

As they came into Fallujah's airspace from the north, the first round of machine gun fire sounded. The *tap-tap-tap* on the fuselage was small-arms fire.

"Raptor eight-nine, taking fire, seven o'clock, two hundred meters," Jolene said into the comm. The other helicopter responded instantly.

"Raptor four-two taking fire, nine o'clock, banking right."

They flew over a small village. A machine gun was set up on a rooftop, shooting at them.

Jolene scanned the area below; her night-vision goggles revealed dozens of greenish-white dots moving through the darkness. The soldiers trapped in the ditch or insurgents looking for them? She reached forward to flip a toggle switch, and everything exploded.

An RPG hit the fuselage so hard she was thrown sideways; her right foot arced up and kicked the instrument panel.

The cockpit filled with smoke. Flames filled the back of the aircraft; she could feel the heat. Jolene called out for her crew, got no response. She clutched the cyclic and tried to keep them in the air, but they were falling—plunging—downward at one hundred and fifty miles an hour.

The power on engine number two went crazy; the instrument panel went dark. Nothing. Not even engine temperature.

She called out to her crew again, told them to brace for impact, and then she tried to Mayday her position, but the smoke was so intense she couldn't breathe. All she got out was "Mayday—" before they crashed.

After a long day spent taking depositions of the police officers who interrogated Keith Keller, Michael came home, dead on his feet, and made dinner for his daughters—one of Jolene's chicken and rice recipes that he found in the overstuffed three-ring binder. Later, when the girls were asleep, he walked out to the empty family room, standing there alone, noticing how quiet the house was.

An unusual emotion rose up in him, so odd that it took him a moment to recognize it. Loneliness.

For so long, he'd felt a kind of simmering anger at being Mr. Mom, felt emasculated by being responsible for his children and the cooking and shopping. He'd blamed Jolene for leaving him adrift on a sea of responsibilities he didn't want and which he barely knew how to perform. But in the last few weeks, it had changed. He'd changed. He'd found a new side of himself; he loved reading to Lulu before bed, hearing her quirky questions about the stories, watching her small finger point at the pictures. He loved it when Betsy sat by him at night, watching TV and telling him stories from school. He loved how they'd become a team at the grocery store, working together, how a game of Candyland could make them all laugh.

He missed Jolene. How was it he hadn't foreseen what his life would be like without her?

She was so far away, and every day she was getting shot at, dodging IEDs, changing in ways he couldn't imagine. And what had he given her to take with her? *I don't love you anymore.*

He walked over to the TV, turned it on. Her latest tape was in the machine, as always; the girls watched it endlessly.

He hit Play.

And there she was, Jolene in uniform, smiling at the camera, pointing out landmarks around Balad—*here's the place where we get that good pie . . .*

His wife.

The tape ended, and the last image of her froze on screen. She stood with Tami, both in uniform, their arms slung around each other. Jolene was smiling brightly, but he saw the truth in her eyes. She was scared and lonely, too.

He wanted to talk to her so much it was an ache in his chest.

There was no way to call her, though. All he could do was write her a letter.

The thing he'd never done. He'd started several in the past weeks, but he'd deleted them all before sending. He was so ashamed of how he'd acted before; how could he just drop her a letter now and pretend that everything was different?

He walked through the family room and into his office, where he sat down at the computer and booted it up.

Jolene, he typed, then stopped, deleted that, and began again.

My Jo—

> *Do you remember when I first called you that? We were at the arboretum, in a rented rowboat, watching baby ducks float through the reeds. You said, "I wonder how they find their mom," and that made me understand how hurt you'd been by your childhood. It took you a long time to tell me what it had been like, and when you finally told me . . . that's when I knew you loved me. I used to look in your eyes and see my own dreams. When was the last time we really looked at each other? I wonder. Anyway, back to the ducks. I said, "They just know. Like I know you're my Jo."*
>
> *"I want to be yours," you said.*
>
> *I loved you so much it hurt. I used to lie in bed and imagine losing you in terrible ways. Sick, huh? But I did it. I loved you so much it was as if I had to think about losing you or I would have lost myself instead. Did you love me like that?*
>
> *I think you did.*
>
> *So what happened? When did we stop being lovers and start being just the girls' parents, and then roommates? When did I start blaming you instead of myself? I think a lot of it started with my dad's death. I*

had never lost anyone before—I didn't know how it felt to be ripped apart like that, and I didn't handle it well. I think I blamed you for everything that was wrong in my life.

   Is it too late to go back?

   I hope not.

   I thought I had it figured out, that we had run our course, but I see how wrong I was, and how I hurt you, and I'm sorry.

   I'm sorry. That's what I know now. For so many things. I guess war doesn't only change the warriors. Those of us on the home front go through our own stuff.

   I miss you.

He stared at the e-mail. It was so short. What good was *I'm sorry* with what she was going through?

Could she forgive him? There was only one way to know.

He hit Send.

Jolene woke up, coughing, her eyes watering, the taste of blood in her mouth. She called out for her crew again, got no answer. Tami was beside her, strapped in her seat, slumped forward, unconscious.

Jolene tried to unhook herself from the seat. On the third attempt, she saw the problem. Her right forearm was a bloody mess. She could barely lift her hand, and her fingers didn't work right. Using her left hand, she leaned forward over the scorched and blindingly hot instrument panel to do an emergency shutdown.

"Mayday," she said, finding it hard to talk, to concentrate. The radio wasn't working. She passed out again. When she awoke, she gave her coordinates over the radio, hoping it was working now. She needed the CSEL radio. Where was it? *Think.*

"Tami," Jolene said, trying to reach out for her best friend, but she couldn't move. She tried to unhook herself, but she couldn't; something was wrong with her. Her body wasn't responding. Something was wrong with her right foot.

Tap-tap-tap.

They were taking fire again. From a distance, she could hear the guttural sounds of men talking, their footsteps thundering forward.

I have to get out, establish a perimeter.

Tap-tap-tap.

We're still taking fire.

She tried to unholster her weapon, but her right hand wouldn't work.

Finally, she unhooked from her seat and crawled painfully through the cockpit. She grabbed Tami, unhooked her from the seat and pulled hard. Tami slid sideways, her eyes blank, her lips slack. Jolene fumbled with Tami's helmet, got it off, and saw the huge wound in her head, the blood gushing out of it.

"Stay with me, Tami . . ."

She looked back into the bay. The right side of the fuselage was gone; bits of metal were melted and smoldering. The canvas straps and netting were on fire. Smitty, slumped sideways, had a black, gaping hole in his chest; it was bleeding and smoking. His eyes were flat, blank. Dead. Jamie lay crumpled in the corner. "Jamie! Jamie!"

She had to get them all out of the helicopter.

When she moved, a wave of nausea rolled through her. The pain in her foot was staggering. Jolene threw up and tried again. She unholstered her weapon with her left hand and brought it up, shaking in her hand, and tried to see through the smoke. "Tami, I'm going to get you out; then we need to establish a perimeter. We need the radio. Jamie, wake up. *Jamie!* Get Smitty out. Help me."

She lifted up on her good arm, tried to aim out the ruined fuselage. The *tap-tap-tap* grew louder, more insistent. She grabbed Tami, hefted her limp body on her back, and crawled slowly out of the cockpit, falling to the ground, hitting hard. Pain exploded into her thigh.

"Chief—"

It was Jamie. Or had she imagined his voice? "Jamie," she said, but her voice was barely a croak of sound. She lay there, breathing hard, Tami's body a deadweight on top of her. "Come on, Tami, wake up, *please . . .*"

She heard the alarm on her wristwatch bleat its lonely sound, but it wasn't real. She knew it wasn't real. She couldn't have heard it above all this noise—the shooting, the screaming. "I'm sorry, Tam," she said, dragging her friend through the dirt. Her vision swam, blood pounded through her head.

Behind her, the helicopter exploded. She threw herself on top of Tami, covering her friend's body with her own. Something hit Jolene hard, knocked her sideways . . . she lay in the dirt, stunned, staring up at the night sky, seeing burning bits of metal falling like fireworks through the blackness, raining down on her.

She heard the bleating of her watch alarm again . . . or was it something else? A scream? A bomb whizzing past her? A shout? She thought, *BetsyLuluMichael,* and then she was falling, fading . . . and there was nothing.

Fifteen

Michael stood at the kitchen window, staring at the coming night. It was mid-September and cool, with a whispering breeze that made the skirts of the giant cedar trees dance along the edges of the tall grass. The days of beach walking were coming to a close; autumn was drawing near, with its cold, frosty mornings and endless falling rain. He knew without looking that the plum trees had begun to lose their leaves.

In the lavender light, he stared at the white fence line that delineated their land. *This is us*, Jolene had said as she helped him hammer the slats in place so long ago. *The Zarkades family. Everyone will see this fence and know we belong here.*

Down on the bay road, a car came around the bend, its headlights bright spots against the sunset. He watched the car approach—it was a boxy, official-looking vehicle. At the bend in the road, the car slowed . . . at his driveway, it slowed more and turned in, then parked.

Michael's fingers curled around the smooth, cool white tile counter. *Turn around, drive away . . . you're in the wrong place . . .*

A soldier got out of the car, slammed the door shut, and turned to face the house.

Oh, God.

Michael closed his eyes, breathing so hard he felt light-headed.

The doorbell rang, sounding ugly and discordant.

He walked woodenly to the door, opened it. "Is she dead?"

"I'm Captain Lomand—"

"Is Jolene dead?"

"She's alive."

Michael clutched the door frame, afraid for a moment that his knees were going to give out.

"I'm sorry for coming like this. I knew how it would look, coming up the walk, but I didn't want you to get a phone call from a stranger for . . . this. May I come in?"

Michael nodded numbly and stepped aside, thinking, *But you are a stranger.* The man walked into the house and went into the family room. He acted as if he'd been here before, which probably he had, but Michael had no idea who he was.

The captain stopped by the sofa, remained standing, and removed his hat. When he looked at Michael, his eyes were compassionate. "Jolene's Black Hawk was shot down several hours ago."

Michael lowered himself slowly to the brick hearth. Behind him, a fire blazed. It was too close, and too hot, but he couldn't feel anything.

"She's being transported to Landstuhl, Germany, right now. It's the biggest American military hospital in Europe. She's in good hands."

"Good hands," Michael repeated, trying to will his mind to work. "But how is she?"

"I don't have any details, sir," Lomand said.

"Was Tami in the helicopter with her?"

"Yes," Captain Lomand said. "But I have no information about her condition at this time. Except that she's alive."

"What do I do? How do I help her?"

"Pray, Michael. That's all we can do for her right now. As soon as we have information, a Red Cross worker will call you."

Michael stared down at his hands, saw that they were shaking. Funny things came to him, stupid things—he heard his own heartbeat and the way breath escaped him, the sound of a beam settling somewhere in the house.

"People will stop by later. To help," Lomand said.

Michael had no idea how strangers could help, but he didn't care so he said nothing. Words seemed dangerous suddenly; there was too much he didn't want to hear or think. He wanted this man gone. "I need to see her." That was all he knew for sure.

"Of course."

Lomand stood there a moment longer, looking pained. "She's a fighter," he said quietly.

"Yeah." Michael couldn't listen anymore. "Thank you . . ." He meant to say the man's name, but he'd forgotten it. He got up and headed toward the door, opening it. He heard the captain behind him, heard his heavy footsteps on the wooden floor, but neither of them spoke.

At the door, the captain said, "We're all praying for her."

Michael nodded. He didn't have the strength to speak, not even to say *thank you*. He stood there in the doorway, watching the captain walk down the driveway, his back ramrod straight, his hat fixed firmly on his head, his arms at his sides.

Time fell away from Michael. One minute he was standing there, watching a soldier walk to his car, and the next minute he was alone, standing in the cold of an open doorway, staring at a yard that was slowly growing dark.

In his career, he'd heard dozens of victims and defendants say *I don't remember what I did . . .* and *I just snapped, my mind went blank.*

He knew now how that felt, how a mind could simply shut down, stop working.

Slowly, he closed the door and returned to the warmth of his kitchen. All he could hear was his own heartbeat, his own breathing, and those words, over and over and over again.

Shot down.

She could be dying right now . . . all alone . . .

He closed his eyes, imagining it for a moment, the loss of her, the funeral, the words, the feelings. As much as it pained him, he couldn't stop. He *wanted* this pain; he'd earned it, and how would he survive the worst if he wasn't ready?

The problem was, he didn't know the worst, couldn't identify it. There was telling the children, raising them without her, failing at it, stumbling; there was standing in front of their friends—a widower who had let his wife go to war on a tide of bad words, broken promises; there was coming home without her and learning to sleep alone.

Missing her.

That would be the worst. How was it he hadn't thought of all of this when he'd so foolishly said *I don't love you anymore*? Then, he'd thought of the worst of who they'd become. She'd seemed to him to have grown so big and so small at the same time—the lynchpin of his existence in an irritating way. He'd resented her strength, her independence. He'd wanted to be needed by her, even though he knew he was unreliable. He'd blamed her for his unhappiness, when all along he had been the one to let go of what mattered.

And now maybe he would have to live without her. The idea was over-whelming. He could consider the symptoms—the talks, the responsibili-ties, the public moments—but the real truth of it, the imagining of a life going on with no heartbeat, was more than he could bear.

He stumbled over to the kitchen counter and picked up the cordless phone. It took him three tries to dial his mother's number—his fingers were shaking so badly he kept hitting the wrong numbers. When his mother answered, sounding breathless and happy to hear from him, pain rushed in, tightened Michael's throat until he could hardly speak.

"Hey, Michael. It's good to hear from you. I'm just unpacking some boxes at the store. Are we still on for—"

"Jolene," he said, his eyes stinging.

"Michael?" his mother said slowly. "What is it?"

He leaned forward, rested his head on the kitchen wall (papered in sunny yellow, *shouldn't a kitchen be sunny, Michael? It's the heart of a home*). He couldn't see anything now. "Jo's been shot down. She's alive—on her way to a hospital in Germany."

He heard his mother's indrawn breath. "Oh, my God. How—"

"That's all I know, Mom."

"Oh, *kardia mou*, I am so sorry . . ."

The endearment, spoken so softly, cracked his composure. He drew in a great, shuddering breath, and then he was crying as he'd never cried before, not even at his father's death. He thought of Jolene, smiling, laughing, sweeping their daughters into her strong arms, twirling them around, and putting her arms around him, holding him close at night.

He cried until he felt empty inside, hollow, and then, slowly, he straightened, wiped his eyes. His mother was still talking, saying something . . . her voice droned on, but he couldn't listen. There was nothing to comfort him now. "Give me a little time, Ma. A couple of hours to tell the girls," he said.

She was still talking when he hung up.

He leaned over the kitchen sink, thinking for a second that he might vomit. He'd done that before at bad news—when they told him his father's cancer had metastasized. He swallowed thickly, trying to calm his heart rate by force of will. *She could die.* The silver drain blurred before his eyes, and fresh tears formed, burned, fell down his cheeks, splashing on the white porcelain.

How long was he there, bent over, crying into the sink?

When he could breathe again, he dried his face and forced his spine to straighten. Moving slowly, he went through the house, up the stairs. Every riser he took was a triumph, like bicycling up the Rockies. By the time he reached Betsy's door, he was breathing hard, sweating.

He paused at the door, wishing more than anything that he didn't have to tell them this . . . Then he went inside, remembering a second too late that he was supposed to knock, that adolescent girls demanded privacy.

They were on the bed together, watching the videotape of Jolene reading a bedtime story.

Michael wanted to stop right there, on the threshold to his daughter's room, and turn around. They wouldn't be the same after he gave them this news. They'd know, from now on, that bad things could happen, and they could happen fast, while you weren't even paying attention. Helicopters could be shot down. Mothers could be hurt . . . and worse.

He actually stumbled.

"You wanna watch Mommy read to me, Daddy?" Lulu asked.

Michael tried to move, but he just stood there, swaying slightly, holding the door frame for support. Then he lurched forward and snapped the TV off.

Betsy frowned. "What's the matter?"

In the silence that followed the question, Betsy's face drained of color. "Is it Mom?"

"Mommy's home?" Lulu said. "Yippeee! Where is she?"

Hope, Michael thought. He had to put his own fears aside and give them hope.

But what if it turned out to be false hope? He had no idea how injured Jolene was, or even if she would survive.

Shot down.

He swallowed hard, wiped his eyes before tears formed.

"Tell me," Betsy said grimly. It broke his heart to see how afraid she was and how hard she was trying to be grown-up. He picked his way past the clothes heaped on the floor and climbed up onto the bed. Lulu leaped onto his chest without warning.

"Where is she, Daddy?" Lulu asked, bouncing.

Michael sat up, stretched his legs out. "Come here, Betsy," he said quietly.

She moved cautiously across the bed, eyeing him the whole time, her mouth trembling, although she was trying to stop it, he could see.

"Mommy's been in an accident," he said when he had both of his daughters in his arms. "She's on her way to a really good hospital right now. And . . ." *She'll be fixed up.* He couldn't say it, couldn't make himself say the words.

Lulu pulled free, sat on his thighs, and looked at him. "Mommy got hurted?"

"Is she going to be okay?" Betsy asked softly.

Never in his life had Michael felt so painfully inadequate. "We have to believe she will be. We have to pray for her."

Betsy looked at him, her composure crumbling. The tears started falling; her whole body shook.

Lulu burst into tears.

Michael took them both in his arms, clinging to them, holding back his own tears.

They cried for what felt like hours. Finally, Lulu pulled back. Her black curly hair was damp and stuck to her pink cheeks. "If Mommy's hurted, will they give her ice cream? Remember how Mommy gave me ice cream when I fell down the stairs, Betsy?"

"Strawberry," Betsy said and Lulu nodded.

"With sprinkles."

Betsy wiped her eyes, sniffed hard. "Remember when she twisted her ankle at the beach last summer, Lulu? It got all swollen and purple and gross, and she said it didn't hurt at all. She only stopped running for, like, a day."

"And when that dog bited her at the grocery story, she was bleeding but it hardly hurted, remember? Cuz she's a soldier, that's what she said. She's army strong. Right, Daddy?"

Michael could only nod. To them, these stories were a comforting way to bring Jolene home, where she belonged, but all he could think about were helicopters hurtling to the desert floor, crashing, exploding—catastrophic injuries. He thought about the letters he hadn't sent to her during her deployment and the things he hadn't said and the things he had—*I don't love you anymore*—and he felt sick to his stomach.

He was grateful as hell when his mother showed up two hours later.

"Mommy's hurted, *Yia Yia*," Lulu said, starting to cry again.

His mother moved purposely forward. "Your mother is a warrior, Lucy Louida, and don't you forget it. She needs our happy thoughts right now. How about if you guys get into your pajamas and I read to you a story?"

Michael extricated himself from his daughters and got up. He was shaky on his feet as he moved toward his mother.

"Oh, Michael," she said softly as he approached, her voice wavering, her eyes filling with tears.

"Don't," he said, sidestepping her outstretched hand. He couldn't be comforted right now, not in front of his children. At his mother's touch, he might just crumble. He moved past her and kept walking out into the hallway.

He closed the door on them and went downstairs. For some time—he had no idea how long—he wandered around the house, just staring at things. The wedding picture in the bookcase, the end table they'd refinished together, the *You Are Special* plate that hung on the kitchen wall.

The phone rang, and he lurched for it. "Michael Zarkades."

"Hello, Mr. Zarkades. This is Maxine Soll, from the Red Cross."

He gripped the phone more tightly, thinking, *Please God, let her be okay.* "How is my wife?"

"Her helicopter was shot down in Al Anbar province last night. Because of heavy fighting, rescue was difficult. I don't have much in the way of details, and I can't give you information on the rest of her crew. But I do know she's alive and stable. She has been treated at Balad and is now on her way to Landstuhl, Germany."

Michael's relief was so great he actually sank to his knees on the kitchen floor. "Thank God," he murmured. He heard the Red Cross worker talking about the hospital, but he was barely listening.

He hung up the phone and went outside, where a cold black night surrounded him. *Jo, you'll be coming home now ... you'll be okay ...*

He was so caught in his own thoughts that it took him a moment to see the man standing on the dock across the street. Although he couldn't really make out the figure—could just see a silhouette in the glow from a distant streetlamp, he knew who it was.

He closed the door behind him and walked down the gravel driveway, hearing his footsteps crunch on the small gray stones. The night smelled of low tide, vaguely sulfuric.

"Carl?" he said, drawing near. "Lomand came to see you, too?"

Carl nodded. "I needed to get out of the house. Seth is . . . I don't know what the hell to say. Tami's mom is with him now."

"Yeah. My mom is with the girls, too. How is Tami?"

"Damn military and Red Cross haven't told me shit. She's alive. In critical condition. That's what I know. Jo?"

"Alive and stable. That's all I know. Nothing about the rest of the crew."

"I found a letter from Tami today. She'd e-mailed it before the mission, I guess. She sounded so . . ." Carl's tired voice trailed off for a moment. Then, quietly, he said, "Afterward, I read it again and thought, are these her last words?"

Michael had no idea what to say to that, so he said nothing. But he couldn't stand the silence, either. "You catching a flight tomorrow?" he finally asked.

"Yeah. You?"

"Yeah." Michael stared out at the black water, listening to it lap at the shore. The longer he stood there, the more ill at ease he felt. Finally, he and Carl had something in common, but it didn't exactly bring them together. "Well, I better get back to the girls. I'll see you tomorrow."

"Right." Carl paused, turned. "Thanks for coming down here, Michael."

Michael nodded and headed back up to the house, but once inside he almost wished he'd stayed with Carl. Everywhere he looked, he saw Jo.

I found a letter . . .

He went into his office and turned on the computer, then pulled up his e-mail.

And there it was in the in-box: Jolene's military e-mail address in bold, black type.

When had she written it? Yesterday, just before her flight?

He clicked on it.

My loves.

> *Thanks so much for the care packages you sent this week. I was the Queen of Dpod, I can tell you! Everyone wanted some of my tasty treats and the baklava was awesome. I took one bite and thought of*

all of you. Ask your Yia Yia *to tell you the story of when she taught me to make it. I was not her best student, that's for sure. Not as good as Betsy.* ☺

You know what else makes me think of home? The weather over here. It's September and that means rain, even in the desert. The base is one big mud hole. You'd love it, Lulu. Splash! Splash!

Things are pretty much routine over here these days. I've been flying a lot. Recently we flew to a place called the Green Zone and had made-to-order milkshakes. Yum!

The Black Hawk is getting to be my home away from home. It has so much equipment, the whole world is at my fingertips. Whenever I look at the GPS, I think of you guys and home and I count the days till I'm back.

Until then, I know how much you both miss me, and I want you to know I miss you just as much. You are the first thing I think of every morning and the last thing I think of at night.

Lulu, I can't wait to hear every little thing about your first day of school. I know you still feel a little scared, but try to remember that everyone feels the same way. Have you made any new friends? How is your teacher? Tell me everything!

Betsy, I know how lonely you sometimes feel these days. Middle school isn't easy for anyone, especially not for a girl who is worried about her mom and having troubles with her friends. Life is messy—especially now—it will help if you accept the mess and let it be. Don't be afraid to talk to Sierra about what scares you. Or Seth. Or your dad. You never know who will say just the thing you need to hear. And remember, a girlfriend can get you through the worst of times. I know because Tami is helping me every day over here.

One thing I see from here, from a distance, is how lucky we all are to have each other.

I love you both to the moon and back.
Mom

He sat back. I love you . . . *both*.

He deserved that, of course, but still it hurt. He'd thought his letter might have made a difference, but why would it? One letter—coming so late—could hardly undo the harm he'd done.

"Michael?" his mother said behind him, coming into the office.

Slowly, he turned. His chair squeaked. "There's a letter from Jo. The girls will want to read it in the morning."

"Come with me," she said.

He followed her out of the office and into the family room, where she sat down in the overstuffed chair by the window. He sank onto the sofa's deep cushions. Between them was an antique coffee table—Jolene's first "faux finishing" project—pale blue and covered with the detritus of family life. A pencil, two photographs in drugstore frames, a poorly fired thumb pot from one of the girls, an unread magazine. If Jolene had been here, it would have been cleaner.

"You need to be strong for your girls," his mother said. "All of them."

"Before she left," he said, knowing even as he formed the thought that he shouldn't speak it aloud—it would make her ashamed of him— but he couldn't help himself, "before she left I told her I didn't want to be married to her anymore."

His mother's face seemed to fall at that. "This is what she took away with her?"

"Yes."

"Oh, Michael." She sighed heavily. "I wondered. Her letters . . ."

"Are to the girls. Yeah."

"Well," she said. "You are an idiot, of course. But we've all been idiots when it comes to love. It's not as if your father and I never had our prob- lems. He once moved out—for six months. You were young. I made ex- cuses. I waited. It is a long story that doesn't matter anymore, except for this: he came back, and I took him in. We found a way to be happy again. So will you." She got up from her place and stepped around the coffee table. Sitting down on the sofa, she put an arm around him and pulled him against her, soothing his tattered nerves in the way that only a mother could. "I'll take care of the girls. You go to her, Michael."

They sat there a long time. When his mother finally fell asleep, Michael got up. He covered his mother's sleeping body with one of her own hand-knit blankets and wandered through the dark house. He checked on his daughters repeatedly, standing in the doorway and watching them sleep, hating the new life to which they would awaken. Unable to sleep, he started drinking coffee at 5:00 A.M., mostly because, although he couldn't sleep, he was so tired he kept stumbling, hitting things, knocking them over. Sometimes an image of Jolene, smiling, flashed through his mind, and it caused a kind of temporary blindness. That was when he'd stumble into a chair or knock over a family photo.

He was awakened by the doorbell. At the sound, he jerked upright—realizing he'd fallen asleep in a wooden kitchen chair. He got unsteadily to his feet and went to the door, opening it.

Three men stood there. They introduced themselves as Jolene's fellow guardsmen and offered to do whatever they could to help out. Out on the road, he saw a car turn into Carl and Tami's driveway. No doubt there were three more soldiers in that car, ready to render aid.

Michael tried to get rid of them—couldn't—and ended up showing them to the family room, where they stood together along the wall. They said they were prepared to do anything—drive carpool, grocery shop, mow the lawn.

"Ma?" he said, bending down to waken her.

"Huh?" Bleary-eyed, she sat up.

"There are some of—"

Before he could finish, the doorbell rang again.

This time it was four wives, standing on his porch, each holding a foil-covered casserole dish and a bag full of groceries. They gave him sad, knowing smiles and hugged him—all without tears—and then started organizing the food they'd brought. In no time the house smelled like frying bacon. They were making breakfast for the girls.

By nine o'clock, the girls had walked into this quiet, crowded house of theirs. Lulu had taken one look at the commotion and crawled up into her grandmother's lap. Betsy had put in her iPod earbuds; she sat in the corner, listening to music and playing some electronic game.

Michael was about to go say something to her when the doorbell rang again.

Exhausted by the thought of more help, he went to the door and opened it.

In his rumpled state, it took him a moment to process what he was seeing. A familiar-looking woman with a pert little haircut, wearing too much makeup, stood on his porch. She was holding a microphone. "I'm Dianna Vigan from KOMO TV. Are you Michael Zarkades?"

He nodded dully, noticing that people had begun to place bouquets along the fence line. Someone had tied a yellow ribbon around the stanchion beneath their mailbox.

"Your wife flew into battle with her best friend as her copilot, Warrant Officer Tamara Flynn? I understand they met in flight school when they were still teenagers. You must be so proud of your wife. How do—"

"No comment." He slammed the door and stepped back, so upset that it took him a minute to notice that the room had gone quiet. The guardsmen and the wives—and his family—were all staring at him. He had failed in some way; that was obvious. What was it they wanted him to say? That he was proud of her? *Proud* that she'd been shot down?

How could they expect that of him? How could he even form the word now, when his world was falling apart?

Sixteen

It was one of those foggy days in Seattle, where it seemed there was no sky at all, just layers and layers of gray. Jolene could hear the ferry's foghorn in the distance, rippling like the water it floated above; a seagull cawed.

Betsy loves feeding those gulls. How many times had they stood on the ferry deck, hand in hand, lashed by a cold wind, throwing food to the beady-eyed birds who seemed to float so effortlessly?

A car horn honked.

She frowned, confused.

The sound changed, became an insistent *beep-beep-beep.*

She realized suddenly that her eyes were closed. Her mouth was so dry she couldn't swallow. No. There was something in her mouth.

She came awake slowly, fought to open her eyes.

Overhead, instead of sky, was a white ceiling tracked with harsh lighting. She blinked. There were machines clustered around her, tall stands with monitor heads, like thin washed-out mourners, clucking and beeping.

The something in her mouth was a tube. Another tube went into her chest from the machine to her right.

A giant sucking sound came and went, rising and falling.

She heard footsteps, then a door opened, closed.

She needed to *think*. Where was she? What had happened?

A tall man in a white coat came to her bedside. He was wearing purple gloves and a white mask over his nose and mouth. He pushed back the curtains that created a semicircle of privacy.

A bed. Yes. That was it. She was in a bed.

"Chief," the man said. "You're awake."

She tried to speak, but the tube made her gag.

Pain. She was in *pain*. It came to her suddenly, swallowed her; had it been there all along? Beside her, a monitor started to beep faster.

"Calm down, Chief," the stranger said through his mask. "You've been in a terrible accident. Do you remember? Your helicopter was shot down."

His voice drew out the word, elongated it: ac-ci-dent.

Smoke. Burning bits of metal. *Tami.*

Adrenaline surged through her. Pain spiked—where was it coming from? She couldn't tell, couldn't isolate it.

She wanted to ask about Tami, about her crew, but she couldn't make anything work. She stared up at the stranger, thinking *please . . .*

She imagined herself reaching out, grabbing the man's arm, demanding to know how her crew was, but she couldn't do any of it. She thought of Tami, remembered holding her, promising her they'd be okay.

Blood on her face . . . everywhere.

The man did something to the bag hanging by her bed, and, slowly, the fog came back, rolled around her, softened the view until she was far away from here. She was on her own back porch, with her feet up on the railing, listening to the high squeak of Lulu's voice as she ran around the yard and to the even, reliable whooshing of the distant waves.

Pain snapped her awake.

Jolene opened her eyes, gasping, desperate to fill her lungs with air.

The tube was out of her mouth now. How long had she been here, drifting in and out of consciousness?

She couldn't track the passing of time. When she woke, it was a barely there kind of waking; she was foggy, confused. A few times nurses had come into her room, and she'd pleaded with them for news, but all she ever got were *poor you* looks of sadness and a promise to call the captain, but if he'd ever came back, she'd been asleep.

She was awake now, though. Her bed was angled up a little, and some of the machines were gone. The overhead lights were harsh, unforgiving. In the small window to the right she could see that it was rainy. For a muddy, drawn-out second, she thought she was home . . .

She studied the room—saw the small metal chair positioned by the window, and a TV tucked up in the corner between the wall and the ceiling, and gray-painted walls. Then she slowly looked down. Her right arm was in a white plaster cast from elbow to wrist. But that wasn't what got her attention.

Her right leg hardly looked like a leg at all. It was positioned on top of the crisp white covers, bent just a little at the knee. From midthigh down it was a swollen, blackened, festering mess; it looked like an overcooked sausage against the snowy sheets. Four big metal screws held it together, kept it a leg at all. A hose connected the leg to a vacuum of some kind that sucked fluids from the wound, collected them in a plastic bag. At the ankle, splinters of bone jutted out. And the smell . . . it was terrible, part burn, part rot.

She gagged at the sight of it, clamped a hand over her mouth; bile pushed up her throat. "Oh, my God . . ." she whispered.

Her door opened, and a tall man in a white coat walked into the room. "You're awake," he said, pulling a mask up over his mouth and nose.

He came up to the other side of the bed, stood beside her. "I'm Captain Sands."

"H-how's my crew?"

"Chief, you need to stay calm."

Jolene struggled to move, but she had no strength in her upper body.

The meager effort left her breathing hard, sweating. "My crew ... and Tami," she asked quietly, looking up. "Chief Flynn?"

"Chief Flynn is upstairs."

"She's alive," Jolene said, slumping back into the pillows. "Thank God. Can I talk to her?"

"Not yet, Chief. She suffered a traumatic brain injury. We're monitoring her very closely."

"Hix?"

"Sergeant Hix is here, too. He took some shrapnel to his thigh, but he's healing quickly. Your other gunner, Owen Smith, didn't survive the crash. I'm sorry."

"Oh, my God." Smitty. She remembered his bright smile ... and the gaping hole in his chest. *I'm holding this space for you, Chief. I'd want to talk to my mom.*

"Now, Chief, can we talk about you?" the doctor asked gently.

She looked up at him blearily, hating the pity she saw in his eyes. "I'm dying. Is that what you're going to tell me?"

"You were seriously injured, Jolene. I won't lie to you about that. Infection is the biggest concern in blast injuries like yours. Everything gets embedded—dirt, glass, bits of metal. We're worried about gangrene in your leg. We're debriding it every day. And you lost so much blood, we're concerned about your liver and kidney function. You're also scheduled for surgery today on your right hand. Shrapnel damaged a nerve in your wrist. We're hopeful you'll regain some use of it, though."

Some use of it.

"The wounds on your face should heal in time, but we're watching them closely. Again, it's the blast injuries."

She fought the urge to touch her cheeks. *My face.*

She closed her eyes so that he wouldn't see how scared she was, but it was a mistake. In the darkness of her fear, she saw her children standing together, crying out for her, begging her to come home. "Please," she whispered, hating the tremble in her voice. She was a *soldier,* for God's sake, and she couldn't make herself look this man in the eyes. "I can't die. I have children, Captain. Please."

He touched her left hand. She felt the cool rubber of his glove on her skin—no human contact; but what difference would it have made? What good was a stranger's touch when everything she was hung in such precarious balance?

She needed Michael here now. He would take care of her.

Michael, whose love had saved her once before. In the back of her mind, she knew there was a problem with Michael, something that had gone wrong, but then the morphine kicked in and began soothing her, and she was with her husband again, holding his hand, walking along the beach with the man she loved . . .

At two o'clock, on the day CNN announced Jolene's accident to the world, Michael and Carl boarded a plane bound for Germany.

They landed in Frankfurt on a cold black night, where rain drizzled anemically on the endless concrete buildings and runways of the airport.

When they finally emerged from customs, carrying their suitcases, Michael looked around. "They said they'd send someone to meet us," he said to Carl. Moments later, a young uniformed man approached them. "Mr. Zarkades? Mr. Flynn?"

"That's us," Carl said. "I'm Flynn."

The young soldier handed Michael a small clear plastic bag. In it were Jolene's wedding ring and her dog tags and her old watch, its face cracked. He stared down at them. In twelve years, he'd never seen Jolene without her wedding ring. *This is real,* he thought. He was going to see his wife who'd been wounded in war. "Thank you," he said hoarsely.

The soldier led them through the airport and into a waiting car. A short drive took them to the Landstuhl Regional Medical Center.

Rain blew in windy sheets across the entrance. Inside the neon brightness of the lobby, Michael and Carl were immediately sucked into a whirlwind of military protocol—there were doctors, nurses, chaplains, and liaison officers waiting to greet them. Everyone stood tall and straight and unsmiling, wearing purple rubber gloves. More than once, Michael demanded to be taken to see his wife, but there was always a reason to wait.

He began to pace, then to get angry. "Damn military," he muttered, moving up and down the busy aisle. When a neurosurgeon came to take Carl away, Michael had had it.

He marched up to the nurse's station again. "I'm Michael Zarkades. I've flown halfway around the world to see my wife, Jolene Zarkades. She's a warrant officer, if that matters. I'm sick to death of waiting. Just tell me where her damn room is."

The nurse glanced up from a file. "Captain Sands has asked you to wait. He wants to brief you himself. I'm sorry, sir—"

Behind them, pandemonium broke out. Michael turned just in time to see a stream of soldiers on gurneys coming through the front doors. Doctors and nurses appeared instantly; a priest came, took one soldier's hand in his own, made the sign of the cross.

Michael leaned over the counter, saw Jolene's room number on her file, and headed for the elevators.

"MAYDAY!" Jolene screamed, waking up from a nightmare. She jack-knifed to a sit, and at the movement pain exploded on her right side. Gasping, she slumped back into the pillows.

As usual, the first thing she noticed when she opened her eyes was her horrible, stinking excuse for a leg. The *whoosh-thunk* of the wound vacuum was so loud it drowned out everything else, even the pounding of her heart. The pain was excruciating, overwhelming.

But more than her own pain, she thought about Tami: Tami and Smitty and Jamie.

All her life she'd been an optimist, forced herself to be. That shiny hope was gone now. What if Tami didn't survive? And what in the hell would she say to Smitty's mother? *He showed me your picture about a dozen times ... that one where you were playing tennis ...*

It was her fault. All of it. How would she live with this guilt? Did she even want to?

She reached for the morphine-drip button, thinking that she could sleep through this horror.

Then, through a break in the curtains around her bed, she saw him. Michael.

Michael argued with the nurse and lost.

"You should wait for Doctor Sands. But either way, you are not going in there without a mask and gloves," the woman said firmly.

"Fine." He snatched the mask and gloves and walked away. Putting them on, he paused outside his wife's door, took a deep breath, and went inside.

It occurred to him suddenly, sharply, that maybe he shouldn't have come rushing in like this, maybe he should have waited to hear about Jolene's prognosis . . .

There was a curtain around half of her bed; he couldn't see her from here. "Jolene?"

He closed the door behind him. The first thing he noticed was the smell. There was a putrid stench in the air that made him almost sick to his stomach. Bile rose up in his throat, choked him.

He wet his lips nervously and moved forward, opening the curtain.

He hardly recognized his wife. The right side of her face was scored with bloody, oozing sores, and the left side was bruised and swollen. A deep gash along her jaw had been stitched. Her lips were dry and cracked. Lank hair hung lifelessly from a side part.

But it was the leg that startled him. If you could even call it a leg. Blackened, peeling, bent, and broken, it was twice its normal size; huge metal screws held it in place at the knee and ankle. A pale bone jutted out from blue-black flesh. And the smell . . .

For a terrible, humiliating second, he thought he was going to be sick.

He breathed shallowly, and only through his mouth, through the mask, but still the smell was there. He knew he needed to be stronger right now, to think of her, but it felt as if he were drowning. He couldn't catch his breath, get steady.

"Jo," he said softly, his voice creaky, his breathing accelerated. "I'm so sorry," he said finally—*finally*—finding the strength to look at her. He knew pity and horror were in his eyes; there was nothing he could do about it. He shouldn't have come in here, not so unprepared. She needed him to be strong and certain now, and he couldn't do it. "I didn't talk to the doctor . . . I didn't know. I should have waited . . ." He started to reach for her hand and saw the bruising, then drew back. "I don't want to hurt you."

"Too late for that," she said quietly, tears glittering in her eyes.

"Jolene—"

She turned her bloody, swollen face away from him. "Tami was wrong," she said softly, more to herself than to him.

"What? What about Tami?"

"It's too late for us, Michael. You were right about that." Her voice broke on the sentence, made him feel even worse. She reached out and pushed the morphine button, and in no time, she was asleep.

Seventeen

He'd let her down, again. He'd seen her injured leg and panicked, just panicked. Why had no one warned him? If he'd known, maybe he would have been able to mask his initial reaction.

Maybe. But honestly, he doubted it. Her injuries had overwhelmed him. How was he supposed to help her?

"Mr. Zarkades?"

He turned, saw a tall, gray-haired man in a white coat walk into the room. Above a surgical mask, his gray eyes were serious.

"I'm sorry for the delay, Mr. Zarkades. Emergencies happen fast around here. I'm Captain Sands. Jim. I wanted to talk to you before you saw her."

Michael felt a rush of shame again, then anger—at himself, at the military, at this man who hadn't shown up in time, at God. "That would have been nice."

"Come with me," Sands said, leading him out into the busy hallway. There were nurses everywhere out here, running from room to room.

"As I'm sure you can tell," Sands said as Jolene's door clicked shut. "Your wife has sustained some serious injuries. There are a lot of concerns now but the biggest is infection. Blast wounds, such as hers, are particularly dangerous. You can't imagine what finds its way into the wound. Bacteria is rampant. We're debriding the leg daily—taking her into surgery and cleaning it—but to be honest, I'm not hopeful."

"What does that mean, not hopeful?"

"There's a chance she'll lose her leg. We don't know about her right hand yet, whether she'll regain use of it."

"How can I help her?"

"We're doing all we can. The injuries to her face will heal quickly."

Michael thanked the doctor and went back to stand by Jolene's bed. He was there for hours, staring down at her, waiting for her to waken. He felt sick with the need to apologize to her, to recast his reaction. To be a better man. He'd grown so much in her absence, and then, at the first chance to show her those changes, he had failed. Utterly.

Finally, exhausted, he left her room and headed out of the hospital. But as he approached the elevators, he thought of Carl and Tami. He asked a nurse where the ICU was and then took the elevator up one floor to Tami's room.

Through the window, he saw Carl standing at his wife's bedside, his head bent forward, tears running down his cheeks. Michael was about to leave, but Carl looked up and saw him. Wiping his eyes, straightening, Carl walked away from the bed, came to the door, opened it.

"How is she?" Michael asked.

"Traumatic brain injury." Carl shrugged. "It means she may wake up and she may not. She may be perfectly fine and she may not. They took out a piece of her skull because her brain is swelling. How's Jo?"

Michael was surprised at the tears that stung his eyes. He didn't bother wiping them away. "She may lose her leg, and her right hand is useless for now."

They stared at each other. It should have been comforting, but it wasn't. Michael couldn't stand here with this man he hardly knew, trading fear back and forth. "Well. I'm heading to the Landstuhl House," he said. It was a place built by some American philanthropist to house the families of wounded soldiers.

"I'm going to sleep here tonight. I had them bring me a bed."

Michael should have thought of that. He mumbled something about seeing Carl tomorrow and headed out of the hospital. Less than thirty minutes later, he was settled into a small, well-appointed room with a bathroom en suite and a double bed in the Landstuhl House.

As he sat on his uncomfortable bed, staring at nothing and remembering everything, he tried to figure out a way to undo the mistake he'd made today. How would he convince Jolene that he'd changed when he'd acted exactly as she must have expected him to?

At the time they'd agreed upon, he called home. Betsy answered. In the middle of his hello, she said, "How's Mom?"

What should he say? The truth would probably give her nightmares, but she needed to be prepared for the worst, didn't she? He might have handled it better if he'd been prepared. He leaned back against the cheap, wobbly headboard. "She says she's feeling a little better and she can't wait to talk to you."

"But what's wrong with her?"

He paused. Now was the time to say something, the right thing, to calm his daughter's fears and allow her to hope. He turned through the choices—lies or the truth—and came up with half-truths. "Her right hand and ankle are . . . hurt. They're working to fix them up now."

"She's left-handed, so that's good," Betsy said.

"Yeah," he said hoarsely.

"Dad? What aren't you telling me?"

He cleared his throat. "Nothing, Betsy. We don't know everything yet, that's all. They're still running some tests. I'm sure that soon—"

"You think I'm a baby. Lulu!" she yelled, "Dad's on the phone. He wants to tell you that Mom got shot down but she's fine."

"Betsy—"

"Daddy?" Lulu squeaked. "Mommy's all better? Did they give her ice cream?" He ran a hand through his hair and sighed. He talked to Lulu for a few minutes, although, honestly, he had no idea what either one of them said, and then his mother was on the phone.

"How is she, Michael?"

"I let her down, Ma," he said softly, more to himself than to her. He knew instantly that it was a mistake, not the sort of thing he should have said to his mother, but he needed advice right now, and what good was advice based on bad information?

"She'll let you know what she needs, Michael. Just listen to her."

They talked for a few more moments. After he hung up, he closed his eyes, thinking that he would never be able to sleep, but, before he knew it, sunlight was streaming into the room, and he was blinking awake.

The bedside clock said seven fifteen.

He got out of bed, feeling old and tired. By the time he'd showered and shaved and dressed for the day, he felt a little better.

Until he stood at Jolene's bedside, and it all came rushing back—the fear, the guilt, the anger. He was afraid she would lose her right leg and use of her hand, and in losing them become someone else. He couldn't imagine how it would feel to be so wounded, to lose so much. How could she get back to who she had been?

He felt guilty that he worried about her limbs when her life hung in the balance, and he was pissed off that she'd put herself in harm's way and been wounded and now neither one of them would be the same.

He hated his own weakness, felt as if he were stewing in this pot of his own worst traits. He wanted to be the kind of man who just wanted her to live, in any condition—and he did, he was that man—but he was the other man, too, the one that couldn't imagine looking at her in the same way if she lost her leg and couldn't use her hand.

He moved in closer, careful not to disturb the tubes coming out of her.

Her face looked flushed; beneath the yellow and purple bruising, her skin had a reddish cast, and she was sweating profusely, breathing shallowly. Dirty, greasy hair flanked her injured face. Her lips were chapped and cracked and peeling, colorless. It made him think that he should have ChapStick with him. The smell was worse today, like garbage left out on a hot day. He fought the urge to gag.

He glanced down the blanket. Her right leg, on top of the blanket, was still swollen and awkward looking, the foot turned almost unnaturally to the right. That vacuum sucked and wheezed, drawing viscous yellow liquid from the wound.

He heard her come awake, heard the catch in her breathing.

"Mi . . . chael," she said, her head lolling sideways to look at him. Her gaze was glassy, unfocused. "You're . . . here . . . thass nice . . ."

"I was here before, remember?"

She frowned, licked her lips. "You were?"

"Jo?" He had so much to say to her, but where should he start? It was hard enough to undo damage done in a marriage without all of this. He brushed the hair from her face and felt her forehead.

She was burning up.

"Wait . . ." she said, drawing the word out. "You doan love me . . ."

Michael hit the nurse's button. When a woman came in, he said, "She's burning up."

The nurse pushed him aside so hard he stumbled back. Within seconds, the room was full of people, taking Jolene's temperature, pulling back the covers. A nurse unwrapped the gauze on her leg.

The smell almost made him sick.

"Get her to the OR, stat." This was Dr. Sands. When had he come in?

"Wait," Michael said, surging toward her, bending down. "I love you, Jolene . . . I do."

It was too late; she was unconscious. He stood there while they wheeled her away.

She is crawling through the thick, sucking mud, carrying her best friend. "Hang on, Tami . . . don't you die . . . I'll get us there . . ."

But where are they going, where is she taking Tami?

Somewhere close by a bomb hits. The sky is full of fire and bullets and burning bits of steel. A helicopter hits the ground and bursts into flames.

She throws her body over Tami's, trying to protect her, but when the night stills and she draws back, Tami is shriveling up in front of her, bleeding through her nose ... her mouth ... her eyes. There's blood everywhere, and smoke. Jolene screams, "NOOOOO!"

She came awake, still screaming.

It took her a second to remember where she was: in a hospital. In Germany.

She moved with extreme caution, lifting her head off the pillow. She felt woozy and unfocused, a little sick to her stomach. Through slitted lids, she saw the machines around her. That whooshing, sucking vacuum was gone. So was the smell of rotting flesh. Now she smelled antiseptic and plastic.

She tried to rise on one elbow, but the effort winded her. Breathing hard, dizzy, she stared down at her legs.

Leg.

From about the knee down, the right side of her bed was a flat expanse of white blankets. She had a distant, watery memory of recovery, of seeing nurses and doctors come and go, monitoring her progress.

They had amputated her leg. Cut it off at the knee.

She grabbed a pillow and covered her mouth and howled in grief and pain; she screamed until her throat was parched and her eyes were stinging and her chest ached. She imagined her new life, off-balance, differently abled, broken, and each image was a scab she had to pick—no more flying Black Hawks or running along the beach or picking up her children and twirling them around on a summer's day.

Finally, exhausted, she slumped back into the pillows and closed her eyes. The grief gave way to a yawning sense of despair. Here she was, her leg cut off, lying in a hospital bed far from home, without a best friend to talk to or a husband to hold her.

Michael.

She released a heavy breath at the thought of him.

He would stay with her now; that was who he was. Michael Zarkades had a strong sense of duty. He would see that she was broken, and he would step back into the marriage where he belonged. Pity would bring him back to her; duty would make him stay. That was why he was here, after all. The dutiful husband standing by his broken wife.

Someone touched her face gently. She opened her eyes slowly, worked to focus. The meds were still in her system, making her unsteady.

Michael smiled tiredly down at her. The shirt he wore, an expensive black turtleneck, hung strangely, as if he'd been pulling on the fabric at his throat, stretching it out. Of course he touched her gently. She was damaged now, crippled; he would be afraid to touch her, afraid that what was left of her would break. "Hey, sleepyhead," he said, "welcome back."

"Michael," she said, feeling inestimably sad. "Why are you here?" She had to concentrate to make her voice work. She felt so groggy.

"You're my wife."

She swallowed; her throat was dry. Her thoughts jangled around her head. "You wanted a divorce."

"Jo, I've been trying to tell you since I got here: I love you. I was an idiot. Forgive me."

It was what she'd waited months to hear, dreamed of almost every night in the desert, ached for, and now . . . she didn't care. His words were meaningless. She pushed her morphine pump and prayed for the drug to work quickly.

"Give us a chance, Jo. You need me now."

"I've never needed anyone." She sighed. "And thank God for that."

"Jo, please . . ."

"You want to help me, Michael? Go home. Get the house ready for a cripple. Get my girls ready. It won't be easy for them to see me like this. They'll need to be prepared." She closed her eyes, feeling useless tears again. Thankfully, the morphine kicked in, and slowly, slowly, she felt herself drifting away.

Michael leaned down and kissed her cheek. The soft, familiar feel of his lips on her skin nearly did her in. She almost reached for him, almost told him how scared she was and how much she needed him.

Instead, she said, "Go . . . way . . ." She refused to need him anymore.

As if from far away, she heard his footsteps as he walked away, heard the door swoosh open and click shut. At the last minute, she thought: *Come back.* But it was too late. He was gone, and she was falling asleep.

Her last conscious thought was a list of what she'd lost: Running. Flying. Being beautiful and whole. Being strong. Picking up her children. Michael.

Eighteen

Twenty-four hours after they cut off Jolene's leg, they wanted her to get out of bed. At first she fought with the nurses who came to put her in a wheelchair, and then she realized the opportunity it presented: she could see Tami.

Now she was out of bed and in a wheelchair.

"Are you comfortable, ma'am?" the young nurse asked, helping Jolene settle into the chair.

How many days had passed since she'd climbed into the pilot's seat of a Black Hawk helicopter? Now she needed assistance just to sit in a vinyl chair. Her gauze-wrapped stump stuck out in front of her. "I'm fine. Thank you. I'm going to see Chief Tami Flynn. In ICU."

"I'll push you."

She couldn't even do *that* by herself because of her bum right hand. The nurse positioned herself behind the wheelchair and rolled Jolene out of the room.

The ortho ward was full of patients like her—their limbs shattered or broken or gone. Most of them were men, and so young. Just boys, by the looks of them; one even wore braces.

That made her think of Smitty.

Smitty, with his bright smile and gawky walk and horsey laugh; Smitty, who drank Mountain Dews one after another and swore that girls were dying to get into his pants. Smitty, who had been so excited to go to Iraq.

We're going to kick some ass over there, Chief. Aren't we?

Too young to have a beer but old enough to keep his head calm in battle and die for his country.

In the elevator, she had nowhere to look except down—at the part of her that jutted out, bandaged white, useless.

Stump.

She looked away quickly, feeling sick. And ashamed. How could you live when you didn't have the courage to look at your own body? The doctors and nurses seemed unconcerned with her cowardice. Repeatedly they'd told her it was normal to be squeamish and afraid, that it was normal to grieve for a lost limb. They assured her that someday she would be her old self again.

Liars.

On the third floor, they rolled out of the elevator and headed through the busy ICU hallway. Here, as before, the personnel were in constant motion.

The nurse stopped outside a closed door. On the metal surface, someone had taped up the soldier's creed. Not someone. Carl. He had put up these words for his wife, because he understood her so well. He knew what Tami would want everyone coming into her room to know: a soldier lay in this bed.

Jolene hadn't read these words in years.

I am an American Soldier.
I am a warrior and a member of a team.
I serve the people of the United States, and live the Army Values.
I will always place the mission first.
I will never accept defeat. (This had been underlined.)
I will never quit.
I will never leave a fallen comrade.

*I am disciplined, physically and mentally tough, trained
and proficient in my warrior task and drills.
I always maintain my arms, my equipment and myself.
I am an expert and I am a professional.
I stand ready to deploy, engage, and destroy the enemies
of the United States of America in close combat.
I am a guardian of freedom and the American way of life.
I am an American Soldier.*

Jolene swallowed hard.

The nurse opened the door and wheeled her into the small high-tech room. Carl sat by the bed, his hands in his lap.

"Jolene," Carl said, getting to his feet. She could tell by the way he moved that he'd been sitting a long time. "I'll take her from here," Carl said to the nurse, who placed a hand on Jolene's shoulder, left it there long enough to make a point, then left the room.

Carl bent down and lightly kissed Jolene's bruised cheek. She reached up with her good hand and held his hand. "How is she, Carl?"

He shrugged. "Apparently no one can say anything for certain when it comes to brain injuries. She's in a coma. We'll know more when she wakes up."

He wheeled her to the bedside. Jolene hated how low she was, like a kid looking up. Already she'd learned how different the world looked from a seated position. Still, she saw Tami's profile. Her friend's face was black and blue and misshapen. She looked like she'd gone twelve rounds with Mike Tyson. A gash split her swollen upper lip. Bandages covered her head, the gauze darkened here and there by blood soaking through. "Help me stand," Jolene said quietly.

Carl helped her out of the chair, positioned himself beside her, holding her upright.

"Hey, flygirl," Jolene said. She wanted to touch Tami's hand, but it took all her strength and concentration to hold herself upright. She clutched the bedrail with her one good hand. "I'm sorry," she whispered.

"She would be pissed to hear you say that," Carl said quietly.

Jolene nodded. It was true. Tami would have hated to hear that Jolene felt guilty about the crash, but how could she not? "I wonder if she knows we're here?"

"She knows."

Jolene wanted to believe that. She felt a sudden rush of loss, of grief. They had been best friends for more than twenty years. Tami was as rooted in Jolene's soul as Michael and the girls. The thought of losing her . . .

No. She wouldn't think that way. "You'll come back to us, Tam. I know you will. You're probably just doing this for attention."

She told Tami about her own injury, and about Smitty, and about Jamie, who was recovering in a room just one floor down, and who asked about Tami every day. She talked about home, and the beach, and the summer they would spend collecting sand dollars and flying kites.

"We'll run along the beach again, both of us." She heard her own words and lost steam. Tears scalded her eyes, fell, and all she could do was plead. "Come back, Tam."

"What if—"

"*No.* She's not going to die," she said softly. "You hear me, flygirl? No dying allowed. If I have to live with one leg and one arm, I will need you." At that, she realized the gravity of it all, the looming loss, and she closed her eyes, thinking, *come back.*

She held on to the slick metal rail. Her leg was starting to ache, but she didn't move. She wanted to stand here until Tami woke up.

She stared down at her best friend, seeing the whole of their lives in a second—the girls they'd been together, in uniforms, in cockpits, wanting so desperately to prove themselves . . . and the women they'd become and the battles they'd weathered together, the jokes they'd shared. They'd been together forever, side by side, listening to everything from Madonna to Tim McGraw, keeping each other strong. Army strong.

"They're sending me home soon," she said to Carl.

"That's great news," he said.

Jolene looked at him. The thought of going home, of leaving Tami behind, was more than she could bear. "How can I leave her?"

"You have to," he said gently. "She would want you to. Go home to your kids, Jolene."

How long did she spend with Tami and Carl? Minutes? Hours? She didn't know. As she stayed with her friend, time lost all meaning, even the pain in her leg was put aside. She kept trying to find the right words to say to Carl, a perfect way to package hope and hand it over, but as the minutes passed, she faded. There was no other word for it. Finally, they ended up sitting in a painful silence, and Jolene called the nurse and asked to be taken back to her room.

In her own bed, she closed her eyes and tried not to think about the worst things—about Tami not waking up and Smitty never coming home.

She was vaguely aware of people coming and going, checking on her, adjusting her medications and tending to her residual leg—lifting, wrapping, cleaning. Hours passing. She tried to keep her eyes closed and ignore it all.

"Jo?"

She heard Michael's voice and felt a wave of exhaustion. "I thought I asked you to go home."

"You didn't mean it. I've been trying to tell you I love you, Jo. And I'm sorry."

She didn't care. Not anymore. What good was an unreliable love? Slowly she turned her head, looked up into his eyes. "Go home and take care of our children, Michael. Please." Her voice broke. "Please. They'll need you. I don't."

"Jolene—"

Tears stung her eyes. "Go, Michael. I'll be home in a few days. They're getting ready to release me. You know that. You can't fly home with me anyway. Go. Take care of our children. That's how you can help me."

"Okay," he said slowly, as if maybe he knew it was the wrong thing to do, but he was glad to get the chance to do it. "I'll go. But I'll be home, waiting for you, when you get there."

"Lucky me," she murmured, closing her eyes.

On the long flight home, Michael told himself he was doing what Jolene had asked of him, and there were moments when he believed it. But most of the time, he knew the truth: he was running away, just as he'd done when his father was dying. It was a failing in him, bruise-like, purplish and ugly. He couldn't stand seeing people he loved in pain.

Worse than the shame was the guilt. He kept thinking that he'd caused all of this. He'd broken Jolene's heart with careless words and then sent her off to war while he simmered in righteous anger and blamed *her* for making a dangerous choice.

He would give anything to take back that one night when he'd ruined everything. If he'd sent her off to war with love, would she have come back to him whole? Would she have been stronger then? Would she have turned her helicopter a split second faster?

He knew the answer to that question was no. Jolene was an outstanding pilot, and if she had one great skill from her screwed-up childhood, it was the ability to compartmentalize pain and keep going.

Now he was almost home. When the ferry docked on Bainbridge Island, he drove off the boat and over the Agate Pass Bridge, past the fireworks stands—empty now until Christmas, when they would become tree lots—and through the postcard-perfect town of Poulsbo.

On the bookstore marquee, he saw the first sign: *JOLENE ZARKADES AND TAMI FLYNN, YOU ARE IN OUR PRAYERS. COME HOME SAFELY.*

There were similar signs everywhere, and big yellow ribbons decorated telephone poles and porch rails and fence posts.

On the way out of town, the yellow ribbons continued—on mailboxes and front doors and autumn-leaved apple trees.

As he approached the house, he could see that the fence line was decorated with more yellow ribbons. The flag on their porch hung slack on this windless night. Bouquets lay on the ground beneath one of the posts, like a grave site, their petals dying and turning brown.

He pulled into the garage and sat there, alone, in the dark. Sighing, he finally went into the house.

His mother was seated on the hearth, in front of a bright fire. At his entrance, she peered up at him from above the jewel-encrusted reading glasses she bought in a six-pack from Costco. Putting down her book, she stood, opening her arms.

He walked into her embrace, not realizing how much he needed a hug until her arms were around him.

"Tell me everything," she said, leading him to the sofa.

He started with: "I should have waited for the doctor, but you know how impatient I am," and he told her everything, ending with, "She asked me to come back here and get the house—and the girls—ready for her homecoming."

"You shouldn't have left her," his mother said.

"You told me to listen to her, that she'd tell me what she needed."

"Michael," his mother said, shaking her head.

"I know." He raked a hand through his hair, sighing. "She threw me out."

His mother made the tsking sound he knew so well. "Men are stupid. I'm sorry, but it's true. *Please leave* doesn't mean she wanted you to actually do it."

"I'm not a mind reader."

"Clearly."

"I don't want to have this conversation. I feel shitty enough. I don't need you making it worse."

She looked at him. "Your wife is in Germany, wounded and afraid, and you left her there alone, grieving for her lost crewman and worried about her best friend. Do you really think it can get worse, Michael?"

"I don't know what to do, Ma. I've never been good at this shit."

"Here's what you do, Michael. You go upstairs and tell your children about their mother. Then you hold them when they cry and you get your family—and this house—ready for your wife's return. You don't make the same mistake again. Next time, you look at Jolene—all of her, Michael, even what's missing—and you tell her you love her. You do love her, don't you?"

"I do. But she won't believe me. Not now."

"Who would? You have been foolish. You will have to swallow your pride and convince her . . . and yourself, perhaps. It will not be easy, nor should it." She patted his thigh. "And now, you will go up and tell your daughters that their mother is coming home from war."

"Are they in bed?"

"They're waiting for you."

He sighed at that, feeling instantly tired, weighed down by this new burden that seemed to be his alone to carry. He leaned sideways, kissed his mom's cheek, and headed for the stairs.

Outside Betsy's room, he paused, gathering up his courage. He knocked on the door and went into the room. The girls were on the floor, playing some board game.

Michael knelt between them. Lulu immediately climbed onto his bent knees and looped her arms around his neck, leaning back like a pair's ice-skater in a twirl. "Hi, Daddy!"

"How is she?" Betsy asked warily.

Lulu bounced on his lap. "You wanna play Candyland, Daddy?"

"Dad?" Betsy said. "How is Mom?"

He drew in a deep breath. "She lost her leg."

Lulu stilled. "Where is it?"

"They cut it off, stupid," Betsy said, scrambling backward, getting to her feet.

"What?" Lulu shrieked.

"Betsy," Michael snapped, "don't scare your sister. Lulu, Mommy's going to be fine, she just lost part of her leg. But she'll still be able to walk and everything. She'll need our help for a while, though. She's coming home in three days."

"Mom lost her leg and Tami is in a coma, but everyone is going to be fine. We're all going to be fine, just like we were." Betsy's voice broke, and she ran to the door, yanking it open. "You and Mom are both liars," she said, wiping her eyes. Then she walked out of the room and slammed the door shut behind her.

"But where's her leg, Daddy?" Lulu said, starting to cry.

"Jo?"

She heard Jamie's voice and opened her eyes.

Jamie stood in the doorway, dressed in his ACUs.

"Hey." She smiled at him, tried to look strong. She had no courage these days, it seemed, no inner strength. It was just so damned good to see him up and walking, even if it was with a limp. He'd visited her yesterday, too.

Closing the door behind him, he walked into the room. The look in his eyes was so compassionate she almost started to cry again. He knew what she was feeling.

"It's not your fault, Jo," he said.

"Smitty's gone. Tami's in a coma. I was flying the aircraft," Jolene said.

"You carried her out of the helicopter, Jo. You." He looked down at her amputated leg. "On that. You carried your best friend. I saw you, as I was scrambling, trying like hell to get Smitty out. I got him out, but it was too late."

She saw the guilt Jamie carried.

"I saw him, Jamie. He was already gone."

He stared down at her. "Don't you give up," he said in a hoarse voice.

"I don't know how to be this woman." She indicated her ruined body.

"You're a soldier, Jo. That's inside."

"Is it?"

"I've been ordered back to Iraq," he said at last.

She nodded, a lump in her throat. It occurred to her that she had just been more honest with this man than she'd ever been with her husband. "Be safe, Jamie."

He stared down at her a long time. "You're my hero, Chief. I want you to know that. And I'll miss you up there in the sky."

Then he was gone and she was alone.

SEPT.

I'm supposed to be glad I write with my left hand. I hear that a lot. But how can I be happy about anything?

I'm going home tomorrow and Tami still hasn't woken up. Carl says the doctors have started to shake their heads and "prepare" him for her death. How can we prepare to lose her?

Tami, who sings off-key and loves mai tais and never knows when to quit. My best friend. She won't quit now. That's for sure.

Carl came to say good-bye to me this morning and the fear in his eyes was enough to make me sick to my stomach. He said, "Her heart stopped today. They got it going again, but . . ." and by then we were both crying. He doesn't know what Tami thinks of "heroic measures," and I told him she was a hero herself and you never stop trying. Never.

Jolene came awake with a start. She had a perfect instant in which she forgot where she was—then the truth muscled its way in. Tami lay in a bed down the hall, and Michael was gone, and she was getting ready to go home.

Home.

She opened her eyes and saw a female soldier in dress uniform standing at the end of her bed reading the latest issue of *Stars and Stripes*. Jolene hit the button beside her bed, which slowly angled her up until she was looking at the marine.

"Hello, Chief," the woman said, putting the newspaper down on the flat blankets at the foot of the bed. Not quite where Jolene's leg should be, but close.

"Do I know you?"

"No. I'm Leah Sykes. From North Carolina," she said in a pretty, rollingly accented voice.

"Oh."

"This is the first time I've been back to Landstuhl in more than nine months. Some things take a while to confront."

"You're a morale officer?"

Leah laughed. "Hardly. My husband would certainly tell you that I'm far from an inspiring kind of woman. But you. I hear you are a helicopter pilot."

Jolene looked down at the place where her leg should be. "I don't want to be rude, Leah, but I'm tired—"

"You ever hear of the Lioness Program?"

Jolene sighed. "No."

"It started a while ago, a few years, I think. I'm no historian. The point is, when the marines did their ground searches, they encountered real resistance from the Iraqi women, who refused to be searched by men. Women soldiers were needed, so they asked for volunteers. A bunch of us who were tired of supply work and such signed up. I was one of the first."

Jolene looked at the woman more closely. She looked like a sorority girl, with her dyed-blond french braid and mascaraed eyelashes.

"We were attached to marine combat units and sent out. We got some special training—not enough, really, a week—but we went. I liked it. Combat, I mean. Who would have thought? Not my cheerleading coach, that's for sure. But *you* know." Leah moved away from the end of the bed. Her movements were awkward. She had a strange, hitching way of walking, and as she did her pretty face grimaced.

Then Jolene saw her legs: two steel rods that ended in hiking boots.

Jolene felt ashamed of herself for complaining. She still had one leg left. "You lost both legs?"

"IED. I'm not going to lie to you, ma'am. You have a hard road in front of you. I was a bitch like nobody's business. I don't know how my husband stayed."

"Will I fly helicopters?"

Leah's sad look was worse than an answer. "I don't know about that. But you'll be you again. In time."

It should have meant something to her, seeing this woman's courage in the face of such adversity. It would have once, in a time that already felt long ago. Now all she wanted was to be left alone. She wanted to snuggle back into the warm, dark waters of self-pity, and so she did; she closed her eyes.

Every time she woke up, Leah was still there, standing beside her.

Part Two

A Soldier's Heart

We don't receive wisdom;
we must discover it for ourselves
after a journey that no one can take for us
or spare us.
—MARCEL PROUST

Nineteen

Michael and the girls had spent all day at the mall. They'd been like search-and-rescue dogs sniffing out the things on their list with relentless purpose. A new bed, new sheets and bedding, lots of pillows. Acrylic paint, a roll of butcher paper, a set of multicolored markers, both fine-tipped and fat.

By the time they'd had lunch at the Red Robin and piled back into the car, the trunk full of their purchases, Lulu was skating on the narrow edge of an adrenaline high. She was talking so much and so fast it was impossible to keep up. Michael had stopped even trying to answer her questions. Each one started with, "When Mommy comes home—"

"—We'll sing her favorite song. What's her favorite song, Betsy?"

"—We'll yell SURPRISE!"

"—We'll dance. She loves dancing. Oh, she losted her leg. What can we do instead of dancing?"

"—We'll give her ice cream."

Even Betsy couldn't keep up.

Back in Poulsbo, they picked up his mother from the Green Thumb.

She brought dozens of flowering plants with her—roses and orchids and bright yellow mums. She wanted to fill Jolene's room with flowers.

"We got everything, *Yia Yia!*" Lulu squealed as Mila slid into the passenger seat and slammed the door shut. "Mommy is going to be SO happy."

His mother smiled. "She's going to be so happy just to see her girls again."

Lulu started talking again—something about painting this time—and they were off. Michael drove through town, quiet again in the off-season, and turned onto the bay road. It was late afternoon, and sunlight gilded the Sound.

Once at home, they dove into preparations. Betsy unfurled the butcher paper on the kitchen floor and knelt in front of it. Carefully organizing her acrylic paints, she began work on the WELCOME HOME, MOMMY sign that had required so much discussion. Lulu had demanded that there be suns all over the paper, and pink hearts; Betsy wanted rainbows and American flags. By the time they were done, there was barely a square inch of paper left to be seen.

"What do you think, Dad?" Betsy said at last, frowning, sitting on her knees and studying the banner. "Will she like it?"

It was a burst of images and color and love. Best of all was the painting in the corner—a man and woman holding hands, with two frizzy-haired stick-daughters beside them. The four figures were inside of a huge pink heart.

Is that who'll we'll be again, Jo? he thought, trying to hold on to his smile. "It's perfect."

"Now we need to make the cake," Betsy said. "Lemon is her favorite."

"I get to help!" Lulu said.

Betsy gave Michael an irritated look. "All she does is lick the spoon, Dad. And she sticks her fingers in the frosting."

"You two can work together," he said. "This is a big day. The biggest day. Your mom is coming home from war, and we need to let her know that she's the most important person in the world to us."

Betsy got to her feet and walked over to Michael. "Is she excited to come back to us, Dad?"

It surprised Michael to hear his own worry voiced aloud by his daughter. "Why would you ask that, honey?"

"I wasn't very nice to her sometimes."

I know the feeling. "She understands that. She knows how hard it was for you."

"She hasn't been writing us many letters lately."

"She's been so busy. The war really heated up in September."

"Is that why?"

"What do you mean?"

Betsy looked up at him, her gaze sharp and assessing. "Maybe it's because of that fight you had. When you said you didn't love her anymore."

He flinched. So, Betsy remembered that; maybe she would remember it her whole life, no matter what happened from here on. Had she been worried about it all this time? And what should he say? "Grownups fight; I told you that."

"You never wrote to her. And she didn't write to you. I'm not stupid, Dad."

"Of course you're not. But—"

"What if she's changed?"

Michael had worried about that, too. He smiled down at his daughter, hoping it looked more genuine than it felt. "Your mom is excited to come home, Betsy. Don't you worry about anything. We just have to show her how much we missed her."

"I did miss her, too. I can't wait to give her a huge hug. And to hear her tell me she loves me to the moon and back."

He pulled her into a hug. "We're going to be happy again, Betsy," he said, his voice as strong as he could make it. "You'll see. Starting tomorrow."

Nine days ago Jolene had walked across the base with her best friend, complaining about the weather, saying, *It's hard as hell to walk in this mud.* She'd grabbed the rim of the Black Hawk cockpit door and climbed easily aboard, putting her feet to the pedals. She had known irrevocably and completely who she was.

Now she was in the air again, but everything about her world had changed. She was in a transport plane, flying home with six other wounded soldiers, as well as some medical staff and a few civilians. The patients were in the front of the plane, in beds bolted to the aircraft's interior walls. A pale, flimsy curtain separated them from the other passengers. In the old days, Jolene would have found a way to smile through the pain and loss; she would have worked to make sure than everyone else was comfortable. Those days were gone. She lay in the bed, gritting her teeth against a phantom pain that made her missing foot throb.

When the plane landed in Seattle, the nurse seated beside her said, "You're almost home, Chief. That must feel good."

She turned her head away and said nothing. The nurse was right; it should have felt good, coming home. For months she had dreamed of this moment, of seeing her daughters again. Of course, she'd imagined herself walking through her own front door, dropping to her knees, and opening her arms for an endless hug.

What was wrong with her?

She should be glad she was coming home at all. What would Smitty give to trade places with her? Or Tami? The thought made her feel guilty and small. But what could she do about her feelings? They were inside of her, uncontrollable now, festering.

She simply couldn't look the other way this time or pretend everything was fine. She had a numbness inside of her that was new and frightening. Maybe she was afraid to feel too much, afraid that if she let her emotions go, she would start screaming and never be able to stop.

The plane touched down, taxied. The nurse said, "Welcome to Boeing Field, Chief. We'll be transporting you to an ambulance, which will take you to the rehab center."

Jolene wanted to say thank you but her heart was beating so fast she felt dizzy. She wasn't ready for this. She was actually afraid to see her children. What in the hell was wrong with her?

A major appeared beside her, in full uniform, and pinned a medal to her tee shirt. He talked down at her, said words she barely heard. Medals shouldn't be given to a woman who'd gotten her aircraft shot down and a young man killed.

Still, she didn't bother saying anything, not even, "Thank you, sir."

They rolled her on the gurney from the belly of the plane, down a bumpy ramp and onto Boeing Field, where a row of ambulances waited to take the patients to different hospitals and rehab facilities. Rain fell on her face, the first real reminder that she was back in the Northwest. She stared up at the swollen gray sky, and then she was in an ambulance, lying next to an earnest young paramedic, who thanked her for her service to the country.

On the way north, she must have fallen asleep, because when she awakened again, they were stopped. This time, the paramedics lifted her as if she were a child and carried her over to a waiting wheelchair. They positioned her carefully in the chair, draped her lap and legs in a blanket.

Her family stood clustered in front of the rehab center's entrance. Michael and Mila were holding flowers. Even from here, she could see how Lulu was bouncing on her feet, grinning. The girls were holding up a WE MISSED YOU sign painted in drippy blue acrylic, with glitter sprayed in rainbow colors above.

She loved her daughters with every ounce of her soul; she knew that, *knew* it, but somehow she couldn't feel it, and that inability scared her more than anything ever had.

"MOMMY!" Lulu screamed, running toward her, leading the charge. Betsy was right behind her.

Betsy rammed into Jolene's residual leg.

Pain sliced through the limb. Jolene said, "Damn it, Betsy, be careful!" before she could help herself.

Betsy stepped back, her eyes glittering with tears.

Jolene gritted her teeth, breathed shallowly until the pain subsided. "Sorry, Betsy," she said, trying unsuccessfully to smile.

"Sorry," Betsy mumbled, looking hurt and angry.

Lulu was on the verge of tears. "Mommy?"

Jolene felt a wave of exhaustion. She didn't know how to rewind the past minutes and start over, how to be her old smiling self, and her leg throbbed in pain now.

Michael moved in beside her, taking control of the wheelchair. "Ma, take the girls into Jolene's room. We'll check in and be there in a second."

Mila herded the confused-looking girls into the building.

"Thanks," Jolene said.

"They've been really excited to see you."

She nodded.

Michael wheeled her into a brightly lit lobby and up to a receptionist desk. There, he introduced Jolene, who smiled woodenly, and he signed a few papers. Then he wheeled her down a hallway and into a small room with a giant WELCOME HOME, MOMMY banner strung across one wall. There were enough bouquets to stock a flower shop, and family photographs covered every surface. Again, her daughters and Mila stood by the window, but this time their smiles were hesitant, uncertain.

Jolene wanted to reassure them, but when she saw the triangular-shaped trapeze thingy that hung from her bed, she thought, *That's my reality now. I need help to sit up,* and the numbness was back and spreading . . .

Come on, Jo, smile, pretend to be who you used to be . . . a smile is just a frown turned upside down. You can do it.

Michael rolled her close to the bed and then stopped so suddenly she lurched forward. He stared down at her stump, covered by the blanket. "Can you get into bed?"

Before she could answer, there was a knock at the open door. Jolene turned to look as a big black man with gray dreadlocks walked into the room. Dressed in pink scrubs, he smiled like a lottery winner as he sidestepped past Michael. With exquisite gentleness, the man lifted Jolene out of the chair and placed her in bed. He removed her slipper, set it aside, and then covered her with the bright purple blanket on her bed. When he was done, he leaned down and said softly, "Just breathe, Jolene. You'll get through it. I hear you're tough as nails."

She looked up at him in surprise. "Who are you?"

He smiled. "I'm your physical therapist, Conny. I'll see you tonight at six for your orientation."

"You don't look like a Conny."

"Honey, I been hearing that all my life." Still smiling, he introduced himself to the family, shook Michael's hand, and left the room.

And then she was alone with her family.

Jolene looked at her loved ones. She wanted—desperately—to feel joy, but she didn't, and the absence both terrified and depressed her. She felt nothing.

Lulu broke free of the pack and walked over to the bed. She looked at the flat place on the blanket where Jolene's leg should be. Frowning, Lulu leaned over her, patted the empty spot. "Yep, it's gone. Where is it?"

"Not there, Lulu. My leg got really hurt and they fixed me right up. I'm perfect now." Jolene's voice caught on the lie.

Lulu got up on her tiptoes and peered at Jolene's casted arm, with its swollen, pale, useless fingers sticking out. "But you still got two hands," she said, turning to Betsy. "She gots two hands, Bets. So we can still play patty-cake."

Betsy didn't respond. She just stood there, staring at Jolene, her eyes wide with hurt. She was scared, too. And why wouldn't she be? Her mother had come home missing a piece of her body. It didn't exactly paint a comforting picture for the future. And the first words her mother had said to her had been in anger.

Jolene knew this was the time to set the tone, to say hey, *I'm missing a leg, but who needs two, anyway* and make them all feel better, but she couldn't do it. She just couldn't. She hadn't found the courage to even look at her leg. How could she act like it didn't matter?

Mila came up behind Betsy, put a hand on her shoulder, and pushed her forward. "Your girls were so excited to see you again. They hardly slept a wink."

Jolene heard the hesitancy in her mother-in-law's voice, and the subtle rebuke. Jolene should be handling this differently.

"You will be yourself again," Mila said after an uncomfortable silence in which Betsy stared down at the floor and gnawed on her thumbnail.

Jolene nodded. She wanted to believe that. "Of course I will. It's just been a long flight, and my leg hurts."

"It will just take time."

She gritted her teeth. Hopefully it looked like a smile.

"Well," Mila said, "we should get home and let your mom rest."

"Yeah," Betsy said too quickly.

"Kiss me, Mommy!" Lulu said, opening her arms for a hug.

Michael picked her up and Lulu leaned forward, throwing her arms around Jolene's neck and burrowing into her neck like a little bunny. "I love you, Mommy."

And there it was. The love. It filled Jolene's heart to overflowing. She didn't even realize she'd started to cry. She held on to her daughter so tightly neither one of them could breathe. "I love you, too, Kitten. And I love you, Betsy and Mila. I'm sorry I'm so tired. It's been a long flight."

"We understand, don't we, girls?" Mila said, patting Betsy's shoulder.

"Betsy?" Jolene said. "Do you want a kiss good-bye?"

"I wouldn't want to hurt you," Betsy said, sounding sullen.

"Betsy," Mila said warningly.

Betsy walked woodenly forward and leaned down to kiss Jolene's cheek. It was lightning fast, that kiss, over before it began, and then Betsy was edging away from the bed.

Jolene waved good-bye with her left hand and watched them walk away. Only Betsy didn't pause at the door, didn't look back and smile.

Michael stayed at her bedside.

"The house is almost ready," he said. "Your friends from the Guard helped me build a ramp. We turned my office into a bedroom. No stairs."

"The separation you wanted."

"Don't do that, Jo. Please. I'm trying."

And really, Michael, it's about you. She sighed, too tired suddenly to do anything—to fight, to pretend, to feel. This day had gone from bad to worse and there was no end in sight. She'd thought the worst of her injuries was her amputated leg, but there was something else wrong; this numbness inside of her. She wanted to do the whole reunion over and be a better mother this time. "Good-bye, Michael," she said.

"You keep pushing me away."

She laughed bitterly; it turned into a sob. Throwing back the covers, she showed him her half leg, swollen to twice its size, cut off above the knee, and wrapped in gauze and elastic bandages. "Look at it, Michael. Look at *me*."

The pity and sadness in his eyes was her undoing. "Jo—"

"Get out, Michael. Please. *Please*. I'm tired."

"My mom read me the riot act for leaving you in Germany. Apparently when a woman says go, it means stay."

"Not this woman. Go means go."

She wanted to cross her arms and sigh dramatically, but of course she only had one good arm. She used that hand to pull the covers up, and she closed her eyes.

She heard him move toward her, felt his breath on her cheek as he leaned forward and kissed her temple. The gentleness of it made her want to cry. She swallowed hard and said nothing.

Finally, he left her, and she was alone again.

It was a long time before she fell asleep.

Jo! Don't leave me—

Tami is screaming, crying . . . blood is spurting from her nose and her mouth . . . her eyes. Jolene is trying to get to her, trying to reach out, but a bomb falls . . . exploding. The black night is full of fire and falling shrapnel, and now she can't find Tami. Somewhere, Smitty is yelling out for her, saying he's trapped. Jolene is yelling for them, coughing through the smoke, dragging herself through the dirt, looking . . .

Jolene woke up, gasping in pain. It felt as if someone was twisting her foot in the wrong direction, as if the bones were snapping in protest.

She grabbed the overhead bar in her one good arm and hauled her body upward until she was sitting up. Breathing hard, she stared down at the flat blanket. "You're not there," she screamed. "You shouldn't hurt anymore."

She flopped back onto the bed, staring up at the speckled white acoustical tile ceiling, gritting her teeth. Tears burned her eyes. She wanted to give into them, maybe cry so hard she washed away on a river of tears and disappeared. But what was the point of crying? Sooner or later she'd wipe her eyes and look down and her leg would still be gone.

"It's common, you know."

With a sigh, she turned her head. Through the billowy wave of her pillow, she saw the black man standing in her doorway and knew why he was here. To *help.*

"Go away, Conny," she said.

He came into the room anyway.

As he moved, he took something out of his pocket—a rubber band, maybe—and pulled his gray dreads into a ponytail. Diamond earrings glinted in his dark ears.

"It's not every man who can wear pink scrubs," she observed wryly.

"Not every woman can fly a helicopter." He stopped at her bedside. "May I?"

"May you what?"

"Help you to sit up," he said gently.

She swallowed hard and met his gaze. The compassion in his black eyes hurt as much as the phantom pain in her leg. "Go away." The words were a croak of sound.

"You just gonna lay here and feel sorry for yourself?"

"Yeah," she said. That was exactly what she wanted now—to be left alone. She'd spent a lifetime being Pollyanna, believing in the power of positive thinking, and where had it gotten her? Tami was hurt, her marriage was broken, and she couldn't even get out of bed on her own.

He put an arm around her and eased her upright, positioning the pillows as a comfortable backrest.

She fought him weakly, too depressed to even care, really, then she gave up.

When she was upright, he stepped back just enough to be polite, but not enough so that she owned her space. "Like I said, it's common."

She didn't want to talk, but she was pretty certain that a mulish silence wouldn't work with this man. She'd lay odds that he had the patience of a sniper.

"Fine. What's common?"

"The pain in your lost leg. It's weird, I hear. Feels like it's actually in the foot."

That got her attention. "Yeah. How am I supposed to forget about it if it keeps hurting?"

"I don't suppose you're going to forget about it anytime soon, do you?"

"No."

"It's the cut nerves. They're just as confused down there as you are. Nothing feels right to them; they're looking for that foot."

"Me, too."

"I can help you deal with the pain until the nerves heal completely. Teach you some basic relaxation techniques. Exercise and a nice hot bath can help, too."

"The morphine worked."

He laughed again. "Soldier girl, we aren't giving you any more morphine. You can't just sleep through this."

"I suppose you have a better idea."

"I do indeed. What physical therapy did they start with you in Germany?"

She lifted her casted right arm. "What do you think? It's not like I can use crutches."

He frowned thoughtfully. "Gee, you're right. I guess I won't start you there."

"Look, Conny, as much fun as it is to have you stalking me, I'm tired. I didn't sleep well last night, and I'm exhausted. Why don't you come back later?"

"I'm here now."

"I'm asking you to leave. Telling you to, actually."

"Wait. Are you confused, soldier girl? You think we're in some big-ass helicopter and I'm your crew?"

"Look, Con—"

"No, *you* look. As my grandbaby says, you aren't the boss of me. I'm the boss of you. Your family is paying plenty for you to get rehabilitated, and that is exactly what's going to happen."

"I can't move. Get it?"

He smiled. "Well, I know that. I've got your chart. And then there's the flat blanket and the busted-up arm. I'm not asking you to move. Yet."

"So what *are* you asking of me?"

"Just to start. I thought you wanted to fly helicopters again."

"You going to grow back my leg like one of those sea-monkey kits we had as kids?"

That made him laugh. "I have to say, they told me you were nicer."

"Yeah, well. I lost a part of me. Nice went with it."

"Here's what we're going to do. We're going to start real easy, with something you can do."

"Hopscotch?"

"I'm going to show you how to wrap your bandages. The pressure of a good, tight wrap helps with the pain. Think of it like swaddling one of your baby girls."

She tried to scramble away from him but there was nowhere to go. "No. Go away."

He put a hand on the headboard and leaned toward her. His lopsided ponytail fell to one side. "It's normal, not wanting to look, but it's part of you, Jolene, part of your body. You have to learn how to take care of yourself. I'll go slow."

"I don't want to look. Go away," she said, quietly now. She was having trouble breathing. Panic had a good, strong hold on her.

He let go of the headboard and moved down toward her legs, peeling back the blanket as he went.

She reached for the blanket, grabbed it, tried to hang on; he pulled it free.

She saw her lower half—the blue pajama bottoms on one leg, with its perfect pale foot at the end, and the other, jutting out beneath the fabric that had been cut away with scissors and now was fraying.

It was grossly swollen, huge, rounded at the end, wrapped in white.

"Take a deep breath," he said.

"I . . . can't."

"Look at me, Jolene," he said.

Her one good hand curled into a fist. She tried to catch her breath and couldn't.

"Just look at me."

As he said it, his hands moved to what was left of her leg—her residual leg, they called it. Wouldn't want to say *stump*; that was an ugly word.

You've got this, Jo, she thought desperately. *You can handle anything. Just don't look away. The first time is the hardest.* But that was the old Jo talking, and her voice was quiet, easy to ignore.

He unwrapped the elastic bandage slowly, so slowly she knew he was giving her the time to readjust with every motion. He lifted her leg a little, unwrapping the back, then moving across the front.

She thought she was going to be sick. *Hold on, Jo. Hold on.* Her fingernails bit hard into her palm. She felt herself starting to sweat.

He pulled the last of the bandages away, set them on the sheet beside her good leg. All that was left was a soft, gauzy dressing. Through it, she could see the discoloration of her swollen, bruised skin. She closed her eyes.

"Jo?"

"I'm not looking," she whispered. "I can't."

"Keep breathing. Just listen to my voice. I'm going to massage your leg, okay? It's good for circulation. When you're ready, I'll teach you how to do it."

When his hands touched her skin, she flinched, felt a ripple of revulsion. She couldn't help herself; she made a little whimper of sound.

"Breathe, soldier girl."

She let out a heavy breath.

Slowly, she felt his fingers moving, massaging, releasing the clenched muscles, and it was a kind of magic. She felt her shoulders let go, her fists open. Her head lolled forward the slightest bit.

"There you go," he said at last, and she had almost fallen asleep. "You can open your eyes now, Jolene."

"Is it covered?"

"Yes. *You're* covered."

She heard the slight emphasis he put on the word, and she lifted her head slowly, opened her eyes.

The elastic bandage was back in place, wrapped more tightly now, the tiny silver closures angled in a pair, almost like officers' bars.

"Thanks," she said. "That helped with the pain."

"You *will* get better, Jolene. Trust me."

"I didn't used to be such a bitch."

He came back up to the head of the bed, stood beside her. "You're not a bitch. You're just scared. My wife, now *she's* a bitch." He smiled. "And I love her like a crazy man."

"I didn't used to be scared, either."

"Then you were lying to yourself. We're all scared sometimes."

To that, she had no answer. She *had* lied to herself about a lot of things over the years, lied or looked away. It had been the only way she knew how to survive. And she'd been right to do it—this fear was unbearable. It unwrapped who she was, as neatly as he'd unwound her bandage, leaving too much pain and ugliness exposed.

Nerve endings; he'd said they were the problem. Things that got cut off, that ended abruptly or died—like parents and marriages—kept hurting forever.

She knew he expected her to be stronger, to try harder, to believe she could get better. But she didn't want better. She wanted her old life back, her old self back, and both were gone, amputated as cleanly as her leg.

"Just try. That's all I ask."

Try. It was another word for believe, and she was done with that.

"Go away, Conny," she said, sighing, closing her eyes.

OCT.

It's raining outside my window. All I can see is tears. There's something seriously wrong with me, and it's not a missing leg.

I'm being weak, falling into this pit of self-pity, and it

embarrasses me, but I can't help myself. Conny comes into my
room, wearing this big-ass smile, and he says all I have to do is try.
He shows me pictures of women playing tennis on artificial legs, and
I get the point, really I do. I just can't seem to make myself care.
What right do I have to walk when Tami is lying in a bed, fighting
for her life, and Smitty is buried in some box deep in the earth, never
to smile again, never to say, Heya, Chief, you wanna play cards?

I've been here eight days, and Michael has visited almost every
day. I pretend to be asleep when he comes. I lay there, listening to
him breathing beside my bed, and I keep my eyes closed. What a
coward I've become. He hasn't brought the girls to see me again. I
know why. They're afraid. They see me and they know I've changed
and it makes them wonder if their world will ever be the same. I
yelled at Betsy when she hit my leg. I didn't mean to, but what could
I do to change it? I know it's my job to comfort them, but I can't. It's
just not in me. Every time I think of them I want to cry.

Maybe if I could sleep, I'd be okay. Or better, anyway. But my
nights are full of nightmares. I hear my crew screaming for me, over
and over and over. I see Tami reaching for me. It's getting so bad I'm
trying not to close my eyes.

Michael sat in the plush leather chair in his office, staring out the window at a bleak October day. It was 10:42 in the morning, nine days after
his wife's return.

She would be in physical therapy now, trying to learn how to do
things she used to take for granted.

His intercom buzzed. "Michael. Dr. Cornflower is here to see you."

"Send him in," he said, rising.

Chris walked into the office.

"Chris," Michael said, trying to get his mind back in the game.
"Hello. Thank you for coming."

Chris tucked a straggly strand of hair back into his messy ponytail.
Today he was wearing a black tee shirt, a fringed suede vest, baggy

cargo pants, and black plastic clogs. An expensive leather messenger bag hung across his body. He took it off and burrowed through it, pulling out a green folder, which he set on the desk. "I don't think there's any doubt that Keith is suffering from an extreme case of post-traumatic stress disorder and probably was in a disassociative state when he killed his wife."

"And you'll testify to that in court?"

Chris sat down, crossed one leg over the other. "I would."

"In a suit?"

Chris smiled. "You'd be surprised how well I clean up, Michael."

"Good. So tell me what I need to know," Michael said, sitting down behind his desk again.

"I've included a detailed report that you can study, so I'll just go with the highlights here. First let me explain how we diagnose. We start with questions designed to determine whether the patient witnessed or experienced an event involving serious injury or death. Some of the events in combat most likely to lead to PTSD are being attacked or ambushed, receiving incoming rocket or mortar fire, being shot at, being responsible for the death of a civilian or an enemy combatant, and seeing or handling seriously injured Americans or their remains. Obviously, many of these are heightened when one is talking about seeing a buddy die or get hurt. As you know, Keith's unit saw some of the worst fighting in the war. The insurgent gunfire and mortar fire was almost nonstop. Sixty-four soldiers from his brigade died in his first year's tour. What you don't know is that Keith was often on 'bagging' duty, which means he was charged with picking up body parts. *Friends'* body parts."

"Jesus," Michael murmured.

"I think the trip to the public market triggered him. The crowds and the movement made him hypervigilant, put him in attack mode. He started drinking to calm himself, but it didn't work. When the homeless man approached, Keith reacted as he'd been trained. He attacked. He has no substantive memory of what happened at home, but I theorize that another trigger—a loud sound, a flash of light, something like that—caused him to flash back to the war. In this dissociative state, he reacted as he'd been trained—he defended himself and killed his wife."

"In a dissociative state of this kind, can a person think rationally at all?"

"If you're asking me if one can form intent, my answer is no. Further, it is my professional opinion that Keith Keller specifically was incapable of forming the intent to kill."

Michael sat back, thinking.

"He's a good man, Michael, a man who saw and experienced things his mind simply couldn't handle. It would be a tragedy to compound his—and his family's—tragedy by locking him away for life. He needs residential treatment."

Michael opened his own file. "You know the Department of Veterans Affairs deemed that he had a 'slight anxiety disorder.' They did not diagnose PTSD."

"The VA," Chris said, shaking his head. "Don't get me started on the government and its failings with regard to our soldiers. It's criminal. The military tends to equate PTSD with weakness or cowardice. But they're going to have to get on board, especially because troops are doing multiple tours. We need to make the VA and the government start addressing the needs of its soldiers at *home*. We need to shine a light on this and erase the stigma. This case is important, Michael. Maybe you can help another broken soldier and save some lives."

"We haven't found a case to date where PTSD was argued successfully."

"There has to be a first time." Chris smiled.

Michael nodded, looked out the window, where a steady rain was falling, in threads so thin they were like gray silk, blurring the sharp steel edges of the buildings. Like tears.

He understood suddenly what this case meant to him, why it mattered so much. "My wife," he said slowly. "She lost a leg over there. One of her crew was killed. Her best friend is still in a coma. Anyway, Jolene just got home and she's different. She was reserved with our kids—angry and edgy, really—and she adores them. I want to help her, but I don't know how."

There was a pause; in the silence, Michael could feel Chris studying him. "She's an army helicopter pilot, right?" Chris finally said.

Michael turned to the doctor. "Yes. Does that mean something significant?"

Chris smiled. "You're such a civilian. It means your wife is tough, Michael. She's a strong woman who has spent a lifetime getting what she wants from a system that really doesn't want to give it to her."

"That's Jo."

"A woman like her won't ask for help easily."

"She keeps pushing me away."

"Of course she does. That's the army way, the military mentality. Be strong, do it all yourself, finish the mission. Don't let her push you away. She needs you now, even if she doesn't know it. And watch out for PTSD symptoms. Nightmares, lack of sleep, hypervigilance, sudden bouts of anger or depression or apparent numbness."

"Thank you, Chris," Michael said.

This time, the doctor stood. They shook hands.

The doctor walked over to the door, opened it, and looked back. "Polyester or corduroy, by the way?"

"What?"

"For my suit."

"I can get—"

"Hugo Boss it is," Chris said, grinning as he left the office.

Twenty

The next day, Michael woke early, exhausted after another sleep-less night. He stumbled out of bed and tried to reanimate his sluggish body with a hot shower, which only made him more tired. He dressed for work in the clothes from yesterday, which he'd left lying over the back of a chair. It was easier than going into his closet and starting fresh. As usual these days, his clothes were strewn everywhere, hanging on chairs, folded in heaps on the floor, draped over the bench at the end of their bed.

He walked down to Betsy's bedroom door, knocked, and opened it just wide enough to say, "Get dressed, Betsy. Breakfast in ten minutes."

Then he shut the door and went down to Lulu's room. Inside, it looked like some kind of toy-and-clothes bomb had detonated. Probably, he should make her pick her stuff up, but, honestly, it seemed easier to do it himself. Then again, that was what he thought every morning, and he had yet to do it. Thank God a cleaning woman came in once a week to help; otherwise, they'd be living in a dump.

"Hey, Lulu," he said, leaning down to kiss her cheek.

He picked her up and carried her to the bathroom, standing beside her for the endless amount of time it took her to brush her tiny teeth. When she was done, she smiled at him triumphantly. "I'm a big girl."

"What do you want to wear to school?" he said. He'd learned in the past few months that telling a girl what to wear—even one the size of a golf club—was a bad idea. Histrionics often followed.

She went back to her room, stood in the pile of stuff with her hands on her hips, studying the disarray.

He counted silently to ten.

Finally, she chose a pair of pink pants decorated with daisy appliqués and a blue *Toy Story* tee shirt. The green striped socks added a clownlike touch, but what did he care? Together they walked down the stairs. In the kitchen, Michael checked Jolene's meal board—another thing he'd learned made life easier. While he got out the ingredients for french toast, Lulu started setting the table. They worked in a companionable silence that was broken only by the tinkling of silverware.

He was pouring himself a second cup of coffee when Betsy walked into the room, saying, "That TV lady is talking about Mom and Tami again."

Michael wasn't surprised. In the last week, the local news had been in a frenzy over the female helicopter pilots and best friends who were shot down together. "Sit down for breakfast" was all he said.

While the girls ate french toast and he drank coffee, he thought about all the things he had to do today. Discovery on the Keller case was in full swing, and he was gearing up for the start of the trial. His mind ought to be teeming with questions and strategies.

And all he could think about was Jolene. He was failing her. Maybe they all were. Since Jolene's return, Betsy had become sullen, silent. She was certain that her mother was damaged in some essential, life-changing way, and, worse, she was angry at Jo. Angry that she'd gone to war, angry that she'd been wounded, angry that she'd come home changed.

By 8:20, both kids were on the bus and on their way to school. Michael drove down to the ferry and rode it across; in Seattle, he headed north.

Fifteen minutes later, he pulled up in front of the rehab center. Pausing just long enough to take off his coat and sling it over his arm, he headed inside.

"Mr. Zarkades?"

He saw the physical therapist coming his way. As usual, Conny was dressed in baggy pink scrubs and his gray dreadlocks swung with every step, sort of like the alien in *Predator*.

"Hello, Conny," Michael said. "How's Jolene doing? I'll bet she's keeping you busy."

"Hardly."

"What do you mean?"

"She won't get out of bed except to go to the bathroom—and she hates that because she needs help. She refuses to learn how to care for her residual limb. She won't even look at it. That's not unusual, of course. Acceptance can take years. But she won't even try."

"Jolene won't try?" He frowned.

"She's hurting," Conny said, "and not in her missing leg. I get it, but it's been ten days. She needs to get started on her PT."

Michael nodded. Turning away, he walked down the long, bright hallway to Jolene's room. There, he knocked once and opened the door.

She sat up in bed, staring blankly at the TV screen. Her long blond hair was tangled, uncared for, dark at the roots. He saw how pale she looked, how thin. Weight loss had sharpened her cheekbones until they looked like knife blades, and her full lips were colorless and chapped. The violet shadows beneath her eyes attested to sleepless nights. He didn't even notice the flat place in the blanket. He looked at *her*, his wife.

She was scared; he saw that now. And depressed.

"Conny tells me you won't start physical therapy," he said, closing the door behind him and moving toward the bed.

"Get out of here, Michael."

"You don't give up, Jo."

She threw back the covers, exposing her bandaged half leg. It was still huge and swollen. "I do now."

He heard the tremor in her voice and felt so sorry for her it was an ache in his heart. He wanted to tell her that, make her understand how deeply he felt her pain, but they'd grown so far apart. She wouldn't even hear him.

"Why are you here?" she asked.

"I love you, Jolene."

"Do you think I can't see the pity in your eyes right now?" she said. "Do you think I don't know that you're standing here because you have to? I've become your duty."

He swallowed hard. He had earned this anger, and he would have to take it. For now, there was something more important than their broken marriage to think about.

Don't let her push you away.

Cornflower was right. If Michael wanted his wife back—and he did—he was going to have to fight for her. And it wouldn't be pretty.

"Enough," he said sharply. "This isn't just about you. This is our life. You're being selfish."

"How dare *you* say that to me?"

"You can't just lie here and grieve for what's gone."

"What's been *cut off*, you mean. Say it. Look at it, Michael."

"*You* wanted to fly. You, Jo. You wanted combat and war and to be all that you could be. Well, you got it, and this is who you are now."

She paled. "Shut up."

"I remember all your boot camp stories and your flight school stories. And how about all those times men climbed into your Black Hawk, saw your ponytail, and got out, saying they wouldn't fly with a woman. You told me you made them eat their words. You said you were tough."

She picked up the blue plastic water pitcher by the bed and threw it at him. It missed his head by inches and cracked against the wall, splashing water all over him. "Get the hell out of my room. You're the last person on earth who can help me."

"Jo—"

"Get out!"

"Why? So you can go back to wallowing in self-pity?"

"You have no idea what I'm feeling, Michael."

"I want you back, Jo. And if that doesn't matter, think about this: your girls need you."

At the mention of their daughters, she slumped forward. He wanted to say more, push harder, but at the sight of her, looking so defeated, he couldn't do it.

With a sigh, he left the room and closed the door behind him.

Conny was waiting for him. The big man was leaning against the wall, with his dark, beefy arms crossed in front of him. "She's a spitfire, our soldier girl. How did it go?"

"She doesn't want me in there."

"Is Jolene the boss of who comes into her room?" Conny asked thoughtfully. "I mean, the woman can't get out of bed. And she needs some motivation, don't you think?"

Michael looked at the therapist. "I don't suppose she'd throw anything at her children."

Conny grinned. "Nope. I don't suppose she would."

On Saturday, Jolene sat in bed, watching visitors stream past her open door, holding balloons and carrying flowers, talking animatedly to the family members they'd come to visit.

She had thrown Conny out of her room and then tried to read a book. But she kept forgetting the sentence she'd just read. Finally, she gave up and closed her eyes.

In that split second, she was in the Black Hawk again, going down.

We've been hit. Tami—

She opened her eyes. God, she was tired of this, tired of the pain, tired of the nightmares . . . just tired.

"Hello, Jolene."

She turned slightly, saw Conny at the door. Before she could tell him to get the hell out of her room, Michael walked in, ushering the girls in with him. They moved all together; he had a hand on each girl's shoulder. Lulu was wearing the small camouflage fatigues that Jolene had made for her last year, with the wings pin on her collar. Her long black hair was a bird's nest of tangles that framed her small face. Her socks didn't match.

"Hi, Mommy!" Lulu said, beaming. She walked right up to the bed, grabbed the metal rails, and rattled them. "Daddy said we needed to be good little soldiers to help you get better. I'm all ready. See?" She twirled around to show off her outfit.

Michael patted Betsy, gave her a little push. She stumbled forward. "Hi, Mom." She wouldn't look at Jolene, kept tilting her head forward so that hair fell across her face.

Jolene stared into Betsy's wounded, angry eyes. "I'm sorry I yelled at you the other day," she said quietly.

Betsy shrugged and looked away. Obviously, she didn't know where to look—not at Jolene's face, which was still scraped up and bruised, or at the missing leg. "Whatever," she mumbled.

Jolene didn't know how to fix what she'd done. The silence in the room expanded. Then Michael said, "Conny said you needed some motivation to get started on your PT. I knew you wouldn't let the girls down. They know it will be hard work—and scary—and they want to help."

"We wanna help! Like when you help us when we have nightmares," Lulu said, eager to show off her understanding of the plan.

Jolene could picture what had happened last night. Michael had gathered the girls close and told them their mom was hurt and scared and that they needed to help her.

She looked at her children and it hurt so much she couldn't breathe. She knew what Michael was counting on; he expected her to be the woman she'd been before all this. That woman was gone; she'd been shot down and died in the desert.

Lulu pulled off her Dora the Explorer backpack. Burrowing through it she pulled out her yellow blanket—the special one she used to stroke as she sucked her thumb. "Here, Mommy," she said solemnly, coming up to the bed. "You can have my blankee."

Jolene's heart seemed to break open at that. For a second, she *felt* it, all the love that used to fill her up. She took the sad, worn yellow blanket, remembering how pretty it had once looked in Lulu's white spindle crib. And she wanted it back, all of it, her life, her ability to love, her sense of motherhood. "Thank you, Lucy. I'll be careful with it."

"But I get it back when you're more better, right?"

"Of course."

They stared at her expectantly.

Come on, Jo. Fake it.

She finally managed a smile. She refused to let her children down. "Okay, Conny. What do I do?"

"You know the answer to that, Jolene. You're going to learn how to wrap your leg."

She nodded, hating the sick feeling that clutched her stomach. "Okay. But the kids don't need to be here for this."

"Why not?" Michael said, coming to the side of the bed.

"They shouldn't see this," she told him, her eyes pleading. She could see that he was afraid, too.

"This? You mean *you*, Jo? We talked about it," he said, nodding down at the girls. "It's you, and we love you, and you're hurt. We're not afraid. We're more afraid of what we can't see."

"Like nightmares and monsters in the closet," Lulu said. "When you turn on the light, poof! They're gone and you're safe."

Jolene stared at Michael, mouthed *please.*

We're staying, he mouthed back.

Conny moved down to the center of the bed, opposite her family, and pulled back the covers. Jolene saw Betsy flinch at the sight. Her daughter edged toward the door.

Jolene gritted her teeth as long, dark fingers began slowly unwrapping the elastic bandage. "It's in a figure-eight pattern, see? That's how you wrap it back up, keeping it tight to help with the swelling."

Then the bandage was off; beneath was a soft white gauze.

She clutched at the blanket in her left hand, squeezed the fabric in her fist. Michael put his hand over hers, held it.

She saw her half leg for the first time, and it made her sick to her stomach. It was huge and swollen. Ugly. Tears flooded her eyes, and she fought to hold them back.

"I have to go to the bathroom," Betsy said, grunted really, and ran out of the room, slamming the door behind her.

"It looks like a football," Lulu said, frowning curiously.

Michael looked at Jolene; she saw her own emotions mirrored in his eyes: fear, loss, sadness, pity.

"Come on, Jolene," Conny said.

She drew in a shaky breath and slowly, slowly bent forward, picking up the new gauze Conny had put beside her.

"Carefully," Conny said, putting his hands over hers, showing her how to bandage it.

Her skin was taut and sensitive; swollen; not hers, somehow. Bile rose in her throat; she swallowed and forced herself to keep going.

For Betsy and Lulu, she thought, over and over. *Act like it's nothing, like it doesn't hurt and make you sick. Be their mom again.*

She wrapped her leg back up tightly, placed the small silver hooks in place, and then sat back, her eyes stinging as she yanked the blanket back up.

"Beautiful job," Conny said. "Practically perfect." He looked down at Lulu. "You and your mom are so brave."

"We're soldiers," she said. "Well, I'm just pretend."

Conny smiled. "That explains it. And now, young lady, I need to get some things to help your mom exercise. You want to help me get them?"

"Can I, Daddy?" Lulu asked.

"Sure."

When they were gone, Jolene flopped back into her mound of pillows, exhausted.

"You okay?" Michael asked, leaning over her.

She didn't have the strength to deal with him right now. She felt so weak and vulnerable, and in that split second when their gazes had met, she'd imagined love. Nothing could scare her more. She'd given him her heart long ago, and for so many years, and then he'd crushed it. With her body so broken, she couldn't let anything else be hurt. "Why are you even here, Michael? You know we're over."

"We're not."

She struggled to sit back up, hating how she looked doing something so simple, all off-balance and breathing hard. She threw back the covers. "Is this what you want?"

"Yes."

She drew in a sharp breath. "Don't lie to me, Michael."

"I'm not lying. I learned a lot while you were gone, Jolene. About you . . . about me . . . about us. I was an idiot to tell you I didn't love you. How could I not love you?"

She wanted it to be true, wanted it so badly she felt sick with longing. But she was broken now, and Michael had always had a keen sense of duty. It was one of the things they'd shared. He wouldn't let himself walk away from his wounded wife, no matter how much he wanted to.

"We're back, Mommy," Lulu said, coming back into the room with Conny. "And Conny says we get to play catch!"

Jolene drew in a tired breath. She wanted to say, *Really? With one hand? Won't it be more like fetch?* but she didn't. Keeping silent felt like a minor triumph. She managed a small, hopeful smile. "Okay, Lulu," she said. "I love playing catch. So let's get started."

Michael stood by Jolene's bedside.

She had fallen asleep almost immediately after her PT session. He was hardly surprised. She must be exhausted. Today he'd seen the woman who flew helicopters. The warrior.

He stared down at her scabby, bruised face. Always, from the beginning even, when she'd come into his office that first day, he'd seen Jolene as a powerhouse, a woman with steel in her spine.

He saw her vulnerability now. Maybe for the first time ever she needed him. It surprised him how much that meant to him, how much he wanted to be there for her.

He touched her face gently. "Have I lost you, Jo?" he whispered.

He heard Lulu's helium-high voice in the hallway, and he turned, realizing too late that he had tears in his eyes. He wiped them away as Lulu said, "Look, Daddy, we have ice cream."

Smiling as best he could, he turned again to his wife, kissed her cheek, and lingered there just a second. Then he straightened and walked away, leading his girls toward the car. All the way home—on the long ferry wait and crossing—Lulu chattered. She wanted a wheelchair of her own.

As they turned onto the bay road, Lulu started singing and clapping her hands together; then she started pretending she was playing patty-cake with her mother. "Help me make one up, Betsy, like Mommy does. Patty-cake, patty-cake—"

"She only has one good hand now," Betsy snapped. "How do you think she's going to play patty-cake with you?"

Lulu gasped. "Is that true, Daddy? Tell her to shut up. They'll take off the cast and Mommy will be fine, right?"

Michael pulled the car into the garage and parked next to Jolene's SUV. "Leave each other alone."

Lulu wailed.

Betsy bolted from the car and ran out of the garage, slamming the door behind her.

"Great." Michael unhooked Lulu from her car seat and pulled her into his arms.

In the house, she immediately wiggled out of his grasp and ran upstairs, probably to torment her sister.

Michael went to the kitchen, poured himself a drink, and stood by the counter, drinking it, gathering strength for what was to come. When he finished the drink, he set down the glass and headed upstairs.

He knocked on Betsy's door. "Betsy, it's Dad. Can I come in?"

She waited almost too long, then muttered, "Whatever."

A phrase he'd come to loathe.

Inside the room, Betsy stood with her back to him, at her window, woodenly rearranging her plastic horses. He didn't need Cornflower to tell him that it was a desperate attempt to create order from chaos.

"She's in pain, Betsy," he said.

She went still. Her hand hovered above a black-and-white pinto, her fingers trembling. "She's different."

He went to her, took her hand, and led her to the bed, where they sat side by side. "It's okay to be afraid."

"But it's her fault. She *picked* the army—"

"Betsy, honey—"

"Sierra's dad says it's Mom's fault. He says women shouldn't be flying helicopters in wartime anyway. If she hadn't been flying, none of this would have happened. I told her I wouldn't forgive her . . . and I can't."

Michael sighed. "Sierra's dad is a dick who doesn't know shit. And you can tell him I said so."

"I'm scared, Dad."

"Yeah," he said, putting an arm around her. "Me, too."

Then the door burst open and Lulu stood there, frowning furiously. "There you are. Were you hiding from me?"

Betsy turned, sniffling. "I'm sorry I was mean to you, Lulu."

Lulu grinned, showing off her tiny teeth and bright pink gums. "I know, silly," she said. "Can we play patty-cake now?"

Twenty-One

Yesterday, Jolene had worked harder than she'd ever worked in her life—army-ranger training hard—and for what? So that she could sit upright in a chair, to stretch a leg that wasn't there, to hold a rubber ball with fingers that barely worked.

Now, she lay in bed, too exhausted and depressed to reach for the trapeze and pull herself to a sit. How pathetic was that? She called Carl at the hospital in Germany, but he didn't answer the phone. She left a message and hung up.

Tami, girl, where are you? Why aren't we going through this shit together?

There was a knock at her door, and she knew who it was. Conny the dreadlocked torturer. She didn't open her eyes.

"I know you aren't sleeping," he said, coming into the room.

She rolled away from him. Even that was hard to do with only one good leg. The motion was pathetic and lurching. "Go away."

He came over to the bedside. "You can't hide from this, soldier girl."

"I rolled over. Why don't you give me a treat and we'll call it a day?"

He laughed at that. It was a bold, rich, velvety sound that clawed at her already-frayed nerves. "I can just pick you up and haul your scrawny white ass outta that bed."

"You would, too."

"What happened to the woman who made it through boot camp and flight school?"

"Her leg is in Germany and she needs it."

"She's not getting it back."

Jolene glared at him. "Do you think I don't know that?"

"You want me to go, Jo?"

"Yes," she said, almost cried it.

"Then get out of this bed and start working with me. Let me help you."

She looked up at him, knowing there was fear in her gaze and unable to mask it. "This is killing me, Conny."

He brushed the hair from her eyes with a gentleness that brought tears to her eyes. "I know that, soldier girl. I been there."

"How have you been here?"

"Pain's pain. I have had my share—more than my share, really. My son died. Elijah. I'll tell you about him someday. He was a beautiful boy, had a smile that could light up the room. After he passed, I was full of anger. Darkness. Started drinking and yelling. Well, I imagine that's all you need to know. Took me a long time—and a hell of a wife—to find my way back. I know about hurting all the way to your bones. And I know about giving up. It ain't the way."

"I used to be the kind of woman who never gave up."

"You can be her again."

Jolene turned away from the compassion and understanding in his dark eyes.

"Come on, Jolene," Conny said, reaching for her. She didn't pull away but let him lift her out of the bed and into the wheelchair.

The physical therapy room was a huge bright space with four broad, vinyl-covered beds along one wall and windows along another. There were two sets of silver parallel bars anchored to the linoleum floor. Scattered throughout the rest of the area were a variety of steps with and without handrails attached to them, yoga-type mats, physio balls in all sizes and colors, stacks of hand weights, Thera-Bands, and a collection of walkers and crutches.

First, Conny had Jolene warm up. She rolled onto her side on one of the bright blue yoga mats on the floor, and stretched out as far as she could, imagining her foot still there, pressing out, reaching for the end of the mat.

With each movement, Conny charted her range of motion and encouraged her to do better.

"I don't think that's possible," she said, breathing hard.

"Oh. It is. Stretch farther."

Jolene gritted her teeth and kept at it, stretching her stump until pain made her scream out. Sweat dripped into her eyes and off her face, making the mat beneath her slippery.

"One more inch," Conny said.

"I hate you," she said, trying to give him what he wanted.

"I wouldn't be doing my job if you didn't," he said, laughing. "That's good." He patted her shoulder. "Now let me see some sit-ups."

"You are worse than any drill sergeant I ever had. You know that?"

"I aim to please." While she did her sit-ups, he went to get her wheelchair and rolled it toward her. "Okay. That's enough. Get in."

She looked up at the chair, hating it. Sweat dripped down from her hair. She wiped her hands on her tee shirt, leaving damp streaks behind.

Conny lifted her onto the workout bench, got her seated, then rolled the wheelchair closer. "I'll show you how to get into your chair. Here, make sure this brake is set. Wipe your hand so you don't slip, and remember, don't put any weight on your right hand. Just use it for balance. Let me help you, Jolene . . ."

She licked her lips nervously. "Who would have thought it took all this work to sit down. I used to run marathons. I tell you that? One time—"

"You're stalling."

She steeled herself again and began the work it took just to get from the bench into a wheelchair. Groaning at the exertion, she angled herself forward, stood slowly on her good leg. Balancing, she waited until she felt steady, holding the chair in her good hand. Already she was breathing hard again, sweating. And afraid she would fall. It wouldn't be the first time.

Before, she could have lifted one leg and balanced with ease. Now her equilibrium was as shaky as her sense of herself.

With exaggerated care, she turned on her good foot and sat down in the chair; her bandaged residual limb stuck out like a bowsprit.

"You did it," Conny said, smiling brightly.

He gave her about ten seconds to revel in her triumph, and then he had her back at the yoga mat, working again. She didn't have the core strength to lower herself to the mat on her one good leg, so Conny helped her. "More sit-ups," he said when she was ready. "Two hundred."

"Two hundred? Are you mental?"

"I told you you'd hate me. Quit whining and start."

She lay down, wishboned her arms behind her and pulled upward. "One . . . two . . . three . . ."

She hadn't noticed before how your feet anchored you for sit-ups. Now, she was constantly moving, sliding, feeling unsteady on the ground as she went up, down, up, down.

"Two hundred, Jolene," Conny said. "Don't slow down."

"Screw . . . you," she said in between breaths. She wanted to give up, wanted it badly, but every time she considered quitting, she thought about her children, and her family, and how much she wanted to be herself again, and she kept trying.

When she finished, Conny wheeled her back to her room. "I'll send an aide to help you shower," he said, positioning her wheelchair by the window.

"Conny?" she said, looking up at him.

"Yeah?"

"I'm sorry about your son."

He gave her a slow, sad smile. "I'm sorry about your leg, soldier girl."

. . .

For the next week, Jolene spent her nights battered by memories, and her days pretending she was getting better. She called her daughters every evening and let them tell her about their day; at night, she called Germany and talked to Carl about Tami. Most of all, she kept working. Every morning, when she woke, her first thought—in the split second when she hadn't yet remembered the truth—was *I wonder if it's too cold to run.*

By the time she opened her eyes, that question was gone, tossed onto the pile of lost chances that made up Before.

Now, her room was dark; the door was closed. She turned her head just enough to see out the small window. Beyond the glass, she saw a bare tree, its spindly limbs sporting puffs of green moss and a few tenacious, multicolored leaves.

She grabbed the trapeze and pulled herself to a sit. By the time she was upright, she was breathing hard. Tired again. She couldn't believe how much muscle mass she'd lost in such a short period of time.

Today she would get fitted for her temporary prosthesis. Her new leg. She wanted to be excited about it, but the truth was that she was scared. The new leg meant that she would be up and around, that she would be walking, that she would go home, to her ruined marriage and her frightened children and a life that had no foundation. She wasn't a pilot anymore, wasn't a soldier, wasn't really a wife. Who was she?

She wanted to talk to someone about her fears, but it had never been her way, and God knew it wasn't the military way. Whatever new fears and ragged nerves and residual images she'd carried home from Iraq, she was expected to deal with them herself. Besides, she'd learned as a kid how futile words could be. With Michael she'd always held back, even in the best of times, afraid to let him see how damaged she was beneath the bold surface. It was a trick she'd learned young, in that house full of alcoholics. Say nothing.

Only with Tami had she ever been truly honest.

She lay back down and closed her eyes, thinking, *Tami.*

How are you, flygirl? Do you need me as much as I need you? You

thought I was screwed up before—you should see me now. I can't even
trust my own mind and I can't sleep without nightmares . . . God, I miss
you . . . wake up . . .

Jolene sighed. As she lay there, feeling scared and (admit it, Jo) sorry
for herself, she heard the sounds of the rehab center waking up. In no
time at all, an aide had come with her breakfast, and another had
helped her into the bathroom and in and out of the shower.

At nine o'clock, Michael showed up. He walked into her room without knocking.

She was almost afraid to look at him; she felt so vulnerable right now.
"I thought you had a deposition today."

"I didn't want you to be alone for this."

The easy way he said it was an arrow to the heart, as if they were
Michael-and-Jolene again. *Don't believe it.* "Thanks," was all she could say.

Conny rapped sharply on the door and walked into the room. If he
noticed the silence between them, he made no sign of it. "Good. You're
here, Michael. Let's go."

Jolene felt uncomfortable getting into her chair in front of Michael—it
was all so pathetically difficult for her—but it quickly became apparent
that Conny had no intention of helping her. So she grabbed the bar and
hauled herself upright with her left hand, then scooted over to the side
of the bed and swung her legs over.

It was still a shock to land on one foot, but she concentrated on keeping her balance. Michael started to roll the wheelchair into range; she
shook her head and hopped one step, then grabbed the rubberized
handles and sat down with a sigh. She could feel how red her cheeks
were from the exertion, and she was breathing hard—again—but she
had done it herself, and there was some small satisfaction in that.

Conny smiled at her, then took his place behind the chair. The three
of them set off down the hallway. For the first time, she saw how big this
place was. Finally, they rolled up at a door marked *Prosthetics.*

Inside, it looked like Frankenstein's laboratory. There were plastic
hands and feet and arms and legs hanging from the ceilings and the
walls, in every size and color and composition.

A small Asian woman with huge glasses came out from the back room. "You must be Mrs. Zarkades," she said.

"Call me Jolene. This is my husband, Michael."

The woman nodded crisply. "Let's get started."

For the next hour, the woman worked in concentrated silence. She measured Jolene's residual leg and made a plaster cast of it.

While the plaster was drying, Michael asked questions. "Why can't she get fitted for her permanent leg now? Why a temporary?"

The Asian woman blinked through the saucer-sized glasses. "Her stump will continue to shrink, which means that the socket will have to be changed often. It saves time and money this way, and it has the added benefit of letting her learn to be mobile while her leg shrinks. Bearing weight on it actually helps speed recovery. It will also help with desensitization." She carefully removed the plaster mold, which Jolene had trouble looking at, and took it into the back room.

Afterward, they headed back to Jolene's room.

"You'll be walking in no time," Conny said as he wheeled her up to the bed.

She maneuvered herself onto the mattress and remained sitting up, covering her legs with the blanket.

"I'll be back at noon for PT," Conny said.

"Lucky me."

Conny's laughter boomed and then faded as he walked away. Then she and Michael were alone.

"Well," Jolene said. "I need to sleep before Genghis Khan throws me to the mat again and tells me to give him two hundred sit-ups."

"You can do it, you know," he said. "Whatever he asks."

Jolene looked up at him, remembering how much his support had once meant to her. She wanted to tell him how scared she was to come home, how uncertain she felt about everything, how terrible her nightmares were. "Thanks for coming today, Michael. You didn't have to."

"I've let you down a lot in the past."

"Yeah," she said quietly.

"Let me make it up to you," he said.

She thought about that, about opening herself back up to him, expecting something, and the idea was terrifying. He'd already broken her heart. How could she trust him again? Especially now.

She didn't answer.

He waited a long time, staring down at her. Then, with a quiet sigh, he left the room and closed the door behind him.

Jolene counted the days until her temporary prosthesis was ready. When it was, Conny strode into her room with a bright smile on his face. "You ready to get a move on, soldier girl?"

"I'm ready," she said.

He rolled the chair up to the bed, and she got into it with less effort than before.

All the way down the hallway toward the physical therapy room, she tried to prepare herself, both for triumph and failure. She didn't want failure to suck her under again.

In the PT room, Conny wheeled her over to a set of parallel bars.

She'd never noticed how intimidating this piece of equipment could be. As she stared at the shiny bars, an aide came up and stood beside her, holding the prosthetic leg.

It looked like a tree trunk with a foot.

"Okay, Jolene," Conny said, squatting down so that he was eye level with her in the chair. "Today isn't about walking. Your right hand isn't ready to really support your weight yet."

"It may never be."

"Let's take one problem at a time." He reached for a thing that looked like a big sock and put it on her residual leg. Then he looked up at her. "Today, you're going to stand."

"Easy for you to say."

He grinned and helped her to her feet. She hopped, holding on to him, and positioned herself inside the parallel bars.

The woman with the prosthetic leg kneeled in front of Jolene and fit the residual leg into the plastic cuplike top of the prosthesis. It felt snug, maybe even tight.

The woman said, "It's on," and backed away.

Conny tightened his hold on Jolene. "You okay? I'm going to put you down now. Just try to stand."

Jolene clutched the left bar in her good hand. With her right, she couldn't really grab hold, but she put her fingers on the metal for balance.

She took a deep breath, trying to calm her runaway nerves. This meant everything. If she could stand, she could walk, and if she could walk, she could run. Maybe she could even learn to fly again. *Just do it, Jo. Stand.*

"Jolene?"

Her heart was beating so hard it took her a moment to hear his voice.

He was standing at the end of the bars, smiling at her.

He'd let her go. When?

Slowly, she looked down.

She was standing. *Standing.*

She could hardly believe it. She looked up at Conny through a blur of tears.

"I know, soldier girl."

She stood there for a long time, working on her balance. She practiced lifting her hands from the bars. It hurt, putting all her weight on the prosthesis, but she didn't care.

She gripped the bar again in her good hand and moved her right leg one step forward.

"You're going too fast, Jo, don't—"

She ignored him. It felt good, making her own choice, pushing on. She had to drag her bad foot. It felt so heavy, unwieldy, but she did it. She *walked.*

She took another step forward. It felt like there were teeth in the socket, chewing her flesh, shredding it. She winced every time she put her weight on it, and by the time she reached the middle of the bar, she was sweating so hard her hands slipped. "I need gloves," she said between breaths.

"That's enough for today, Jo."

Ignoring him, she gripped the bar in her good hand, stood on her good leg, and forced another awkward step.

Pain pushed back.

Focus, Jo.

She loosened her grip on the bar until she had let go completely. She put all her weight on the prosthesis, ignored the pain that shot up her thigh and lodged in her hip like a hot knife blade, and took another step. It took forever but she walked all by herself to the end of the bars. When she finally looked up, sweating and red-faced and breathing hard, she saw Conny smiling at her.

"You know what this means, soldier girl?"

She wiped the sweat from her eyes, still breathing hard. "What?"

"It means she's going home soon," Michael answered.

Jolene glanced to the left and saw her husband standing by the wall, smiling. That was all it took, a look, a tiny adjustment to her balance, and she stumbled. Pain exploded up her right side.

Conny was beside her instantly, catching her before she hit the ground. She bit her tongue so hard she tasted blood.

"I'm tired. Can I go back to my room?"

"Sure." Connie started to reach for the wheelchair.

"I'll walk," she said.

"I don't know, Jolene, that's—"

"She'll walk," Michael said, coming up beside her. His gaze was steady on her face. "She can lean on me."

He gave her one of his old smiles, and she was surprised by how deeply it affected her. She realized all at once how much she'd missed it, missed *him*.

He moved in beside her, slipped an arm around her waist. His hand pressed against her hip bone, holding her steady. She felt his breath against her lips, her cheeks.

"Don't let me fall," she said.

"I won't."

She nodded and took a deep breath. Staring at the open door, she gritted her teeth and began to move like Quasimodo: step, limp, drag; step, limp, drag.

She made it one step at a time, to the door, through the door, down the hall. By the time she reached her room, the pain in her leg was unbearable. She was so tired, she let Michael help her into bed. Neither one of them knew how to remove the prosthesis, so they just covered it with the blanket. She was pretty sure blisters were forming down there, bubbling up and oozing, and she felt no rush to look.

"You're back," Michael said.

She'd been thinking about the pain of her forming blisters so deeply she'd almost forgotten he was there. "What?"

"Back there, I saw the woman who could run a marathon on a high-tech leg."

"That woman is gone, Michael," she said.

The look in his eyes was sad. It spoke volumes about who they'd been and who'd they'd become. "I should have told her I loved her, before she went off to war."

"Yeah," she said hoarsely. "That would have been nice."

Twenty-Two

Jolene woke up screaming, drenched in sweat, shaking hard.

Falling back into the pillows, she worked to slow her breathing. They were killing her, these nightmares. She tried not to fall asleep anymore, but sooner or later, it crept up on her, and the nightmares were always there, waiting for her in the dark. Every morning she woke up feeling drained, already exhausted. Her first thought was always *Tami*.

She stared out her one small window; that was her view now. Her world had shrunk to a single room and a three-by-three-foot sheet of glass that looked out on a tree that was losing its leaves.

From her cockpit, she had seen forever . . . and now she needed help to go to the bathroom.

It was demoralizing. As hard as she tried to be positive, she was irritated and shrewish when the aide finally came in to help her.

"I hear it's a big day for you today," the woman—Gloria—said, pushing a wheelchair into the room.

"Yeah," Jolene said, unsmiling. "I'm getting my cast off."

"I thought you were going home."

Jolene thought again: *What's wrong with me?* "Oh. That, too."

Gloria helped Jolene out of bed and into the wheelchair. Talking all the while about something—Jolene couldn't concentrate on the words—the woman wheeled her into the bathroom, helped her pull her pants down and sit on the toilet seat.

"Do you need help wiping?" Gloria asked in the same voice you'd say, *Would you like fries with that?* Perky. Cheerful.

"No. I'm left-handed. Thanks. Maybe a few minutes of privacy?"

"Of course." Gloria left the bathroom and closed the door behind her, but not all the way. A slice of air showed through.

It took Jolene a long time to empty her bladder—nothing seemed to work as well these days. When she was finished, she was actually winded. And she still had dressing and hair combing and teeth brushing to accomplish. It tired her out just thinking about it.

"Are we done?" Gloria asked.

"*I'm* done," Jolene said, striving not to sound irritated.

She was getting upset. It didn't take Sigmund Freud to guess why.

She was scared to have her cast removed.

With the cast on her arm, there was hope. She could look down at it and think that within that plaster casing, the nerves in her hand were mending, growing strong. But today she would know for sure. Was she a woman with two good hands or just one?

She let Gloria help her back into the wheelchair, as humiliating as it was.

"Conny will be here in a few minutes to take you to get that cast off. Do you want to get back in bed to wait?"

"Could you roll me to the window? I'd like to look out."

"Sure." Gloria rolled Jolene to the window. "It's going to be a beautiful fall day." She patted Jolene's shoulder and left. At the door, she paused and turned back. "Oh, I almost forgot. Maudeen Wachsmith in accounting wanted to ask you what you wanted us to do with your mail."

"I have mail?"

"Guess so."

"Oh. Well. Bring it to me." She turned back to the window.

Outside, the autumn sky was a pale sage green with wispy clouds.

Beyond the parking lot, giant cedar trees screened whatever lay beyond. Up close, an aged cherry tree clung stubbornly to a handful of blackened leaves. As she watched, one lost its grip and tumbled downward.

"There you are, soldier girl. Nice to see you doing something besides sitting in bed."

"I was thinking about trying a cartwheel."

Conny laughed. "You're a firecracker, Jolene, that's for sure."

He came around behind her and wheeled her out of the room. All the way through the hallways, he made small talk: his wife's new hairdo, his daughter's promotion, the way his back ached when he first got out of bed in the morning.

"Well, here we are."

Jolene checked in and was wheeled into an examination room. Moments later came a knock at her door. In walked a stick-thin man in a white coat with messy salt-and-pepper hair and a nose like a portobello mushroom. She could tell instantly that bedside manner would not be his strength.

He came into the room, mumbling an introduction while he glanced at her chart. Then he set the file aside and looked at her. "I'll bet you're anxious to see how your hand works."

She nodded, unable to find her voice.

He pulled up a chair and sat in front of her. Within moments, the cast was off, broken into pieces.

She looked down at her right forearm, shocked to see how thin it was, how pale. An angry red scar ran up from the back of her hand.

The doctor touched her palm very gently. "Can you feel that?"

She nodded.

"Try to make a fist."

She stared down at her hand, thinking, *come on, come on,* and *please,* and then slowly, slowly, she watched her fingers curl into a feeble fist.

Jolene let out a sigh of pure relief.

The doctor smiled. "Excellent. Can you lift your arm?"

She could.

She *could.*

By the time she'd finished the range of motion tests, she was smiling.

At the end of the appointment, she wheeled herself out of the room. It took real effort to make her right hand contribute, but she did it.

"You're looking good, soldier girl," Conny said, getting up from his chair in the waiting room.

He rolled her back to her room and positioned her by the window again. "PT in one hour. We need to start working on your grip now, too," Conny said. "And you can start on crutches."

"I don't think I'm ready to go home, Conny. We should postpone until—"

"Until when?"

She saw the understanding in his eyes. It shamed her to show such weakness to him. "Until I'm ready," she finished lamely.

"Today," he said quietly.

After he left, she sat there, staring out at the sunshiny day, squeezing the ball he'd left with her. *I did it, Tami.*

Yes, you did, flygirl.

Jolene would have sworn she heard the words, but no one was there. She looked out the window. *Was that you, Tam?* She wanted to believe in it, believe in the idea of her best friend finding a way to communicate across all these miles. Maybe it meant Tami had awakened . . .

"Mrs. Zarkades?"

She looked behind her. An orderly stood at the door, holding a few envelopes rubber-banded together.

"I've got your mail."

"Okay, thanks."

He came into the room and put a pair of letters on the table beside her. She stared down at them, surprised. Finally, she picked up the packet and pulled out the top letter. It was from someone in Kansas.

Dear Jolene Zarkades:

I read about your story in the Topeka Gazette. *I can't believe I'm writing to you—a stranger—but my heart won't let me say nothing.*

I close my eyes and I think of you because I know how you're feeling.

I was fourteen years old when I lost my leg. Just an ordinary girl from a small town, worrying about getting pimples and passing tests, and wondering when I would need a bra. Not a helicopter pilot or nothing cool like that.

Then I heard the word: cancer.

My mom cried more than I did. I was more worried about being different. I know you're probably strong, because you're in the army and all, but I wanted to make sure someone told you to be gentle with yourself. I wish I'd known that. It took me a long time. You think life will never be normal again, but it will. You and your daughters will be fighting again in no time—and about her chores or her choices. It won't be about your leg at all!

God bless. I have lit a candle for you and your family in my church. Our prayers go to you.

Sincerely,

Mavis Sue Cochran

Topeka, KS

Jolene wiped her eyes and put the letter back in its envelope, then opened the second one.

Chief,

I'm PFC Sarah Merrin. I'm at Walter Reed, after six months in-country.

I don't really know what to say or even why I'm writing to you. I guess because it's quiet here now. And you're a woman.

I lost my leg last week. Now they're afraid I'm going to lose the other leg. Infection in blast injuries is bad, but I guess you know that. I'm going to be here a long time.

How do you do it? I guess that's what I want to know. They tell me I'll be able to walk again—even run—but it hardly seems likely and when I look down at what's left of me, it isn't pretty. Can't see my husband sticking around after I take my clothes off.

Any words of wisdom you got would sure be helpful.

Sincerely,

Sarah Merrin

Jolene put the letter back in the envelope and stared down at it. She knew how Sarah felt, lying in her hospital bed, so far from home, wondering what part of herself she'd get back and what she'd lost forever.

But wisdom? Jolene had none to offer.

She would just add Sarah Merrin to the list of people she couldn't help, the people she'd let down.

That night, after a long, grueling day at work, Michael left the office and drove to the rehab center. As he drove through the stop-and-go rush-hour traffic, he thought about the jury consultant he'd met with today. They'd begun voir dire proceedings—jury selection—in the Keller case. As every criminal defense attorney knew, cases could be won or lost before the trial even began. Jurors were crucial. He would need to find compassionate, liberal-minded people who believed that a good man's mind could be broken by war. The prosecution would be looking for hard-liners who thought psychiatric disorders were just excuses for criminality.

It was dark by the time he reached the rehab center. He parked close to the entrance and went inside. The minute the bright lights enveloped him, he let go of the Keller case and thought about his wife.

She was coming home tonight. Finally.

He hoped that now they could begin to really heal. Last night, he and the girls and his mother had spent hours readying the house for her return. They'd placed flowers on every surface and filled the fridge with her favorite foods. His mother had spent all day in the kitchen with the girls, making baklava and moussaka; they'd frosted a lemon cake and decorated it with fresh orchids. They'd hung a banner across the front porch that read: WELCOME HOME TO OUR HERO! and moved the WELCOME HOME, MOMMY banner to the kitchen.

Betsy had spent hours decorating Jolene's new downstairs bedroom. There was a new bed and a bright new comforter and literally dozens of pillows to help her position her leg while she slept.

Everything was perfect.

At the rehab center, he walked down the brightly lit hallway to her room and found her sitting in her wheelchair, looking out the window.

She was as beautiful as ever in profile. The scrapes and bruises on her face were almost healed. The only scar remaining was a small pink slash along her jawline. She was frowning slightly, chewing on her thumbnail.

"You look nervous," he said, coming into the room.

She turned, saw him, and didn't smile. "I am."

It was a surprise, that answer. Jolene had never shown fear or anxiety, not when her parents died, not when she gave birth, not even when she went off to war. All of that she'd handled with the stoicism and courage that was as much a part of her as the green of her eyes.

She didn't really want to go home; he could see it in her eyes. It made him wonder sharply if he'd lost her.

He wanted to say something real, but she looked so distant—as if her composure were the thinnest of shells—that he didn't dare. "It's time to go home."

"Home," she said, turning the word into something foreign, a little frightening. "My things are in that duffle bag."

He picked up the big army-green duffle bag, carried it out to the car, and was back to get her in no time. Taking control of the chair, he wheeled her out of the rehab center. In the parking lot, he opened the car door and then turned to her.

Her pant leg fell away from the amputated leg like a flag in no wind. He stared down at it, wondering how he was supposed to lift her. Conny had never shown him. Could he touch her leg or would it hurt her?

For hours, Jolene had been imagining her homecoming. In her mind, she pictured it unfolding perfectly—the girls laughing, her crying, Mila making them all some food. She'd spent the last hour sitting in her chair, in the shadows of her room, telling herself she could do it, she could go home and be the woman she used to be.

Then, at the Lexus, she saw Michael hesitate. He couldn't even look at her leg, let alone touch it.

She gripped the chair's metal wheels and rolled past him, determined to climb into the passenger seat herself.

"Jolene, wait—" Michael said.

She ignored him, set the brake, and reached up for the side of the car. What should she hold on to? What would steady her the best? She hadn't practiced this with Conny.

"Looks like soldier girl is trying to do everything all by herself. I thought we talked about that."

Conny crossed the parking lot and came toward them, his dreadlocks swinging. As he moved, he retied them in a ponytail.

"Hey," Jolene said when he stopped beside her.

"You sneaking out on me? I stayed late to say good-bye."

"It's not good-bye." She looked up, afraid suddenly to leave him, afraid to go home, where everything that she'd lost would be so apparent. With Conny, effort was enough; at home, the expectations would be higher.

"Yeah," he said. "I'll be seeing you three days a week."

She nodded, tilting her chin up. He knew how badly she wanted to be the mother she'd once been, the woman she'd once been—and he knew, too, how scared she was that she would fail. They had talked and talked about it. Or rather, he had talked and she had listened.

He squatted down beside her, his knees popping in protest at the movement. "Everyone is scared to go home," he said softly, so that Michael couldn't hear. "It's safe here."

He reached out for her left hand, held it in his dark baseball mitt of a hand. "Don't tell me you're not tough enough for what comes next, soldier girl, 'cause I know better. It's a new beginning, that's all."

It was true. She *was* tough enough. She always had been, from the moment she'd realized that her parents were unreliable. She'd learned to take care of herself. If she could survive her parents' deaths and Michael falling out of love with her and losing her leg and Smitty dying, she could handle going home . . . she could love her babies again and be a new version of herself.

She swallowed hard. "By this time next week I'll be playing lacrosse."

Conny grinned. "That's my girl." He patted her hand and stood up. "Ten o'clock tomorrow. Don't be late."

"She won't be," Michael said.

"Michael," Conny said. "Here's how you help our girl get into the car."

Jolene let Conny help her to a stand and then she pivoted on her foot and backed into the passenger seat with Conny's hand steadying her. She couldn't help noticing how her half leg stuck forward when she was seated.

Conny patted her shoulder one last time and closed the door.

Then it was just she and Michael, sitting in a car together. She didn't want to remember the look on his face in the parking lot, when it had been time to touch her, but what else could she think of?

He made small talk all the way home. She nodded and made listening sounds and stared out the window.

The familiarity of the landscape sucked her in, reminded her of the life they'd shared in the shadow of these magnificent mountains; when they turned into their driveway and the headlights shone on their white fence, she thought: *I'm home,* and for a split second the joy of that was pure and sweet and intoxicating. She forgot about her leg and her husband and her lost crewman and comatose best friend; she thought how lucky she was to be here at all. She still had what mattered most to her in the world: her daughters. And now, finally, she would be Mommy again.

There, just next door, was Tami's house. *You should be there, Tam,* she thought sadly.

As they drove up to the garage, the security light came on in a burst of brightness—

And she was in the helicopter suddenly, turning back around to look at Smitty. All she could see was the gaping, smoking hole in his chest and the flatness of death in his eyes . . .

"Jo? Jo?"

She snapped back to the moment and found that she was shaking. Swallowing hard, she clasped her hands together to still them. A banner hung across the front door—WELCOME HOME TO OUR HERO!

Hero. Heroes brought their people home.

She knew then she was in trouble.

"Jo?"

"I'm fine," she said woodenly. "The banner is great."

"They worked really hard on it."

Michael pulled into the garage and parked; the overhead light came on. He went to the trunk of the car and wrestled her wheelchair to the ground and brought it to her side, then opened the door.

He looked at her and frowned. "Are you okay?"

No, she wanted to say, but she didn't know how, and she wouldn't have said it to him anyway. She gripped the car frame and pivoted on her butt, so that her legs were facing out. Michael moved in awkwardly, looked at her, and then slid his hand beneath her, anchoring her, helping her into the wheelchair. For that moment when he was in control of her body, she felt unsteady, but she made it.

He wheeled her into the house.

"She's home!" Lulu shrieked, running down the stairs. Mila and Betsy came down behind her.

"You're here, you're here!" Lulu said, dancing. "Did you see the stuff we made for you? Betsy? Let's show her the stuff we made for her. Are you hungry, Mommy?"

Jolene gripped the rubberized handles of the wheelchair, tried to slow her racing heart. *What was wrong with her?* She wanted to be here, wanted it with every molecule in her body, and yet . . .

"She looks weird," Betsy said, crossing her arms. "What's wrong with her?"

Lulu walked up to her, cocking her head. "You care about all the stuff we did, don't you, Mommy?"

Jolene forced a smile. "Of course, Lulu. I can't wait to see everything. It's just . . ." She looked around, saw the evidence of her former life, everything that had once mattered to her, and she couldn't make herself care about it. She felt numb and distant, a woman wrapped in gauze and peering out through the pale, sheer fabric, a ghost moving among the living.

Mila came over to her, bent down so they were eye to eye. She reached out, squeezed Jolene's hand, and said simply, "You're home."

Jolene's eyes stung. "I'm glad to be here," she said in a tight voice.

"Remember, your mom gets tired quickly," Michael said, coming up beside her.

"In ten minutes?" Betsy said.

Jolene could feel the homecoming fraying around her. She'd disappointed them instantly, despite her best intentions. *Focus, Jo. Be the mom they expect. How would she have acted before?* "Why don't you wheel me around, Betsy and Lulu? Show me what you've done."

"How come you aren't walking on your fake leg?" Betsy asked.

"Conny thinks I should wait a while. Our floors might be uneven. I'll need to start slowly."

"Oh." Betsy sounded disappointed at that. No doubt because she wanted a mother who looked normal, at least. Betsy positioned herself behind the wheelchair; Lulu tucked herself against its side. For the next hour, they rolled her through the house, showing her the changes they'd made for her—the food in the fridge, the cake on the counter, the banner on the wall, and a new bedroom in what had once been Michael's office. All through dinner, Lulu never stopped talking.

By eight o'clock, Jolene could barely keep her eyes open. She had a pounding headache, and her stump hurt so badly she had trouble concentrating. Twice Betsy had accidently banged her into the door frame.

"Quit sleeping, Mommy," Lulu demanded. "I'm showing you your new nightgown. See?"

"Yeah, like that's important," Betsy said. "She doesn't care about any of it."

Jolene looked up. "I'm sorry. I do care. I'm a little tired."

Mila stood up from the sofa. "Come on, girls, upstairs. Time to get ready for bed."

"Come on, Mommy," Lulu said. "I'll show you how I brush my teeth."

"Girls," Michael said. "Your mom has had a long day. Just kiss her good night."

Lulu looked like she was about to cry. "Isn't she coming up to read us a story?"

Betsy rolled her eyes. "Wheelchair, Lucy."

"Oh." Lulu pouted. "I am not liking any of this."

Jolene opened her arms. "Come here, Lucy Lou."

Her youngest daughter scrambled up into her lap; it hurt. Jolene gritted her teeth and hoped her grimace looked like a smile. "I'll be able to go upstairs someday. Just not yet, okay?"

"O-kay," Lulu said, drawing the word out to show her displeasure. Betsy mumbled good night and left the room. Mila took Lulu's hand and led her up the stairs.

Jolene let out her breath. She was in the open doorway to her new bedroom. All that was left of the previous décor was Michael's old college desk, tucked in beneath the window, with his computer on it. The door to the en suite bathroom had been widened; the molding hadn't yet been replaced, so it was bracketed by raw wood.

An antique queen-sized bed filled the center of the room. Bright pink and yellow Hawaiian bedding attested to the girls' shopping trip. There were several down pillows scattered about and a thick white blanket lay folded at the foot.

She could see how hard they'd worked to welcome her home, and she wanted to be moved by it, but, honestly, all she felt was tired. It had only been a few hours and already she'd disappointed them.

She heard Michael come up beside her. "I shouldn't have let the girls badger you so much," he said. "They were so excited to have you home."

Jolene could barely say, "It's fine." All she wanted now was to be left alone. She had failed tonight. Failed.

"I added a bunch of handicapped stuff to the bathroom in there—railings and handles."

"Great. Thanks."

He glanced down at her half leg, sticking out there, ending in a flap of fallen material and then looked quickly away. "If you need help . . ."

"Don't worry, Michael. Your duty ends at the bedroom door. I can handle myself from here," she said tightly.

"That's not fair, Jo."

"Fair?" That pissed her off. "None of this is fair, Michael." She gripped the wheelchair and rolled away from him. She was almost to the bathroom door when he said her name. She stopped, looked back at him.

"Do you want me to sleep with you? In case you need something?"

In case I need something. How romantic. "No, Michael. I'd rather be alone."

"Maybe I didn't say that right. Maybe—"

"Good night, Michael," she said firmly, rolling into the bathroom, closing the door behind her.

She told herself she wasn't disappointed as she set the brake and stood up, gripping the tile counter for support.

It took forever to brush her teeth and wash her face. She was so tired, she kept losing her concentration and her balance. Once she almost fell over. When she looked at the toilet, she felt a wave of exhaustion. Gritting her teeth, she hopped over to it, grateful for the side rails Michael had installed. She gripped it in her one good hand and lowered herself to the seat, realizing too late that she still had her pants on. She sat there a minute, too tired to move, then slowly she stood. It was harder than she'd anticipated to unzip her pants and pull them down without falling, but she did it, finally.

Who would have thought it was so damned hard to go to the bathroom? *Welcome home, Jo.*

While she was seated, she pulled off her top and bra and slipped into the floor-length flannel nightgown the girls had bought for her. After that, she got carefully to her feet.

Foot. Unsteady, she grabbed the counter again and caught sight of her reflection in the mirror above the sink. Cautiously, she turned to look.

Her face was disturbingly thin, her cheekbones high and sharp. The bruises and scrapes had healed; the only sign of her accident was the small pink scar along her jaw.

Her *accident.*

Would she think or it every time she looked in the mirror? And why shouldn't she? With a sigh, she turned away. She didn't know the woman in that mirror anymore.

It took another decade to get out of the bathroom, and when she wheeled back into the room, she saw Michael standing at the door, looking worried.

Before she could even try to do it herself, he was beside her, helping her into the bed. The minute she lay down, she felt the starch drain out of her. She sank into the softness with a sigh. He helped her position pillows around her residual leg.

"Your sleeping and pain pills are right there, on the nightstand. And your water. And a sandwich, in case you get hungry."

He brushed the hair out of her eyes.

She hated how her body reacted to his touch. It had always been that way for her, from the beginning. Even now, as tired as she was, she found herself being drawn to him.

Dangerous, Jo.

"We're going to have to talk about us, you know," he said at last.

"There's nothing to talk about, Michael. You said it all before I left. Now let me sleep, I'm exhausted."

He stared down at her so long she thought he was going to say something else. But in the end, he left her alone in the room, closing the door behind him.

Twenty-Three

As tired as she was, Jolene couldn't fall asleep. She felt as if she'd drunk a carafe of espresso; her whole body was taut, her nerves jangling. It was so quiet here—too quiet. No mortars falling, exploding; no alarms blaring or helicopters taking off or men talking. It scared her, all this quiet, and that was wrong. She was *home*. She shouldn't even be thinking about Iraq anymore.

She lay in the new bed, on the new sheets, in her new room, and all she felt was achingly, frighteningly out of place. Every noise in the house upset her fragile equilibrium. At every sound, she jackknifed up, her heart pounding, listening.

The last time she looked at the clock, it was three thirty. When she finally fell asleep, the nightmare was waiting for her.

Tami! We've got to establish a perimeter . . . Smitty . . . Jamie, help Smitty . . .

She woke up, heart pounding, sweating. A bleary-eyed glance at the clock showed it to be five thirty. She threw the covers back and started to get out of bed.

And remembered: she'd lost her leg. She stared down at it, still swollen and wrapped in gauze and bandages. Closing her eyes, she flopped back into the mound of pillows and sighed. Somewhere, on the other side of the world, her best friend lay in a bed, too . . .

Outside, not far away, a coyote howled. Upstairs, the floorboards creaked, then a toilet flushed. She wasn't the only one awake.

As she lay in bed alone, she tried to draw strength from what she had left. She was home; she was a mother. For the first time in months, she could focus on her children and be the mother she'd once been to them, the mother they needed. Tami would kick her ass for giving up.

She could do it. She *could*. Today was the day she would reclaim her life and herself.

She imagined herself making them breakfast, getting them off to school, kissing them good-bye for the day.

That was her last conscious thought. The next thing she knew, she was waking up again, and beyond her window, the world was pale and gray, rainy.

The first day of her new life. She sat up in bed, looking longingly at the crutches leaning against the wall. She wished she was ready to use them, but Conny had been adamant that she wasn't ready for them in the house yet. Too many hidden dangers. She maneuvered into her wheelchair and rolled into the bathroom. Again, it was a struggle. She balanced on one foot and brushed her teeth and washed her face, then hopped over to the toilet. By the time she was dressed and ready for the day, she was tired. Settling into her wheelchair, she rolled out into the family room and found the remote.

She turned on the TV and flipped to CNN, waiting for any news on the troops.

Michael came downstairs, carrying Lulu, who was chatting animatedly about something.

"Oh, you're up," Michael said. He was already dressed for work.

"Put me down!" Lulu squealed, wiggling in his arms. As soon as she hit the ground, she ran over to Jolene, accidentally bumping into her residual leg. It hurt so bad Jolene cursed before she could stop herself.

Lulu stopped dead, her eyes widening. "You said a bad word, Mommy. Daddy! Mommy said a bad word."

"Sorry," Jolene said grimly.

"What does everyone want for breakfast?" Michael asked.

Jolene looked up at him. "I'll make them breakfast and get them off to school."

"That's too much work for you, Jo. Take it easy. I'll—"

"Please," she said, hearing the pleading tone in her voice and unable to temper it. "I need this, Michael. I have to get into my life again. I can handle making my two girls breakfast."

He eyed her as if she were a bomb that might go off. "If you're sure . . ."

"Sure about what?" Betsy said, coming down the stairs.

"Your mom is going to make you girls breakfast and help you get ready for school," Michael said.

"She is?" Betsy said, clearly suspicious of Jolene's ability.

"Today's definitely special," Lulu said, eyeing Jolene as if she were unsure about this whole turn of events. "Cap'n Crunch."

Betsy groaned.

"You sure, Jo? Because I can do it." Michael asked again.

"I'm sure."

"The girls catch the bus these days. They know the times," he said.

Another change. It was just as well. Jolene could hardly drive carpool.

"Okay. I have voir dire today, so I'll be in court most of the day. Mom is going to pick you up for PT in an hour. I'll be home no later than six."

"You never get home by six."

"People change, Jo," he said, giving her a pointed look.

"Kiss Mommy good-bye," Lulu said when he picked up his coat.

Michael and Jolene looked at each other. Then he moved toward her, leaned down slowly.

The kiss he gave her was butterfly light. The kind of kiss a man would give an old woman, or a dying one.

From her chair, she watched him leave the house. When she heard his car start up, she snapped out of it. "Okay, girls, go get dressed for school. I'll have breakfast ready in no time."

She rolled into the kitchen, surprised to realize how small it was from chair level. There was barely room for her to maneuver, and the counters were too high; she couldn't reach them easily.

She was still trying to figure out the logistics when the girls returned to the kitchen and sat down at the table. Jolene glanced at her calendar, the one she'd left for Michael. Today was oatmeal and wheat toast with sliced bananas.

She climbed out of the chair and clung to the counter with one hand while she tried to dig through the cabinet for a pan. The clanging of metal got on her nerves, made her think of gunfire and cement cracking . . .

"You want help, Mom?" Betsy asked.

"No," Jolene said. "I can make a damn pot of oatmeal."

"Well, excuse me," Betsy said, stung.

"Mommy said a bad word again," Lulu said.

Jolene found the pot, grabbed it, and looked over at the sink. There was no more than ten feet between her and the faucet, but the distance seemed to swell before her eyes. God, how she wanted to just walk over there like she used to, laughing with her girls as she cooked.

Instead, she gritted her teeth, lowered herself to the chair and wheeled herself to the sink. There, she climbed to her feet again, turned on the water, and held the pot under the faucet.

Blood spurted out, poured down the soldier's face. Jolene yelled, "Smitty, get the medic, this man isn't going to make it—"

"It's seven fifty-seven," Betsy said sharply.

Jolene came back to the present. She wasn't in Iraq, flying a medevac mission. She was in her kitchen. She looked down; the pot was overflowing with water.

"Mom, it's—"

"I know," Jolene said. She turned off the water and set the pot on the counter. Pivoting on her foot, she repositioned the wheelchair.

"Dad has oatmeal ready by now," Betsy added.

Jolene grabbed for the pot without thinking, using her right hand. It happened in an instant, her losing her grip, but she saw it in slow motion: the grab, the turn, the fingers failing her, opening, the pot falling . . .

It hit with a *clang*.

"You got water all over me!" Betsy screamed, scrambling back from the table. "Oh my *God*. I have to change—" She ran out of the room.

Jolene slumped into her chair.

"You made a mess, Mommy," Lulu said, frowning. "The floor looks like a lake."

Jolene just sat there, stunned.

"Mommy? You made a mess," Lulu said again, sounding scared. "I want my daddy."

"Who gives a shit?" Jolene snapped.

Lulu started to cry. "I want my daddy NOW!"

Betsy came back downstairs, dressed now in jeans and a white hoodie. She picked Lulu up. They stared down at Jolene.

"Well?" Betsy said to her mother.

"Well what?"

"What's wrong with you?"

Jolene felt bitterness well up. She wanted to hold it back, be a good mother, but she couldn't stop herself. The anger and edginess overtook her. "What's wrong with me?" She held back from screaming *do you not see?*

Outside, the school bus chugged up to the driveway, gearing down to a stop.

Betsy screamed and dropped Lulu, who hit the ground hard and started to cry. "She hurt me! She hurt me!"

Betsy ran to the kitchen door and flung it open. "Wait! Wait!"

But it was too late. Jolene heard the bus driving away.

"I'm *late*," Betsy shrieked, stomping over to her. "Now I'll have to walk into first period *late*. Everyone will stare at me."

Lulu wailed. "I'm hungry. I want my daddy."

"Well?" Betsy demanded. "Are you just going to sit there?"

That did it. Jolene grabbed the chair's wheels and spun around. "What the hell did you say to me? Believe me, being late to school is not a tragedy, Betsy." She lifted her residual leg up. It twitched upward; the empty pant leg did a little dance. "*This* is a tragedy. Make your sister breakfast. *Yia Yia* will be here in a little while. She can take you to school."

"You said you'd be fine," Betsy yelled, her cheeks pink. "But you're not. You can't even take care of us. Why did you even come back?"

"And you're a spoiled brat." Jolene gripped the wheels and rolled away from them. As soon as she was in the office, she slammed the door shut. Getting up, she hopped over to the bed and fell into it with a groan.

She wanted to call her best friend, say *I just yelled at my daughter and she yelled at me. Tell me I'm not a bitch . . . tell me she is . . . tell me I'm going to be okay . . .*

Through the closed door, she could hear Lulu's crying. Betsy was trying to soothe her. They were probably huddled together, looking at the closed door, wondering who in the hell the woman behind it was. They knew their mom hadn't come home from war. Not really. The woman who'd come home was a stranger to all of them, herself most of all.

I want my daddy.

When had Lulu ever wanted comfort from Michael?

It was yet another change. While Jolene had been gone, the heart of her family had shifted. She'd become marginalized, unimportant. Michael was the parent who comforted and cared for them now. The parent they trusted.

She heard a knock at the door and ignored it.

The door opened. Mila came into the room. She was dressed for work in jeans and an oversized denim shirt and the green canvas apron. Her black hair was hidden beneath a blue and white bandanna. She walked toward the bed, sat down on its edge. Leaning forward, she brushed the tangled hair from Jolene's eyes. "A warrior doesn't run to her bedroom and hide out after one lost battle."

"I'm not a warrior anymore, Mila. Or a wife, or a mother. In fact, who the hell am I?"

"You've always been so hard on yourself, Jolene. So you're having a hard time and you dropped a pan of water and you yelled at your daughters. Big deal. I yelled at Michael all the time when he was a teenager."

"I didn't used to yell at them," Jolene said quietly, feeling a tightening in her stomach.

"I know. Honestly, it wasn't natural."

"They're scared of me now," she said, sighing. "*I'm* scared of me."

Mila gave her a knowing smile. "We all knew it would be hard to have you gone, but no one told us how hard it would be when you came back. We'll have to adjust. All of us. And you'll have to cut yourself some slack."

"I've never been good at that."

"No, you haven't. Now, get up and get dressed. We're leaving for PT in twenty minutes."

"I'm not going today. I don't feel well."

"You're going," Mila said simply.

Jolene thought about making a scene, getting angry, but she was too worn-out and depressed to do anything but comply.

Michael spent most of the day in court, questioning potential jurors. Of one person after another he asked probing questions, trying to get to the heart of bias. When court was adjourned for the day, he returned to his office and worked for an hour or so on his opening statement.

He knew the prosecutor's opening in the Keller trial would be matter-of-fact. Brad would begin with the damning facts of the murder, repeating often how Emily had trusted her husband and loved him and how Keith had shot her in the head. He'd hammer home that Keith had never denied shooting his wife. He'd lay out the forensics of the case, layer fact upon fact until the jury would more than halfway believe that there was no reason for them to be there. They would be told that Keith's memory loss was "convenient" and no doubt a bald-faced lie. He'd probably close with something along the lines of: "Who wouldn't want to forget that he'd shot his young wife in the head? Well, ladies and gentlemen of the jury, I'll tell you who *won't* forget." Then he'd turn to Emily's weeping parents. "I don't want to tell *them* their daughter's murderer will go free. Do you?"

Usually, Michael would refute every piece of evidence in the opening, try to plant doubt about the case both in its specifics and in its entirety. In this case, however, Michael was going to take a calculated risk. He wouldn't refute that Keith had killed his wife. What he wanted the jury to understand was why. In Washington State, it fell to the state to prove each element of the crime, including intent. Put simply, the state had to prove beyond a reasonable doubt that Keith had intended to kill his wife.

Intent.

That was the crux of it.

He was still mulling it over at five thirty, as he drove off the ferry and headed toward home. As he turned into his driveway, he wondered how Jolene's day had gone. For once, Mila wouldn't be here, taking care of the girls after school. They were with Jolene again for the first time.

Pandemonium greeted him.

Every light in the place was on, the TV was blaring some movie with teenyboppers dancing together, and the girls were fighting. He could tell by the wild look in Lulu's eyes that she was seconds away from a screaming fit, and Betsy looked pissed.

At his entrance, they stopped shrieking at each other and started screaming at him.

"Whoa," he said, raising his hands. "Slow down."

"Mommy doesn't like us anymore," Lulu said.

"She was a bitch, Dad. I know that's a bad word, but it's true," Betsy said. "And now she's in her room and she won't come out. When I went in, she said, 'Not now, Betsy.' She hasn't even apologized for this morning."

"This morning? What happened this morning?" he asked.

"We were *late* to school. We missed the bus," Betsy said, her voice shrill with the remembered horror of it.

"She dropped the water for oatmeal and said a bad word," Lulu added solemnly, her mouth trembling. She was seconds away from crying.

"Now, girls, you remember we talked about this. It isn't going to be an easy transition. We've talked about being patient, remember?"

"Yeah, well, you should have talked to *her* about it. I even offered to help with breakfast and everything," Betsy said. "There's something wrong with her, Dad."

Through the blustery anger, he heard his daughter's fear, and he understood it. Jolene wasn't the same woman she'd been before, and none of them knew quite how to deal with her. "We'll be okay, Betsy."

"You know what, Dad? I'm sick of hearing that. It's a big fat lie."

"She's different," Lulu whispered, crying now. "She didn't even talk to us after school."

Michael knelt down and opened his arms. The girls ran at him, throwing themselves into his embrace. He held them tightly.

When they finally drew back, Michael saw the tears in Betsy's eyes. "I'm so sorry, Betsy. I know she hurt your feelings—"

"Mine, too!" Lulu said.

"Both of your feelings," he corrected. "But just think of how bad it feels when you get a cut or a bruise. She lost her leg. It's going to take a while for everything to get back to normal. I should have prepared you for that. Hell, I should have prepared myself for it."

"You said a bad word," Lulu said.

"Thank you, Miss Word Police."

"What if she never gets better?" Betsy asked.

"She will," he promised. Then he kissed each daughter's cheek. "Now, go order a pizza, Betsy."

"She might as well still be gone," Betsy mumbled, walking away.

Michael went over to the office. Knocking softly, he waited for an answer. Not getting one, he opened the door just a crack.

The room was dark. Pale gold light from the eaves outside provided an ambient glow, illuminating the sharpness of her cheekbone. Beside the bed, the silver handles of the wheelchair glinted like strands of mercury. On the nightstand was an opened bottle of wine and an empty glass.

Frowning, he went to her bedside, stood beside her. In all their years together, he'd never seen her take more than a sip of wine. He picked up the bottle—it was half empty, at least.

He wanted to wake her up, talk to her about what had happened today—why she was drinking wine—but he knew how precious sleep was to her.

And would she talk to him about it, anyway? Even before the deployment, back when their marriage had been intact, Jolene wasn't one to talk about bad days or failures or disappointments. With the exception of love, which she showed exuberantly, she kept her emotions to herself.

It was part of why they'd gone so wrong. She'd never needed him.

He closed the door and left her alone.

He spent the evening with his daughters, eating dinner with them, playing a game, watching a Discovery Channel special on dolphins. They were still hurt and angry and confused when he put them to bed.

When the house was quiet again, he put on some sweats and went back to work on the Keller opening. The trial was set to start soon, and he still hadn't figured out how to make the jurors really understand PTSD, how to put them in Keith's shoes. He was making a note about that when a bloodcurdling scream echoed through the house.

He threw the papers aside and ran out of his room. Another scream rose up from downstairs, swelling, spiking.

He ran down the stairs and pushed open the office door.

Jolene was screaming in her sleep, writhing so much the sheets and blankets had come free of their moorings and were twisted around her. Pillows lay scattered on the floor.

She screamed, "Mayday! Tami—I can't lift you. Damn it—"

"Jolene!"

"We need a perimeter," she yelled, crawling across the bed toward the nightstand.

"Jo!" He grabbed her by the hand and she elbowed him hard in the gut. His breath rushed out and he let go for a second. She kept moving, toward the edge of the bed.

He lunged at her so she wouldn't fall off, put his arms around her. She punched him in the eye so hard he lost his balance, and they fell to the floor together, landing with a thud.

She came awake with a gasp, frowned in confusion. "Michael?"

Betsy and Lulu stood in the doorway, looking terrified.

"WHAT'S WRONG WITH HER?" Betsy shrieked.

Jolene was shaking; he could feel her trembling.

"Your mom had a nightmare, girls. That's all."

"A nightmare?" Betsy shook her head. "Do we look stupid?"

"Go upstairs," Michael said, helping Jolene stand. She was breathing like a freight train beside him. "I'll take care of your mom."

"Can I sleep with you?" Lulu asked her sister. There was a tremble in her voice.

"Sure." Betsy took Lulu's hand and led her away.

Jolene climbed into bed and leaned back against the headboard so hard it banged against the wall. "Sorry about that," she said shakily.

He sat down beside her.

"I'm having . . . trouble, Michael," she said, swallowing hard.

It was the closest Jolene could come to asking for help. "I know, Jo. We'll get you some help."

"Are they safe with me?"

He wanted to say *yes, sure, of course they are,* but he was sitting here, his eye throbbing from a punch she probably didn't remember throwing, feeling his wife tremble beside him. And the truth was, he didn't know.

Twenty-Four

The next morning, Jolene was up before Michael.

He found her in the family room. She had a mirror set up at one end, and she was walking in front of it, studying her gait, trying to walk as naturally as she had before.

As he watched from the doorway, she tripped, fell hard, and cursed. He went to her side, reaching out. "Jo—"

"I have to do this myself," she said through gritted teeth, shoving his hand aside. "I have to be me again."

He heard the desperation in her voice and saw the fear in her eyes, and he drew back. It actually hurt to watch her climb to a stand and waver, grab the back of the chair for support.

She fell three more times while he stood there. Each time, she curled her good hand into a fist, breathed hard, and got back to her feet. She didn't curse again, didn't say a thing about her pain. And he knew it had to hurt like hell; Conny had told him she'd been working so hard she had blisters on her stump.

"You look great," he said when she made a good pass and an apparently easy turn.

She smiled at him, but he saw past her can-do attitude and was startled by the sadness in her eyes. He saw what it cost her to fall, to trip, to need help with the simplest things. She frowned. "You have a black eye."

"Very Jack Sparrow, don't you think?"

"Did I do that?"

"Not on purpose, Jo."

"I'm sorry."

"I know. Don't worry about it."

"Right," she said tiredly.

He saw how fragile she was, how scared by the idea that she had hurt him—and that she didn't remember doing it. He wanted to talk to her about the nightmares, but she'd just put up one of her walls, and how could he scale it? He had no idea what she'd been through in Iraq. What would he even ask?

The girls came running down the stairs. At the sight of Jolene, they stopped so fast Betsy shoved Lulu forward.

"Girls," Jolene said, looking as sad as he'd ever seen her. "I'm sorry about last night. It was just a nightmare."

"A nightmare that gave Dad a black eye," Betsy said tightly. "What's wrong with you?"

Jolene sighed. "I'll be fine. Honest. I just need to try again."

"I'm hungry," Lulu said. "Daddy, are you going to make us breakfast this morning?"

Michael saw Jolene's reaction to that. She looked disappointed; her shoulders slumped. She turned and limped away, walking resolutely toward the mirror again.

"Okay," Michael said, "let's get breakfast going." He ushered the girls into the kitchen, made them breakfast, and then followed them upstairs, where they got ready for school. "Tell your mom good-bye," he said as they headed for the door.

"Bye, Mom," they said dutifully together. They didn't look at Jolene, and she kept walking toward the mirror, gauging her gait. Michael walked them both to the end of the driveway and stayed until the buses came to take them away. Then he returned to the house. When he approached Jolene, he saw the sadness in her eyes.

"Hey," he said, touching her arm.

"Don't be nice to me this morning," she said. "I can't take it."

And there it was: the reminder of how far apart they'd drifted. She didn't want to be comforted by him, even now when she was terrified and depressed and her heart was breaking.

"Come on, Jo, it's time to leave for rehab" was what he ended up saying. It was all he could think of.

On the ferry, she didn't want to leave the car. So they sat there in silence until Michael looked at her. "It must have been terrible over there," he said tentatively, feeling like a fraud. He had no idea, and both of them knew it.

"Terrible? Yeah."

"Were you scared all the time?"

She stared out the car window. "Not all the time. I don't want to talk about this, Michael. It doesn't matter now."

"You're home, Jo," he said.

She nodded but didn't look at him. Neither did she speak again on the drive through Seattle. She just stared out the car window and shrugged in answer to his questions.

When he dropped her off, he said, "Jo? We need to really talk about all this, you know."

"Yeah," she said. "I know." She sounded exhausted by the very idea of it.

He watched her limp into the rehab center and then he drove away. Instead of going straight to his office, he turned onto Aurora and drove to Cornflower's office.

There, he walked up to the desk, saw the girl with the hardware all over her face and the purple hair. "I know I didn't call. But I'd like to see Chris, if that's possible. I'm Michael Zarkades."

"Yeah," she said, "just a sec." She got up and walked down the hall. A minute or two later, she was back. "He'll see you in the sunroom. It's that way."

Michael followed the hallway out to a pretty little glass-walled sunroom decorated in 1950s rattan furniture and overflowing with greenery and flowers. It reminded him a little of his parents' living room, with its wide-plank wooden floors and floral cushioned furniture. A framed, yellowed poster of "Desiderata" hung on the only solid wall. *Go placidly amid the noise and haste, and remember what peace there may be in silence.* He couldn't help smiling. His mother had once had the very same poster on her bedroom wall.

"I don't have long, Michael," Chris said, closing the door behind him. "A patient will be here in ten minutes. Is it Keith? Are the nightmares getting worse?"

Michael sat down in one of the floral cushioned chairs. "It's my wife, Chris. She's . . . different. Last night she drank a few glasses of wine—I know that doesn't sound like much, but her parents were alcoholics. I've never seen Jolene have more than a few sips of alcohol. And she woke up screaming."

"She give you that shiner?"

"She's always had a hell of an arm. You should see her pitch."

Chris smiled and sat down. "Obviously, we need more than ten minutes for this discussion. I'd be happy to talk to Jolene if she'd do that."

"She's not a big talker in that way, but she did say she was in trouble."

"She's a soldier, Michael, which means she won't want to appear weak, and it will be difficult for her to admit that she's having trouble adjusting. As you know, nightmares and trouble sleeping are common symptoms of PTSD, but they're also a normal reaction to having been at war. In most cases, these nightmares will diminish over time. We really need to worry if she's still experiencing acute symptoms in three months. But she's going through a lot of emotions right now—she's probably grieving over her lost crewman and her comatose friend; she's probably feeling some guilt—misplaced—that it's her fault the bird went down; she's probably afraid that your family is irrevocably broken and that she doesn't have the strength to hold you all together again. Add to that the fact that she's lost her leg and most likely her career, and you have a woman in crisis."

"So how do I help her?"

"She feels like she's coming apart," he said quietly. "You think you're one person, and then suddenly you're not. You don't know who you are. And the nightmares can be absolutely terrifying."

"I saw that."

"Make sure there are no weapons in the house."

"Jesus . . ."

"And watch her drinking very carefully. That can really exacerbate the problems she's having. Mostly, Michael, get her to talk to you. Listen without being judgmental."

"Jo and I have never been particularly good at talking."

Chris gave him an understanding nod. "This would be a good time to change that, Michael."

On the ride home from rehab, Jolene wanted to talk to Mila, but she couldn't form the words. She kept reliving last night, when she'd woken from her nightmare, on the floor, screaming, with her children staring down at her in fear. It was eating her up inside; it had been all day. She'd barely been able to concentrate in PT.

What in the hell was wrong with her? She needed Tami more than ever. The thought of that only made her feel worse.

As they pulled up to the house, Mila turned to her. "Are you okay, Jolene? You're awful quiet."

She imagined herself saying *I'm afraid, Mila, something's wrong with me,* but she couldn't do it. She was terrified of opening the floodgates, of revealing the depth of her fear. For the first time in her life, she was really, truly afraid. More afraid than she'd been in Iraq.

"Rehab was a bearcat today. The blisters are killing me." She smiled tightly, hating the lie.

"Do you want me to stay with you until the girls come home?"

"No. I'm getting better. Honestly. I'll take a nap and then I'll be stronger. I'll have snacks ready for them when they get home from school. Maybe we'll play a board game."

"Okay," Mila said hesitantly.

Jolene managed a smile. Giving her mother-in-law a quick kiss, she got out of the car and went into the house. When the door closed behind her, she sagged forward on her crutches, and finally released the breath she'd been holding.

She needed a glass of wine. That would calm her jagged nerves, still the trembling in her hands. Just one glass. There was nothing wrong with that.

Her hands were shaking again. She went to the refrigerator, poured herself a glass of wine, and sat down. By the time she'd drunk two glasses, she felt slightly better. The wired feeling had dissipated somewhat. But the fear remained.

She needed help.

There. She'd thought it. Nothing mattered more than her children, and she was losing them, pushing them away, frightening them. She'd punched her husband in the face and didn't remember doing it. What could she do to her children? She went to the phone. After a quick look in the phone book, she dialed the Department of Veterans Affairs.

"I think I need to talk to someone," she blurted out when the receptionist answered.

"About what?"

"I'm an OIF vet. Injured. I need to talk to someone about the nightmares I'm having."

"Just a sec."

Breathe, Jolene. Don't hang up.

"Can I help you?" a man said abruptly.

"Oh. Yes. I hope so. I'm a returning Operation Iraqi Freedom vet, and I'm having some trouble sleeping."

"Are you thinking of hurting yourself or others?"

"What? On purpose? No. No, of course not, but I just—"

"I can make you an appointment with a counselor."

She sighed in relief. "That would be great. Thanks."

"How is December fifteenth?"

"I'm sorry. Did you say December fifteenth? It's October."

"Yes. That's how long the wait is. We're backlogged. A lot of returning soldiers need help. If you're thinking of hurting yourself, however . . ."

She knew what would happen if she answered in the affirmative. They'd stamp whacko on her file. "No. Thank you. I don't need the December appointment. I'm sure I'll be fine by then." She hung up the phone and sat there.

Her phantom pain was back, twisting her ankle hard.

She made her way to the family room and collapsed on the sofa, trying to gut it out. Sweat itched across her scalp. She closed her eyes and concentrated on breathing through the pain.

Later, a knock at the door interrupted her thoughts. She came awake sharply. How long had she been asleep? Were the girls home already? She glanced at the clock. It was only three. She got up, retrieved her crutches, and limped slowly to the front door, opening it.

Ben Lomand stood on her porch, holding a bouquet of flowers.

"Ben," she said, smiling for the first time in days. "It's so good to see you, come in." She led the way back into the family room and sat down on the sofa.

"I came to see how you're doing," he said, sitting beside her. "Michael said you'd be home now."

"I'm getting better every day," she said.

"That's good."

She steeled herself. "Have you spoken to Smitty's parents?"

He nodded. "At the funeral."

"Do they blame me?"

"Of course not, Jolene. They know their son was a hero and that he died serving his country. They're proud of him."

"I tried to get to him."

They fell silent, each knowing there was nothing to say.

"Jolene," the captain said at last, a pained look on his face. "I've got some news for you."

"What is it?"

"I've got your physical profile from Captain Sands in Landstuhl. It assesses your FFD."

FFD. Fitness for duty.

"Oh," she said softly. With all that had happened in the past weeks, she'd forgotten about her career. About flying.

How could she have forgotten? "And?"

"You're a pilot," he said, his eyes filled with compassion. Maybe some soldiers could fulfill their job assignments with one leg. Not a pilot.

He was going to say she could never fly again. She closed her eyes for just a moment, feeling as great a pain as her missing leg. "I don't meet the retention criteria," she said. "Of course I don't. I only have one leg."

"You could appeal. Go on probation, see if you could meet the criteria for duty after rehab."

She looked at him. "They won't let me fly again, though, will they?"

The answer was in his eyes. "No. No flight status. But you could stay in the Guard maybe. Or if you retire, you'll have full benefits."

"Benefits," she said softly, trying to imagine her life without the military, without her friends, without flying . . . but she was a pilot. A *pilot*. How could she be in the Guard and not fly?

What was left to her now?

"I'm sorry, Jo."

She nodded, looked away before he could see the sadness in her eyes. "Thank you, sir," she said in a thick voice.

After he left, she grabbed the bottle of wine and went into her bedroom.

The ferry was docking on Bainbridge Island when Michael's cell phone rang. "Hello?"

"Mr. Zarkades? This is Principal Warner, from the middle school. I'm afraid there's been an incident with Betsy."

The ferry banged into the dock; stilled. He started up his car. "What? An incident, did you say? What does that mean?"

"Betsy was in a fight."

"You mean a *fistfight?*"

"Yes."

"I'll be right there," he said, hanging up. He followed the line of cars off the boat and across the ramp and up onto the road. Out on the highway, he hit the gas.

Twenty minutes later, he pulled up in front of the middle school and parked. Inside, the bright white walls were decorated with dozens of Science Fair and History Day banners. In the principal's office, he found Betsy in the waiting room, her arms crossed tightly, her mouth pressed in a flat line. At his appearance, she looked up, her eyes widening.

"Dad, I—"

He gave her the Hand and kept walking. At the front desk, he introduced himself and was led into the principal's office.

Principal Warner, a petite, pretty woman with kind eyes, noticed his black eye and frowned.

"I fell off my bike," he said tightly.

She smiled, but only a little. "I'm sorry we had to call you. We're all aware of the struggles your family is currently facing. Please, sit."

He sat down. "She got in a fight? With whom?"

"Sierra Phillips and Zoe Wimerann. From what I hear, they were teasing her about her mother. It seems Sierra's dad made some comments about women's ability to fly helicopters, and Zoe responded by laughing. Betsy swung the first punch."

He sighed. No wonder Seth called them the bitchwolves. "There's a lot of water under the bridge with these girls. Beyond that, Betsy's having some issues dealing with her mother's return. It hasn't gone as smoothly as we'd expected."

"Her teachers tell me she's been acting out in the past few days. Snapping at friends and not turning in her homework. We have an excellent school counselor, if you'd like her to see someone."

"Thank you, Principal Warner. I'll let you know if that becomes necessary. And now, I'd like to speak to my daughter, if you don't mind."

She stood. "Certainly. And . . . how is Jolene?"

Michael didn't know how to answer that. He was getting sick and tired of pretending that everything was fine. "She's not good. That's the problem."

"Perhaps she needs some time."

"Yeah," he said. "I hear that a lot."

Principal Warner walked him out of her office, led him to where Betsy sat, looking mulish now, both scared and angry.

"Betsy," the principal said, "I'm going to let your father handle this for now, but if you're caught fighting again, I'll suspend you from school. Do you understand?"

Betsy nodded glumly. She followed Michael out to the car without saying a word.

"Is this the whole frenemies thing?" he said, opening his door. "Because I thought Sierra was your BFF."

"Don't try to sound cool, Dad. It's weird."

"These girls are not worth your friendship, Betsy."

"I know that," she said, sighing. "I'm done with them."

Michael got into the car. "What happened, Betsy?"

She got into the passenger seat and looked at him. Her face was flushed. "I just lost it, Dad. I don't even know what happened. But it wasn't my fault. Zoe totally started it. She hit me first."

"And why did Zoe hit you?"

"I called her a bitch. But she is, Dad. She really is. You always say truth is a defense."

"Nice try. Look, Bets, I know you're upset with your mom, but—"

"Not everything is about her, you know."

"This is. You punched a girl for saying something mean about her. But, you know, Betsy, you've been a little mean to her yourself. Maybe you feel bad about that."

"You were mean to her before she left."

"Yes, I was. And I feel bad about that. But I don't go around punching people."

"She barely looks at me. Mom, I mean. I don't think she even likes me anymore."

Michael sighed. And there it was. The real problem. "I know, baby. Your mom is different, and it hurts all our feelings, so you're acting out. I get it, I do. But you can't go around hitting people."

Betsy looked at him. "I'm scared, Dad," she said quietly.

"Yeah," he said. "We all are."

.   .   .

Jolene heard the door open, heard footsteps coming toward her bed. She knew it was Michael.

She pretended to be asleep. The three glasses of wine she'd drunk had sedated her, given her solace from the grief and fear and anger. She couldn't face the family who wanted her back. And Michael would be the last person on earth she could talk to about her lost career anyway; he'd always hated her service. He'd probably say, *good,* and let it go at that. He couldn't possibly understand how it felt to know that she'd never fly a Black Hawk again.

Even as she had the thought, she hated herself for it. Smitty was dead, for God's sake, and Tami lay in a hospital bed far away, fighting for her life. What right did Jolene have to bemoan a lost career?

"Jolene, I know you're awake."

She lay perfectly still, trying to slow her breathing. She didn't dare look at him, not tonight, when her sense of loss was as deep as a mountain cavern, bottomless.

She kept her eyes closed until finally—finally—he left her alone.

Twenty-Five

For the next week, Jolene hid from her family. It was surprisingly easy to do. She spent days at the rehab center, working hard, becoming increasingly self-sufficient, and then she came home, begged Mila for help, and disappeared into her bedroom. Wine and sleeping pills dulled her pain enough that she could sleep. Night after night, she heard her family beyond the door—talking, laughing, watching TV. They were going on with life, living it without her, and at each bit of laughter, she felt herself fall deeper into this sweaty darkness, until she began to have trouble even imagining a way to crawl out.

She lay in her solitary bed, cut off from everyone and everything, knowing she was giving up, giving in, but unable to change. What could she reach for? Who would help her to stand in her newly precarious position? Her children were afraid of her, and she was afraid of herself, afraid of her own crumbling, unreliable mind. Tami was too sick to offer help, and that was another of Jolene's sins. No matter how often she told herself the crash wasn't her fault, guilt was always there with her at night, a vulture waiting to pick at her bones. She called Germany often, talked to Carl, but they both knew his wasn't the voice she wanted so desperately to hear. Their conversations had become stilted lately; hope had worn thin.

Michael scared her, too, perhaps most of all. He kept saying the right things, words she'd longed to hear, but he didn't really love her. How could he? He had stopped loving her when she was at her best; how could he possibly love her now, at her worst?

She was terrified that if she let herself believe him in a moment of weakness, it would ruin what small bit of pride was left to her.

Every morning, she vowed to do better, but each night found her back in her room, taking sleeping pills to help her sleep. And still she had the nightmares.

"You're going to court with me today," Michael said one morning in mid-October, coming into her bedroom without even knocking.

"No, thanks," she said.

He walked over to the nightstand and picked up the empty wine bottle. "You can walk or I'll carry you."

She sat up in bed. "I haven't come to court with you in years."

"You will today. Mom said she'll handle the girls. We'll need to be on the seven fifty boat."

"But, Conny—"

"Has agreed."

She stared at him. "Fine," she said at last.

It took her a long time to get ready—naturally—and when she was done, she returned to her bedroom and looked at herself in the full-length mirror.

From a distance, she would probably draw no attention. It wasn't until you came near or saw her walk that you noticed the ugly plastic prosthetic foot.

"You look beautiful," Michael said from the doorway.

She pivoted awkwardly on her good foot.

His gaze swept her from head to toe, taking in the hair that fell free to well past her shoulders, the green boatneck sweater that showed off just a little skin, and the black pants that covered the part of her that was gone.

"Maybe I'm not ready to go out in public," she said.

"You're ready. Conny says so." He offered his arm. She clung to him, let him steady her as she made her slow, hitching way into the family room, where the girls and Mila were waiting. It broke her heart all over again to see how warily her children stared at her.

Mila rose at her entrance. "You have her pills, Michael?"

"I have everything," he said.

Mila came forward. Jolene couldn't help noticing that the girls hung back.

"You can do this," Mila said.

Jolene felt a rush of remembrance at that, a sweet longing for her life before. How many times had Mila encouraged her over the years, and then stayed by her side? It had been Mila who had told Jolene, over and over again, in the barren years after Betsy, *keep trying, there's always hope. You'll have another baby, I know it.* An old, ragged desire to make her mother-in-law proud rose up in Jolene; it was tattered and torn, but *there,* and it felt good. "Thanks, Mila," Jolene said in a hoarse voice.

And then they were moving, she and Michael, making their way through the family room and the mudroom and into the garage. Jolene got into the car with some effort—her damned temporary leg was unwieldy and heavy.

She wanted to take off the prosthesis and massage her leg in the car, but she didn't have the room. On the ferry, they stayed in the car. Jolene sat there quietly, staring out at the island's coastline while Michael read his notes.

When the ferry rounded the bend, Seattle was in front of them, a steel and gemstone tiara set above the waters of Elliott Bay. The sky on this early morning was rose-colored, tinged in aqua blue at the horizon. Mount Rainier rose elegantly above the city, deigning on this day to be visible.

She'd forgotten how beautiful it all was and how big. From here, she could see the stream of headlights snaking along Alaskan Way, zipping over the antiquated concrete viaduct.

Please be strong enough for this, she thought, realizing suddenly that she'd be moving in a crowd—could get jostled and bumped.

On Third Avenue, Michael pulled into a parking place right in front of the courthouse. She knew he'd have to have an associate move the car later, but she was glad he understood that the shortest distance was best for her.

He came around to her side and opened the car door.

She panicked.

"You can do it," he said evenly, reaching for her hand. She clung to him, stepped out onto the sidewalk. As she stood, clouds wafted overhead, blocking out the ineffectual sun, sending a smattering of rain to the sidewalk.

"Can you carry my crutches?" she asked. "I might need them later."

"Of course."

She began the long, slow walk to the courthouse. In no time, she was breathing hard, sweating. She concentrated on each step, ignoring the pain caused by her blisters.

She was slow, and none too pretty in her movements, but she was doing it: walking by herself to the courthouse. Michael's hold on her arm was only a balance point.

At the start of the stone steps, she paused, winded, and looked up. The concrete stairs rose like Chichén Itzá into the gray sky. "If you're going to be late—"

"They'll wait for me," Michael answered easily.

This time she held his arm and let him steady her as she slowly, slowly climbed upward. Step. Lift. Swing. Plant.

She didn't know how long it actually took—minutes probably—but it felt like hours. Finally, though, they were in the courtroom. Michael guided Jolene to a seat behind the defense table.

"Good luck," she said.

He smiled down at her. "Thanks."

And then he was moving away from her, joining the eager young associates gathering at the table.

The courtroom filled up around her. She saw reporters milling about outside, microphones at the ready. It must be a big case. She should have asked him about it.

At the same time the bailiff entered the courtroom, so did four marines in dress uniforms. They moved in unison, sat down shoulder to shoulder beside Jolene, their backs straight, their faces grim. Before she could wonder about it, really, the defendant came into the room.

He was just a kid, probably no more than twenty-five. But she knew by looking at him that he was a vet. She could see it in his eyes.

The judge entered the courtroom, banged his gavel, and began the proceedings. The prosecutor stood and began to tell the state's side—a story of bloodlust and anger, of a love gone tragically wrong, of a girl shot in the head by the man who had vowed to love her. For a simple story, it went on for more than an hour, so long Jolene's leg started to ache. Pain pulsed in her missing foot.

Finally, it was Michael's turn. He stood and addressed the jury. Unlike the prosecutor, Michael was relaxed with them, almost friendly. "Keith Keller is no monster. That would be easy, a monster. We could put a monster away and feel good about ourselves. Keith is something scarier. Keith is us. He is your brother, your son, your next-door neighbor." He looked at the jurors one by one. "He was a popular kid at Wenatchee High, a star football player. After a year of college, he married the girl of his dreams, Emily Plotner, and found a full-time job at a local feed store. His employers and fellow workers will tell you what a great guy he is. Keith thought his life was going along on a pretty good track. He and Emily had begun to talk about children.

"Then came September Eleventh. I'm sure you each can remember where you were when you heard about the attacks. Keith was at work. He learned almost immediately that his best friend had been on Flight Ninety-three."

Jolene found herself leaning forward.

"Most of us wanted to do something. Keith actually did. He joined the marines and went to fight terrorism in Iraq, where he saw some of the worst fighting of the war. Every day he saw friends killed or maimed; every day he wondered if the next step he took would be his last. He saw children and women smile at him and then blow up. He picked up the pieces of his best friend after a roadside bomb blew the young man apart.

"Keith is a Marine. I didn't used to know what that meant, but I should have, because my wife is a soldier. I sent her off to war without a clue as to what that meant." Michael turned, looked at her. "I'm proud of her service."

Jolene caught her breath. He was talking to *her*. That was why he'd wanted her here today. So that she would listen.

"Heroes," Michael said softly. The world seemed to fall away until it was only them, looking at each other across a crowded courtroom. "They are heroes, our soldiers, the men and women who go into harm's way to protect us, our way of life. It doesn't matter what you think of the war, you have to be grateful to the warriors, of whom we ask so much. To whom we sometimes give too little."

Slowly, he turned back to the jury.

How long had it been, when he'd been talking to her, only her? A few seconds? A moment? It felt like forever. How long had she waited to hear that from him—I'm proud of you? Tears stung her eyes; she wiped them impatiently away.

"A Marine is taught to be strong and brave," Michael said in a voice in which only she would hear the hoarseness, the emotion. "Not to need anyone. But Keith Keller did need help. He came home damaged beyond repair, suffering from nightmares." Here, Michael looked at Jolene again, and there was an understanding in his eyes she'd never seen before, a compassion that had nothing to do with pity. "He wouldn't let anyone help him, although his wife tried. But how do you help someone deal with horrors you can't imagine? And how does a warrior come home from war, really? As a nation, these are questions we need to ask ourselves. In the case of Keith Keller, he might be sitting right there in front of you, but in a very real way he never came home from Iraq . . ."

For the next hour, Michael went through the facts of the case from the defense's perspective, outlining PTSD and the failure to help him and the escalating anger and fear Keith had felt. "Keith's friends and family will testify that he came home from the war changed, mentally broken. He tried to get help from the VA but he couldn't, as so many other returning soldiers have discovered. He suffered terribly—

nightmares, insomnia, flashbacks. He drank too much to mask these symptoms, and unfortunately alcohol only exacerbated the condition. It's called post-traumatic stress and it is a recognized psychiatric disorder. It was around long before we had such a serious-sounding clinical name for it. In the Civil War, it was called a 'soldier's heart,' which I think is the most accurate of the descriptions; in World War One, it was 'shell shock,' and during World War Two, 'battle fatigue.' In other words, war changes every soldier, but it has always profoundly damaged some of them.

"Like so many other warriors before him, Keith came home jumpy, prone to violence, hyperalert, and angry. The facts will show that on the terrible day when he took his wife to the Pike Place Market, events occurred which reminded him of the war. Too much. In a single, tragic second, he forgot where he was, who he was, and he reacted on pure adrenaline and warrior training. In this fuguelike state, he shot his wife. Why? We don't know because Keith doesn't know, but expert witnesses will help us understand."

Michael finished with: "Keith Keller didn't have the ability in that moment to decide to kill his wife. In his mind, he was in Iraq, doing what he was trained to do. He never intended to kill Emily. Keith doesn't need to go to prison, he needs help. This man who went to war to defend *us* needs our help now. How can we turn our back on him? What happened in his house on that terrible, terrible day was a tragedy, certainly, but it wasn't murder. Thank you."

Jolene finally released a breath. She had been mesmerized by her husband, transported, and she could tell that the jury felt the same way. It was obvious in the way they watched him, didn't look away.

When he sat back down, Jolene felt the spell break, and she leaned back against the hard wooden seat. His words—his understanding—surprised and moved her. Deeply. She had spent all of her adult life in the service, and yet never had she been able to share that world with her husband. It had been the start of her loneliness, that separation, the start of their marriage's fall.

The prosecution called its first witness, and for the next hour, Jolene forgot about herself and Michael and listened to the testimony on the stand.

At noon, the judge released them, and Jolene stood, remembering a second too late that she was on her prosthesis. The marine beside her steadied her.

Their gazes caught. He looked down.

"Al Anbar," she said.

He nodded and reached for her crutches, handing them to her.

"Thanks," she said. Positioning her crutches, she stood in the row, letting people sidle past her. She needed something to steady her in this crowd.

The courtroom was practically empty when Michael touched her arm. She looked up at him. In that instant, all the love and passion she'd once felt for him came rushing back; she could no more hold it back than she could stem the tide. "When did you learn all that?"

"My wife went off to war," he said. "And while she was gone, I remembered her. I'm sorry I let you go on . . . those words. There are so many things I should have said. I understand why you didn't answer my letter, but I want another chance."

"Your letter? What—"

"Can you give me another chance, Jo?"

She swallowed hard. She couldn't have found her voice even if she had known what to say.

An associate came up to Michael, whispered something in his ear.

Michael nodded. To Jolene, he said, "Keith would like to talk to you."

"To me? Why?"

"I've mentioned you to him. I guess he has something he'd like to say." He led her through the courthouse to a room in the back, where Keith sat in front of a scarred wooden desk, his ankles and wrists shackled. At her entrance, he stood up; the chains rattled.

He was so damned young, and the pain in his eyes drew Jolene forward. She set her crutches against the wall and walked the last ten feet to the desk, where she sat down across from him. When she took the weight off her prosthesis, she felt instant relief.

"Chief," he said.

"Call me Jolene." She reached across the desk to shake his hand. He hesitated, then brought his manacled hand forward, shook hers.

"Ramadi," he said. "Mostly."

That was all he had to say. She knew what it had been like for him, how he'd served his country. He'd patrolled streets lined with IEDs, day after day, watching people—friends—blow up. He'd been on bag duty. How many hero missions had she flown for his buddies?

"Is there something I can do to help you?" she asked gently, leaning forward.

"Help yourself, Chief. That's what I wanted to tell you. We both know what's in our heads, how hard it is to think sometimes, how bad the nights can be. I should have told Emily everything and held on to her. Instead, I pretended I was okay. I could handle it. I'm a marine. And here I am . . . and there she is." He leaned forward. "You have kids, right?"

She nodded, sitting back.

"Don't be who you needed to be over there. Come home to the people who love you. I wish to hell I'd figured out a way to do that." He leaned forward, lowered his voice. "Talk to Michael. He's a good man. He wants to understand."

There was so much she could say to this wounded young man, but in a way, he'd said it all in those few sad words. He understood her: her pain, her fear, her reluctance to show weakness. He'd been there, and because of that, he was here.

A soldier's heart.

No wonder they'd called PTSD that in days gone by. It was true. *We can come home broken,* she thought. *No matter how strong we are . . .* The military should have prepared her for it. There was so much training before one goes to war, and so little for one's return.

Keith rose. Staring down at her, he bent his arm in a salute. To her horror, she felt the sting of tears. She shook her head. "I'm not a soldier anymore."

Keith's smile was heartbreaking. "We'll always be soldiers, Jolene."

. . .

When they got home, the house was empty. Mila had taken the girls out for dinner and left a *back by 8* note on the kitchen table.

Jolene limped into her bedroom and sat down on the edge of the bed. Although she was in considerable pain, she felt jittery, edgy. Michael's opening statement had been seductive, romantic, and it scared the hell out of her to believe—even a little—that he'd changed. On the long ride home from court, she and Michael had made small talk. She listened to his questions and formulated answers, but both of them heard the echo of all their unspoken words.

Michael knocked at her bedroom door, walked into the room.

She stared up at him. "There's something wrong with me," she said quietly. Her heartbeat kicked up. "I'm afraid." It was as honest as she knew how to be, as honest with him as she'd ever been. "What if I'm like Keith?"

"You're not."

"How do you know?"

He walked toward her, came to her side. Taking her hand in his, he pulled her to a stand. His gaze was steady, and in the darkness of his eyes, she saw the shadowy reflection of their whole lives, the good and the bad. He leaned slowly, slowly forward, saying, "I'm going to kiss you, Jolene . . ."

She knew he was giving her a chance to stop him, and there was a part of her that wanted to push him away and run and protect what was left of her heart. But she couldn't.

His kiss was everything she remembered, everything she'd ever wanted. Her body responded to him in the way it always had, wholly and completely.

When he drew back, she could see that he was as shaken by the kiss as she had been. His breathing was ragged.

"Tell me it's not too late for us," he said. She heard the desperate plea in his voice and knew she'd never heard it before.

"It's not too late," she said, trying to catch her breath. "But I'm not ready . . ."

He smiled at last, and it was his smile, the one that had swept her away all those years ago. How long had it been since she'd seen it? He walked over to the nightstand by the bed, opened the drawer, and took out a small plastic bag.

She heard the jangle of metal as he opened the baggie, and she knew what was inside of it. Why hadn't she thought about it before? Her belongings. They'd given her jewelry to him in Germany—her dog tags, her watch, her wedding ring. He took something out of the bag before putting it back in the drawer, closing it with a *click*.

She drew in a shaky breath.

He moved toward her, reached for her left hand. Without looking away, he slipped the wedding ring back onto her finger. "You will be," he said, and the certainty in his voice struck a chord deep within her.

She watched him walk away, close the door behind him. Twice, she almost called him back, almost said, *I was wrong, I am ready,* but she was too afraid.

She hobbled into the bathroom and got ready for bed. Climbing under the thick comforter, she positioned the pillows around her residual leg and closed her eyes. The simple golden band added a forgotten weight to her hand. For the first time in weeks, she went to sleep without a glass of wine or a sleeping pill. Keith was right. She would take his advice. She would *come home to the people who loved her—her husband, her family.* She had to be able to do it. She'd gone to Iraq, for God's sake, she'd flown helicopters in combat. How could it be harder to come home than to go to war?

Her last thought, as she drifted off to sleep was, *Tomorrow I'll start over, Tami. I'll be Mommy again. I'll come home at last.*

Twenty-Six

Jolene woke to watery yellow sunshine pouring through her window. It illuminated everything in the room—including the empty wineglass on her nightstand and the collection of orange pill bottles.

Today was the day she would give all that up. No more sleeping pills, no more wine to calm her jangling nerves. She closed her eyes and imagined it in detail—she would rise confidently and go into the kitchen and make breakfast for her girls. Then she would take them aside and talk to them openly, tell them that the war had hurt her mind for a while and sucked out some of her spirit but that she could handle it now. She was ready to be Mom again, and that she'd always, always loved them, even when the numbness was at its very worst. They wouldn't understand, perhaps, wouldn't believe her completely, but it would be a start. From there, she would prove it to them by improving every day, by getting strong and showing her love more freely. She wouldn't be afraid anymore.

She got out of bed and grabbed her crutches, hop-swinging into the bathroom. Emerging only ten minutes later, dressed for rehab, with her prosthesis on, she limped out into the kitchen and started breakfast. Pancakes today—like the old days. She got some blueberries out of the freezer and started the batter. Every now and again she caught sight of her wedding ring and it made her smile. Hope felt as close as it ever had.

As she poured the batter in dollops on the hot griddle, she heard Michael come up behind her. He moved in close, leaned over her shoulder. "Pancakes, huh?"

"A peace offering. I could have learned quantum physics in the time they took to make." She smiled at him, and for a second they were Michael-and-Jo again, and she thought: *We can do it.*

"Jo—"

She wanted to know what he was going to say, leaned closer to hear the words, but the phone rang. Michael went to answer it. "Hello?" It was obviously the office; he frowned, sat down, and lowered his voice to say, "When?"

The girls came thundering into the room.

"Mommy's making pancakes!" Lulu said, her frown turning into a smile when she saw that the pancakes looked ordinary.

Jolene turned slightly, saw Betsy's narrowed gaze. "The griddle's too hot," her daughter said.

"Thank you," Michael said, hanging up the phone.

Jolene smiled. "Michael, Betsy thinks the griddle is too hot. Will you tell her I was making pancakes before she was born?"

Michael stared at her, unsmiling. "Maybe you should sit down, Jo."

"Sit down? Why? My leg feels great."

"Betsy, finish the pancakes," Michael said.

"Why me?" Betsy whined. "Why do I always have to do everything?"

"Betsy," he said so sharply Jolene frowned.

"Michael?" she said. "You're scaring me."

He took Jolene by the arm and led her through the house, toward the bedroom. When she sat down on the bed, she looked up at him.

"It's Tami," he said quietly, sitting beside her. "She died last night."

Jolene couldn't breathe. As if from a distance, she saw Michael holding her, soothing her, rubbing his hand up and down her back, but none of it reached her.

For more than twenty years, Tami had been there for her, keeping her strong when she felt weak. *I've got your six, flygirl.*

And Seth . . . he would grow up without a mom . . .

She made a great gasping sound and started to cry.

"It's okay, Jo," Michael said, stroking her hair.

"No." She felt wild suddenly, feral. "It's not okay. My best friend died and it's my fault. Mine. She died and then I left her behind . . ." Her voice broke. "I'm never supposed to leave anyone behind."

"Jo—"

"I'm sick of people telling me it will be okay. It won't be okay. It'll never be okay."

She couldn't take this pain. It was consuming her, devouring her. She stumbled to the nightstand and grabbed her sleeping pills. Opening the container, she spilled three into her shaking palm. "A nap will help," she said, her voice shrill. "I'll feel better after a little nap."

It was a lie. She wouldn't feel better, but she needed to close her eyes and get away from this grief. She couldn't bear it. Not anymore; she wasn't strong enough. Her heart might just stop . . . and would she care?

She swallowed the pills, dry, and sank to the bed, hanging her head, willing them to work.

Michael moved closer, took her in his arms again. She knew he was judging her for taking the pills, thinking that she was pathetic and damaged, but she didn't care. It was the truth anyway; she'd been snapped in half and her courage was gone.

She looked at him through her tears. "We were supposed to grow old together. We were going to be old women, sitting on our deck in rocking chairs, remembering each other's lives . . ."

On the day of Tami's funeral, Jolene couldn't get out of bed.

As soon as she woke up, she poured herself a glass of wine. Downing it quickly, she poured and drank another. But there was no help in the bottle today.

She heard the shower start upstairs. Michael was up.

Throwing the covers back, she got out of bed, put on her prosthetic leg, and made her way across the family room slowly; aware of every step, every bump and line and scar on the wood floor. In the past few weeks, she'd made excellent progress with her prosthesis, she was able to wear it almost all the time now, and her movements were getting stronger every day.

At the rag rug, she positioned her fake foot carefully so she wouldn't slip and then kept going. Up the stairs. Grab, lift, thrust, place, step. Each riser took phenomenal concentration and resolve. By the time she got to the master bedroom, she was sweating.

She shouldn't be up here. It was off-limits, really, this second floor. No one trusted her to use the stairs. No one trusted her to do much of anything, really. She could hardly blame them.

She limped over to the closet and opened the louvered doors. Her clothes were all still there, neatly aligned.

The first thing she saw were her ACUs, the combat fatigues, with the black beret pinned to the chest. She and Tami had worn that uniform almost every day in Iraq . . .

Beyond it were her class As—dress uniform: a jacket, knee-length skirt, and white blouse. She pulled it out, stared down at the jacket with its gold detailing, surprised by the emotion that washed over her.

"Jo?" Michael said, coming into the room. He was bare-chested, wearing a towel wrapped low on his hips; his hair was still wet. "You're crying," he said.

"Am I?"

He came over, took the uniform from her. "Let me help you get downstairs. Mom should be here by now."

"I can't do this."

His gaze was steady, warm. "You can." He held on to her arm, steadied her as she moved through the bedroom and went down the stairs, where Mila was waiting at the kitchen table, sipping coffee.

"I came to help you get ready," she said gently.

Jolene felt as empty as corn husk, hollow, dried-out. She was shaking when her mother-in-law took her by the elbow.

Mila helped her into the shower. When Jolene was done, and wrapped in a big, thick towel, Mila positioned her on the toilet, then brushed and dried her hair. Her residual leg stuck out like a baseball bat, still swollen and decorated with bright-pink stitch marks. Mila wrapped it expertly in the elastic bandage and then covered it with the gel sock.

"A little makeup would be nice today, don't you think? You're pale and you've lost so much weight . . ."

Jolene nodded but didn't really care.

"Sit up straight and close your eyes."

Jolene closed her eyes when asked, opened them when prompted, and pursed her lips. She couldn't have cared less how she looked, but neither did she have the strength to protest.

"There. All done. Let's get you dressed. Here." Mila knelt in front of her, holding the waistband of the skirt open.

Jolene lifted her left foot and guided it through the opening, gritting her teeth when her mother-in-law slipped the skirt over her stump. Then she stood dutifully and sat again, zipping her skirt before she opened her arms for the blouse, fixing the smart dark neck tab at her collar.

Mila talked the whole time, about gardening and recipes she'd tried and the weather. Anything except the thing they were getting ready for. "Okay. All done. How did I do?"

Jolene lifted the skirt and put her prosthetic limb on. Grabbing the handrail by the toilet, she got to her feet. Turning with care, she faced the mirror on the back of the door.

In her crisp white shirt, dark neck tab, and jacket decorated with honors and trimmed in gold, she was a soldier again.

We're graduating, flygirl, stand up straight . . .

Mila took Jolene in her arms, holding her tightly.

Jolene drew back. She couldn't be touched right now; she was like fine antique china. The smallest pressure in the wrong place and she'd crack. She limped out into the family room, where Betsy and Lulu and Michael were waiting, all of them dressed in black.

When she looked at them, the membrane between what had happened and what could have seemed as fragile as a spider's web. She was lucky to be here. It could easily have been her funeral that had made them wear black. They were thinking the same thing; she could see it in their eyes.

She managed a smile, wan though it must be, because it was expected of her.

Her family came forward, bookended her. She knew that Michael had already loaded her crutches and wheelchair into the SUV. He also knew how much she wanted to walk on her own today.

Perhaps he thought she wanted to look whole, unharmed, soldier-like. But the truth was that it hurt her to walk still, and she wanted that pain today, welcomed it. It was proof in some sick way that she'd given her best that night, that she had barely survived.

She walked—limped, really; she'd gotten new blisters on her trip to the courthouse—out to the garage.

She climbed awkwardly into the passenger seat of her SUV and forced her prosthesis to bend at the knee. The ugly ankle boot on the clunky foot hit the car's rubber floor mat and stuck there.

She knew she should say something to her family now. They needed her to put them at ease and let them know she was okay.

But she wasn't okay and they knew it. They were afraid of her now, afraid she'd blow up or start crying or yelling or maybe even that she'd hit someone.

She didn't even care. The numbness was back, and this time, she was grateful for it.

Michael started the engine and opened the garage door. It clattered up behind them.

Outside, rain fell in broken threads, strands so slim and pale you only knew it was raining because you could hear it pattering the roof. Michael didn't even bother to turn on the wipers.

The radio came on. "Purple Rain" blared through the speakers.

Jolene glanced to her left, and for a split second Tami was there, moving side to side, tapping her fingers on the steering wheel, singing *pur-ple rain . . . puur-urr-ple rain . . .* at the top of her lungs.

Michael leaned forward and clicked off the radio. It wasn't until he looked at her, laid his hand on her thigh, and squeezed gently that she realized she was crying.

She looked at him, thought, *How am I going to get through this?*

Michael squeezed her leg again.

She turned away from him, looked out the window. They were still on the bay road, and the water was calm today, as shiny and silver as a new nickel. By the time they turned onto Front Street, the sky had cleared. A pale sun pushed its way through the layer of cottony gray clouds, limning them with lemony light. In an instant, colors burst to life: the green trees on either side of the road seemed to swallow the sun and glow from within.

In town, there was bumper-to-bumper traffic.

"They all have their lights on," Michael said.

"But it's not night," Lulu said from the backseat.

"It's for Tami," Mila said quietly.

Jolene climbed out of the darkness of her own grief and looked around. The hearse was about three cars in front of them, crawling forward. There had to be a hundred cars behind them.

They were going through town now. On either side of the street, people stood in front of the shops, gathered in clusters, waving at the passing hearse.

There were flags everywhere—on posts and poles and streetlamps. Yellow ribbons fluttered in the breeze—from doorknobs and flower boxes and car antennae. A sign in the window of Liberty Bay Books read: GOODBYE TAMI FLYNN. SAFE JOURNEY HOME.

By the time they made it to the end of town—only a few blocks later—there were hundreds of people waving at the hearse as it passed.

Then the honking started. It sounded like a symphony as the snake of cars turned up toward the cemetery. Once there, on the crest of the hill above Liberty Bay, you could see forever—the Sound, the town, and the jagged, snow-covered Olympic Mountains.

After they parked, Jolene sat there long enough that her family started to worry. They threw questions at her like tiny darts until she said, "I'm fine," and sighed and got out of the car.

The family merged into the crowd of mourners, many of whom were in uniform.

Behind them, Jolene heard the throaty roar of Harley-Davidson motorcycles.

She shouldn't have turned, but she did. The cars were still streaming in, lights on. There, in the middle of traffic, were about thirty motorcycles, moving in formation; huge flags flapped out behind the riders—Guard, army, American. They created a blur of flying colors. She could see from here that the riders were of all ages and most were in uniforms.

Patriot riders.

Jolene stumbled; Michael caught her, steadied her. Giving him a tight smile, she squared her shoulders and kept walking.

As they rounded the bend, she saw their destination. Perched out on a lip of land that overlooked the Sound was a peaked green tent roof supported by four glinting silver poles. Beneath it was a casket draped in an American flag.

Already there were hundreds of mourners standing around. Behind them stood a row of flags—the Guard, the United States, the army. Last was the Raptor flag.

She wanted to lean into Michael and feel him take her in his arms, but she stood tall, lifted her chin just the slightest amount. This might be the last moment she would ever be Chief Warrant Officer Zarkades, and she'd be damned if she'd disgrace the uniform.

At the side of the casket, she saw Carl and Seth, both dressed in black, looking blank and confused. Beside them was Tami's weeping mother.

She went up to Seth, put her arms around him. She saw the tears glaze his eyes, and it took every ounce of willpower she had not to cry. She concentrated on each breath, remaining composed by sheer force of will.

And then it was beginning. Michael led her to one of the folding chairs reserved for the family. It hurt to look at Seth and Carl as they took their seats beside her, but she did it, wanting desperately to say *I'm sorry* to each of them. Amazingly, they looked at her with sadness, but not blame. That only made her feel worse.

Somewhere a bagpipe started to play.

This time Jolene closed her eyes. She heard the high, mournful notes of the instrument, heard the muffled sound of boots marching along behind, and knew the soldiers were making their way down the hill, toward the casket.

"We are here to say good-bye to a special woman. Chief Warrant Officer Tamara Margaret Flynn . . ."

Jolene dared to open her eyes.

The minister from Tami's church stood by the casket. He had no microphone—no one had expected such a crowd—but the people quieted instantly, until all you could hear was the wind fluttering the flags out front. "But she wasn't Tamara to us, was she? She was just Tami, the girl who used to climb trees with the boys and run wild along the beach. I remember when her mother despaired that she would ever slow down enough to find a career." He looked up the hill.

Jolene knew what he was seeing—hundreds of people, and more than half of them in uniform. "She did find that career, though, and I have to say, I wasn't surprised that she found her passion in the sky. She loved flying. She once told me that it was as close to God as she could imagine being."

He looked down at his hands, then up at the crowd again. "We lost her, and that is a wound that won't heal. We lost her in a faraway land, doing something that most of us can't begin to understand. We ask how we could have lost her in such a way. But then we know: that was Tami. If someone needed help, she was the first to show up. Of course she put herself in harm's way. That's who our Tami was."

Jolene heard Seth make a sound beside her. She reached for his hand, took it. He held on tightly.

"We thank Tami for her service today, as friends and as Americans.

She gave the full measure to protect, and she is a hero. But we knew that, didn't we? We knew she was a hero long before today. To Seth and Carl, whom she loved with a fierceness that was matched only by her courage, I say, remember her, all of her. And when you look at the sky, think of her up there, in her beloved blue, with our Lord beside her. She would not want you to mourn." He looked up at the sky and said quietly, "Good-bye, Tami. Peace be with you."

He stepped aside and one of the uniformed soldiers marched up to the casket. The soldier removed the flag from the casket, and, along with another soldier, carefully folded it into a near triangle. Then he offered it to Captain Ben Lomand, who stood nearby. The soldier saluted and handed Ben the flag. Ben turned crisply on his heel, pivoted, and brought the flag to Carl.

Jolene saw that Carl's hands were shaking as he reached out.

On the ground, two rows of soldiers pointed their guns skyward and shots rang out. A twenty-one-gun salute. Carl stood, walked toward the casket. He stood there a long time, his head bowed; then he placed a red rose on the gleaming mahogany top. Seth followed. The rose he placed on the casket slipped off, and he bent to retrieve it, placing it next to his father's. One by one Tami's relatives came up to say their last good-bye and put a rose on the casket.

When it was Jolene's turn, she stood slowly. She felt awkward, uncertain that her legs would hold her up.

"You can do it," Michael said.

She moved cautiously forward. At the flower-strewn coffin, she stopped, and put her hands out, touching the smooth wood. The rose she held bit her with its thorn. *Good-bye, flygirl. I'll miss you . . .*

She put her rose with the others and then joined the five soldiers who'd gathered at the casket. The bagpipes started to play again, and Jolene watched as the soldiers—her friends from the Guard—picked up the casket. The soldiers carried it down the grass toward its final resting place. Jolene limped beside them, an honorary pallbearer.

Tears glazed her eyes, and she couldn't see well, but she kept moving, gritting her teeth against the pain. The uneven grass threatened to break her stride at every step, but she kept going. Finally, they came to the grave site.

The bagpipes wound down, their music fading away. In the sudden silence, three helicopters roared into the airspace, rotors whirring, engines purring, and hung there.

Good-bye, Tam. Fly safe . . .

And it was over.

Twenty-Seven

❊

For the next week, Jolene hung on by the thinnest imaginable thread. The grief was so overwhelming she forced herself to ignore it completely. With a combination of wine and sleeping pills, she found numbness. She went to rehab three days a week and tried to concentrate on her recovery, but to be honest she barely cared. At home, she drank two or three glasses of wine and crawled into her bed, pulling the covers up to her chin. When she was lucky, she slept at night. Other times, she lay awake in the darkness, acutely alone, remembering her best friend. She knew how her family felt about her lethargy—Betsy was pissed, Michael was saddened, and Lulu was confused.

She knew she was letting them down again, and sometimes she found the energy to care. Mostly, she just . . . looked away. Even on Halloween, she'd been unable to rouse herself. She'd waved good-bye to her princess and her gypsy and watched them leave with Mila and Michael for trick-or-treating.

"Okay, Jolene," Michael said one morning in early November. He came into her bedroom and flung back the curtains, letting light steamroll over her.

She had a pounding headache. Had she had an extra glass of wine last night? "Go away, Michael. It's Saturday. I'm not going to rehab."

"You're going somewhere else."

She sat up, blinking wearily. "Where is it you think I'm going?"

He stepped aside. Seth walked into the bedroom. He was dressed all in black—wrinkled black corduroy pants and an oversized black short-sleeved shirt with an envelope stuck in the breast pocket—and his hair pulled back in a samurai topknot that only Johnny Depp could pull off. *My kid's a fashion disaster, what can I say?* She heard Tami's voice so loudly, so clearly, that Jolene caught her breath. For a split second, she thought she saw her friend standing in the corner, her arms crossed, her face lit by a smile.

"Miz Z," Seth said, coming forward.

"Seth," she whispered, feeling a stab of guilt. "I should have come over to see you. I've just been . . ."

"Yeah," he said. "Me, too."

Jolene wanted to fill the sudden painful silence, but she couldn't.

"Her locker," Seth said at last.

Jolene knew what he was going to ask of her, and she couldn't do it.

"They want us to clean it out. Dad doesn't even know where it is. Will you take me to the post, help me get her things?"

She wanted to say no. Instead, she nodded, her eyes stinging again, and said, "Of course, Seth. Maybe next week—"

"Today," Michael said. "We'll all go." He came to the bed, held out his hand.

She stared at it, afraid to let him touch her. She felt so breakable right now. But Tami had asked this of her—take care of Seth—and she'd be damned if she'd let her best friend down. In an act of will, she took Michael's hand, let him help her to her feet. She stared into his eyes for a moment, seeing the strength that was offered there, unable to take it for her own. "I'll get ready." She gave Seth a weak smile.

In the bathroom, she stared at herself in the mirror. Her face was healed now, but even so, it was different. Sharper. Harder. Her cheek-bones were bony ridges above hollow cheeks; her lips were chapped and pale. And there was that slightest pink scar along her jaw. "You can do this."

Of course you can.

It was Tami's voice again, so close, Jolene turned sharply, looked behind her. There was no one there.

She limped toward the shower. When she was done, she dried her hair, coiled it in a bun, and went to her closet.

Her ACUs were right there in front. Michael must have brought them down. But she wasn't a soldier anymore.

The thought came to her before she could guard against it.

She gritted her teeth and dressed in a pair of black pants and a gray turtleneck. When she went out into the living room, Betsy and Lulu were standing by Michael. Seth stood off by himself, his arms crossed tightly.

"Okay," Jolene said. "Let's go."

She limped into the garage and opened the passenger door of her SUV. She opened it and hoisted herself up into the plush seat.

In no time, the kids were in back: Seth and Betsy were sitting together, with Lulu on the left side of them. In the rearview mirror, Jolene saw Betsy poke Seth's upper arm. He blinked in surprise and pulled the earbuds from his ears. Betsy leaned closer to him, whispered something. He looked at her, his eyes widening at her smile.

Jolene turned away, looked out the window, watching the gray landscape blur past her. Now and then Michael tried to begin a conversation, but she didn't bother to answer, and soon he gave up.

All she could think about was Tami. Her friend should be in the car now, cranking the music up, saying, *Hey, flygirl, Prince or Madonna today?*

When they drove up to the guard post, Jolene felt a sharp stab of emotion—longing, disappointment, loss.

So much of her life had been spent here. With Tami beside her, always.

They parked in front of the hangar. Jolene steeled herself. It would be a tough day—and not just because hours on the temporary prosthesis came at a price. She climbed out of the SUV and stood there, both feet firmly planted, waiting for Seth.

Michael said, "Lulu has to go to the bathroom."

Jolene nodded. "It's in that building right there. First door on the left. We'll meet you back at the car. It . . . won't take long."

Michael leaned forward, kissed her lightly on the cheek, whispered, "You got this, Jo."

She shivered at the touch of his lips.

"I'll go with Mom and Seth," Betsy said quietly.

Seth looked at her. "Really?"

She gave him a shy smile. "Really."

Jolene moved closer to Seth, placed a hand on his thin shoulder. "You ready?"

"I don't know," he said.

"Yeah, well that makes two of us."

Jolene led the way to the hangar. The last time she'd been here, she'd been deploying . . .

As they crossed the threshold, moving into the giant space full of helicopters and cargo planes and people in uniform moving from place to place, Jolene stopped.

She didn't mean to. She just saw the Black Hawk and couldn't move.

My turn to fly. It's right seat for you today, no arguing.

"Jolene?"

She looked down at the boy beside her, seeing how pale and sad he looked, and she forgot about her own loss for a minute. *You make sure he knows who I was.* "She loved to fly," she said quietly. "She would want you to know that. She loved to fly, but . . . you . . . you were her whole life, Seth. She would have done anything she could to get back to you." She forced a smile. "And she sang off-key. Did you know that? I swear, dogs joined in when she sang."

Tears brightened his eyes.

Jolene stared up at the helicopter, with its open door and back bay cluttered with straps and metal boxes. She let go of Seth's hand and walked forward. She didn't mean to, didn't really think about it; she just moved forward and stared up at the cockpit.

Her residual limb ached, as if in reminder.

"Can you still fly?" Seth asked, coming up beside her.

"Not a Black Hawk," she said, and for a split second, she remembered all of it—flight school, Tami, flying into the blue, looking down on the trees in bloom. "I loved it, though," she said, more to herself than to Seth.

How long did she stand there, staring up at her past, grieving for both the loss of her leg and the loss of her friend and the end of an era?

"You'll never be able to fly again?" Betsy asked, sounding surprised.

Jolene couldn't answer.

"My mom would say you can do anything," Seth said.

Jolene nodded. Those few words brought Tami into the hangar so clearly she could practically smell her gardenia shampoo. "Yes, she would. And she'd kick my ass if she saw us standing here with tears in our eyes."

He wiped his eyes. "Yep."

"Come on, guys." She led him through the building to the locker room. Betsy followed a pace behind.

Jolene limped through the narrow area, lined with metal lockers. At number 702, she stopped.

"Is that my mom's?"

Jolene nodded, feeling Betsy come up beside her. Jolene hesitated a second, and then spun the lock into its combination. It clicked open.

At the bottom of the locker were a pair of sand-colored boots, a green tee shirt, a helmet, and a silver water bottle. A picture of Seth and Carl, its edges curled up, was taped to the inside wall. Jolene reached in and took the items out, setting them aside. She handed Seth the picture.

That was when she saw the envelope. There was just one—a long, business-sized white envelope with one word written across it: *Jolene.*

"I knew she'd write you one," Seth said. His hand made its way to his pocket; he fingered the envelope that stuck up. "It's her 'in case I die' letter."

Jolene couldn't reach for it.

"Do you think she knew?" he asked, looking at her.

"No," Jolene said thickly. "She thought she'd come home. She wanted to, so much. For you and your dad." She took a breath. "I know I'm not her, Seth, but I will be here for you your whole life. If you need anything—advice with girls, driving lessons, anything. You come to me. We can talk about anything. When you're ready, we'll talk about your mom and how much she loved you, and what her dreams for you were. I'll show you some pictures and tell you some stories."

"When I'm ready?"

Jolene knew what he meant. She wasn't ready yet, either. She couldn't read Tami's letter until she was stronger, until she was sure the goodbye wouldn't break her. Hell, maybe she'd never be able to read it.

The Keller trial ended amid a flurry of icy rain in downtown Seattle. Michael fought for the jury instructions he wanted, and he got them. The prosecution had amended the charges to include both murder in the second degree and manslaughter to the charges—a good sign for the defense. For weeks, Michael had put on witnesses and offered evidence about PTSD. He'd argued fervently that Keith had been incapable of forming the specific intent necessary to commit the crime of murder in the first degree. One witness after another had confirmed Keith's deep and abiding love for his wife. Even Emily's mother had tearfully confessed that she had known something was wrong with Keith, that he'd come home "messed up in his head somehow," and that the killing was terrible and tragic but that she didn't see how prison would help. "We just have to live with it," she'd concluded, dabbing at her eyes.

Keith's own testimony had been the defense's best weapon. It had been a big gamble to put him on the stand, but Michael had known by then that the jury would only believe Keith if they heard the story firsthand.

With Keith, there were no previous crimes, no barroom fights or petty shoplifting charges in his youth, nothing that his testimony would open the door to. He had been a good kid who had grown into a fine man who had been broken by war. He testified about trying to get help from Veterans Affairs and the helplessness he felt. He cried when he talked about his wife, although he seemed to be unaware of his tears. When he said, "If I hadn't gone to Iraq, maybe I'd still be working at the feed store and we'd have a baby by now. Theresa. That was the name Emily picked for our daughter. It haunts me, thinking stuff like that," several of the jurors had shiny eyes.

Michael had hoped—as all defense attorneys did—for either a lightning-fast verdict or a very slow one.

This time, he got his wish. The jury's deliberation went on and on. For six days, Michael went into the city, sat at his desk. He read reports and conducted depositions and drafted pleadings, but all the while he was waiting. The worst part of it was that he needed to be at home, and yet here he was.

Since Tami's funeral, Jolene had fallen into a despair he couldn't imagine, gone to a dark place he couldn't follow. The tiny footprints of their reconciliation—that one kiss—had been lost in the rubble of her grief. She drank too much and took sleeping pills and slept the days and nights away. She woke screaming at night but wouldn't let herself be comforted. When he tried, she pushed him away, looking at him through eyes that were wide with pain. The girls steered clear of her. Lulu cried herself to sleep, wondering what had happened to her mommy.

Michael was literally at the end of his rope. He was trying to give Jolene space and let her grieve, but she was pulling them all under water, drowning them, and he didn't know what to do.

His intercom buzzed. "Michael? The jury's in."

Michael thanked his secretary and grabbed his coat. Within minutes, he was walking up Second Avenue in the spitting cold rain. Damp bits of paper and black leaves skidded along the wet streets, plastering themselves to windows and bus stops and windshields.

Inside the courthouse, he stomped his feet on the stone floor and shook the rain from his hair.

Not far away, a knot of reporters had gathered. More would probably follow. In the past week, both CNN and Fox News had done stories on the case.

"Michael!"

They called out to him, waved him over.

He paused just long enough to say, "No comment yet, guys," and then walked into the courtroom, where he took a seat at the defendant's table.

The Kellers had been staying in a local hotel, waiting, and they arrived a few minutes later.

Every seat was taken by the time a guard led Keith into the courtroom. He looked pale and drawn after his months in jail. He was allowed to hug his parents—briefly—and then took his place beside Michael.

"How are you doing?" Michael asked.

Keith shrugged. For once the marine posture was gone; Keith was just a kid now, facing life in prison and worse—life in the prison of what he'd done.

"All rise." The judge took his seat at the bench.

The jury filled in. Michael tried to see the answer in their eyes, but they wouldn't look at him—not a good sign.

"Have you reached a verdict in the matter of the *State of Washington v. Keller*?"

"We have," said the jury foreman.

"What say you?"

At first there was the legalese of case and crime, and then: "On the count of murder in the first degree, we, the jury, find the defendant not guilty."

Michael released a breath. He heard a rustle of noise behind him. People were whispering among themselves.

"On the charge of second degree murder, we find the defendant guilty."

The gallery erupted. Once again the judge tried to take control. Michael heard Mrs. Keller cry out.

"We'll appeal, Keith," Michael said quickly.

Keith looked at him, and for once he looked old. "No, we won't. I deserve this, Michael. And it's not murder one. You did a good job. They know I didn't mean to kill her. That matters to me." He turned away, was enfolded in his parents' arms.

The associates who'd worked on the case surged around Michael, congratulating him on beating murder one. He knew this case would set precedent here in Washington and carry weight nationwide. It was a statement about the jury's belief in PTSD. They believed Keith didn't intentionally kill his wife. For the young lawyers, who hadn't yet learned the chasm that sometimes existed between justice and the law, this would be cause for much celebrating. For them, it was simply a win, a victory against formidable odds. They wouldn't think about this case again, except in technical terms. They wouldn't think of Keith sitting behind bars, suffering through nightmares.

"I deserve to go to prison," Keith said to him. "I said that from the beginning. Maybe you're right and the war messed me up, but Emily is dead and I killed her."

"You didn't mean to."

"It's not intentions that matter. It's actions. My drill instructor used to say that all the time. We are what we do and say, not what we intend to. I meant to tell Emily a thousand times that I was in trouble, but I never did. If only I'd told her the truth, maybe we would have had a chance. Thank you, Michael. Really."

Then the bailiff came and took Keith away.

Michael stood there until everyone else was gone and the courtroom was empty. The Kellers thanked him, as did the Plotners, and he didn't know what to say in response. He had done his best for their son, and it had been almost enough. He remembered his father saying once that ghosts were the curse of the criminal defense attorney, and he knew that this case would haunt him. He would wonder forever if he could have done something more, if he shouldn't have put Keith on the stand.

All the way home, he replayed the trial in his mind, tried to follow the threads of different choices, wondering if any one of them would have changed the outcome. Then he began to construct his argument for the next phase of the trial, how he would ask for mercy in the form of a lesser sentence . . .

When he walked into his house, though, all of that fled. He could tell instantly that Betsy and Lulu had been fighting. Lulu's eyes were red and puffy, and Betsy was shrieking at her.

"She's NOT the boss of me," Lulu wailed at him, running, throwing herself into his arms.

Betsy rolled her eyes and stomped off.

Michael couldn't handle this tonight. Not tonight. "Where's your mom?" he said more sharply than he intended.

Lulu looked at him through her tears. "In her bedroom. She hates us."

"I need to talk to her." He tried to put Lulu down, but she clung to him like a burr on wool, crying harder.

"Damn it, Lulu . . ."

"You s-said a b-bad word."

"I know. Sorry." He kissed her damp cheek and forced her to stand on her own. "Stay here," he said, leaving the room. He went to Jolene's room, knocked, and opened the door.

She was sitting up in bed, her hair a mess, holding Tami's unopened letter, staring down at it.

"Read it," he said harshly.

She ignored him.

He saw the open wine bottle on the nightstand. Without thinking, he walked over to her, grabbed the bottle, saying, "Enough, Jo."

She reached out. "Don't—"

"Don't what?" he yelled at her. "Don't love you anymore? Don't want you? Don't care if you drink yourself into a coma?"

She flinched at the obvious reminder of Tami.

He saw her eyes go blank again. She was retreating, pulling her pain into that dark place inside of her, the place to which he'd never been granted access. "Enough," he said again, yelling it. "I was an asshole before you left. I admit it. I was an asshole and I broke your heart and I might have ruined us. Maybe I did ruin us. But I've changed, Jo. I've changed and you don't seem to care. I'm sick of throwing myself against the concrete wall of your defenses. You're giving me nothing. You're giving your children nothing. *Nothing.* And you know what that's like, don't you, Jo, getting nothing from your parents. If we're broken now and this family is ruined, it's on you. On you. I can't try any harder."

She looked at him through tears. "You think I don't know that?"

"Give me something," he said, his voice breaking. Her tears brought it all home to him, pulled the fire from his anger and left him shaken, cold. "Reach out, Jo. Talk to me. Be my wife again."

"I can't."

"So we're done . . . after all this . . ."

She rolled away from him, pulled the covers up around her.

He stood there, uncertain, feeling as lost and alone as ever in his life. It was worse even than standing at his father's graveside. Jolene, he realized right then, realized it to the marrow in his bones, was his life.

Behind him, there was a knock at the door. He said nothing, but the door opened. Lulu stood there, her face wet with tears. "I'm scared, Daddy," she said.

With a sigh, he went to her, took her in his arms. "It's okay, Lulu," he lied, leaving Jolene's room, closing the door behind him.

Twenty-Eight

The next day was Carl's "celebration of Tami's life" for friends and family.

All day, Jolene had been shaky, angry. She'd snapped at her children and cried at the drop of a hat. The fight with Michael had pushed her to the very edge of control. She kept her emotions in check with the fiercest grip of her life. A headache throbbed behind her eyes. She drank two glasses of wine, but it didn't still the trembling in her hands. She should have been at Tami's house at three o'clock, setting out food and plates and utensils, making sure that everything was ready. It was a best friend's job to help out the husband at a time like this.

Jolene had nothing to give. She was so empty inside she was surprised every time she looked in the mirror—how could her veins not be showing through her pale skin, how could her bones not be visible?

At seven, Michael knocked on her bedroom door and came inside, closing the door behind him.

She sat on the bed, dressed in jeans and a white blouse, her hair still damp. She knew by the look on his face that her eyes were red-rimmed and bloodshot.

"You don't have to do this if you can't," he said tiredly, but he wouldn't meet her eyes. She saw how much she'd wounded him, hurt him, and it shamed her. She thought of the letter she'd written to Michael before she left for Iraq. *I loved you, beginning to end.*

"I have to." She got unsteadily to her feet.

He was there in an instant, holding her arm. At his touch, she felt a surge of loss. Had it only been a few weeks ago that he'd kissed her? That she'd thought *maybe?* and began to fall in love with him again? It all felt so far away now, like memories held under water.

He kept hold of her arm as they went into the family room, where Mila and the girls were waiting. Mila and Betsy both held foil-wrapped casserole dishes, and Jolene thought, *I should have cooked.*

Tami's seven-layer dip. She loved it . . .

She almost stumbled; Michael held her steady. They walked out of the house and across the yard. On this cold November evening, it was already darkening. Soon, there would be frost on the fence posts and across the green surface of the grass.

Michael opened the gate. They walked through the opening and over the hump of grass and up the Flynns' gravel driveway. At the house, there were dozens of cars and trucks parked out front. Lights blazed from the windows.

I love a party.

She heard Tami's voice, her throaty laugh . . . or was that the wind through the cedar boughs?

Seth welcomed them into the house; he looked as dazed and shaky as Jolene felt. She saw the envelope sticking out of his pocket. It was a reminder of her own last letter from Tami, which lay hidden in a drawer in her nightstand, still unopened. He wore his mother's dog tags around his neck.

"Stay with your mom," Michael said to Betsy. He and Mila worked their way through the crowd, taking the food to the table.

"Lucky me," Betsy muttered under her breath.

Jolene barely heard. She remained by the door. She heard talking, even laughing, but it made no sense to her. *Tami should be here. It was her house . . .*

The narrow manufactured home was too full of people; food covered every surface in the kitchen and dining room. Most of their Guard unit was here. Oh, God, there were Smitty's parents, their faces different now, lined by the kind of grief that constricted blood flow and tightened skin. What would she say to them? What would they say to her?

An easel in the center of the room held a poster-sized picture of Tami in her ACUs, smiling brightly for the camera, waving to the folks back home. Jolene had taken that picture only a few weeks before the crash . . . *Give me your real smile, Tam, come on* . . .

She closed her eyes, trying not to remember. *Count to ten. Breathe.* She needed to go talk to Smitty's parents, to tell them how sorry she was for their loss and how brave their son had been. *He didn't suffer.* Was that what they would want to hear? Or that he'd been courageous or funny or thoughtful?

Behind her, a door slammed shut. *Bam!* Jolene screamed. In an instant, she was in Balad again, and the base was under attack, and a rocket whizzed by her head. She reached for Tami, told her to take cover, and threw herself to the ground.

She hit so hard it knocked the breath from her lungs, made her dizzy.

When she opened her eyes, she saw a pale white patch of linoleum and a sea of feet. Not boots . . . not sand. Nothing smelled like smoke or mortar fire.

Feeling sick with shame, Jolene realized that she was on the floor of Tami's house.

Her family and friends—and the soldiers from her unit—stood around her, beers in their hands, smiles faded, peering down at her with concern. They were talking. Was it to her or themselves? She couldn't tell; their voices were a chain-saw buzz of sound. Michael was in the kitchen, standing beside Carl. A song—"Crazy for You"—blared through old speakers in a distant room.

"Oh, my GOD," Betsy yelled, distancing herself from Jolene. "What's WRONG with you?"

Jolene saw how mortified her daughter was. "I'm sorry, Betsy," she whispered, crawling slowly to a stand. She was shaking now; she couldn't breathe. She hated the pity she saw in the eyes around her.

She knew she should say something, make some pathetic excuse, but what was there? She could see by the way her friends were looking at her that they knew, all of them; they knew she was damaged now, broken. Crazy.

She limped for the front door, pushing through it, going out into the night.

"Jolene, wait," she heard Michael yell from inside the house.

She slammed the door shut behind her and kept going, limping down the gravel driveway and across the grass field that separated their properties.

She was almost home when Michael caught up with her. He took her by the arm, tried to stop her.

She pushed him away. "Leave me alone."

"Jolene—"

"Don't say anything," she hissed. She was losing herself as she stood here, falling apart by degree. "Leave me alone."

"Jolene," he said. "Let me help you."

She pushed past him and went into the house, then limped into her bedroom. She turned to slam the door shut and stepped wrong, came down hard on her blisters, and a rage exploded inside of her, made her shake it was so powerful. Suddenly she wanted the prosthesis off—*off*—she couldn't stand looking at it. She leaned against the dresser and took it off, screaming as she threw it across the room. The ugly plastic leg hit a vase Mila had given them last Christmas, and the pretty blue and white Chinese porcelain cracked into pieces.

She started to laugh even though it wasn't funny, was the opposite of funny, but she kept laughing. *Look, Tam—no leg!*

She wanted to sink to her knees, but she couldn't do it. One of the many things she couldn't do anymore. It took everything she had just to stand here, storklike, swaying.

She laughed harder at that. Then she realized she had to go to the bathroom and she'd thrown her leg and the wheelchair wasn't here and her crutches were in the mudroom.

Cursing, she hopped awkwardly forward, balancing on the furniture. In the bathroom, she caught a glimpse of herself in the mirror and looked away. Her hands were shaking as she unbuttoned her jeans and shoved them down to her ankles. She realized too late that she wasn't close enough to the toilet.

"Damn it."

She hopped closer, stepped down on one pant leg, and lost her balance; her ankle twisted. Falling sideways, she grabbed the towel rack. It ripped out of the wall, and she crashed to the floor, hitting her shoulder on the edge of the sink hard enough to make her cry out.

She lay there for a moment, dazed, her shoulder and ankle throbbing, and suddenly she was screaming in frustration.

The bathroom door banged open. "Jolene?"

"Go away."

Michael knelt beside her, touched her face. "Baby," he said softly, in the voice she had once loved—still loved—and it made her feel so lonely and lost she couldn't stand it.

"Are you okay?"

"Do I *look* okay?"

"Baby," he said again, and suddenly she was crying. *Sobbing.* She tried to stop, to hold back these useless, useless tears and be strong.

Michael took her in his arms and held her tightly, stroking her hair.

Once she'd started to cry, she couldn't stop. Great, gulping sobs wracked her body, shook her like a rag doll until her nose was running and she couldn't breathe. She cried first for Tami, but then it was for everything she'd lost, all the way back to her parents, and even before that, for the family she'd longed for as a child and never had. She cried for Smitty, and her lost career and her missing leg and her best friend and her marriage.

When she finally came back to herself, she felt weak, shaky. She drew back and saw that Michael was crying, too.

He gave her an unsteady smile and she needed it—needed him. Telling herself anything else was a lie. "I take it you need to go to the bathroom."

It made her laugh. Only she could have the breakdown of her life on the bathroom floor, with her jeans down around her ankles. *Ankle.*

"Yeah."

He got up and picked her up as if she weighed nothing and set her on the toilet, then he reached over and unspooled a wad of toilet paper, handing it to her like a perfect white rose.

She'd peed in front of him a thousand times in their marriage, but now the act felt painfully intimate. She thought about asking him to leave and changed her mind. Whatever was happening now between them, she didn't want to ruin it.

She flushed the toilet when she was done.

He knelt in front of her, helped her pull her panties back up.

She saw him look at her gel-socked stump and felt sick to her stomach. He would look away now . . .

Instead, he slowly peeled off the gel sock, and there it was—the ugly, rounded stub of her once-beautiful leg. He leaned forward and kissed the bright pink scar.

When he looked up, she saw the love in his eyes—there was no denying it anymore. Impossible as it seemed, he'd fallen in love with her again. She'd known on that day in the courtroom, hadn't she? Known it and feared it.

"You know, right?"

She nodded.

"No arguments," he whispered, then he picked her up and carried her out of the bathroom. She expected him to set her down on her bed, but he kept walking, out of her room and up the stairs.

"Where are you taking me?"

"Our bed," he said, climbing the stairs with her in his arms.

She clung to him. All the way up the stairs she thought of why it was a bad idea for them to make love. The doctors had told her she could "resume sexual activity" when she felt ready, but what would it be like?

She wanted to say *stop, I'm not ready*, but even as she had the thought, pushed up by a lifelong fear, she knew it was a lie. She had been ready to love this man from the moment she first saw him. In all these years, that had never changed. They'd hurt each other, let each other down, and yet, here they were after everything, together. She needed him now, needed him to remind her that she was alive, that she wasn't alone, that she hadn't lost everything.

She had to believe in him again; it was their only chance. Her only chance. There was no protection from being hurt except to stop loving all together, and she couldn't do it. She'd tried. She wanted love—reckless, unpredictable, dangerous. Even with her damaged body and her even more damaged heart. She wanted it. Wanted him.

He shoved the bedroom door open and then kicked it shut behind him. At the bed, he stopped, breathing a little hard from the exertion of carrying her up the stairs. In his eyes, she saw the same intense passion that had jolted her body at his touch, brought her back to life, but she saw fear, too, and worry. They lay down together.

"I love you, Jo," he said simply, although they both knew there was nothing simple about such a declaration.

"I love you, too, Michael," she said brokenly. "I always have."

He took her in his arms and kissed her. Her body came alive at his touch, opened to him, and she moaned his name, pressed against him. She drew him close, wanting him more than she ever had.

His hand slid under her shirt, unhooked her bra.

She took a deep breath, trying to gather her courage. She wanted him, wanted this to happen, but it frightened her, too. What would love be like with this new body of hers? Would he really still want her?

Moonlight came through the window, illuminating her pale legs. Her thighs were the same size—the swelling had gone down—one tapered to a knee and a shapely calf and a foot. The other . . .

She so rarely let herself really look at it. Now she did, and she knew Michael was looking, too, at the amputated leg, with its rounded end and Frankenstein stitches, still an angry pink. Lulu had been right: it kind of looked like a football.

"We might have to be . . . innovative," she said.

"I love innovative," he whispered, letting his hand move across her jutting hip bone and along her thigh. His touch electrified her. She pulled off her blouse and undressed him and lay against him, every part of her needing to be touched by him. She ran her bare hand along his chest, feeling him, remembering. Their kiss turned desperate. Her fingers slipped beneath the waistband of his boxers.

Had she ever felt this sharp, aching need before? She couldn't remember, but it was in her now, fueling her, straining to be released.

He knew her body as well as he knew his own, knew when to touch her and where, knew how to bring her to this edge that was both pleasure and pain. It didn't matter at all that they had to do things a little differently than before, that she sometimes needed to position herself with pillows. Lying on her side, she clung to him, her breath coming fast and hard, feeling him inside her again, filling her; she arched up, kissed him, and their cheeks were wet with each other's tears. Her release was so powerful she cried out; it felt as if her entire body were being lifted up, carried on some dark wind, and then floated back to the softness of the bed she'd shared with this man for so much of her life. In the aftermath, she curled against him, her body sweaty, spent, and as he stroked her arm, she lay there, her cheek against his chest, remembering the feel of his tears on her face, the salty taste of his kiss.

"Can I ask you a question?" he said afterward, as they lay together, still breathing heavily.

"Of course."

"How come you never answered my letter?"

"What letter?"

"The one I sent you in Iraq, a few days before your crash."

She frowned. "I never got a letter from you over there. We were crazy that last week, missions constantly, and the Internet was always going down. I opened my e-mail once after I got home; there were hundreds of condolence messages about my leg. I couldn't stand reading them. I haven't gone to the computer in forever. What did it say?"

"That I wanted another chance."

She tried to imagine what that would have meant to her then, when she was so far from home. Would she have believed him? "How did it happen, you falling in love with me while I was away?" she asked, her body tucked up against his, her chin resting on his shoulder.

He slid his arm beneath her, pulled her closer. "After Dad's death, I was depressed, and you were always so damn cheerful. You gave me the kind of advice I couldn't follow—like think 'good thoughts, remember his smile.' Honestly, I hated that shit." He looked at her. "I was unhappy, and it was easy to blame you."

"I thought you could will grief away. That's what I did with my parents. At least that's what I thought I did. The truth is, I knew loss. I didn't know grief. Now, I do." She tilted her chin to look up at him. "I let you down."

He kissed her forehead slowly, lovingly. "And I let you down."

"We need to talk more this time," Jolene said. "Really talk."

He nodded. "I want to know about Iraq. Can you do that?"

Her instinct was to say *no, you don't want to know* and protect him. "I'll tell you what I can do. You can read my journal," she said. "And I need to talk to that doctor of yours, too. I need help with this, I think."

"You'll make it through, Jo. You're the strongest person I've ever met."

"What about Betsy? How will I convince her to forgive me?"

He smiled. "You flew helicopters in combat. You can handle one angry twelve-year-old girl."

"I'll take combat anytime."

They were laughing when someone knocked on their door. Pounded, actually.

Michael got out of bed, snagged his pants and stepped into them. He was buttoning the fly as he opened the door. "Ma," he said, grinning.

"It's Betsy," Mila said. She was holding Lulu, whose head rested on her shoulder. "She's gone. We can't find her anywhere."

"What do you mean?" Michael said, picking a tee shirt up from the floor, pulling it over his head. "I'm sure she's in the backyard or somewhere close."

"Gone?" Jolene sat up, clutching the sheet to her bare breasts. She didn't know how Michael could sound so calm.

Mila glanced sympathetically at Jolene. "After the . . . incident at Tami's, there was a lot of talk. People are worried about you, Jo. Anyway, I was soothing Lulu, who kept wanting to know why you'd thrown yourself to the ground, and when I got her settled, I looked for Betsy. It took a long time to work the room. The point is, she and Seth are gone. We've looked everywhere. Carl is frantic."

"I'll check the house," Michael said.

He rushed out of the room. Jolene got out of bed and went to her dresser. Finding jeans and a white sweater, she dressed as quickly as she could. Michael returned with her prosthesis, and they went down the stairs. Hold-limp-step. Hold-limp-step. Never had the unwieldiness of her fake leg bothered her more.

Carl was waiting for them in the family room, looking harried. Mila was beside him, holding Lulu in her arms.

"They ran away," Carl said to Jo. "I heard them talking, and I thought, 'Good, they're friends again,' and I went for another beer. I don't know how long it was before I went looking for him again. It wasn't until people started to leave that we noticed. I should have noticed."

"The Harrisons' tree," Michael said. "Remember the last time Betsy ran away? Seth found her at the tree by the Harrisons' dock."

Jolene stared at her husband. "The last time she ran away?"

Michael barely responded. Carl nodded and the two men set off. Jolene followed them as far as the porch.

Out there, it was cold and black. No stars shone through. She stood at the railing, trying to will herself to see through the darkness. Mila came up beside her, carrying Lulu. "We'll find her, Jolene," she said. "Teenagers do this sort of thing."

This sort of thing; running away in the dark, where God only knew what waited. If Jolene had been a better mother in the past weeks, they wouldn't be here, staring out at the cold night, praying. She heard Lulu's small sob, and she turned.

"She ranned away again," Lulu wailed.

Opening her arms, Jolene whispered, "Come to me, baby. Let Mommy hold you."

Lulu's teary eyes widened. "Really, Mommy?"

Jolene's voice cracked. "Really."

Lulu hurled herself forward so hard Mila stumbled sideways. Jolene caught Lulu in her arms and held on tightly, breathing in the familiar little-girl smell of Johnson's Baby Shampoo and Ivory soap.

She felt Lulu's sobs, and all she could do to help was hold on tightly, to tell Lulu over and over again that she was safe in Mommy's arms. Finally, Lulu drew back. Her dark eyes were swimming in tears, and her cheeks were glassy-looking with moisture. "You scared us, Mommy."

Jolene smoothed the damp hair from Lulu's face. "I know, Kitten. The war made your mommy a little crazy. I'm going to get better, though."

"You promise?"

The trust in Lulu's eyes was a balm to Jolene's battered spirit. She wanted to say *I promise*. That was what she would have done in the old days; deflect and pretend. But promises were fragile things, and the future even more so. "I promise I'm going to do everything I can to be the mommy I used to be. But I might need your help. Sometimes if I'm . . . you know, crazy, you'll have to just raise your hands and shrug your shoulders and go, 'That's my mom.' Do you think you could do that?"

Lulu raised her small pink palms and shrugged and said, "That's my mom."

"Perfect," Jolene said, her smile unsteady.

Then Carl and Michael emerged from the darkness across the street and appeared in the driveway, walking slowly toward them. Betsy and Seth weren't with them.

"Where is she?" Lulu said.

Jolene's fear kicked up a notch, edged toward panic. She kissed Lulu and handed her back to Mila, "Will you put her to bed, Mila? Please?"

Mila nodded. Taking Lulu, she carried the little girl back into the house. The screen door banged shut behind her.

Jolene met the men at the end of the porch.

"They weren't there," Carl said. "There was no sign that they'd been there, either." He looked down at his watch. "It's ten o'clock. Should we call the police?"

Jolene felt a chill go through her. Betsy was out there, somewhere, in the night, running away from a family that made no sense to her anymore, from a mother who could no longer be trusted. She went to the railing, stared down toward the road. *Come back, Betsy. I will explain it all to you, please . . .*

Michael came up beside her, put an arm around her shoulders. She couldn't help thinking that before all of this, she would have shrugged his comfort away, would have been pacing now, trying to control a situation that wasn't hers to control. Now, she leaned against him.

How long did they stand there? Long enough for Michael and Carl to call everyone they knew, long enough for Mila to put Lulu to bed and come out to the porch, wrapped in a purple and pink afghan. Long enough to see their friends and family walk over from Carl's house and stand clustered along the fence line. Long enough to see the red and yellow flash of police lights coming their way.

Jolene saw the bursting bits of color, and she tightened her hold on the railing, freezing cold now, shivering. She was reminded of another night like this, long ago. She'd stood on another porch, all alone, watching her parents drive away. She'd never seen either one of them again.

Tami, bring her back to me.

The police cruiser pulled into the driveway and stopped. The colorful lights snapped off, leaving darkness behind.

Two uniformed officers got out of the car.

Michael tightened his hold on Jolene's waist. Was he thinking about the night he'd been told about her accident? Hadn't Ben Lomand come up at night with the news?

The older of the two officers opened a pad of paper. "We're here about the missing children?"

Missing children.

Jolene gripped the railing so tightly her hands went numb. *Think, Jolene. You know Betsy. Where would she be?*

She heard the questions being asked and answered beside her; descriptions, names, favorite places, reasons they might have run away. She heard the pause after that question, and then Carl's halting answer.

"We were having a memorial for Seth's mom tonight. She was killed in Iraq. Jolene had an . . . um . . . flashback and threw herself to the floor. It caused some . . . I don't know . . . upset to the kids, I think. Later, I heard Seth say to Betsy, 'That picture doesn't even look like my mom.' That's the last time I remember seeing them. It was, maybe, eight thirty or nine. I can't be sure. There was so much going on."

Jolene looked up sharply. "What did you say, Carl? What did Seth say about Tami?"

"He was mad at me for using the picture from Iraq. He yelled, 'That's not my mom. It's not even her real smile.' I should have listened to him, and then Betsy said, 'My mom hasn't smiled since she got back.'"

"I know where they might be," Jolene said.

"Where?" Carl asked.

"They want the last pictures of us," she said, her throat tight. "The last time they saw their moms."

"The Crab Pot," Michael and Carl said together.

"You go," Carl said to Michael. "I'll stay here in case you're wrong."

Jolene and Michael were already moving, going into the house, grabbing the car keys. In no time, they were in the car, backing down the driveway and turning onto the bay road. Neither spoke as they drove along the water. At some point, Jolene reached out and put her hand on his thigh, needing to touch him. "If anything happens to them . . ."

"Don't say it, Jo," he pleaded.

They pulled up into the Crab Pot parking lot, which was empty. Two solitary streetlamps threw spots of light down on the asphalt.

Michael ran and Jolene limped as fast as she could to the front door, which was ajar. The window beside it was broken. Shards of glass lay on the weathered silver boards at their feet.

A pinprick of light shone in the shadowy interior.

Michael opened the door slowly; it creaked in protest.

Seth and Betsy were huddled together at the wall, holding Polaroid pictures in the beam of a flashlight.

Jolene heard Seth say quietly, "See her smile, Betsy? That's her."

Jolene's relief was profound, but short-lived. She should have been truthful with her children from the beginning. She should have warned them that war could hurt her, change her, change them. Protecting them from the inevitable had only increased their pain and confusion and caused all this collateral damage.

"Hey, Betsy," she said quietly.

Betsy saw her and grimaced. "We'll pay for the window. Don't worry."

"We aren't worried about the window," Michael said.

"I had to get out of there," Seth said, tears filling his eyes. "They were all telling these stories about her in the Guard. And I missed her so much I couldn't stand it. I wanted to see her the way I remembered her. Betsy was the only one who understood."

"A good friend is like that," Jolene said quietly.

Betsy swallowed hard, staring at her. She held out the Polaroid picture of their family; it shook slightly in her grasp. "*She* never came back."

"Come here, Betsy," Jolene said.

Betsy looked terrified by the request. She clung to Seth's hand as if she thought she might be yanked into a whirlwind if she let go. After all that had happened in this year, that was smart thinking on her part. They'd all become Dorothys, hurtling through a tornado. Who knew where they would land?

"I'll tell you what," Jolene said at last. "We'll take Seth home, and then you and I will talk."

"Are you going to lie to me and tell me everything is fine?" Betsy asked.

"No," Jolene said quietly. "I'm not going to lie to you anymore."

It took them almost an hour to get everything settled down and taken care of back at the house. All the while, Jolene thought about the advice young Keith Keller had given her: *Come home to the people who love you.* It was time, finally, for Jolene to do that, and, to be honest, she was more than a little afraid.

When Carl and Seth and the police finally left, Jolene looked at Betsy, who was standing on the end of the porch, wrapped in a big blanket.

"Can we talk now?" Jolene asked quietly.

Betsy nodded, although she didn't look happy about it.

Jolene took her daughter by the hand and led her into the family room. At the sofa, Betsy tugged her hand free and hung back while Jolene sat down. Michael kissed them both and went upstairs.

She heard his footsteps on the stairs, then creaking on the second floor.

They were alone.

"What do you want to say?" Betsy said, standing back. Her cheeks were still red with cold and her eyes were wary. For the first time, Jolene noticed the small pink pearl earrings.

She frowned. "Are your ears pierced?"

"I wondered when you were going to notice. I guess you have to look at me to see them."

"I know, but—"

"You weren't here. And I'm practically thirteen."

It was a sharp reminder of all the time Jolene had lost with her daughter, and of the problems that lay between them now. In Jolene's absence, life had gone on; Michael had stepped up to the plate and guided their family, and he'd made decisions along the way. Jolene had never wanted to leave her children for any reason, and yet she had; she'd abandoned them in a way, and Betsy couldn't forgive her.

"No," Jolene said slowly. "I wasn't. I'm sorry about that, Betsy."

"I know you're sorry."

"It's not enough. What is?"

Betsy looked away. "I don't want to have this conversation."

"Come here, baby," Jolene said gently.

Betsy moved forward woodenly.

"Closer," Jolene said.

Betsy shook her head.

"You're mad at me for leaving . . . and for getting hurt."

Betsy shrugged, said, "Whatever."

Jolene didn't look away, even though the pain in her daughter's eyes was a terrible thing to see. "I know I'm not the mom you remember, the mom you want. I know you're mad at me. And I deserve it, Betsy. Not for going to war. I had to do that. But for who I've been since I got home." She got up, trying not to limp, and reached out, taking hold of Betsy's warm, soft hand. "I'm sorry I scared you. Or embarrassed you."

Betsy's eyes filled with tears. "I read Tami's last letter to Seth. Did you write me one?"

Jolene wanted to lie, to say *no, of course not, I knew I'd never leave you alone,* but she was done with wrapping her life in pretty paper and pretending. "I did. It was the hardest thing I've ever done, thinking about leaving you and Lulu and your dad."

"What did it say?"

"There were a lot of words and stories and advice, I guess. I tried to tell you everything you would need to know without me. I told you about my life, my parents, the kind of childhood I'd had, and how love—and motherhood—had changed me. I told you I was afraid to leave you. Things I should have told you before I left." She looked at Betsy. "It said I love you in a thousand different ways."

"Do you still?"

Jolene felt tears come to her eyes. She couldn't help wondering how long it would wound her, the memory of this question. "I will love you forever, Elizabeth Andrea Zarkades. I might screw up, I might embarrass you, I might yell at you, but I will never, *ever* stop loving you. You're my firstborn. The first time I held you . . ." Her voice broke on that; the tears started to fall. "I fell in love so hard it cracked my bones."

The hug came so fast, Jolene stumbled sideways, almost lost her balance, but she clung to her daughter until they steadied. She held her daughter tightly, breathing in the familiar, girly scent of her corkscrewed blond hair, feeling Betsy's sobs.

Jolene knew there would be more fights, probably lots of them, and screaming and hurt feelings and wrong things said, but there would be this, too.

Finally, Betsy drew back and looked up. Her beautiful, heart-shaped face glistened with tears. "I love you, Mom. To the moon and back. I should have said it when you left."

Jolene didn't know it until right then, this second, but those were the words she'd been waiting to hear. "I knew, baby," she said, holding her close again. "I always knew . . ."

Twenty-Nine

�֎

The psychiatrist's office was a boxy little midcentury house that backed up to the fury of Aurora Avenue. Michael pulled up out front and parked next to an electric car. "Are you ready for this?"

"Honestly? No."

Michael smiled in encouragement. "I'm pretty sure that's the right answer."

Jolene got out of the car. In the week since Tami's memorial service, she had relaxed a lot. The talk with Betsy, the reunion with Michael, the return of Lulu's laughter—all of it had combined to restore Jolene's sense of self. She'd poured her wine down the drain and put her sleeping pills away. But she still had a long way to go. Even in Michael's arms, she sometimes woke screaming for the crew that had been lost, for the helicopter that had crashed. Sometimes she still found herself standing somewhere—in the kitchen, in the bathroom, on her own back porch—and loss would overwhelm her. Maybe that sadness would be a part of her now, a weave in the fabric of her soul; or maybe it had been there all along and she'd never let herself see it. All she knew was that it was time to dig deeply into her own psyche, to figure out how to come home from war figuratively as well as literally, how to forge a new life after a sharp bend in the road. Since she'd given up drinking, it was easier to see the path of her own life more clearly.

An older man greeted them in the main room of the house. He was tall and gangly-looking, with long, unkempt gray hair and an angular face. He was wearing baggy black pants, orange clogs, and a Grateful Dead tee shirt. "Hello, Jolene," he said. "It's nice to finally meet you."

This was her doctor? "Oh," was all she could think of to say.

He smiled broadly. "I'm Chris Cornflower. I see Michael didn't prepare you."

Michael laughed. "There's no preparing someone to meet you for the first time, Chris. It's an experience."

"He told me you were a Vietnam vet," Jolene said.

"And I am. A POW, too." He reached out and shook her hand. "I'm thrilled to meet you, Chief."

"I'm not that woman anymore."

"And there's our job, Jolene, to find out who you are now. Would you like to come back to my office?"

She hesitated, looked back at Michael, who smiled and nodded. "Okay," she said.

She followed Chris into a small, nicely decorated room in the back. She was glad to see that there was no couch. "I don't know exactly how to do this," she said, taking a seat in the comfortable chair positioned near his desk.

"I have some experience," he said, giving her a smile. "We could start so many places. Your childhood, your experiences in Iraq, your best friend, your civilian future. Whatever you want to talk about first."

She laughed nervously. "When you put it like that, it makes me think we'll be doing this for a while."

"Only as long as you want to, Jolene. You're the chief here; I'm the private. You lead, I follow."

She was afraid to dive into this conversation. They both knew it. But she'd already let fear guide her before, and that hadn't worked. "People see my lost leg and they think that's the problem. But I lost more than that. Sometimes I have no clue who I'm supposed to be or what my life will look like from here on. I was good at being a soldier. I like answers."

"Why did you join the military, Jolene?"

"I was eighteen and alone in the world with no money. It gave me a place to belong."

"A family."

"Yes," she said after a pause.

"But it's an easy family to belong to, isn't it? Rules guide every situation and behavior. There are no hurt feelings or broken hearts in that family. You always know who you are and what your job is. When you're in trouble, your unit is always there for you. You know you'll never be left behind."

Jolene felt herself relax a little. He understood. Maybe finally— *finally*—she could talk honestly about the pain in her past, and maybe if she could tell him, she could tell Michael, and she could begin to heal. "Can I ask you something?"

"Of course."

"You were a POW. So, you endured a lot. How did you know when you were out of the woods?"

"An excellent question. There were a lot of angry years after I got home. Lost years. I guess I knew I had begun to heal when I was ready to help someone else."

Jolene knew how that could happen, how you could sink into a pool of anger or grief or sadness or guilt and simply drown. She thought about the letters she'd received in rehab, especially the one from the young marine, Sarah, who'd lost her leg. She'd ignored the young woman's plea for help. "I used to be the kind of woman who helped people."

"You can be that woman again, Jolene."

"Okay," she said slowly. "I want to start with the nightmares . . ."

. . .

On the second Friday in December, Lulu woke early and went straight to her bedroom window, pressing her nose to the glass. "No snow," she whined.

"Maybe God's waiting 'til Christmas Eve," Jolene said. "A white Christmas would be great, wouldn't it?"

Lulu's little shoulders slumped as she turned away from the window. "I was hoping for no school."

"But, Lulu, you love kindergarten."

"I know," she said miserably. "But I wanted to go with you today."

Jolene pulled her youngest into her arms and kissed her cheek, then patted her butt. "Get dressed, Kitten. You'll just have to wait to see my new pretty leg. Surprises are good, right?"

"I guess so," Lulu said, although clearly she didn't believe it.

"Good. Now let's go wake up your sister. You know how cranky she gets if we're late."

Jolene and Lulu walked down the hall and awakened Betsy, and then the three of them went downstairs.

Today was supposed to be oatmeal.

"Cap'n Crunch," Lulu said, climbing onto her chair. "Cuz it's a special day."

Jolene smiled at her daughters. "You know what, Lulu, it *is* a special day."

Michael stumbled into the kitchen after the girls, looking tousled and a little bleary-eyed. A five o'clock shadow chiseled his jaw, gave him that rock star look she loved.

She handed him a cup of coffee.

He took it gratefully. "Thanks."

"You look tired," Jolene said, pressing against him. He leaned back against the counter, and put the cup down so he could grab her by her butt and pull her against him.

"I *am* tired," he said, grinning. "I'm not getting much sleep lately."

"Gross," Betsy said from the table.

Lulu sat up, looked around. "What's gross?"

Jolene laughed and pulled free, executing a pretty decent twirl on her clunky fake foot. She poured the girls some orange juice, then started packing lunches.

Michael kissed the girls good-bye and went upstairs to take a shower. Jolene moved through the morning routine with an ease that belied her inner excitement.

All week, she had tried to tamp down her expectations for this day. Repeatedly, she'd warned herself not to want too much, not to let hope run away with her, and honestly, until this morning, she'd done pretty well.

"Good luck, Mommy," both girls said, one after another, as they left the warm house and ran down the wet driveway to the yellow school buses that pulled up out front. Jolene stood on the porch for each, waving until the bus was gone around the bend.

She felt Michael come up behind her. "Hey, you," he said, holding her shoulders, kissing the back of her neck. "You ready?" he said from behind her.

She turned to face him. "I've been ready for months."

"Then let's go."

They got into the car and drove away. All the way to the rehab center, Jolene stared out the window at the falling rain. Hope was an elevator right now, broken from its cables. She could feel herself plunging with it.

At the center, she and Michael met Conny in the lobby.

"Well, well, look how good you're walking on that ugly clunker of a leg."

"You said it wasn't so bad," she teased.

"I lied." He held out his hand. "Come on."

The three of them walked down the wide white hallway to the prosthetic center.

Jolene smelled plastic. Artificial arms and legs and hands and feet hung on the walls and around her.

"Jolene Zarkades is here," Conny yelled toward the back room.

A moment later, the Asian woman came into the front area, holding an artificial leg.

Jolene stared at it in awe. It was shapely, almost pretty, with a foot that could be adjusted for heels.

Conny took the limb from the woman and knelt before Jolene. He took off the heavy, unwieldy temporary leg and tossed it aside. Because her limb had shrunk so much in the last few months, she'd needed more and more gel socks to keep the fit tight in her prosthesis. Conny peeled the socks away, dropped them in a pile, until there was only one left, which he smoothed carefully to remove any wrinkles. Then he fitted her into the new prosthesis.

"Wow," she said, shaking her head. It didn't look exactly real, of course, but it was close enough. She took a step forward, amazed at its lightness, its ease of movement. "It's almost like having my leg back," she said, looking at Michael, her eyes shining. "I could dance on this leg." She turned to Conny. "Can I run?"

Conny said gently, "One mountain at a time, Jolene."

For the next hour, she worked in the PT room with Conny, while Michael made notes on a deposition.

Jolene discovered that she could skip. She hadn't skipped since childhood; now she couldn't stop. She laughed so much and so often the other patients probably thought she was loony tunes, but she didn't care.

"Well, Jolene," Conny said at the end of the day. "It's been good knowing you."

Jolene felt a tightening in her throat. How could she ever thank this man, who had been there for her every step of the way? She walked to him, barely limping at all, feeling no pain in her stump. "You saved me, Conny. Without you—"

"It was always you, soldier girl. You have the heart of a champion." He leaned over and kissed her cheek. "I'll miss you, too, but don't make a scene."

"I never used to be a scene-making gal," Jolene said, her eyes bright.

"Life changes us, that's for sure."

Jolene stared at him a moment longer, thinking that he was like the men and women in her unit. The job was what mattered, not the thanks. She nodded one last time, letting her gaze say it all, then she took Michael's hand and they walked outside.

Rain engulfed them, splashing beneath their steps. Jolene amazed herself—she ducked her head, held on to Michael's hand, and ran for the car.

Ran.

It wasn't perfect, of course, her leg didn't bend like it should, but she did it. Her hair was dripping wet by the time she got into the car.

"That was a pretty sexy bit of running on your new leg, Mrs. Zarkades."

"Everyone's going to want one, I can tell you."

She couldn't help looking at her new leg; she kept lifting her pant leg and staring at it. It was almost impossible to stop smiling.

He stopped at the mailbox, picked up the mail, and drove up the driveway. When they pulled into the garage, she turned to her husband. "You'll be home for dinner?"

He handed her the mail. "Before that, even. As soon as the Byer dep is done, I'm coming home. How about dinner at the restaurant above the marina?"

"Perfect." She leaned over and kissed him, then got out of the car and practically skipped into the house.

Inside, it was quiet. Jolene made herself a cup of hot tea and went through the mail.

There was another letter from Sarah Merrin, the young marine who had lost her leg in Iraq.

Jolene sat down at the kitchen table and opened the letter.

Chief,

I understand why you haven't written to me. You probably feel as crappy as I do. I guess I'm just hoping there's a silver lining out there. Ha.

I'm still at Walter Reed. I'm thinking of painting the walls, that's how long I'm going to be here. They had to amputate the other leg. Infection.

Honest to God, I don't know why I'm telling you all this.

How do you do it? I guess that's all I really want to know. They tell

me I'll be able to walk again—even skate—but I think they're full of
shit. And my husband couldn't get out of here fast enough.
Again, any words of wisdom you got would sure be helpful.
Sincerely,
Sarah Merrin

Jolene sat there a long time, staring down at the words.

On a cold, rainy mid-December day, Jolene and Michael boarded an airplane for Washington, D.C., and took their seats in the third row.

Michael settled back into the comfortable blue leather and buckled his seat belt.

Jolene was turned away from him, looking out the small oval window, watching the ground crew do its job. He could see by the tightening of her mouth that she was missing her old life now: the military, flying, the woman she'd been before the war.

He reached over, took her hand in his. It was rare these days for her to be sad, but at times like this, when the melancholy seized hold, she gave in to it, let it be. The watch he'd given her for her birthday encircled her small wrist, the faceted face glinting in the light. It was an odd contrast with the plainness of her gold wedding band. When he'd first seen her wearing it, he'd been embarrassed. He'd offered to replace it. *I shouldn't have bought it for you,* he'd said, *that was when I was different. I should have gone with you to the damn party.*

Old news, she'd said with a smile. *We're both different now, and thank God.*

It was true. They had all been changed in the past year.

Jolene most of all. She'd learned in the last few weeks—they all had—not to gloss over sadness. She squeezed Michael's hand.

The plane's engines started up, rattling the seats slightly. She was probably remembering how it felt to climb into the pilot's seat, to put on a helmet, to go through the preflight check.

The plane backed away from the Jetway and rolled across the airport

to the runway. It picked up speed, rocketed forward, rose up . . . up . . .
up into the air.

Blue sky filled the windows.

"Did I ever tell you about the plum trees?" she said quietly. "We used
to see them when we took off from the post. You'd look down through
the blue sky and see these blurry pink trees, and it was so beautiful."

It took his breath away, how easily she said it, how good she sounded.
After a moment he said, "I want to take the girls to my dad's grave."

She looked at him. "You've never gone there, not since the funeral."

"I guess I'm not the only one in this family who has trouble letting go."

"Yeah." She sighed. "I still haven't read Tami's letter."

"I know."

She leaned against him.

"By the way, I talked to Ben Lomand last week," he said.

She turned. "You did?"

"I was going to save it for Christmas, but here we are, up where you
belong . . . so, I talked to him about you flying again. He doesn't see any
reason why you couldn't do it on your snazzy new leg. He said something
about a smaller chopper—there were a bunch of weird words and letters,
and, well, he lost me. But he's willing to work with you. When you're
ready. Maybe you could fly a news helicopter someday. Who knows?"

"Who knows indeed?" She smiled. "I love you, Michael Zarkades."

In the abstract, Jolene had known that Washington, D.C., was a city of
monuments. She'd read about the various places dedicated to the country's history, but until she stepped out onto the busy streets, she didn't
quite understand how they all joined one to the other and told a story.
Everywhere she looked—on tiny slivers of snowy ground, on plaques on
park benches, on white marble statues—there was a memory, a reminder. The scale of the city surprised her, too. She'd imagined a New
York–type city, full of thrusting skyscrapers. But this city felt grounded
in a way she hadn't expected; there were no high-rises, no canyons of
concrete that made passersby feel small.

New York was a city that showed off its greatness, sought to make tourists look at man's accomplishments with awe. D.C. knew that man's greatness lay not in stone and steel, but rather in ideas and decisions.

"Are you ready?" Michael asked.

She turned away from the hotel room window, which overlooked a quiet street covered in snow.

Behind Michael, a gilt-framed mirror hung on the wall above a sleek French reproduction dresser. In it, Jolene saw herself from the waist up.

A soldier again—if just for this moment—in her class A dress uniform, with her hair pulled back and a black beret positioned with care. Medals and insignia decorated her chest, reminding her of who she used to be. This was probably the last time she would wear this uniform. She was in the process of taking a medical retirement from the military. Soon, this uniform would be like her wedding dress, a memory hanging in plastic in the back of a closet.

That part of her life had ended. The future lay cloudy in front of her, full of possibilities.

"Jo?"

She smiled. "I'm fine, Michael. It's just weird, that's all." She slipped into the coat he offered her.

She held Michael's hand as they walked to Constitution Avenue. The whole city was gray and white, with slashes of black, a moody chiaroscuro. They walked through the Constitution Gardens; snow glazed the tree branches and benches.

They strolled past one last bare tree, and there it was: the Wall. Even on this frigid, snowy day the black granite seemed alive, reflecting the images of those few visitors who had ventured out in today's cold; an endless expanse of glossy black stone engraved with the names of soldiers who'd died in Vietnam. She reached out with her gloved hand, let her fingers trace the names in front of her. Dotted along the wall were mementos and flowers and gifts left by loved ones.

There were more than 58,000 names.

She didn't realize she was crying until Michael put his arms around her. She leaned against him, barely noticing the snowflakes falling on her cheeks and eyelashes.

They stood there until Jolene was shaking with cold, and still she hated to leave. "I want to bring the girls here in the summer."

"Summer is a great idea," Michael said, "but now, let's go. I can't feel my hands."

She nodded and let him lead her away. In front of them, distant, the Lincoln Memorial rose up through the gloom and snow, pearlescent, lit by beams of golden light. *A house, divided against itself, cannot stand.*

Michael flagged down a cab, and they climbed in. "Walter Reed," he said, clapping his gloved hands together.

Jolene settled into the seat and stared out the window at the white-coated city blurring past. By the time they pulled up to the imposing medical center entrance, it was snowing so hard she could barely see.

When she stepped into the busy hospital, she had a sharp, sudden memory: she was on her back, strapped to a gurney, staring at hot lights, trying not to cry or scream, asking, *How is my crew?* until she lost consciousness. The pain was overwhelming. It was all in her head in a second.

Michael squeezed her hand, reminding her with his touch that she was here, standing; the worst was behind them. She took off her heavy woolen coat and handed it to her husband.

For a moment, as she stood there in her dress uniform, decorated with the medals she'd earned and the patches that had defined so many years of her life, she felt tall again, steady. It didn't matter that the skirt revealed what she'd lost; the uniform revealed who she had been for more than twenty years. She wore it with pride.

"Are you okay?" Michael asked.

She smiled. "I'm fine."

"I'll wait for you?"

"Okay." She let go of his hand and went to the desk, where the nurse on duty gave her the information she needed.

"Are you family?" the nurse asked.

"No."

"Is she expecting you?"

"No. My visit is a surprise. But I've cleared it with the hospital."

The nurse studied her for a moment, then nodded. "Room 326. You're lucky. She's leaving in two days."

Thanking her, Jolene headed down to room 326, in the orthotics wing.

The door was open.

Jolene moved through the buzz of medical staff with the ease of someone who had learned the routine of a place like this.

She paused at the open door and knocked.

Inside the room, a woman lay in a hospital bed, angled up. Jolene recognized the look in the woman's eyes: a combination of fear, anger, and loneliness. There were few lonelier places in the world than a hospital room. Even with loved ones beside you, there was no escaping the frightening, isolating truth that neither love alone nor family could make you whole.

She went to the end of the bed and stood there. "Sarah Merrin?"

"What's left of me is."

Jolene's heart ached for this woman—this girl, almost; she couldn't be more than twenty years old. She saw the empty blanket where Sarah's legs had been. "You're still Sarah, even though it doesn't feel like it. It feels like you left her somewhere, over there, right?"

Sarah looked up.

God, she was so young.

"Do I know you?"

Jolene moved slowly away from the end of the bed. As she walked, with only the slightest hitch in her gait, she felt herself gliding back in time, and for a second she was the woman in the hospital bed again, and a young marine named Leah Sykes was coming up to her bed, smiling, offering hope in the fact of her stance. Jolene hadn't appreciated it enough then—she'd been so broken—but she had learned, over time, how much that support had meant.

She moved to the side of Sarah's bed.

Sarah looked down at Jolene's prosthesis, then up at her face.

"I'm Jolene Zarkades. You wrote me a letter. Two, actually. I'm sorry it took me so long to get here. I was . . . depressed and pissed off for a while."

"Chief?"

"It's just Jolene these days. Hi, Sarah," she said gently.

Sarah's eyes filled with tears.

"I'm a runner," Jolene said softly. "It took a while, but I'll be a runner again. I ordered a tricked-out new metal prosthesis. It's called a blade. Supposedly, I'll be able to run like the wind."

"Yeah, I hear a lot of shit like that. People actually say, 'Oh, it's just your legs, thank God it wasn't worse.' They wouldn't say that if they had a stump. Or two."

"You'll lose things, I won't lie. But you'll find things, too."

Sarah lay back in her pillows, sighing. "Teddy's coming back today. He's just finishing his tour, and I'm what's waiting for him. Lucky guy. I don't know what to say to him. Last time . . . well, he had trouble looking at me, if you know what I mean."

Jolene knew better than to hand out some shiny bit of optimism. She understood now that some things had to be fought for to mean anything. There were journeys in life no one could take for you. She couldn't tell this girl, this soldier, how to handle her life or her injury or her marriage. All she could do was be here, standing as tall as she knew how, and hope that down the road, this would be remembered, as she remembered the woman who had stood by her bedside in Germany, all those months ago. "I'm just going to stand here, okay?" she said to Sarah. "Be here with you."

"I've been alone," Sarah said, sounding young, almost childlike.

"You're not alone now." Jolene stood a few inches away from the wall, listening as Sarah talked about her childhood in West Virginia and the man she'd loved since ninth grade and the fear that she would be in a wheelchair for the rest of her life.

Jolene said very little. She listened and nodded and stood there. Not once did she sit down, even though her hip started to ache.

As night fell, she saw Michael come up to the open door.

He saw her standing there by Sarah's bed, and he smiled. She thought about the letter she'd written him all those months ago, those few simple words: *I loved you beginning to end.* No wonder she hadn't been able to say anything more. What else was there?

She'd had to go to war and lose almost everything to find what really mattered.

I'm so proud of you, he mouthed. At that, she felt something open up inside of her, in the deepest, most untouched part of her heart that for years and years had been hers alone.

Tears stung her eyes, blurred her vision until he was the only solid and true thing in this bright, unfocused world. She could feel her tears, streaking down her cheeks, taking years of hurt with them. She wiped them with the back of her hand until her tears were gone, a memory.

Epilogue

S ummer comes, as it always does, in a wash of light and expectation. One day it is cool, wet spring, and then, as if at the turn of a
switch, the sun returns. Long, hot days bake the pebbled shores of
Liberty Bay, turn the already-weathered dock into brittle, silvery slats of
wood trimmed in dune grass. Shorebirds call out to one another, swoop-
ing and flapping above the peaked blue waves.

Jolene sits in the Adirondack chair on her small deck, watching
Michael and Carl teaching Lulu how to fly a kite. Betsy and Seth run
along behind, laughing, waving their hands in the air. Mila is their
adoring, cheering audience. The day smells of kelp steaming on the
rocks and charcoal burning down to ash in the barbecue pit.

Every few seconds, someone yells: "Look, Mom!" and she looks up,
smiling and waving. It isn't that she can't walk along the beach. In her
new prosthesis, she can do almost anything—she runs, she skips, she
chases after her five-year-old. She even wears shorts and rarely feels self-
conscious.

She is here, separate from them, because she has something to do . . .

something she's been putting off. She can't do it with them, but neither can she quite do it without them.

Lulu's giggle floats on the air.

Jolene reaches down for the letter in her lap. Her hand shakes as she picks it up and sees her name in her best friend's handwriting.

At last. After months of therapy, she is past the time when words can break her. Or, she hopes she is.

She eases the seal open, feels it resist for a second and then give. The letter is written on plain copier paper. She can imagine Tami on that last day before they left, with her clothes piled in a heap on her bed and her duffle bag by the floor. She would have rushed around, looking for something to write on, and probably curse that she'd forgotten to buy stationery. Tami was like that; she remembered all of life's big things, but the little details had often passed her by.

> *Jo*
>
> *If you're reading this, it didn't go the way I wanted over there. It's funny, I never thought I'd die. I pictured you and me lasting forever, sitting on your deck, watching our kids grow up while we managed to stay young. I hope that's where you are now. In a deck chair, with a fire going in the pit. I hope Michael and Carl are down with the kids on the beach. Is my chair empty beside you?*

Jolene looks up, into the clear blue sky. An eagle flies past, dives deeply into the blue water, and comes up with a bright silver salmon in its beak, dripping water on Jolene as it soars to the top of an evergreen.

> *Don't be whining about how much you miss me. Of course you miss me. Wherever I am, I miss you, too. But you know all that. From the time we met, we knew everything that mattered about each other, didn't we? We just knew. I guess that's what best friends are: parts of each other. So you'll have that with you, have me with you.*
>
> *I don't want to get maudlin. I'm sure you've cried enough tears for me to fill the bay. I know I would cry for you.*

God, Jo, we had it all, didn't we? That's what I'm thinking about now, on a sunny day when I've been asked to think about my death.

Here's what matters: take care of my baby. My Seth. It's hard to even write his name. My damn pen is shaking. Make sure he knows me. Me. There are bits of me that only you can share. Tell him about my dorky sense of humor, how I used to cry when he hit a baseball in Little League, what dreams I had for him. Make him know that I was more than his mother; I was his champion. Tell him that sometimes when I laugh too hard, I sound like a seal. Help him remember me. That's my last request of you.

And that you take care of yourself. That, too. Michael loves you and you love him. I hope to shit you haven't blown that. If you have, I will definitely haunt you.

I know that sadness has stalked you in your life, Jo, from early on. I saw you fight it and win. You always won. But maybe now it's harder. Maybe you should give in to it just enough. We're all sad sometimes. I'm sad right now, thinking of you reading this letter. But I want to look down (God—I hope it's down and not up) and see you flying, running, laughing, living your life to the fullest.

Play without a net, flygirl. Because even from here, I've got your six.

Always.

I love you.

T

Jolene folds the letter into thirds and slips it back into the envelope. She knows she will read it a hundred more times in her life. Whenever she needs to remember.

For a brief, beautiful second, she looks in the chair beside her and sees Tami there, her head thrown back, laughing, saying something Jolene can't quite hear.

"Look, Mom!" Betsy says running up to her. "We found a yellow ribbon on the beach."

Jolene smiles and rises to her feet. She takes the ribbon in her hand, feeling its satiny softness between her fingers. She can't help thinking of Tami's ribbons. Of Smitty's ribbons. Of yellow ribbons on trees all across the country. To her, yellow will always be the color of good-bye.

"Mom?" Betsy says, looking up at her. "Are you ready to come to the beach yet? We're waiting."

Jolene holds up the ribbon, watches it flutter in the breeze; then she loosens her hold on it, lets it fly up into the blue, blue sky. Sunlight blinds her for a moment, swallows the strip of fabric, and takes it away. *Good-bye.*

"I'm ready," she says quietly, taking her daughter's hand.

Smiling, she walks down to the beach to join her family.

Acknowledgments

I n the research and writing of this book, I felt a little like Alice, tumbling into a strange and foreign world full of acronyms and unknown words. I knew very little about a soldier's life—or a family's sacrifice—beyond what I saw on the news each night. On my journey, I encountered three very special people, and to them, I offer my endless gratitude.

To Sergeant Andrew Wanamaker, thanks for getting me started and pointing me in the right direction.

To Captain Keith Kosik, thanks for answering a cold e-mail from a strange woman who claimed to be a writer. And for answering endless questions, many of which probably made you want to laugh.

Finally, to Chief Warrant Officer 5 Teresa Burgess. I can't tell you how much your support, help, and friendship has meant in the past year. You repeatedly took time away from your busy schedule to read and reread drafts of this manuscript, and each time you helped me make the story better. More honest. Your comments were always helpful and insightful. You are an inspiration, Teresa, in so many ways. Somehow you balance it all—being a soldier, a Black Hawk helicopter pilot, a wife, and a mother—and you do it with grace and courage. You are truly an example of everything that is right with our country.

Reading
Group
Gold

HOME FRONT

by Kristin Hannah

About the Author

- A Conversation with Kristin Hannah

Behind the Novel

- Interview with Chief Warrant Officer 5 Teresa Burgess
- Greek Culinary Traditions and Recipes

Keep on Reading

- Ideas for Book Groups
- Recommended Reading
- Reading Group Questions

A
Reading
Group Gold
Selection

For more reading group suggestions,
visit www.readinggroupgold.com.

ST. MARTIN'S GRIFFIN

A Conversation with Kristin Hannah

The prologue really jostles the reader into dispelling any thoughts of "pretty daffodil borders"; this story is about battle, for love and everything else that truly matters. How hard was it for you to begin writing this book?

I began this book as I begin all of my novels, with a combination of absolute fear and boundless enthusiasm. Usually I know with some clarity where my stories will go and who will populate them. Although that original road map always gets revised along the way, this book, more than most, consistently messed with my head. The book I envisioned and researched simply didn't work. When I first began to write *Home Front*, it was about two estranged sisters brought together by the deployment. It took me a long time to really grasp that Jolene's story—and to me, she was always the heart and soul of the story, the one character who never changed—needed to be part of a bigger tapestry, that of a marriage that was tested to the limit by the wife's deployment. I literally threw away hundreds of pages before I gave in to this new version of the story. Once I created Michael and let the marriage be center stage, I knew I was on my way. The story unfolded beautifully…until I hit the ending. It took a surprising number of drafts for me to "bring Jolene home" the way I wanted to.

The prevailing themes in *Home Front* delve into perhaps the most controversial and demanding issues you've explored in your writing so far. What inspired you to take this on? And how were you, in turn, inspired in the writing of it?

Quite simply, this story was inspired by the nightly news. As the war in Iraq went on, I watched the stories—night after night—our troops lost or wounded in battle, and the stories of their families left behind, waiting for them to return. As a mother,

I was heartbroken for the men and women and their families. So many of the young soldiers on the news were the same age as my own son, and that hit me really hard. As an American, I was grateful, and as a woman, I began to wonder what it must be like to go off to war and leave your children behind. I can't imagine anything that would be more terrifying and difficult. I realized that I had never read that story, and I wanted to. I wanted to explore the idea of a woman torn between love and honor. So I decided to write it.

I never thought about the potentially controversial nature of the themes in *Home Front*. I simply set out to write a story about a female mother and soldier who went to war. Although Michael is fairly antimilitary and antiwar, the book is ultimately less political and more personal. I didn't set out to take a stance on the war itself. This was really about supporting and understanding the troops and realizing the extent of the sacrifices they make.

How was a typical day spent while writing this book? On a good day? On a bad day?

Fortunately for me, I have a lot more good writing days than bad ones. I'm really glad about that because a bad writing day is an ugly thing. Usually, a bad day means that either: I can't think of what to write about (which means that something *major* is wrong and I need to go back to the beginning to diagnose and correct the problem), or I write a scene that I end up throwing away before I even finish it.

A good day writing is a beautiful thing. It's a day when the words and ideas flow from the end of my pen and collect in a gorgeous swirl of blue ink on yellow paper. Yes, that's right—I write my novels longhand on yellow legal pads. I do this because I can write anywhere—on the beach, in a deck chair, in my living room. A typical day, of course, is somewhere in between. With *Home Front*, I had to stop often to do extended research, and that was often frustrating. I wanted to write a scene, knew what it was, but I needed the facts to get it all correct.

You've said that you've never had such a difficult time writing a novel. Why was it so difficult, and how did you ultimately find your way to the emotional end of this story?

There were two difficulties that this book presented. First was the burden of authenticity. It was important for me to capture the spirit of the true American soldier in my portrayal of Jolene and Tami and their colleagues. Because I knew so little about the military when I began, creating these characters, and indeed the world they inhabit, was often an uphill battle. And then, as the writing continued, I fell so in love with Jolene—she has become my favorite character of all time—that I really wanted not to "ruin" her by doing anything wrong. Second, I was fairly undone by the emotional component of this novel, and honestly, even though I have often written about difficult, heartrending situations, no story has ever affected me personally so deeply. No novel of my own has ever so consistently brought me to tears. It was difficult to maintain my balance as a writer in this one.

What about Jolene made her such a favorite for you?

In a word, heroism. I can elaborate on that, but you'll have to bear with me. At first, my answer may seem to make no sense. I have always been a geek girl at heart. I grew up reading a lot of science fiction and fantasy novels, and a quick trip to my Web site will let readers know that *Harry Potter* and *The Lord*

of the Rings are two of my favorite stories of all time. Harry standing up to Lord Voldemort and Frodo climbing Mt. Doom with the increasing weight of the ring…these are two of the greatest reading memories for me. When you read about a hero's quest you feel it all: fear, horror, hope, faith. In a way, Jolene is my version of the hero, fighting nearly insurmountable odds, with only her heart to defend herself. We wives and mothers are heroic every day, but rarely do we get to be a *hero*. Jolene, as a Black Hawk pilot in combat, gave me a new kind of heroine.

About the Author

How was it for you to write a character that was so richly nuanced in her conflicted loyalties to her family and career? Do you ever feel similarly conflicted in your own life?

I absolutely loved writing about a character as conflicted as Jolene. I think that's what real life for a woman is all about—balancing the needs of our families with our own desires. Nothing is ever easy for a working mom, or for an at-home mom, for that matter. Motherhood is a minefield of worry. We tend to live with a certain amount of guilt because we want to do so much. In that way, Jolene was very much like any other working mother. She was trying to balance the demands of her job with her responsibility to her children.

Home Front **is a startlingly honest account of the true costs of war. What were your views on the war in Iraq and the military in general before writing this book? Did your views change through the research leading up to and the writing of it?**

I don't come from a military family, nor do I know a lot of military families personally, so I would say that I was woefully uninformed about all of it. Prior to *Home Front*, I would have said that I understood something about their lives and their service, but I was wrong in almost everything. I only understood the thinnest layer. I learned so much in the writing of this novel and in researching it. I went to a deployment ceremony and honestly, I think every American should attend one. Watching our military men and women preparing to go off to war, and their families standing alongside to say good-bye, really brings their sacrifice into sharp focus. It is a powerful reminder that whatever one feels about any particular war, we need to always respect and honor our servicemen and -women and their families. Honestly, I felt a little ashamed that I hadn't attended one before. Although, boy, was it difficult. I was humbled by their pride and strength in the face of such an undertaking. It makes you truly consider what heroism is and reminds you to be grateful.

The vast dimensions and effects of PTSD must have made it a tricky subject to research. How did you go about learning about PTSD, and what were the greatest challenges in writing about the disorder?

As I mentioned earlier, *Home Front* was a research nightmare. I didn't anticipate that to be the case, either. I was actually fairly cavalier about this particular aspect. I mean, I'm a lawyer, so research is something I'm comfortable with, and additionally, I have tackled breast cancer, brain tumors, the Siege of Leningrad and World War II Russia, and DNA testing to exonerate convicted prisoners. I didn't think that the themes and issues in this book would require any more research than I was used to. I couldn't have been more wrong. Researching and writing *Home Front*, with its military theme, was a mammoth undertaking. I was a bit like Alice, falling down the rabbit hole, into a world where nothing was quite the way I imagined it.

I think the depiction of PTSD is one of the most important and relevant portions of the book. I tried to really bring it home in a way that allowed readers to understand how it feels to suffer the symptoms. I also tried to inform readers, which was the point of the Keller trial. The reader learns the truth of PTSD along with Michael. Ultimately, one of the points of the novel is a reminder to all of us. As a nation, we have to care for our warriors upon their return from duty. And their families. It's just that simple.

Having gained so much insight into your subject through firsthand accounts of people who entrusted you with their stories, did you find it difficult to deal with the expectations (of yourself and others) of honesty in your portrayal of Jolene's story?

I was consistently terrified that I would do a poor job in portraying soldiers and their lives and their families. I felt a very keen responsibility to "get it right." They sacrifice so much for the safety of the rest of us, so I really hope I wrote a book that resonates both with military and nonmilitary readers. I would love it if the novel sparked a dialogue about the price of war on our troops and our obligation to them upon their return.

You've written much about the bonds between women, and mothers and daughters in particular, in your previous books. Was it a joy or a pain (or both?) to depict Michael's changing relationship with his daughters?

Michael was really a constant surprise to me in this novel. First of all, as I've said, I spent months researching and devising a version of the story in which Michael didn't even exist. I envisioned a book about women in a family and a daughter's relationship with her distant father. Obviously none of that made it into the final draft. Once I decided to give a marriage a try, Michael appeared fully formed. I liked him from the get-go, and I liked the complexity of both his character and his relationship with Jolene. I never saw the problems in their marriage—or in their reconciliation—as wholly one-sided.

The twist in Michael's story is that he fell in love with his wife while she was gone, and became a better man by becoming a better father. I loved this story arc, and I loved how he evolved from a distracted, disinterested parent into an invested one.

Who was the first person to read this book?

The first person to read this book was Megan Chance. She is always my "first line of defense." She is an extremely talented historical fiction novelist, and we have been friends and critique partners for the duration of both of our careers—more than twenty years. She's always the first person to brainstorm with me, and to read early drafts. We have learned to share the kind of honesty that is rare in writing. She loves telling me when I've made a misstep or missed an opportunity—almost as much as she loves telling me when I've done something well.

Do you ever have conversations with your characters? Do they ever surprise you?

Well, if I had *actual* conversations with characters, I think that would be the sign of a real problem ☺. That being said, I do "listen" to them an awful lot. I can often see scenes unfolding in my mind, and in those lovely moments when my subconscious is working hard, I pay very close attention. I do a lot of my best thinking when I'm actually doing something

else, like running or skiing or swimming.

In a way, my characters always end up surprising me just a little. They become more real than I had anticipated, with backstories and concerns and foibles that I didn't see when I began. I have often said that I really learn who my characters are the same way the reader does—through dialogue. It is true that we learn who people are through words and deeds, and that's true of characters as well.

What do you hope readers take away from this novel?

At its core, *Home Front* is a novel about two ordinary people who have lost their way over twelve years of marriage and then find themselves separated. I think this is a story we can all relate to. You don't have to be a military family or even know someone serving in our military to relate to the powerful emotional themes in the book. We can all imagine how it felt for Jolene to hear her husband say, "I don't love you anymore," and we can understand how lost Michael felt after the death of his father. A marriage is a tricky thing that hangs on hooks both big and small. Every little thing can matter. Words spoken and unspoken carry a tremendous weight, and in a way it requires as much commitment and honor to hold a marriage together as to go off to war. In that way, we all understand sacrifice. It's no surprise that I'm a romantic, and to me, there's nothing more romantic than a husband and wife falling back in love with each other.

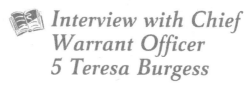

Interview with Chief Warrant Officer 5 Teresa Burgess

I'm still not entirely sure how I got the idea to write about a female Black Hawk pilot, but one thing I know for sure is that without the help of Chief Warrant Officer 5 Teresa Burgess, I would have been in a world of hurt. The military was as foreign to me as the face of the moon. Teresa was everything I could hope for in an advisor. She was honest and open and straightforward. More than that, she turned out to be a lot of fun to hang around with, and I am proud to call her a friend. Not long ago, I was fortunate enough to sit down with Teresa and have a nice old-fashioned girl-to-girl chat. I hope you enjoy this small glimpse into her extraordinary world.

How did you become a helicopter pilot?

I visited the career center during my senior year of high school. I found some brochures on joining the Army. My father was in the Air Force, and I thought I would play a joke on him by telling him I joined the Army. After looking at the brochures a little more closely, I saw one was on going to flight school and becoming a Warrant Officer. I really had no interest in college at the time, and flying interested me. I had grown up around it. I went to the Army recruiter with my dad, completed all the necessary tests, and was accepted. I attended Basic Training at Fort Dix and then went to Fort Rucker for Warrant Officers candidate school followed by flight school.

Tell me a little bit about what it was like to be a full-time/active-duty soldier and the mother of two boys. Did your kids understand your service? Were they always proud of you?

I was active-duty Army for only a year after the birth of my first child, Matthew. It was hard juggling schedules since my husband was active-duty National

Guard. I was in a Medevac unit at the time, and
we did a lot of shift work, twenty-four hours at a
time. I had Andrew, my second son, while I was a
"traditional" guardsman—the typical guardsman is
known as traditional. That is your "one weekend a
month, two weeks in the summer" soldier. Pilots have
extra requirements for duty to keep proficient at their
flying duties. Luckily, I could schedule those based
on when I could get child care. The best part-time job
for a stay-at-home mom. I became a full-time Active
Guard Reserve, AGR, soldier when Andrew started
school. The timing was perfect. My husband, Bryon,
was still AGR, and scheduling could still be difficult,
but it was much more manageable. We had a lot of
support from family and great babysitters—Ruth,
Amy, Nicole, Emily, and Katie.

I am not sure it was a matter of my kids
understanding my husband's and my service. It was
just our way of life. As they got older, I think they
began to understand what it was we did and became
increasingly prouder as they understood more.

**How did you tell the kids—and your husband—that
you were being deployed? What was your greatest
fear upon learning of the deployment?**

By the time I deployed, Bryon was retired from the
National Guard. He worked closely still with the
National Guard, so he knew it was coming.
It was a matter of confirming it when it did become
official. He was very supportive. I think my greatest
fear was just leaving Bryon to take care of everything.
Not that I didn't think he could do it. I just felt bad
leaving him to do everything. The kids were at a stage
of life where they played a lot of sports. There was
a lot of chauffeuring to do. We were very fortunate
to have support from many of the families the kids

played ball with.

You reacted very strongly to a sentence in *Home Front*. Jolene says that she wants to go to war, but she doesn't want to leave her family. What was it about this remark that touched you so deeply? Can you explain how that conflict feels to a woman who is both a soldier and a mother?

You want to go be with your "guys"—the people you have trained with for years. You also want to test yourself and your training. The unit I deployed with has since deployed again. I changed jobs and did not go with them. I felt terribly left out.

When you deploy you are a soldier first—your mission is first. That's the way it has to be when you are in charge of an aircrew and are being counted on to complete a mission. You don't want to let anyone down, least of all the ground soldiers who we are there to support.

Leaving your family is another thing altogether. It is something you just do not want to do. You're the Mom, something that just doesn't go away. You still want to feel like a part of the family.

How was parenting different when you were in Iraq? How was it the same?

Bryon made most decisions while I was gone. It was hard. I still wanted a say, but I wasn't there. Bryon and I had been married twenty-three years when I deployed, so we knew each other's parenting styles pretty well. He did a great job. I am very thankful for his support.

Do you think being at war is different somehow for women? If so, how?

I don't think so. Women, just like men, join for many different reasons, but when it comes down to it, they

just want to do their job and be part of a team. They want a chance to do their duty just like everyone else.

Can you speak at all about the idea of women in combat?

When I joined, women were not allowed to fly in combat. That changed in 1993. I have no issue with women doing a job as long as they are qualified and can perform the job. I don't think women should be put in a job just because they are women in order to equal things out.

What was your homecoming like? How easy was it to get back onto the track of your ordinary life?

It was very nice. I came home after a ceremony at the Post. My family had made a nice sign that was hanging in the kitchen. There were lots of flowers. The pitcher of margaritas was pretty good, too. I had commented to Bryon during one of our phone calls after a particularly long, hot day in the cockpit that the other pilot and I had been talking about how nice margaritas would have been that day. Bryon remembered that and had them waiting.

My parents had come in from out of town and some neighbors had made dinner for us. It was very nice.

In what ways did your tour in Iraq change you? Your marriage? Your family?

At first I think it is hard on every marriage. There are a lot of adjustments to make. Bryon or one of the kids would mention an event or people they had met while I was gone, and I would have no idea what they were talking about.

How did your husband handle being the parent at home? Were routines changed when you returned?

Bryon did great. Some routines I am sure changed when I left in order to suit his routines better. It helped that Matthew got his driver's license while I was gone. He probably ran more errands and played chauffeur to his brother more than most sixteen-year-olds.

Your husband was in the military also, and a pilot. Do you think that helped make your deployment go more smoothly?

Yes and no. It made it easier to talk to him about what was going on; he understood the lingo and the mission. Then again, he understood the mission and what could happen.

Tell me what it feels like to fly a Black Hawk in peacetime... and in wartime.

In peacetime you are training, practicing, and honing your skills. In war you get to apply those skills. If you hone your flying skills and knowledge in peacetime, it becomes second nature in war. Of course, flying in the Pacific Northwest is great. It is beautiful and we have many different environments to train in: mountains, desert, beaches, and cities. The flowering plum trees are beautiful from the air.

How do you feel when people call you a hero?

Uncomfortable. I am not a hero. The guys on the ground are. I am there to make their job easier.

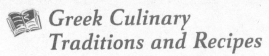 

Greek Culinary Traditions and Recipes

To the Zarkades family matriarch, Mila, food is love. And this is a story about love, and all of the ways we show it. Discovering, tasting, and experiencing Greek food is truly a joy for me to share with my readers.

SPANAKORIZO *Serves 6–8*

This Greek spinach and rice pilaf is bright and full of promise, yet hearty enough for cool evenings. It's often likened to a Greek risotto, creamy and starchy but without the constant stirring required by its Italian counterpart. It's sentimental Greek comfort food, and healthy to boot!

½ cup olive oil
½ onion, chopped
2 cloves garlic, minced
½ cup freshly chopped dill weed
1 cup cooked rice
10-ounce package frozen
   chopped spinach, thawed
1 lemon, juiced
2 TB tomato paste
Salt

Heat ¼ cup olive oil in the bottom of a large pot.

Add onion and garlic, and sauté for about 5 minutes.

Add dill weed and cooked rice.

Add package chopped spinach. Be sure to thaw it first.

Add the lemon juice and salt to taste.

Slowly add ¼ cup olive oil and stir.

Add tomato paste (about a tablespoon at a time) and stir.

Keep stirring until it looks and tastes delicious!

FINIKIA

Yields about 5-dozen cookies

This cookie is made of almonds, coated in a honey syrup, and sprinkled with crushed almonds. They're particularly delicious if combined with a mug of steaming tea, a big comfy chair, and a good book.

<u>Cookies</u>

½ cup butter, softened
½ cup superfine sugar
Grated zest of one orange
½ cup corn oil
2 ½ cups all-purpose flour
1 ½ cups semolina
4 TSP baking powder
1 TSP ground cinnamon
1 TSP ground cloves
½ cup orange juice

Preheat oven to 350 degrees F (175 degrees C) and grease cookie sheets.

In a large bowl, cream together the butter, superfine sugar, and orange zest.

Gradually mix in the oil and beat until light and fluffy.

Combine the flour, semolina, baking powder, cinnamon, and cloves; beat into the fluffy mixture alternately with the orange juice.

As the mixture thickens, turn out onto a floured board and knead into a firm dough.

Pinch off tablespoonfuls of dough and form them into balls or ovals. Place cookies 2 inches apart onto the prepared cookie sheets.

Bake for 25 minutes, or until golden. Cool on baking sheets until room temperature.

Syrup

1 cup water
1 cup white sugar
½ cup honey
1 cinnamon stick
2 TSP lemon juice
½ cup finely chopped walnuts

In a medium saucepan over medium heat, combine the water, white sugar, honey, cinnamon stick, and lemon juice.

Bring to a boil and boil for 10 minutes.

Remove the cinnamon stick. While the mixture is boiling hot, dip the cookies in one at a time, making sure to cover them completely.

Place them on a wire rack to dry and sprinkle with walnuts. Place paper under the rack to catch the drips.

Keep finished cookies in a sealed container at room temperature.

Do You Know?

The first cookbook was written by the Greek food gourmet, Archestratos, in 330 B.C., which suggests that cooking has always been of importance and significance in Greek society.

Modern chefs owe the tradition of their tall, white chef's hat to the Greeks. In the Middle Ages, monastic brothers who prepared food in the Greek Orthodox monasteries wore tall, white hats to distinguish them in their work from the regular monks, who wore large black hats.

To a large degree, vegetarian cuisine can be traced to recipes that originated in Greece.

Many ingredients used in modern Greek cooking were unknown in the country until the Middle Ages. These include the potato, tomato, spinach, bananas, and others, which came to Greece after the discovery of the Americas.

KEFTEDES

Yields about 25 meatballs

This fried meatball—with its unique flavor provided by the herbs—is a versatile dish that can be served in many ways: on a platter of *mezedes*—small plates of food served in Greece with ouzo that are often compared to tapas—with pasta, or as a main meal with salad, *tzatziki*, and chips. *Keftedes* are especially good when served with a little bit of *mizithra*, a traditional Greek cheese, grated on top. That's the Greek way!

Meatballs

2 pounds ground meat (combination of veal, pork, and beef)
4 pieces torn up white bread, or a half cup of bread crumbs, or a half a cup of crushed saltines
2 eggs
1 onion, minced
4 cloves garlic, minced
½ cup fresh mint, finely chopped
½ cup fresh parsley, finely chopped
1 TSP oregano
½ TSP allspice
Salt and pepper
¼ cup olive oil

Mix all ingredients together and form the meatballs.

Heat olive oil on medium heat in a skillet.

Briefly fry the meatballs, about 20–30 seconds on each side.

Set meatballs aside.

Sauce

½ onion, minced
2 cloves garlic, minced
2 TSP salt
2 cinnamon sticks
6 cloves
16-ounce can plain tomato sauce
4 TB tomato paste
1 TSP apple cider vinegar
1 cup water

In the same pan you used to fry the meatballs, sauté the onion and garlic.

Add salt, cinnamon sticks, and cloves.

Add tomato sauce and tomato paste.

Bring all of the ingredients to a low boil for about 5 minutes or until it's all blended.

Add the apple cider vinegar and water. Sauce will be thin. This is normal!

Return the meatballs to the pan. Cover. Cook on medium heat, stirring occasionally, for 45 minutes.

Uncover and cook for 15 more minutes. Serve with the pasta of your choice.

Ideas for Book Groups

In the past year, I've been able to "talk" to book groups via speakerphone during their meetings. What a blast! For so long, I wrote books and never really met anyone who had read them. It is such a joy to talk to women from all over the country. We talk about anything and everything—my books, other books, best friends, kids, sisters. You name it, we'll discuss it. So if you belong to a book group and you've chosen *Home Front* as your pick, please come on over to the Web site and set up a conversation with me. I can't promise to fulfill all the requests, but I will certainly do my best. And don't forget to join me on my blog and/or Facebook. I love talking to readers. The more the merrier!

Thanks!

Kristin Hannah

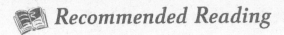 **Recommended Reading**

*Here are a few of the books that helped me understand
the lives of American soldiers—both at war and at
home—and their families. I thank all of these authors
for sharing their personal stories with readers.*

The Other Side of War
Jessica Caputo

Courage After Fire
Keith Armstrong, L.C.S.W., Suzanne Best, Ph.D.,
and Paula Domenici, Ph.D.

Once a Warrior, Always a Warrior
Charles W. Hoge, M.D.

While They're at War
Kristin Henderson

Band of Sisters
Kirsten Holmstedt

The Lonely Soldier
Helen Benedict

Nowhere to Turn
Daniel Hutchison

You Know When the Men Are Gone
Siobhan Fallon

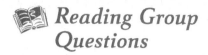 *Reading Group Questions*

1. In the prologue of *Home Front*, we see Jolene's early life and the incident that leads up to her parents' deaths. How does this scene lay the groundwork for her personality and her choices in the remainder of the book?

2. When Michael says, "I don't love you anymore," he wonders fleetingly if he'd said the words so that Jolene would fall apart or cry or say that she was in love with him. What does this internal question reveal about Michael? About Jolene?

3. When Jolene learns of her deployment, she is conflicted. She thinks that she wants to go (to war), but that she doesn't want to leave (her family). Can you understand the dichotomy she is experiencing? Discuss a mother's deployment and what it means from all angles—honor, love, commitment, abandonment. Can you understand a soldier/mother's duty? Do you think it's harder for a mother to leave than a father? Is there a double standard?

4. Jolene and Michael's twelve-year marriage is on the rocks when the novel begins. Did you blame both of them equally for the problems in their relationship? Did your assignment of blame change over the course of the novel?

5. Jolene worries that Betsy will see her deployment as abandonment. Do you agree with this? Think of yourself at Betsy and Seth's age: how would your twelve-year-old self have reacted to your mother going off to war?

6. When Michael sees Jolene for the first time in Germany, he is so overwhelmed by the magnitude of her injuries that he can't be strong for her. He reveals both pity and revulsion. Discuss his reaction. How do you think you would handle a similar situation?

7. At home, Jolene can't cope with her new life. She can't reconcile the woman she used to be with the woman she has become. She wonders how it could be harder to return from war than to fight in it. What does she mean by this? A soldier gets a lot of training and preparation before going to war. Should there be more preparation for returning home?

8. Early in Jolene's homecoming, Mila says: "We all knew how hard it would be to have you gone, but no one told us how hard it would be when you came back." What do you think about this comment? Do we romanticize homecomings and thereby somehow set ourselves up for disappointment? What could her family have done to make Jolene's return an easier transition?

9. At the beginning of her physical therapy, Jolene asks Conny how she is supposed to forget about her injury if it keeps hurting. What does this question reveal about Jolene's personality and her attitude toward her injury? How does this attitude hinder her recovery? How does it help her?

10. Dr. Cornflower describes Jolene as a woman who has spent a lifetime in the Army getting what she wants from a system that doesn't want to give it to her. What does he mean by this? Do you agree? How is a woman's career in the military different from any other career? How is it similar?

11. During the Keller trial, Michael turns in the middle of his opening address to look at Jolene. Why did he choose this very public forum as the time to address the Iraq War with his wife?

12. Although the dire effects of post-traumatic stress disorder (PTSD) are as timeless as war itself, the counseling and support services provided to military men and women returning from war are often insufficient, and the public is often ill-informed about the vast consequences of the disorder. What did you already know about the disorder, and what insights did you gain from reading *Home Front*?

13. Discuss the various relationships formed between parent and child, from Michael's relationship with his daughters and his grief for his father to Jolene's relationship with Mila. Which struck the most resounding chord for you? Why?

14. On page 175, Jolene thinks about the word "heroes" and all that it means in the shadow of loss. For her, heroes were her fallen comrades. What is the definition of a hero to you? Who is one of your own heroes? How do our heroes reflect our values?

15. This book explores a lot of dramatic situations and powerful emotions. Has reading it changed you in any way? What was the most important thing you learned in reading this book? Who would you like to recommend the book to and why?

KRISTIN HANNAH

#1 NEW YORK TIMES BESTSELLING AUTHOR

The Nightingale

AVAILABLE FEBRUARY 3, 2015

ONE

April 9, 1995
The Oregon Coast

*I*f I have learned anything in this long life of mine, it is this: In love we find out who we want to be; in war we find out who we are. Today's young people want to know everything about everyone. They think talking about a problem will solve it. I come from a quieter generation. We understand the value of forgetting, the lure of reinvention.

Lately, though, I find myself thinking about the war and my past, about the people I lost.

Lost.

It makes it sound as if I misplaced my loved ones; perhaps I left them where they don't belong and then turned away, too confused to retrace my steps.

They are not lost. Nor are they in a better place. They are gone. As I approach the end of my years, I know that grief, like regret, settles into our DNA and remains forever a part of us.

I have aged in the months since my husband's death and my diagnosis. My skin has the crinkled appearance of wax paper that someone has tried to flatten and reuse. My eyes fail me often—in the darkness, when headlights flash, when rain falls. It is unnerving, this new unreliability in my vision. Perhaps that's why I find myself looking backward. The past has a clarity I can no longer see in the present.

I want to imagine there will be peace when I am gone, that I will see all of the people I have loved and lost. At least that I will be forgiven.

I know better, though, don't I?

My house, named The Peaks by the lumber baron who built it over a hundred years ago, is for sale, and I am preparing to move because my son thinks I should.

He is trying to take care of me, to show how much he loves me in this most difficult of times, and so I put up with his controlling ways. What do I care where I die? That is the point, really. It no longer matters where I live. I am boxing up the Oregon beachside life I settled into nearly fifty years ago. There is not much I want to take with me. But there is one thing.

I reach for the hanging handle that controls the attic steps. The stairs unfold from the ceiling like a gentleman extending his hand.

The flimsy stairs wobble beneath my feet as I climb into the attic, which smells of must and mold. A single, hanging lightbulb swings overhead. I pull the cord.

It is like being in the hold of an old steamship. Wide wooden planks panel the walls; cobwebs turn the creases silver and hang in skeins from the indentation between the planks. The ceiling is so steeply pitched that I can stand upright only in the center of the room.

I see the rocking chair I used when my grandchildren were young, then an old crib and a ratty-looking rocking horse set on rusty springs, and the chair my daughter was refinishing when she got sick. Boxes are tucked along the wall, marked "Xmas," "Thanksgiving," "Easter," "Halloween," "Serveware," "Sports." In those boxes are the things I don't use much anymore but can't bear to part with. For me, admitting that I won't decorate a tree for Christmas is giving up, and I've never been good at letting go. Tucked in the corner is what I am looking for: an ancient steamer trunk covered in travel stickers.

With effort, I drag the heavy trunk to the center of the attic, directly beneath the hanging light. I kneel beside it, but the pain in my knees is piercing, so I slide onto my backside.

For the first time in thirty years, I lift the trunk's lid. The top tray is full of baby memorabilia. Tiny shoes, ceramic hand molds, crayon drawings populated by stick figures and smiling suns, report cards, dance recital pictures.

I lift the tray from the trunk and set it aside.

The mementos in the bottom of the trunk are in a messy pile: several faded leather-bound journals; a packet of aged postcards, tied together with a blue satin ribbon; a cardboard box, bent in one corner; a set of slim books of poetry by Julien Rossignol; and a shoebox that holds hundreds of black-and-white photographs.

On top is a yellowed, faded piece of paper.

My hands are shaking as I pick it up. It is a *carte d'identité*, an identity card, from the war. I see the small, passport-sized photo of a young woman. *Juliette Gervaise.*

"Mom?"

I hear my son on the creaking wooden steps, footsteps that match my heartbeats. Has he called out to me before?

"Mom? You shouldn't be up here. Shit. The steps are unsteady." He comes to stand beside me. "One fall and—"

I touch his pant leg, shake my head softly. I can't look up. "Don't" is all I can say.

He kneels, then sits. I can smell his aftershave, something subtle and spicy, and also a hint of smoke. He has sneaked a cigarette outside, a habit he gave up decades ago and took up again at my recent diagnosis. There is no reason to voice my disapproval: He is a doctor. He knows better.

My instinct is to toss the card into the trunk and slam the lid down, hiding it again. It's what I have done all my life.

Now I am dying. Not quickly, perhaps, but not slowly, either, and I feel compelled to look back on my life.

"Mom, you're crying."

"Am I?"

I want to tell him the truth, but I can't. It embarrasses and shames me, this failure. At my age, I should not be afraid of anything—certainly not my own past.

I say only, "I want to take this trunk."

"It's too big. I'll repack the things you want into a smaller box."

I smile at his attempt to control me. "I love you and I am sick again. For these reasons, I have let you push me around, but I am not dead yet. I want this trunk with me."

"What can you possibly need in it? It's just our artwork and other junk."

If I had told him the truth long ago, or had danced and drunk and sung more, maybe he would have seen *me* instead of a dependable, ordinary mother. He loves a version of me that is incomplete. I always thought it was what I wanted: to be loved and admired. Now I think perhaps I'd like to be known.

"Think of this as my last request."

I can see that he wants to tell me not to talk that way, but he's afraid his voice will catch. He clears his throat. "You've beaten it twice before. You'll beat it again."

We both know this isn't true. I am unsteady and weak. I can neither sleep nor eat without the help of medical science. "Of course I will."

"I just want to keep you safe."

I smile. Americans can be so naïve.

Once I shared his optimism. I thought the world was safe. But that was a long time ago.

"Who is Juliette Gervaise?" Julien says and it shocks me a little to hear that name from him.

I close my eyes and in the darkness that smells of mildew and bygone lives, my mind casts back, a line thrown across years and continents. Against my will—or maybe in tandem with it, who knows anymore?—I remember.